Elizabeth Drummond hails fr
stint in New York (when she
Carrie Bradshaw) now works
home in Essex. *The Reunion* is he

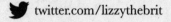 twitter.com/lizzythebrit

# THE REUNION

## ELIZABETH DRUMMOND

One More Chapter
a division of HarperCollins*Publishers* Ltd
1 London Bridge Street
London SE1 9GF
www.harpercollins.co.uk
HarperCollins*Publishers*
1st Floor, Watermarque Building, Ringsend Road
Dublin 4, Ireland

This paperback edition 2022
1
First published in Great Britain in ebook format
by HarperCollins*Publishers* 2022

A catalogue record of this book is available from the British Library

ISBN: 978-0-00-852005-2

This novel is entirely a work of fiction. The names, characters and incidents
portrayed in it are the work of the author's imagination. Any resemblance to
actual persons, living or dead, events or localities is entirely coincidental.

Printed and bound in the UK using 100% Renewable Electricity
by CPI Group (UK) Ltd

*For Neil*

# Prologue

## TWELVE YEARS AGO

Lucas O'Rourke waited outside Headmaster Day's office, unable to take his eyes off the thick oak door that barred his way into the great man's chamber. He checked the stack of notes in his lap, colour-coordinated in order of importance. His fingers trembled as he did so and he shook his hand impatiently. Now was not a time for nerves. After all, the hard work truly lay in the years ahead, didn't it? Just one more year of excelling at school and his path to success was ensured: the best university, the top degree and then the pick of jobs. All Lucas had to do was make certain his CV and academic record was the best it could be, a process that started with this meeting. The meeting due to start in... Lucas checked his watch with a huff. Two minutes! The most important meeting of his school career so far and the other main attendee had yet to show up!

He looked around impatiently but the lobby of the ancient and fine institution that was Arundel College was empty and hushed. The thick-pile red carpet was pristine, the wooden-panelled walls gleaming with scented wax. Under the watchful stares of headmasters past, Lucas fretted. Where was she? His watch beeped a warning – one minute to go. Lucas checked his pockets for his pen and the spares, vexed by the way the costly wool blazer hung limply off his lean form. How Lucas wished his growth spurt would hurry up and make its presence known. He was seventeen, for crying out loud, surely it was time to grow into his feet? He ran his tongue along his teeth, ensuring they were clean and his breath fresh. If only his wilful mop of dark hair would agree to sit straight, he'd look damn near perfect. And perfection was very much needed; nothing could go wrong.

The door from the main corridor opened and Lucas's head whipped around so quickly he made himself dizzy.

"You took your time," he said, unable to withhold the irritation from his voice.

"Would you just chill out? I'm here now." Posy Edwins sauntered over to the waiting area, escorted as ever by her usual acolytes: Desdemona Carrington and Honor Pryce-Demille. Lucas wasn't sure if the two girls had deliberately arranged themselves either side of Posy to permit a kind of symmetry, but one had been created, nonetheless. Where Posy was flowing limbs and long hair, her friends were shorter, overshadowed by the presence of their undeniably more luminous ringleader. Dee had tried to style her dark-blonde frizz the same way Posy had, but where Posy's honeyed locks formed an effortless braid, Dee's was a defiant stub that poked charmlessly out from the back of her head. Posy elegantly lowered herself into the chair beside Lucas, her ever-present camera hanging round her neck. "I'll be all right girls. I'll see you at lunch."

"And leave you alone with Helpboy?" Desdemona simpered.

Lucas didn't let his offence show. He'd heard the demeaning moniker enough times by now. Never mind that his mother was the head chef and his father head of security; they worked in service for the pupils and as such, they were still *the help*. As the only scholarship kid at Arundel College, he was easy fodder for all the gleefully unkind jokes.

"Knock it off, Dee," Posy said. Dee's lower lip jutted in response to the admonition and Lucas was surprised. As one of the most popular girls in school, he'd just assumed that Posy would share in the derision with his nickname, but he was gratified to learn that she wasn't. Posy went on. "You know how Mr Day feels about that word and Lucas is not worth getting a detention over."

Lucas rolled his eyes. Of course. The only thing Little Miss Popular cared about was detention, certainly not his feelings. "Not worth it?" he growled. "I was elected head boy, the same way you were elected head girl."

"Only because no one else went for the job," Dee sniped, a victorious smile carved across her pale face.

"Julian Willoughby did," Lucas corrected her.

"He missed the campaign Q&A because of the rugger match against Caister High and forfeited his chance!" Honor said. "So you actually ran unopposed."

"Julian didn't do the Q&A because he snuck out at lunch to get hammered," Lucas countered, unable to keep the frustration out of his voice. "Although the school put out some rubbish about a match to save face. You're telling me Arundel couldn't move a debate to accommodate the rugby captain and Sir Spencer Willoughby's son?" He shrugged.

"There was competition, just not anything I had to worry about in the end."

"Stop making excuses," Posy laughed. "Like, you think if people had a choice between someone as good-looking as Julian and you, you'd still have won? You're so square your sharp edges will cut someone."

"This isn't a popularity contest," Lucas said hotly. "It's about doing something meaningful to enhance the school that also looks great on your CV." Not that Posy Edwins had a CV, Lucas suspected.

"A popularity contest is exactly what it is." Honor dragged her attention away from her cuticles to look him up and down. "Or at least it used to be."

"Well, at least I have policies," Lucas said. "Actual plans to improve the educational experience for the student body. Exam results could go up by—"

"Oh snore." Posy practically threw herself to the floor in derision. "You really understand what teenagers want, don't you? *Policies.*"

"Yeah, nailed it," Dee giggled unkindly.

"I mean, where's the creativity?" Posy cradled her camera in loving hands. "Not everyone wants to be like, a desk-jockey working for some boring, faceless corporation. Some of us dream of being the next Hamilton Lee or Marina Cano."

"Who?" Honor said. Lucas could only echo her confusion.

"Oh my God, I talk about them all the time!" Posy tutted. "Like, the most famous wildlife photographers ever. The reason I collect *National Geographic* magazines? That print over my bed is a Cano."

Dee wrinkled her nose. "If you say so."

4

Posy was visibly riled. "Not every photoshoot has to be about fashion, Dee."

"They are way more fun though," Honor chimed in with a hair flick. "My aunt is best friends with Annie Leibovitz. You should hear about the parties."

"Whatever." Lucas felt like the conversation was drifting into a place beyond pointless. "What does all this have to do with the prefect roles?"

Glowering at Dee, Posy then turned to Lucas. "The point that seems to keep escaping you is that teens our age want fun as well as a future." Posy inspected her nails – flawlessly manicured, of course. "Like, we want parties, socialising, adventure. You'd have us all learning Latin on a Saturday night."

"At least Latin is useful." Lucas's cheeks burned. Yes, he was studious and sensible, but that was because he had a clear vision for his future. "See how far your advanced-level drinking qualifications get you in the professional world."

"She's Posy Edwins!" Dee exclaimed. "She doesn't need to worry about being a professional."

"Er?" Posy lifted her camera, a wounded expression flitting across her hazel eyes. "Dee? I'm going to do something with my art."

"Of course, Pose!" Dee blustered. "But you know, that's like, a super hard career choice."

"What Dee means"—Honor elbowed Dee—"is that you have a safety net, that's all. So why worry? Just enjoy life the way you're meant to."

"Sure." An unreadable emotion briefly flickered across Posy's face but she tossed her thick braid over her shoulder and beamed. "But mark my words, I will make it. I have to."

"Definitely." Dee nodded.

Lucas turned away, unable to even look at the smug grins that blossomed across their privileged faces. Reluctantly, Lucas had to admit that Posy did seem to have an eye for photography. Arundel insisted that every candidate for the role of head boy or girl ran a quasi-serious political campaign. That meant in addition to trying to win over the student body with their manifesto, it also necessitated the creation of marketing materials in the form of posters and flyers. Students were encouraged to get creative. Lucas had struggled with this aspect but judging by Posy's striking posters plastered all over the school, she'd very much risen to the occasion.

"Ah, there you are." Mr Ranulph Day's emergence from his office startled the four of them and he acknowledged it with a quiet chuckle. Arundel's headmaster was a lean man, his tall frame filling the entrance to his office. He'd been headmaster of the school for decades, ruling with a gentle authority that subdued even the unruliest of pupils.

Lucas rose to his feet, his binders of meeting prep sticking to his clammy hands. He took a deep breath. Posy cooed goodbye to her friends and Lucas followed her into the hallowed space that served as the headmaster's office. It was stiflingly warm, lined with bookshelves compacted with all manner of sporting trophies and framed pictures of prominent alumni. Lucas and Posy followed Mr Day to his desk, their feet making no sound on the plush burgundy carpet.

"Congratulations you two." Mr Day gestured at them to sit and rounded his desk to settle in his leather chair. "This is a great honour your fellow students have bestowed upon you. I'd like to congratulate you both on campaigns well run." He turned to Posy. "I daresay your appointment was no surprise, given your siblings as well as your mother served in the head prefect role during their tenure with us." He smiled. "Celia was quite the artist."

Posy's knuckles tightened around the arms of her chair. "That's right," she said eventually. "It was certainly expected of me."

"I still remember the day I learned she was no longer with us," Mr Day went on. "A real loss."

"It was a long time ago," Posy muttered, and Lucas could see it was taking real effort for her to keep the polite smile affixed upon her face. He didn't know what to say. He hadn't realised Posy no longer had her mum. A mix of pity and sadness rose within him; for all his bullying woes and the pressure to perform, his parents were very much alive and well.

Mr Day regarded Posy speculatively for a moment, then turned his attention to Lucas. "And you! Your parents must be very proud. I do believe you're the first scholarship student to be head boy."

"Thanks." Lucas swallowed, wishing his social status didn't have to be mentioned. He held up his notes. "I have a lot of ideas as you can see. I'd really like to set up some Young Enterprise events, get guest speakers in." He pulled out a chart he was particularly proud of. "I've estimated costs for a September event here. See, if we can get our local MP in we could—" He stopped as Mr Day lifted his hands in a plea.

"There will be time for all this." Mr Day blinked. "Miss Edwins, are you *yawning*?"

"Sorry," Posy said. "It's just… I mean, Lucas presents some really promising ideas, but I was wondering where the socials come in?"

"Socials?" Lucas reeled at his carefully thought-out plans being dismissed as 'promising'. They were dead certs, more like!

"Yeah, like, the parties. Fundraisers, charity events, fancy dress?" Posy turned her startling eyes on Lucas yet again. "My final year of school is not going to be dictated by, like, boring lectures on the joy of spreadsheets and the finer points of stamp-collecting."

"That's not what I'm proposing." Lucas wondered if Posy was being deliberately dense. Every single activity he was planning would enrich the entire student body's experience and maximise their career potential. Give them an edge in job interviews and university applications. But then again, like most of the student body, Posy didn't need to graft to get to live her best life. Her father was so wealthy he could probably buy her her own university to get a degree from. Posy's likely fate was to walk straight into a marriage to a stuffy landowner and pop out a handful of entitled, improbably named little brats who would no doubt rule the roost at Arundel in twenty or so years' time. In Lucas's case, to achieve his goals, every step had to be planned and executed with no errors. Aware of Mr Day's keen observation, Lucas fought to keep his voice steady. "For some of us, Posy, being a senior prefect can mean the difference between first or second choice of uni. We don't all have your limitless options. Just one mistake, one missed opportunity can mean disaster."

"Seriously?" Posy rolled her eyes. "A prefect role, really? With your grades you'd walk into any uni, right? If you manage not to bore them to tears with your personal statement, that is."

"Now, now, Posy. Lucas has a point," Mr Day said.

"Albeit a rather a fatalistic one. Being elected head boy or girl of a school like this really is an achievement. A sign that you have the brightest of bright futures ahead, with a little diligence and perseverance, I might add. But this appointment looks excellent on your CV and proves to employers you're the cream of the crop." He rubbed his chin and turned to Lucas. "I'm certainly glad you're taking it seriously Lucas, but please believe me when I say so long as you work hard and make the most of your time in the role you will reap the benefits. Have some fun with it! Not everything in life can be planned to the tiniest detail. Employers also value flexibility and quick-thinking, rolling with the punches. Life can change so quickly, after all."

Easy for him to say, Lucas thought. Lucas had a mountain of competitors for the university place of his dreams. Competitors with private tutors and bottomless bank accounts. Have fun? If Lucas didn't map out every aspect of his education and career, he'd be sunk. Guaranteed. Even the thought of 'rolling with the punches' was bringing him out in a sweat.

Mr Day placed his fingertips together and flexed them in contemplation. "The two of you have to make this work. There may need to be compromise. After all, both prefects need to be in complete agreement for every single initiative."

Lucas's head drooped. "Every single one?" There was not a chance Posy would agree to his career workshops or his skills seminars. Well, not unless he ordered in a truck-full of Smirnoff Ices to accompany them.

Posy snorted. "Sorry, spreadsheet-boy."

"Mr Day!" Lucas clutched his notes tightly. Posy Edwins could not thwart his plans. Inviting their MP in was just the beginning of what promised to be fruitful networking, all of which would also conveniently serve Lucas's university applications and beyond. "Please! I made these plans to benefit everyone."

"I know. Your focus is on professional development, and I appreciate that. Just as I understand that Posy's campaign focused heavily on friendships and making memories," Mr Day replied gently.

"If that's what you want to call it," Lucas muttered. True, Posy's campaign posters had looked exactly like something out of a fashion magazine, but they had also been pictures of her friends heavily made-up and pouting wistfully in and around Arundel's admittedly stunning grounds. They didn't speak to the academic prowess or the impressive heritage of the place.

"So there has to be a way to combine the two priorities," Mr Day said. "Let's mix things up a little. Who knows? Perhaps you'll both learn something from this? Maybe we'll see a new friendship develop here."

As one, Posy and Lucas's heads swivelled to regard Mr Day with identical scepticism.

"Mr Day, I can assure you that mine and Lucas's relationship will be professional only." Posy's sweet smile barely concealed the revulsion beneath it. "Besides, I doubt he has the emotional capacity to befriend anything besides Excel formulas and bar charts."

"I will certainly do my best to work with what I've got." Lucas ground his teeth so hard it made his head hurt. How on earth was he going to get anything meaningful achieved with such a vapid partner?

"What does that mean?" Posy snapped.

Lucas couldn't resist. "It means the only thing I've seen

you enthusiastic about besides your precious camera is lip gloss and party invites."

"Oh, so you know what a party invite looks like then?" Posy smoothed back a shiny strand of hair. "Because I've never seen you at one."

"Settle down please," Mr Day harrumphed. "My, my. I think it's safe to say Mrs Day won't need to buy a new hat." Lucas and Posy exchanged slow glances. What was the old man on about? The headmaster clocked their consternation and chuckled. "Oh, of course, you probably don't know about the Prefect Marriage bylaw." Lucas and Posy shook their heads. "It's a rather lovely throwback to the early days of this fine institution when it was split into a boys' school and a girls' school. It was decreed that if ever a head boy and head girl who served in the same year got married, the school would pay for their wedding. Honeymoon too, if I recall correctly." Mr Day rose stiffly and moved to the window of his office, his lined face softening as he took in the immaculate, sun-drenched grounds. "In those days it was all about uniting powerful families and ensuring the school could reap the benefits in generous alumni donations."

Lucas didn't even need to look at Posy's face to know she was experiencing the same reaction as him; he could hear the faint gagging sounds from where he sat.

"How quaint," he remarked eventually in a strangled voice.

"Absolutely." Mr Day looked over his shoulder at the pair of them with an apologetic smile. "But I don't think that's something we need to worry about with you two, is it?"

# Chapter One

## PRESENT DAY

Posy's alarm blared obnoxiously from where her phone lay under her bed.

"Fuuuccckkk," she breathed as loudly as her hangover would allow her. Eyes still closed, she swiped an arm frantically, cursing again as her wrist slammed painfully into her bedside table.

"Posy!" her father's voice bellowed from downstairs.

"Just a minute!" Silencing her phone, Posy rolled onto her back and clutched her throbbing wrist. Ruing the multiple absinthe cocktails of the night before, she slid out of her sumptuous emperor-size bed, lowering her brightly manicured feet onto the plush rug. Padding over to the powder-pink dressing table, she rifled through the drawers, certain there were painkillers in one of them. As she fumbled, she knocked over several perfume bottles and the resulting clatter made her grip her head in agony. "Shitshitshit!" Then she caught a glimpse of her reflection and groaned. Her hair resembled a straw bush and there was mascara smeared all down her face. Plus, it felt like something had crawled into her mouth and died a violent, stinky death. With a belch, Posy wondered if it was time to accept that the party days of her early twenties where she could drink her own bodyweight in booze and emerge unscathed were rapidly diminishing. She sagged against the dressing table to fight a wave of nausea.

From the silken pile of her bedsheets, Henry's muscular arm emerged to pull the bedcover off his face.

"Babe. So much noise," he growled.

"Sorry darling," she hissed, resuming her interrogation of the drawers. "Where are they?" She shuffled into the en suite, skidding on sudsy water left over from her and Henry's sensual 3am shower. Despite the raging calamity of her hangover, Posy couldn't stop the smile that took over her face at the memory of Henry's trick with the showerhead. Opening the cabinet, she sighed with relief at the sight of a packet of Anadin and knocked a couple of tablets back with tap water cupped in her hand.

Henry appeared in the doorway behind her, stark naked bar his Rolex. "Your dad likes to shout in the morning."

Posy grabbed his wrist to check the time and grimaced. "It's lunchtime. That'll be why he's shouting."

"Last night was insane." Henry raked a tanned hand through his thick crop of wheat-blond hair. "Is Tara awake? I haven't heard the jaws of hell creaking open yet." When Posy elbowed him defensively, he shook his head. "Just kidding!"

"Yeah, yeah. I'll go and check on her." Posy's best friend had taken the spare room next to Posy's. "And go easy on Tar – the divorce almost finished her off."

"I was joking." Henry lifted his hands in innocence. "She was the one giving me the third-, fourth- and fifth-degree last night."

"That's my Tar." Posy had known Tara Sastri her entire life. Their mothers had been best friends, raising their families on the same street. Tara hadn't attended Arundel however; her super-traditional, super-rich grandparents had insisted on Swiss boarding school, much to a young Posy's dismay.

"How about you check on her then? I need to wash and head out." Henry leaned past her to grab a towel off the rail and Posy resisted running her tongue down his rock-hard abs, knowing she'd have to drag him back to bed if she did. She had to make do with merely revelling in his woody, salty scent. But then his words hit.

"You're not staying for brunch?" Posy jutted out her bottom lip. "You could finally meet everyone." She'd been dating Henry for four months now and although she was happy with taking things slow, her family had begun to question whether her boyfriend actually existed.

"The mood your dad is in?" Henry said. "Not likely. I'll creep out the back door when you go down. Next time, promise." He tapped her bottom to usher her out. "You'd best get Tara up, hey?"

"Fine." Wrapping a tropical kaftan around her body, Posy trudged to the room next to hers and tapped on the door. "Tar? You awake?"

A faint whimper was emitted from behind the door and Posy took that as her cue to walk in. Amongst the mass of bedding she could see an unruly wedge of dark hair, crimson lipstick smeared across the white pillows.

"Rise and shine!" Posy bounced onto the bed next to her friend. She instantly regretted it as her head spun.

"Ugh." Tara dragged her scarlet nails through her hair and licked her lips. "Why do I let you take me on these nights out?"

"Oh, you loved it," Posy said. "How are you doing? I feel like my blood is ninety per cent absinthe at the moment."

"I'm too old for this—" Tara froze, eyes snapping to her Cartier watch. "Is that the time? Is that really the time? Fuck! Ben's dropping the kids off in three hours!"

"Ah, you'll be fine." Posy hiccupped then flinched at the smell. "Let's do breakfast and you'll be right as rain."

"POSY!" Her father's holler echoed around the house and Tara's bloodshot eyes widened.

"Yeah right, there's no way I'm breaking bread with your dad right now." Tara inelegantly rolled off the bed, wincing as her feet thudded against the floor. "Besides, you need to bring up the photography festival with him. Isn't the admission deadline soon?"

"Oh don't." Posy sagged against the headboard. "I'm too hungover for that."

"Well, you do need your dad's money for it." Tara found her bag and pulled out some gum. "Don't you dare waste this opportunity because you were too busy partying."

"I know, I'll ask him for the money today." Posy had blasted through her allowance quickly this month. "I'm so excited about this thing though, Tar. It could be the best thing to ever happen to me."

"As you should be." Tara chewed loudly. "You're, like, the best photographer ever. Jesper pays for everything, doesn't he? I'm sure he'll help with something as important as this."

"I'm sure he will." Posy flapped a hand confidently. Her pops always invested in her.

"Henry still here?"

"Yeah, he's going to try and sneak out though, I think."

"Don't blame him," Tara muttered as she cast her eyes about for her shoes.

Posy studied her friend's face closely. "So, what do you think of Henry?" she asked. Last night had been Tara and Henry's first meeting, totally impromptu on Posy's part, but it seemed like the only way to get Henry to meet the people that mattered to her was to spring it on him. He was always so busy.

"I didn't get much chance to speak to him." Tara's voice was muffled as she looked under the bed. "Kinda loud in that last place."

"He's hot though, right?"

"Oh, yeah. He's got that whole Adonis thing really working out for him," Tara said. "Where's my other shoe?"

Posy noticed Tara was avoiding her gaze. "You like him though, right?"

"Sure, he seems fine. Aha!" Tara emerged with a battered Weitzman pump.

"Just… fine?"

"Yes. Fine." Tara jammed her foot into the shoe and reached for her bag. "Darling, we can do a full debrief when next we meet but I have to get the fuck out of here and sober up before Ben returns the kids."

"Okay." Posy knew when to give up. Tara's relationship with her ex was finally almost becoming amicable and taking receipt of her kids whilst stinking of booze would not help matters. "Brunch soon?"

"Absolutely," Tara replied, her mobile already at her ear.

"Hi, can I get a cab? Ten minutes, yeah, okay, if that's the best you can do. 15 Clifton Mews." She hung up and belched wetly. "Christ."

"Come on, at least grab a coffee," Posy said encouragingly. "Get home and shower. By the time Ben drops the kids off, you'll be fine." With a reluctant nod, Tara allowed Posy to lead her out. At the same time Henry emerged from Posy's room, his blond mane darkened from the shower.

"I'm going to nip off." He indicated the rear stairway that led directly out to the back garden. "Sounds like the gang are all in the kitchen so they won't see me."

"Are you sure you want to sneak out?" Posy pleaded. Henry and Tara would serve as armour against the audible wrath of her father. "I know Pops sounds annoyed but seriously, he'll be delighted to finally meet you."

"I really have to go," Henry said tightly. "Need to head back down to Norfolk, see my folks."

"One of these days you'll have to take me with you," Posy grumbled as Henry leaned in for a farewell kiss. His family home sounded sublime, even if his elderly parents were still in residence. As much as she loved the luxurious flat he kept for work in nearby Leeds, with its minimal and masculine design, the Norfolk property was apparently the last word in taste. He was frequently back and forth between the two locations and it wasn't uncommon for him to be away for well over a week or two at a time.

"Perhaps," Henry murmured into her mouth. He cupped her face and stared deeply into her eyes. Posy's breath quickened. There was very little Henry needed to do to make her body react this way.

"Well, bye then," Tara said bluntly, shouldering her way past.

"Oh, right." Posy stepped back from Henry. The last thing poor divorced Tara needed to see was Posy swooning all over her hot boyfriend.

"I'll call you!" Henry whispered and he darted off down the back stairs.

"You'd better!" Posy then turned to Tara. "Come on. Let's face the music." She dragged a stumbling Tara down the sweeping staircase of Edwins Manor, through the softly lit entrance hall and into the grand kitchen that was the heart of the house. "Do you really need to shout, Pops?" Posy greeted her father moments later. Jesper Edwins was a large man, his ashy hair cropped close to his head. There was no sign of his usual jocular demeanour; he was visibly brooding at the table, thick fingers wrapped around a steaming mug of tea.

"I shouldn't have to wake you up by any measure." He watched as Posy wandered over to where the full and fragrant cafetière sat on the counter. "You're a grown woman, for crying out loud." His eyes moved to a sheepish Tara. "Tara," he greeted her.

"Morning, Mr Edwins," Tara mumbled.

"It's actually closer to lunchtime." Ines Edwins joined her husband at the table with a glint in her eye. "Big night, was it?" She shook back her dark waves and tried to catch Posy's eye.

"Try a big weekend," Posy yawned, reaching for mugs.

"You're almost thirty years old yet still acting like a hedonistic teenager," Jesper said, ignoring the pleading glance from his wife. "Tara, I expected better from you."

"Sorry Mr Edwins." Tara looked as if she might burst into tears.

"Posy, I last saw you two days ago when you said you

were popping round to Tara's for lunch," Jesper went on, his face reddening. "After that, I hear nothing from you for hours, only to see from Tara's Instagram that you were up in Leeds at one point?"

"Ah, you follow me? Thanks Mr Edwins!" Tara beamed, only to shrink back when Jesper shot her a frustrated stare.

"Actually, I was trying to work out what kind of damage Hurricane Posy had caused whilst she was away!" he snapped. Posy sighed. How she hated that nickname! It had been in place for as long as she could remember and deployed with glee by the entire Edwins family whenever Posy made even the smallest error.

"Sorry Pops, time kind of ran away with us," Posy said. "See, it was Tara's first weekend without the kids, so I dragged her out for the day but then Henry had a client party that we ended up crashing." Posy handed Tara a mug of strong coffee.

"It was pretty epic," Tara agreed. "That terrace! Dreamy as—"

"You live under my roof," Jesper interrupted as Posy blithely sipped her own coffee. "You cannot go AWOL like that."

"I'm not a child." Posy shuffled to the fridge. "Anything in here for brekkie?"

"I can make you something?" Ines started to rise from her seat. "Omelette? Porridge?"

"Nah," Posy said. Ines's eagerness to please always grated more when Posy was hungover. Ines nodded wordlessly and dropped back down.

"Goddammit Posy!" Jesper slammed his mug on the table, slopping tea all over it and Posy froze, one hand on the fridge door.

"Actually." Tara cleared her throat. "I think I hear my cab outside so I'm just gonna…" She gingerly placed her coffee on the counter and backed out, arms raised as if placating a grumpy bear.

"Call me!" Posy yelled to Tara's retreating back. Tara flicked a hasty wave before diving gratefully out of the front door. "Happy now, Pops?" Posy said once her friend had left. "Tara's having such a terrible time and all you can do is make her feel unwelcome. She's my oldest friend."

"Well, the pair of you need to grow up." Jesper angrily swiped at his spilt tea with a dish towel.

"Jesper, please." Ines placed a heavily ringed hand atop his. "Let's just remain mellow and—"

"Life is for living," Posy spoke over Ines's platitudes with an eye roll. "It doesn't stop because you have kids. That's all I'm doing. I have better things to do than wake to meet the dawn chorus."

"I'd be happy for you to wake before noon," Jesper snarled. "But really, it is time to settle down. You're getting to that age."

"What age?" Posy pulled a pack of bacon from the fridge. "And what do you mean by settle down? You mean, marry?" Posy baulked. Henry was great for sure. After locking eyes with him across the VIP room of Leeds' hottest cocktail bar, the attraction had been instantaneous. But as they'd not been together long they definitely weren't at the 'meet the parents stage' yet. And as for marriage? Far too soon to even *think* about it, and Posy was fairly sure Henry would agree.

"Not marriage, per se," Jesper said. "I was thinking more career. A vocation. But if you chose to marry, I'd be happy for that to happen too."

"Pops, I am in no way desperate to get married, unlike—"

"I'd be careful how you finish that sentence," a cool voice interrupted her. Posy sighed.

"Hi Flo," she said through gritted teeth. Her sister Florence stood in the doorway, perfection in a floral tea-dress and white plimsolls. Her glossy chestnut hair was waved without a strand out of place and in her delicate hands she clutched an overstuffed binder decorated in white lace and flowers.

"Heavy night, was it? I saw Tara pouring herself into a cab." Flo sashayed over to her father and kissed the top of his head. She then gave Ines a long, loving squeeze before plopping down next to Jesper. "Daddy, I have to go over the catering budget with you. Soren insists that the only suitable meat amuse bouche is actually Iberico instead of duck but that does add an extra squeeze on the amount we finalised last week." Flo batted her large emerald eyes at her father, who simply waved a hand.

"Darling, it's your day. If Iberico is what that extortionate wedding planner is telling you to want, then Iberico you shall have." Jesper Edwins had never been one to worry about the small details. Owning hefty amounts of real estate in England and Scandinavia afforded a certain comfort that his children had got more than a little used to.

"Oh, thank you, Daddy!" Flo bestowed another kiss on him and glared at Posy. "Now then, Hurricane. Have you even *looked* at the latest bridesmaid dress samples yet? Honestly you're being so fussy."

"Oh." Posy stopped halfway through ripping open the bacon packet with her teeth. "I kinda wanted to have another squiz at them, Flo. To check." She spat out a scrap of plastic and kicked herself mentally for not having got back to her sister on the dresses. Despite being the picture of elegance herself, Florence had awful taste in bridesmaid dresses from what Posy had seen so far. Every single dress review had ended in a massive fight between the sisters, and Posy was in no mood to repeat that, especially not today.

"Well, are any of them speaking to you at all?" Florence persisted, flopping down opposite their father. "The pastel tulle? Or perhaps the Liberty print midi?"

"Um, the first one," Posy said gratefully as she threw rashers into a pan. "Really, um, fairy-tale."

"There IS no tulle option!" Florence shrieked. "That was a test! I knew you hadn't bothered to look at the email. God's sake Posy, this is my WEDDING."

"The other one then," Posy hurriedly said.

"The midi?" Florence positively frothed. "Do you really THINK I would have my bridesmaids wear midi-length dresses? What do you think this is, afternoon tea with minor royalty?"

"No, er…" Posy was barely able to concentrate due to the delicious smell of bacon. "I just think… I just think you have, like, a super specific vision for this wedding. You have such an eye." Florence huffed, but Posy sensed a softening and pressed on. "Tell you what, I'll eat my sandwich and go and have a look after that. All right?"

"Fine." Florence sighed. "I need Hettie to order the fabric by the end of the week so please, let me know ASAP." She glanced at her watch and squealed. "Crumbs! I must get to the florist's within the hour. Daddy, could I borrow the Merc?" She fluttered her eyelashes at her father who nodded

23

indulgently. "Thank you! Ines, fancy coming to look at the flowers with me?"

Ines clapped her hands gleefully. "Do I ever! Give me a moment to get ready." She hurried to the sink to rinse her mug. Posy dutifully kept her eyes on her bacon, but she was aware of Ines hovering, hoping to catch Posy's attention. She thought her stepmother might say something, but Ines seemed to think twice and rushed off with Florence.

Groaning with relief, Posy stuffed greasy bacon into soft bread and took a ravenous bite. "Thank God." She sighed. "Flo gives me such a headache."

"Are you sure that's not the gallons of champagne you no doubt inhaled last night?" Jesper remarked.

"As if." Posy chewed with relish. "It was absinthe, actually."

"Anyway, at least your sister has direction," Jesper said. "A life plan."

"What, marrying Inigo Fitzpatrick?" Posy snorted. "The man has about as much personality as a soggy ham."

"Be that as it may," Jesper admitted with a hint of a smile, "Florrie has chosen *him*. They make each other happy."

"Well, hurrah for them," Posy said, with an insouciant shoulder.

"I merely want the same for you," Jesper said.

"What, marriage to a ham?" Posy curled her lip.

"Lord no," Jesper replied, obviously certain his daughter's fate was far removed from that.

"You know I have a boyfriend, right?" Posy said. "He's great. Can't you just wait and see how that goes?"

"I will when you see fit to introduce him to Ines and me," Jesper said.

Posy bridled. She could have done just that if Henry hadn't snuck out the back door. At least Jesper would have backed off a bit. "Why should my boyfriend meet Ines?" Posy's lower lip jutted in petulance. "She's not my mother. Why does she get to weigh in on this?"

"Right, she's not your mother," Jesper echoed, "but she loves you. She's also my wife and has been for a long time now. I trust her on every personal matter. So, until she and I meet this boyfriend, I'll keep on believing he's yet another flash in the pan flirtation. Darling, I simply want you to have purpose."

"I have purpose," she grumbled.

"Beg to differ. You don't have a career." He lifted a thick finger to enunciate. "You don't even have your own income at the moment, not since you quit that restaurant hostess job before Christmas. You don't volunteer for charities, local or otherwise. If you're not partying, you're hungover at home or halfway around the world with that camera of yours."

"And what's wrong with that?" Posy demanded. "My photography means everything to me."

Jesper growled. "That may be the case but you're fast approaching your thirtieth birthday with no career and no real prospects for the future. I mean, is this boyfriend a potential husband or just another person to party with?"

"What is the obsession with me marrying?" Posy cried.

"I don't have an obsession with you marrying," Jesper sighed, "but your mother and I were long married by your age and people might think—"

"Oh, the horror!" Posy feigned a swoon. "How on earth will you hold your head up at the club when it emerges your youngest daughter is a spinster?" She threw herself back dramatically. "For shame!"

"It's not about me," Jesper said, shifting uncomfortably, although Posy would wager it definitely was about him a little bit. "I don't want you to wake up in ten years' time wishing you'd done something meaningful with your life. Whether that meaning is a career, kids, education… you know what I mean."

"I know." Posy paused, regarding her father's craggy face and wished she wasn't so hungover. She took a deep breath. If her pops wanted purpose, well, she'd show him purpose. "Actually, now you mention it," she said, pushing her plate away. "There is something I want to discuss."

"Oh?" Jesper leaned forward.

Posy inwardly cursed the timing. He was not in the best mood but, as Tara had pointed out, the festival's deadline for confirming attendance was very soon. "I've had an interesting offer," she began. "There's this festival that wants to show my art."

"Art?" Jesper looked blank. "You mean your photos? I thought you just used that camera for selfies."

"Selfies!" Posy repeated with a laugh. "You think I use a £1500 camera with Zeiss lenses for *selfies*?" Her father's distanced expression made it evident he'd thought precisely that, and Posy tried not to let her hurt show. "My specialty is documenting landscapes and nature." She pulled out her phone and scrolled through her pictures. "Some portraiture but what I really love is documenting the outdoors. See, here are some shots from the mountains in Mallorca… and here, see? Peruvian jungle? God, that snake bite stung like a bitch."

"Delightful." Jesper nodded tightly. "A lovely hobby."

"Listen Pops, it could be a career!" Posy said. "Look at

all the comments on my Insta account. People want to buy prints of my pictures!"

"Right." Jesper's lips thinned. "So then what does this have to do with me?"

"About this festival," Posy said. "It's the International Photography Achievement Festival. All the top editorial bods and world-famous photojournalists and enthusiasts attend to discuss art, trends, technology. People sell their art or their services… It's like this super-cool celebration of photography and art!" Jesper seemed unmoved so Posy ploughed on. "They have a whole forum dedicated to up-and-coming talent and this year they've selected *me* as one to watch! I'll sit on some discussion panels as well as have an entire Q&A dedicated to my development as an artist. I can sell my work at the fair; they'd advertise my presence on their website… It'd be an amazing opportunity for me."

"And…?"

She licked her lips. "It's in Hawaii."

A resigned expression settled across Jesper's face.

"They confirmed my place but I'm kind of between cash injections right now." Posy's quip didn't land with Jesper, so she quickly carried on. "I only need the airfare, not accommodation. They'll put me up somewhere, so I won't need a hotel but it's Hawaii peak season so—"

"So, you'd need an advance on your allowance to pay for the flights?" Jesper said with a sigh.

"Yes!" Posy said. "Thank you Pops, that's exactly what I need. It's super expensive even if I travel economy class." She thought about doing a comedic shudder but decided against it given her father's stony repose. "Thing is, I spent my reserves on printing some works to display when I'm out there, so I'll need some spends on top of my plane ticket."

"You mean you don't have anything left?" Jesper's resolve gave way to disbelief. "No savings at all?"

Posy shook her head. "No." She'd tried to squirrel away bits of money here and there. But there was always a new adventure draining her best efforts or a new camera lens she wanted to test.

"Oh, Hurricane." Jesper looked away, his face tight.

Posy gulped, an unfamiliar feeling taking hold. Was he about to say no? Her dad never denied her anything. She'd travelled, partied and learned on his dime since a young age and if ever the well ran dry she'd always been able to run to him with open hands. But her new credit card hadn't arrived – weirdly – and it was over a month before the next allowance payment hit her account. "Pops, what's wrong?"

"I'm sorry darling, but how different is this festival to the Cordon Bleu course you took?" Jesper said. "Or the calligraphy camp? The yoga retreat last summer?" He stared into his hands guiltily. "I paid for all of those – outside of your allowance – thinking that these would lead to a career for you. Yet all I have is a shed full of unused pans and yoga equipment, not to mention gallons of ink, and you still have no job. How is *this* any different?"

"But I was always doing the photography in the background, developing my skills." It was dawning on Posy that for the first time in her life, her father might not help her. "That other stuff was like, experimentation. I just fancied learning some new things. But did you not see my pictures? I'm good at this! You do know some of the times that I'm out all night I'm not partying, I'm doing night shoots, see?" She frantically scrolled through her Instagram feed. "This is Harper's Meadow at midnight and—"

"Posy!" Jesper interrupted loudly. She dropped the

phone with a clatter. "I'm still not seeing how this is any different to the last fad."

Posy couldn't believe it. Her pops had always been supportive and generous with her. Yes, there had always been the odd remark about 'getting a real job' or 'when are you going to pay me back for all this?' but said with a loving smile and a wink. She could only conclude that now his middle child was planning her wedding, it had him focusing on Posy, his youngest. "Guide's honour, it is totally different!"

"You got kicked out of the Girl Guides," Jesper recalled.

"That was a misunderstanding," Posy muttered.

"You scaled the roof of the Scout's Hut and refused to come down until they admitted girls," Jesper said.

"Actually, they were required to admit girls, but their leader refused," Posy said defensively. "They were going quad biking and rock climbing instead of the mumsy crap Brown Owl was making us girls do."

"You didn't have to throw all the sewing kits in the quarry though," Jesper said, almost managing to hide his mirth at that. "You could have raised a legitimate complaint instead of going full Hurricane on them."

Posy ignored the blasted nickname. "Seriously Pops. This art festival is super important."

"I don't believe *you* are though." Jesper turned grave again. "Serious, that is."

"What's the problem?" Posy said. "It's just a few grand for the airfare and a little petty cash for incidentals after all."

"*Just?!*" Her father shook his head. "That's what I mean, Posy, I don't think you understand money. How hard it is to come by for so many people and what it means to earn it all yourself. That's my fault though, I suppose."

"Pops… of course I understand money." Posy had never had to beg for something before and didn't know what else to say. "And once I'm a top photographer I'll have my own income, and you won't need to worry about me or pay my way ever again. How can I show you I mean business?"

"She could always attend the big reunion for inspiration," Sebastien Edwins drawled, clomping into the kitchen with his chunky boots, plump toddler on hip. "Hi Posy. Hi Dad." He handed his son Max over to Jesper whose face lit up with grandfatherly love.

"Didn't know you were coming over today!" Jesper said in delight. "And what reunion?"

"Arundel College. The big fundraiser event thingy." Seb dashed his golden curls from away from his eyes as he helped himself to coffee. "I'd go but Angharad and I will be away. Can I drop off the revenue sheets for the last quarter tonight?"

"Yes please," Jesper replied. "And as for the reunion, Posy, that's not a bad idea." A grin spread slowly across his face. "Reconnecting with old friends, getting some inspiration, maybe even a job offer… Arundel alumni are terribly well connected."

"I don't think so." Posy scraped back her chair with a yawn. Arundel was ancient history. She had tried her best to keep in touch with her crew since graduation but one by one they'd married off or emigrated or had dynamic careers that didn't leave time for someone like Posy. She could take a hint. "I'm off back to bed."

"Posy, it's lunchtime!" Seb said with a chuckle.

"And?"

"Posy." Jesper stood, hefting a gurgling Max to his other hip. "I need you to start taking things a little more seriously.

Less of the frivolity. Make some actual, fruitful decisions. And that begins with the Arundel reunion. The whole point of sending you to a school like that was to set you up for life. Do some networking or something. For Christ's sake, do something beyond partying and I'll consider donating to your latest enterprise."

"But…" Posy gaped.

"I mean it," said Jesper. "Sort yourself out, starting with attending this reunion. Until then, consider yourself cut off. No money, no credit cards, nothing." And with a pained nod, he carried Max out of the kitchen, leaving Posy open-mouthed.

"What have you done now?" Seb stared at her in fascination.

"Sod off, Seb!" Posy snapped. "What's it like up there on Pop's pedestal?"

"Oh Posy," Seb chuckled.

"No, seriously, well done you." Posy couldn't stop the sarcasm flowing. "You're running Pops's empire, married to your childhood sweetheart. I haven't even met Henry's parents and I'm reduced to scraping pennies from under the couch."

"My life is far from simple, Posy," Seb said with a gentle smile. "For one thing, Pops has tasked me with organising the new investment funds he wants to set up. Our current wealth manager hasn't been doing so well."

"Yawn," Posy said automatically.

"Seriously," Seb went on. "I have no idea about this sort of thing. Managing property and tenants? Fine. But wealth management? I'm freaking out. That's Dad's thing normally."

"So why doesn't Pops do it?" Posy said.

"Because he wants to test me. He's not getting any younger, Posy. He wants to take more of a background role with his businesses and for me to step up starting in the autumn. Don't suppose your boyfriend could help?"

"He's in insurance, not wealth," Posy said.

"But he must have contacts in this line of work," Seb said. "I know I could ask a few of Dad's friends but they're like sharks smelling blood with me. They know this isn't my area. What if they take advantage?"

"You need someone you can trust," Posy said and Seb nodded miserably. She racked her brain, surprised that in her wide circle of friends she didn't know anyone in the relevant line of work. "I'll have a think."

"Nah, you'll forget all about it," he joked. "If it isn't a camera lens or a fabulous party it doesn't stand a chance."

"Well, not all of us can be the Golden Boy." Posy stuck out her tongue.

"Oi!" He ambled over to her and ruffled her hair. "If you want people to take you seriously and stop calling you Hurricane then you have to settle. Make a plan, stick to it."

"I *have* a plan!" Posy leapt up, aggrieved. "I just laid it all out for him, but Pops won't help me with it!"

"Seems to me that he won't until he sees you really commit to something. You just have to make Dad see you're capable of that."

"But I have no savings, Seb!" Posy grumbled. "And he cut me off – you heard!"

"So be resourceful, sis," Seb laughed, elbowing her. "Sell some of your shoes or something. You can do it." Just then, Max started wailing from the other room.

"Sebastien!" Jesper's voice was filled with the panic only a very dirty nappy could inspire.

"Coming, Dad!" Seb looked back at Posy, blue eyes softening. "You can do it, kid." He dropped a kiss on her head and strode out, leaving Posy to wonder what the hell she could do to score a free flight to Hawaii in just a couple of short months.

# Chapter Two

Lucas stared down at the surface of his immaculately arranged chrome and glass desk. Specifically, he stared at the sizeable diamond ring currently resting atop his leather diary, mocking him with its glittering perfection and costly symmetry. He slowly lifted his head to meet the eyes of the woman who had placed it there.

Sally stood before him, elegant as ever in her Alexander McQueen suit, auburn hair glossed and waved to perfection. But her beautifully shrewd dark eyes were red-rimmed, rosebud lips downturned and trembling.

"You didn't need to return it," Lucas said dully. "I told you to keep it."

"And I told you I need a clean break." Sally tightened her hands around the handle of her tote. "Completely clean. So I have to give this back to you."

Lucas wondered what on earth he was to do with a 2ct emerald-cut diamond ring. One he'd specially requested have a secret ruby hidden under the bridge because his ex-future-mother-in-law's name was Ruby and had died just weeks before he popped the question. It had seemed so romantic at the time. "I'm sorry," he said eventually.

"I tried." Sally's voice was barely a whisper. "I really tried."

Lucas found it hard to form words. Every inch of his being was reminding him what an utter failure he was. "I know you did," he said. "Align became—"

"Became everything to you," she interrupted, her whisper taking on a hard edge that sliced deep. "And where did that leave me?"

"You were always number one," Lucas said. "I just lost my way for a bit." But this was old ground. His assertion that he could focus on their relationship when the business stabilised rang hollow now, a belief that had pushed them further and further apart from each other. The desk between them may as well have been miles of desert. He couldn't believe the stranger before him was the same woman who'd let him lick salted caramel from her bare navel in the Corinthia penthouse suite that Valentine's Day, who used to delight in playing very daring footsie in exclusive restaurants. The same woman who six months ago had ecstatically agreed to marry him.

"I know. And I know that you thought Align would be more established, much earlier. Just like I know you have been struggling for months now to find enough rich people in need of wealth management," Sally said. Lucas knew she understood, intellectually at least. As a corporate lawyer she did her fair share of late nights and stressful meetings. But she also took her private life seriously and until recently, Lucas had featured very prominently in her plans for that. "Thing is, I'm ready for the next stage of our lives and…"

She jutted her chin at the ring. "I don't think you are. Not really."

"Of course I am. Otherwise I wouldn't have asked you to marry me, would I?" Lucas said. But he'd be lying if he told her the only thing that filled his head recently wasn't Align. That even on weekends he'd been focused more on the business than any kind of pleasure. But he hadn't had to tell her. Sally had known and she'd tried so hard to bring him back to her. Lucas wasn't sure exactly when he'd lost his way, but it was painfully evident to both of them he had no hope of finding it. But it didn't stop him trying to make her understand. "The industry has been so unstable recently and we lost a few really important clients of late. I just need time. I have a plan th—"

Sally lifted a hand. "Yes, the plan. The one you've had for years, Captain of Industry and all that. Thing is, I'm tired of waiting around for you to finish it. I don't..." She sniffed. "I don't know you anymore. You've lost yourself in financial planning and budgets and forecasting. Your eyes are always on the horizon and not in the moment. Life is happening *now* and that's what I want. A life."

Lucas reeled. It wasn't the first time in his life that a woman had bemoaned his love of spreadsheets.

"Sally..." He rose to his feet and reached for her.

"I'd best go." Sally took several steps back, eyes shimmering.

Lucas felt his chest tighten. She was so beautiful, and he was simply letting her walk away. "I'm sorry," he said. "You deserve better."

"Don't say that!" Sally admonished him. "Just promise me you won't be this person forever. That one day you'll do something not planned or predictable down to the nth degree, that you'll really live?"

Lucas stared back at her. Planning was his thing. Security. Facts. How could you ever get what you wanted from life if you didn't have a target? He knew she expected some kind of answer, but all he could manage was a half-hearted nod.

"I think it's best we don't speak for a while," she went on. "I need space."

"Whatever you want," Lucas answered dully. Sally's athletic frame wavered, and he knew she had hoped he'd show more fight. But he didn't have any left in him.

Her eyes flashed. "Goodbye Lucas." And with that, Sally whirled on her patent heel, striding out of his city office and his life.

Lucas silently stared at the door she'd just gone through. So that was it. The absolute end of Lucas and Sally. When he'd met her just over two years ago, he'd finally felt that sensation of things falling into place. He had been starting his dream business with his best pal and then along came the exact sort of girl he'd always believed he should settle down with. Clever, ambitious and independent, Sally was endlessly kind despite her high-powered career. She was everything a man should aim for in a partner. And yet. He'd barely seen her this year; he'd had to cancel their two-year anniversary dinner due to a work crisis and had yet to make up for it. There was always next time, he'd told himself, never once stopping to make 'next time' happen. And of late, when her work took her away from him, which it often did, he started to feel relief when once upon a time he'd missed her like crazy.

Honestly, she should have ditched him a long time ago.

Deciding that he'd earned a coffee, he headed to the kitchen. As he trudged down the plushily carpeted corridor, Lucas realised he needed a friend more than ever and on approach to the kitchen he could hear Fred humming a song rendered unrecognisable by his complete lack of any discernible musical ability. Fred Jones was built like a fridge, wide and solid, with a thick cap of blond hair and oodles of barrow-boy-style charm. He was the definition of a perfect salesman and he never failed to make Lucas smile – exactly what was needed right now. Lucas rounded the corner into the kitchen just in time to see Fred discreetly slipping a small white tablet into his mouth.

"Hangover?" Lucas asked in surprise. Fred was a health nut who rarely drank since he'd become a father. To see him taking anything other than a vitamin was unusual.

Fred gulped back water and smacked his lips. "Nah, just something my doc wants me to take. Nothing to worry about."

Lucas regarded him for a moment. "You sure?"

"Very sure," Fred said with a wink. "Was that Sally I just saw leaving?"

"Nice change of subject." Lucas went straight to the gleaming coffee machine in the corner and popped in a pod for a premium espresso. "But yes, it was her. She was dropping this off." He brandished the ring from his pocket.

"Oh mate." Fred clapped a meaty hand on Lucas's shoulder. "I'm sorry. But you knew this was coming."

"Yeah." Something hard constricted Lucas's chest. "Not feeling great about it though."

"I know," Fred said. "She's obviously not the one."

"She was pretty damn close." Lucas shoved the ring back in his pocket, near to his heart.

"To love and to win is the best thing." Fred puffed his chest ostentatiously.

"But to love and to lose, the next best," Lucas finished Thackeray's quote then pulled a face. "At least we learned something from that book club the girls dragged us to. I should be grateful I don't have to endure that again."

"Suzi still nags me about going back but until Jack Reacher is on the list, I ain't." Fred had met his wife at university, and she'd been the one for him ever since. The dreamy smile that briefly flickered across his face was immediately tempered by concern for Lucas. "Seriously, though. Let's get together, talk it out."

"Thanks," Lucas said, blinking hard. "Still can't quite believe this is where I ended up. Like, I sleepwalked into this corner, and I don't know how I can get out."

"You know I'm here for you, yeah?" Fred patted the back of Lucas's neck. "Come for dinner round ours some time. Can't promise the kids won't be absolute tyrants but they do love their Uncle Lucas."

"I'd really like that." But Lucas was pretty sure Fred's kids *would* be tyrants. He loved them deeply and was godfather to all four, but it had taken hours to scrape the crusted snot off his iPhone the last time he visited. Not forgetting the many chiropractor appointments after little Rudy had demanded an hour of piggybacks for his fifth birthday. He took a deep breath, anxious for distractions. "Anything this morning?"

"Call with Dorfman later," Fred replied glumly.

"Yes. We *have* to try and keep him on the books," Lucas said. "Projections for the next year are so bad we need client fees of at least two million before the next financial year if we're to stay afloat. Otherwise, we'll need to consider selling some or all of the company off."

"We said we'd never do that." Fred's mouth turned downward.

"I know and believe me, I don't want to." As young dreamers at university, they'd always imagined having their own empire, their legacy to pass down to their children, affording them a happy, comfortable retirement. But as the strategic brains behind the company, Lucas had concerns.

"We can get the team out pitching," Fred said hopefully.

"Pitch to who?" Lucas knocked back his espresso in one gulp. It was still too hot and burned the roof of his mouth. "We've not had a sniff in weeks."

"Morning!" Jackie chirruped as she bustled into the kitchen. As Align's executive PA, she was the miracle worker who kept the place running. "How are those new pods?" She asked as she selected a latte for herself.

"Delicious, Jackie." Lucas moved to the dishwasher to put his cup in. "Thanks for ordering. Any calls?" For a crazy moment, he hoped that Sally might have tried to reach him in the few minutes he'd been away from his desk.

"Nothing urgent," she said. "Oh, but someone from the Arundel alumni association called for you again."

Lucas paused. "What?"

"About that school reunion? The fundraising one in your calendar?" Jackie replied smartly.

"It's TBD." Lucas's voice was pitched high. "*TBD!*"

"I know," Jackie said quickly. "And I said you hadn't confirmed anything to me but they seemed very keen to get your RSVP in."

Lucas swallowed. He had deliberately been ignoring the emails and calls about the Arundel reunion fundraiser.

What did he care if his old school needed to repair the clocktower? Why should he rush to spend his money on an institution where he'd endured years of bullying and snobbery?

"Lucas," Fred said quietly, "I have an idea."

"What?" Then Lucas caught the gleam in Fred's eye. "Don't say it."

"Hear me out," Fred said. "I know that reunion isn't your idea of a good weekend, but this could end up being quite fruitful."

"I'm not going." Lucas slammed his cup down.

"You always said you went to school with rich idiots who had more money than sense." Fred folded his thick arms. "So why not turn that to our advantage? I bet some of your old classmates could do with our services!"

Lucas gripped the kitchen counter as if it could ward off the anxiety brewing within him. "It's not that simple," he hedged. "You know I wasn't exactly Mr Popularity."

"You were elected head boy!" Fred said.

"Yes, however—"

"Popular enough then. Just start with the head girl and work your way down!" Fred chortled.

"One doesn't start anything with the likes of Posy Edwins," Lucas growled. "One finds a safe quiet spot and waits until she blows over."

"Posy…?" Fred lifted a hand. "As in Jesper Edwins's daughter? *She* was head girl?"

"You know her?" Lucas said with surprise.

"No!" Fred spluttered. "But *him* I do know! Lucas, Jesper Edwins is a multi-millionaire! His real estate interests are off the charts. Jackie, can you do some of your top-notch research on him? Get a bead on what opportunities he

41

might go for?" Jackie nodded excitedly. She had an amazing ability to dig up anything on anyone.

"I know he's a big fish," Lucas agreed. "But I'm not the man to reel him in. Especially if it means pitching to Posy, talking to Posy or, in fact, interacting with Posy in any way."

"Come on, man," Fred said.

"Don't *come on man* me," Lucas said irritably. "You don't know Posy. And Arundel? It's a fucking shark tank and I barely made it out alive."

"Swear jar!" Jackie interjected, rolling her eyes good-naturedly when Lucas flapped an apologetic hand at her.

"Besides, Posy Edwins probably won't even be at this reunion," Lucas said. The image of her startling hazel eyes flickered across his memory. Her constant laughter. "She'll be partying in Bali or photographing festivals in Alaska or something mad."

"Perhaps," Fred conceded. "But if she isn't in attendance, I bet you can still find some prime candidates." He directed shrewd eyes towards Lucas. "Please, just think about it. I know Arundel holds some unpleasant memories for you – Lord knows I get how tough it is being the only scholarship kid amongst a load of toffs – but said toffs could represent a real save for us."

Lucas took a deep breath. "I wasn't well liked." He knew even as he spoke that the battle was lost. "They won't want to work with me because I'm not... well, you know, I'm not..."

"Oh, for Goodness sake, you aren't posh, so what? Aren't you human? Well-educated? Amazing at your job?" Jackie jumped in, slopping coffee on the tiled floor. "You're all *those* things and more."

"What she said," Fred added.

"I went to the roughest comp in Tottenham and I can run rings round most of our clients." Jackie's face creased with pride. "The least *you* can do is go to a flippin' party."

"Fred's the pitch man," Lucas protested. "I'm the numbers man. I work on strategy and projections, not wooing clients."

"Exactly." Fred sighed. "So you know how bad things are. Why not go, have a sniff? If you find someone willing to bite, you can send them to me for the close."

Lucas looked to Jackie for moral support, but she sipped her latte with an unforgiving eyebrow raise and Lucas knew he was cornered. "Fine," he said grumpily.

"Nice one." Fred clapped him yet again on the shoulder. "Right, I've got to see a man about a dog."

"You're paying for my ticket!" Lucas called after Fred as he ambled out.

Fred guffawed back, "You land Jesper Edwins and I'll buy you tickets to anywhere you want!"

"Shall I call your school back and confirm for you?" Jackie asked, talons poised over her tablet.

"Sure," Lucas groaned. "You might as well book me into the nearest therapist's office for the Monday afterwards."

"I'm sure it won't be that bad!" Jackie's earrings jangled as she shook her head.

"I wish that were the case," Lucas said despondently as he wondered what on earth he'd let himself in for.

## Chapter Three

Posy slid out of the taxi and paused to drink in the view of her old school. Arundel College nestled in the green Yorkshire hills like a contented hen, golden brick glowing from the fading sun that caused the mullioned windows to glitter with refracted tones of orange and red. The long gravel drive cracked under the weight of the various vehicles dropping off eminent alumni and the air was sweet with the fresh breeze coming in off the peaks. As a flock of geese streamed majestically overhead, Posy hurried towards the great door. A queue was already forming there and so Posy obediently got in line behind a balding man who she vaguely recognised as being a few years above her. He was braying loudly to his bored-looking wife about the 'silent efficiency' of his brand new Tesla. Said wife was clearly too busy admiring the gigantic sapphire on her right hand to pay him any attention and the man's voice was getting increasingly more grating as a result. Sullenly, Posy checked her phone to see if there were any new messages from Henry, but she'd not heard much from him since he'd gone back down to Norfolk over a week ago. She'd sent him a mirror selfie of her reunion outfit to tease him out of radio silence. It was a dress that always invited a second look: a clingy Halston in coral-pink that fitted her like a dream to mid-calf, teamed with her favourite metallic Choos. But all she'd received in return were thumbs up emojis over an hour later.

Soon Posy was in Arundel's sumptuous lobby. She took a moment as nostalgia barrelled through her, taking her breath away. The carpet was still the same plush burgundy and despite the balmy spring evening, a fire roared in the hearth that dominated the far side of the lobby. Above it, Posy noticed with a pang, was the portrait of the new head-teacher. Mr Day had died years previously and his latest successor was a Mrs Paddington, an icy blonde with a Wintour-esque bob and quizzical, long-lashed eyes behind severe designer spectacles. Posy accepted a glass of cham-pagne from a passing waiter, who was clearly a current sixth-former and very much over this latest assignment he'd been given. As Posy sipped, she strolled over to the right-hand corner where the waiting area for the headteacher's office was. Sure enough, the squat red leather chairs were still there. She remembered sitting there with Lucas O'Rourke, waiting to hear all about her role as head girl. Posy grimaced, recalling their time together. God, he'd been such a drag to work with, always insisting on finding a way to drain the fun from any situation and add extra helpings of boring responsibility. *Because it'll look good on our CVs,* was his constant mantra. Who even cared about CVs anyway?

Posy followed the train of attendees into Arundel's Great Hall. It looked enchanting, she had to admit. Large tables were dotted around the perimeter, artfully decorated with fresh flowers and towering candelabra. The stage where Posy had formally accepted her role of head girl was now where the black-tie-clad string quartet played by the light of yet more candles. The diminishing evening light filtered through ancient stained-glass windows that filled most of the east wall, casting flattering tones across the multitude of guests. One corner of the hall was taken up by a busy pop-up bar, fetchingly decorated with ironic neon brewery signs and yet more flowers. The air smelled heavenly – a combination of perfume, wine and polish emanating from the pristine wooden floor. The elegance of the event could not be denied. And yet it left Posy cold. Around her, people moved with purpose and confidence, bragging about their families, their money and their careers. The way she felt right now after Jesper's scathing admonition, Posy could do none of those things. But she had to endure the evening for a least a little while, if only to make her father relinquish his grasp on the purse strings. Gulping down the last of her fizz, she headed over to the bar, hoping she could drink the awkwardness of the night away.

"Give me your strongest single malt," she demanded of the acne-riddled teen playing bartender. Moments later, she had a tot of Laphroaig and the peaty smell was a welcome transportation from the discomfort she felt within. As she inhaled, the string quartet switched from Vivaldi to Bizet. Posy winced. It wasn't that she hated classical music, it was just that it reminded her so strongly of her mother, particularly Bizet. Celia had loved entertaining and had especially liked curating playlists of classical music for dinner parties. Posy had barely turned four when cancer suddenly took her mother's life, but she remembered the gorgeous ceremony of

Celia's soirees: the cooking smells, the flower arrangements and the music, but most of all her mother's laughter tinkling through the house as Posy lay in bed not sleeping, feeling very aggrieved that she wasn't invited to have fun with the person she loved most in the world. As a little girl, Posy had been determined that as soon as she was old enough, she'd sit by her mother's side and co-host every single party. But the cancer had put paid to that. Across the room she caught a glimpse of Mrs Paddington, a vision in ice-blue Prada. She moved amongst the guests with regal poise, her polite smile unable to unseat that calculating curiosity in her eyes that was evident even from a distance. She was a different breed from the likes of Mr Day, that was for sure.

"Oh, my word! POSE!" Dee's unmistakable squeal rent the air and suddenly Posy was engulfed in a Chanel-scented embrace from behind, snapping her right back to reality.

"Dee?" Posy whirled around to return the hug.

"How the devil *are* you? What's it been, two, three years since we last got together?" Although Dee sounded the same, everything else had changed. The Dee of the past had been a little bird, all sharp elbows and frizzy hair. The latest version was still small, still forcing her hair back into a French braid, but marriage and motherhood had rounded her body into a softer shape, one that was now expensively ensconced in satin and cashmere. Long nails were painted a tasteful pink and diamonds dripped from her ears and fingers. Dee looked Posy up and down with a practised eye, nude lips curving in a knowing smile. "Ravishing as always!" she declared. "No kids, I take it?"

Posy forced a polite smile. Why was it so common for this question to be asked so bluntly of a woman? It was almost as if making it to thirty without spawning offspring was a transgression against everything that was right and good. Posy longed to tell Dee to get stuffed but given that they hadn't seen each other for several years that seemed a little harsh.

"Perhaps one day," she replied diplomatically, hoping that would herald a topic change.

"You should get on with it. I'm afraid your best eggs are far behind you." Seemingly ignorant of her breath-taking rudeness, Dee flicked a wrist to someone behind her. "You remember Lionel, my husband?" A tall, angular man with a receding hairline and non-existent upper lip edged to Dee's side. A glass of water in one hand, he gave Posy a joyless nod.

"Of course, we met briefly at your wedding," Posy said. Which had been almost immediately after university graduation. Dee hadn't wanted to wait for her fairy tale. "How are you, Lionel?"

"He's fabulous! The business is a dream!" Dee shot a glance at her husband. "Li, could you get me a drinky?" Obediently, Lionel ambled to the bar and Dee turned back to Posy. "Was the last time we saw each other at that gallery opening?" Without waiting for Posy to confirm, Dee ploughed on. "And then you went on to Belize on a photography jaunt, didn't you? Gosh, you're always on the move. I mean, I understand, I get it. My life is so WONDERFULLY busy too!" She fished out her phone and pushed it under Posy's nose. "My tinies! Gabriel and Alec. They're five and three now."

Posy squinted. The phone was whisked away almost as quickly as it had been proffered. She caught a glimpse of two small, pale faces posing stiffly by a gleaming Bentley.

48

"Lovely," she remarked, unsure what else she could say, given she'd barely met the boys.

"Have you seen any of the gang?" Dee went on. "Honor is— Oh, I say, there she is!" She waved and all of a sudden Honor was amongst them, glamorous in a slinky emerald sheath, her white-blonde hair sculpted into a chic, retro wave.

"Darling, awesome to see you!" Honor cooed, greeting Posy with a flurry of air kisses, her voice betraying a definite Atlantic twang.

"Honz!" Posy reciprocated the contactless kisses. Honor had emigrated to Seattle with her family not long after turning eighteen. However, Honor's work as a fashion journalist frequently brought her back to London, where she and Posy had managed quite a few debauched and expensively wild weekends. But then Honor had married Edgar Farquharson, the cream of New York society. Between that and popping out three children one after the other, wild nights with Posy had become a thing of the past. "I've missed you."

"You too!" Honor patted Posy's cheek.

"I can't believe you made it," Dee trilled. "Your schedule is impossible!"

"Oh well, thanks to a fleet of nannies and a lot of air miles, anything's possible," Honor purred, showing gleaming teeth. She narrowed her eyes at the bartender who'd served Posy. "Do you have De Brignac?" She plonked her champagne flute on the bar. "Because whatever this is, it's barely quaffable."

"The, uh, champagne is Bollinger and it's the only one we're serving," the young man gulped in reply.

"Leave him alone Honz, you're not in Manhattan now,"

Posy laughed at her old friend. "Besides, Bolly was more than enough for you back in the day."

"I know but since we started summering with the Carters – that is, Bey and Shawn…" Honor paused for effect and Dee didn't disappoint.

"You're friends with *BEYONCE*?" she shrieked.

Posy let out a snort of laughter. "Oh my God, Honor, you still haven't mastered the casual name drop, have you? You're friends with everyone who's anyone."

Honor giggled. "That is true. What can I say?"

Dee virtually swooned against Lionel as he returned bearing a martini. "Li, you must hear this. Honz is only besties with Beyonce and Jay-Z!" Dee said. Lionel's face stayed immobile.

"Very good," he remarked, with all the verve of a wet flannel.

"At any rate," Honor went on, "I've been drinking Shawn's champagne brand pretty much exclusively." She rolled her eyes in an attempt at self-deprecation. "But you're right Posy, I'll make do. Bottoms up!" She snatched up her glass and knocked it back, making sure to wince overtly to convey the depth of her compromise. "Oh, Posy! It's been simply ages since we hung out. I say, do you remember that time we almost got arrested in Harrods?"

"Well, you were making Princess Beatrice feel rather uncomfortable with all the yoo-hooing!" Posy laughed.

"Of course. God, the Royals are so over, I swear it. You should hear the way Megz talks about them. Anyway," Honor shook her head in humoured disbelief, "what's new with you?"

"Um." Posy took her time taking another sip of whisky, the liquid suddenly sour on her tongue. What *was* new with her? As she pondered the least lame response, her father's words about Posy's lack of a meaningful life came floating back. To her horror, tears threatened and she had to fake a cough to explain them away. "Not much," she spluttered eventually.

"Still snapping those little photos of yours, are you?" Dee asked.

"Well, yeah." *Little photos* made it sound as if Posy was farting about doing selfies and nothing else. Her latest project had been a landscape shot of the night sky over the Moors and it had taken ages to work out the shutter speed and filters required. She'd even slept in a tent for that one. "It's a passion of mine."

"Oh, you've made a go of it professionally?" Honor squealed. "Why, that's marvellous darling."

"I'm trying to." Posy's throat tightened. Maybe she never would, if she couldn't get the ticket to Hawaii. Plastering a wide smile on her face she decided to change tack. "Edgar not with you, Honz?"

"Sadly no," Honor said. "He's doing this sailing challenge at the moment, and you know I have no sea legs. Solo trip for me this time. But seriously," she fixed her eyes on Dee and Posy, "it's been far too long; we should have a solid catch-up. A proper, boozy girl's lunch, whaddya say?"

"Absolutely!" Dee lifted her glass.

"Would love that." Posy swallowed what was left of her whisky, failing to match Dee and Honor's enthusiasm. A whole lunch of trying to defend her non-existent achievements sounded like torture more than anything else. But she couldn't let on to such a thing and so the conversation flowed pleasantly. However, after a few minutes of Dee and Honor humble bragging about their marriages and lives of fortune, Posy started to feel a little sick. Excusing herself, she slipped away, weaving through the Great Hall. The mass of bodies and honking laughter was almost too much to bear and it was with relief that she slipped through the French doors and out into the school grounds.

## Chapter Four

L ucas's cheeks ached from so much forced smiling. Entering the school grounds once more had been an oddly visceral experience; he could virtually taste the semolina Froggy St Clair had flicked into his mouth as an April Fools prank and smell the scorched carbon of the traditional Guy Fawkes bonfire night celebrations. As he visited the gents' toilets that adjoined the Great Hall, Lucas even managed to find the burn marks from the time he'd busted two juniors smoking on their last day before summer break. Christ, didn't Arundel ever re-paint?

But Lucas was determined to make good on his £250 ticket. He had on his favourite suit and his dress shoes were polished brighter than mirrors. Now was the time to put aside the past and look to the future. As he walked into the Great Hall, he saw the somewhat familiar face of Julian Willoughby, his one-time opposition for the head boy role.

"Evening Julian," Lucas said brightly.

Julian blinked at him. "Do I know you?" Considering the guy had been the captain of the rugby team, the years had been especially harsh. Gone was the taut chest and super-hero jaw, in their place a burgeoning gut that threatened to pop the buttons on a rumpled YSL shirt and premature jowls that trembled with every move of his head. That once luxuriant mane of blond hair had been replaced by a combover of greying strands working overtime to cover a hot-pink scalp.

"Yeah, Lucas O'Rourke. We both ran for head boy?" Lucas tried not to let his embarrassment show. Surely there had been something memorable about their encounters?

"Oh right, right, right, right." Julian squinted. "You look different. Did you grow?"

Now it was Lucas's turn to blink. "Grow?" He suddenly caught a whiff of the beery tinge of Julian's breath and sighed. "Yes, I did grow in the ten plus years since we saw each other."

"Here." Julian nudged a statuesque creature next to him. "Sooky, meet this chap."

Sooky lifted her bored face from her phone. One look at Lucas saw the device stowed in a Bulgari clutch and her diamond-ringed hand reaching for Lucas's. "Charmed," she purred.

"Lucas O'Rourke. A pleasure," Lucas said. Sooky was immaculate in a tasteful, fitted gown, typically gorgeous in the way that only someone who spent one hundred per cent of their time on their image could be. High cheekbones framed a heart-shaped face with narrow, long-lashed blue eyes. A smile that had no doubt benefitted from chemical assistance was plumply welcoming. "I take it you didn't attend Arundel?"

"No. Marlborough." Sooky was clearly expecting an impressed response and when Lucas gave her the requisite awed expression she beamed. "Yah, good old Katy. Always knew *she'd* nail the top prize." Her eyes pointedly slid to Julian who was quietly belching into his pint and hoping no one would notice.

"Quite." Lucas wasn't sure whether England's future king would appreciate knowing he'd been *nailed* but he was more interested in what Julian had to say about his business. His father had left quite an empire. But years of observing Fred work a room had taught Lucas you couldn't just dive in cold. "So how are things?" he asked Julian. "The family well?"

"Well, Daddy kicked the bucket, as I'm sure you're aware," Julian said.

"I wasn't aware. Terribly sorry." It was a lie. Of course Lucas knew Sir Spencer Willoughby had died – from cirrhosis, if rumours were to be believed. But he felt that feigning ignorance about Julian being in charge of Sir Spencer's money was a good foil for pitching.

"Don't mention it." Julian gulped back his drink. "It was years ago."

"He left Jules in charge of the estate," Sooky said.

"Oh?" Lucas gave them his best wide-eyed stare. "How are you finding being lady of the manor?"

"Ha!" Sooky almost spat out her champagne. A sharp glance from Julian saw her daintily dab at her lips and compose herself. "That is to say, it's not what you would expect."

"I wouldn't know what to expect to be honest," Lucas said truthfully. "But I do know one often needs support managing sudden inheritances or windfalls. Mistakes can be made."

"Yah, they totally can," Sooky agreed breathlessly.

Lucas was buoyed by her words. "Many of my clients have really benefitted from the help—"

"Now I remember you!" Julian's thick finger was suddenly in Lucas's face. "Your parents worked for the school, didn't they?" Julian bobbed his head excitedly. "Yes, your mum was the cook. And didn't your dad mow the lawn or something?"

Sooky's reaction was immediate. Nose wrinkling, she actually took a minute step backwards. It was a discreet reaction to be sure, but to Lucas it was as bold as a slap in the face.

"That's right," he said resignedly. "My parents worked here. But my dad was head of security, not a gardener." He instantly hated himself for making that distinction. It shouldn't matter what his gloriously hard-working parents did. Yet to these people, who had been handed everything they had, those who grafted to achieve modest returns were the kind of people you step back from. As revolted as he was, Lucas needed new business and so he forced himself to stay in their presence.

"Yah and that's how you got your place. Scholarship." Julian was tapping his sloping forehead with glee. "Still got it. The old noggin still works."

"Clearly." Lucas swallowed the urge to snarl back. "But anyway, parents aside, I now own a wealth management business and if you'd ever—" He was reaching for his business card when Sooky laid a hand on Julian's forearm.

"Darling," she said, "the Carruthers are here. We really should say hello."

"What?" Julian had been staring morosely into his empty glass. "Do we have to? Timothy is such a miserable bastard sometimes— Oh!" Sooky's nails were digging into his arm.

Julian lifted his eyes to meet Sooky's and whatever marital telepathy she was conducting worked because Julian nodded and looked back at Lucas. "Sorry, Luke old chap, have to do the rounds, you know how it is."

Lucas slid his card back into his pocket and smiled genially. "Absolutely, crack on." As he watched them leave, he wished he had the balls to yell his correct name at their retreating backs, but he didn't need to be Fred to know that would be a poor show at an event like this.

Taking a deep breath, Lucas headed to the bar and ordered a whisky. He fancied something sweet and steadying and to his delight they had a very fine single malt that would do the trick. Drink in hand, Lucas turned and surveyed the room. It reeked of privilege. And he was standing in it, very much a product of that privilege yet also outside it. He should know how to navigate these troublesome waters, but they were as alien now as they had been when he joined the school as a nervous eleven-year-old. Again, he wished Fred could be here. Then immediately felt guilty for not doing his friend justice.

With another hit of Scotch warming his belly, Lucas decided not to give up. He turned to his left and spotted a pale-faced drip of a man clutching a glass of tap water.

"Very sensible," Lucas said by way of preamble.

The gentleman glanced down at his drink then back at Lucas. "I beg your pardon?"

Lucas gulped. Was it a major faux pas to make such a comment? He hoped the man wasn't a recovering alcoholic. "I mean, it's sensible to stay hydrated," he gabbled. "Warm in here."

"I suppose." The man stretched out a hand. "Lionel Goodman."

"Lucas O'Rourke." Relieved that his introduction hadn't completely scared Lionel away, Lucas relaxed a little. "Were you a pupil here?"

"Oh no," Lionel said. "Gordonstoun. But my wife attended here."

"Really?"

"Yes, Desdemona Carrington," Lionel answered. "Well, Desdemona Carrington-Goodman now."

"Dee?" Lucas's heart sank. Dee Carrington had been a total witch, if memory served. Always cosying up to Posy Edwins. Christ, did that mean Posy was here?

"Yes. Were you pals?"

"We moved in different circles." Although if Dee had had her way she and Lucas would have been moving on different planets. "She was best friends with Posy who I, ah, worked with quite closely."

"Oh yes, Posy. I met her at our wedding," Lionel said. "Mind you, that was some time ago."

"Li, darling!" Desdemona was suddenly upon them in a blur of diamonds and Chanel perfume. "Where did you get to?" She turned to Lucas. "Do excuse me for— Oh, do I know you?"

"Desdemona, allow me to re-introduce a fellow alumnus, Lucas O'Rourke," Lionel said before Lucas could say a word. "Apparently he worked with Posy?"

A merciless sneer spread across Dee's face. "Worked with? If you say so." She allowed herself an appreciative study of Lucas from head to toe. "You have certainly changed since school days."

"Er thanks?" Lucas wasn't sure if he preferred Dee's disdain or her lustful admiration. "I'm in wealth management now." He steeled himself and pulled out a business card.

"You?" Dee eyeballed his card as if it were about to explode. "Wealth?"

"Yes." Lucas was finding it difficult to keep his temper. "I have a successful company in London and—"

"And what, it's so successful you need to pitch for business here?" Dee interrupted with a snort.

"Hang on a minute Dee, this could be really useful," Lionel said measuredly. "You know I've been having issues with Aintree. Couldn't hurt to at least take the man's card."

Lucas could honestly have hugged Lionel in that instant.

"Aintree has been your family's wealth manager for decades," Dee pouted. "And besides…" She leaned in close to Lionel and whispered theatrically. "His parents were the *help*. It would be entirely inappropriate." To his credit, Lionel didn't seem fazed by this. His lack of response only riled Dee more and she turned back to Lucas. "Look, I'm sure your little business is doing just fine but Lionel works with Aintree because Aintree knows the world we exist in. It just makes sense."

"I'm afraid I don't understand." Lucas had been educated privately – as had more than a quarter of students at his university. He'd joined the sailing club and the rugby club – he'd even joined the drama club for a brief and hideous period. Lucas had ingratiated himself into the world of the wealthy because he'd known he could use his skills to succeed there and so far, he had done a damn fine job. What more could he do?

"You're right, you don't understand." Dee patted his arm as if he were a recalcitrant child. "And that's the problem." Dee spied someone across the room and her eyes widened. "Oh my God, that's Jemima! Her husband is a Right Honourable!" And without so much as giving Lucas one last glance, Dee veritably sprinted off across the room, leaving Lucas and Lionel to stand in awkward silence.

"I don't pretend to understand why my wife talks down to you so," Lionel said eventually. "There's no excuse for her rudeness."

"Thank you," Lucas said with surprise.

"But perhaps she has a point." Lionel gestured around him, face impassive. "My father made his money in medicine, as did I. But my roots are very much working-class."

"Really?" Lucas struggled to believe this. For one thing, the man's accent was so genteel it seemed to belong to a different age. That and he had consciously chosen to wear a cravat to this event as opposed to a tie.

"Oh yes." But Lionel didn't elaborate any further.

"Yet Dee married you?" Lucas couldn't help it. Dee, for all her exuberant snobbery, was at best an odd match for the dour, unflappable Lionel, let alone now Lucas knew this fact about his origins.

"She did. Vast sums of new money are an acceptable alternative for old money and titles. At least, in my wife's eyes they are." Lionel took a tiny sip of water. "As I understand it, you are in neither camp."

"I do all right." Lucas bristled. Owning a flat in Central London and driving a nice car counted for something, didn't it?

"My wife's point is… *all right* doesn't cut it amongst this crowd." Lionel dabbed his strangely thin lips delicately. "If you want these people to give you the time of day, you'd better rectify that." Dee's screech echoed across the Great Hall, causing more than one guest to wince in response.

Lionel heaved a sigh. "And that is my cue to attend to her. Take care, Lucas." And with that, the man strolled away.

Lucas took a moment to compose himself. He knew Lionel was right. Unless his business made him richer than God, being accepted by the upper echelons was going to be a difficult task. But understanding that fact didn't make it any less wounding. He'd lived with that understanding all his life and it never got any easier. As Dee's shrill laughter ricocheted into his ears, Lucas's temper rose. He spied the open doors leading to the school grounds and he made a beeline for them. Lucas needed fresh air and he needed it now.

## Chapter Five

Scurrying down the paths to the lake, Posy took appreciative gulps of the fresh night air. The path was meandering, with loose pebbles underfoot and she was grateful that the way was marked with festoon lighting. Ahead of her she could see the looming mass of the old Clary Chapel and the shimmer of the lake before it. From her clutch bag her phone buzzed. With delight, she saw it was Henry, finally.

HENRY: *Evening darling. Just got back to the flat and gagging to see you. Having a good night?*

POSY: *Taxi booked for midnight. Can't come soon enough.*

HENRY: *Fancy coming back here?*

Henry added drooling emojis.

Posy hovered her thumb over the keypad. Did she fancy it? Carefree laughter tinkled from the Great Hall behind her and the sound was so overwhelmingly smug Posy was suddenly very sure she might explode if she didn't get to see Henry soon.

*Maybe.*

She sent her message back with a wink emoji, then shoved her phone back in her leather clutch. Let him sweat a little bit. Of course Posy was going back to his, however she had to endure a little bit more of this night first. Perhaps get some phone numbers to make it seem to Jesper that she'd genuinely tried to network. But for now she could manage to take some time out to enjoy the last few minutes of dusk. She slipped off her heels and drifted across the lawns which were as neatly mown as ever. Drinking in the night-time scents, Posy wandered around the lake edge. How was it possible she'd reached this stage of her life only to feel so lost? Dee and Honor seemed so very content with their lot, Honor over-achieving as ever. But Posy had been head girl; she was an Edwins, after all. Mr Day's proud words echoed back to her from years ago. *The brightest of futures,* he'd said. As she approached the lake shore, its brackish aroma clung to her nostrils. From where she stood, things didn't seem quite so bright right now. "Get over it," she muttered.

"Someone there?" a male voice called from just ahead and Posy nearly fell into the lake.

"Hello?" she replied, once her heart had stopped thudding quite so painfully. Just ahead was a memorial bench and it was on this bench the mystery speaker was sitting. The evening light was almost gone but the man was sitting directly underneath the festoons and soon she was close enough to see him properly.

Even though the man was seated, Posy could tell he was tall, with impressive shoulders and a glossy mop of dark hair that looked as though he'd been continuously running his hands through it. Eyes as dark as bitter coffee regarded her from under a heavy, intelligent brow. "Hello," Posy breathed. Who on earth was this vision?

The man studied her for a moment, then his thick lips parted in surprise. "Posy Edwins?"

"Yes." Posy wished she knew who the hell he was. "Sorry to disturb you…" She dragged out the last word in the hopes that he would supply his name but he didn't; he merely regarded her blankly. "Kind of crazy in there," she said with a grin. "Mind if I join?" She pointed at the bench and he slid over.

"I won't stay long," he said. "You can have the bench to yourself soon."

"Oh, don't leave on my account,' Posy replied airily.

"It's quite all right," he said stiffly. "I'm sure we don't have much to say to each other." He sipped from what appeared to be a double measure of whisky.

Posy stiffened. "Excuse me?" She squinted at him. What was the attitude about? Posy was pretty sure they'd never laid eyes on one another.

The man snorted. "Come on Po—" then he stopped, letting out a humourless laugh. "Oh my God. You don't recognise me." He rose to his feet with a rueful head shake.

"Er, what?" In the few short seconds since Posy had approached this guy, he'd gone from stiff to uptight to angry and she couldn't for the life of her understand why.

"You *really* don't recognise me?" He laughed bitterly.

Posy's face turned hot. "It is a little dark out here." The mystery man tutted and turned sideways to glare out at the

64

lake and at the sight of his profile, a memory twinged in Posy's mind. She hurtled through time to find herself sitting in the headmaster's office, Helpboy next to her. "Oh my God!" she spluttered. "*Helpb*— Lucas? Lucas O'Rourke? Is that you?"

"Try not to sound *too* shocked I turned up to this thing," he said wryly.

"I'm so sorry." She distinctly recalled towering over him at school and that he'd been somewhat weedy. But not only had Lucas shot up to be well over six feet, he'd also managed to fill a suit very, very nicely with broad shoulders and muscles a sharply cut blazer did nothing to hide. "You look so different. And it's dark out here."

"Yeah, sure, okay." He shook his head.

"I see you've retained your sense of humour," Posy muttered. Not everything had changed then. "Have you popped to the library to cuddle the dictionary for old times' sake?"

"Oh, so you do know the library exists then," Lucas said. "Shocking, given that I never saw you in there."

"Well, forgive me for believing that life doesn't happen between the pages of books," she said immediately. "But I had a *life*. Friends. You know, people who want to hang out and have fun with you?" The irony that almost every one of those friends who'd kept her away from her books were now distant memories in the main did not escape her. But Posy wasn't about to let Lucas know that.

"What I had was − is − a life *plan*," Lucas shot back. "You know, the way those of us who don't have rich daddies have to—" he stopped abruptly then, swallowing visibly.

"No, *do* go on," Posy said stonily. She was overdue a lecture on her lack of responsibility and forward thinking.

First Pops and Sebastien, so why not this guy? "I'd love to hear all about what a massively ungrateful, privileged bitch I am."

"Um, er, sorry." Lucas looked down into his glass and took a deep breath. "I don't mean to be rude."

Posy nodded stiffly. "It's okay. And I'm sorry I didn't recognise you. But in my defence, you really have changed a lot."

"That's time for you," he remarked. He looked across the lake to where the Clary Chapel stood, squat in the dimming light. "Although that place is still standing, God knows how."

"I suspect that heap of bricks will outlast us all," Posy said.

"I wonder if it's still as cold in there all year round?" Lucas said.

"Dee swore she caught pneumonia from the last Easter service," Posy replied. "I hope for everyone's sake they've invested in a fucking radiator." She shivered. Speaking of such things had made her aware of the coolness of the night and in her haste to escape the party, she'd left her trench-coat in the cloakroom.

"Here." Lucas grudgingly handed Posy his dinner jacket and as she gratefully took it, she tried not to notice the way his muscles bunched under his crisp white shirt. The jacket was beautiful: Dries Van Noten, silk-lined, and warm from his body. If she wasn't mistaken, the cologne she could smell was Tom Ford. "You're right though." Lucas sat back down next to her. "This place is stuck in time!"

"Too right." Posy rolled her eyes. "All the old traditions and hazing. I wonder if they still do any of them?"

"I'm sure they do," Lucas said. "Like, making all the

First Years swim in there on their first day?" He pointed at the lake, black and ominous in the rapidly approaching night.

"Oh no!" Posy laughed. "I'd forgotten that one. I almost peed myself it was so cold. Did you ever climb the clocktower at midnight? We did that every Halloween. No wonder the thing needs fixing."

"Never did it." He shrugged sheepishly. "I do *not* like heights."

Posy wasn't surprised that Lucas didn't have a daredevil streak. Then she remembered what Mr Day had told them all those years ago in his office. "Speaking of weird traditions, do you remember that old bylaw Mr Day told us about?"

Lucas frowned. "No, which one?"

"The one where if the head boy and head girl ever got married the school would pay?" As soon as she said it Lucas's face twisted.

"Oh yeah." Lucas shuddered. "Must have blanked that from my memory in an act of self-preservation."

"One rule I hope they've got rid of, obviously." A chilly breeze tickled the back of Posy's neck and she shuddered, clumsily adjusting Lucas's jacket around her shoulders. A slim silver case fell out of an inner pocket, spilling business cards along the ground. "Shit, sorry." As she leaned down to pick them up, her foot skidded, casting most of them into the damp earth.

"You're getting mud on them!" Lucas crouched down and gathered up the cards, tutting loudly as the formerly pristine cards were now mostly streaked with mud. Posy caught a glimpse of the company name in the faint glow of the festoons.

"You're in wealth management?" she asked.

"Yes." Lucas was still scooping up his cards. "And I'm sure you have something pithy to say about that."

'Not really." But she did wonder why someone who hadn't fitted in at Arundel had chosen a career that was bound to catapult him back into similar circles.

"These are ruined." Lucas raised a fistful of cards at her. "Premium stock. See that embossing work? Took me weeks to source the supplier."

"I see you still manage to make everything you touch horrendously boring," Posy said. "No wonder your business is struggling."

Lucas stiffened. "What makes you say that?"

"Who brings business cards to a party?" she said. "Only someone desperate to score business, that's who."

"My business is none of your concern." Lucas's voice went tight and Posy knew she'd hit a sore spot. "But thanks for sticking your nose in anyway. And what about you? Did lugging around a heavy camera get too wearing on your manicure?"

Posy instinctively curled her hands into fists to hide her freshly painted nails. "Actually, I am still lugging around that camera, if you must know," she said defensively. "And I'm still pursuing a career with it. Although I have hit somewhat of a snag."

"A snag?" Lucas repeated, raising his brow.

"The financial kind," Posy said.

Lucas looked sceptical. "You? Surely you can get your father to invest in a studio of your very own or something."

Anger surged in Posy's gut. "You'd think so, but he's not convinced enough of my skills. I'm on my own."

Lucas seemed far from sympathetic. "Like the rest of us,

then?" he said and Posy could have sworn the smile on his face was victorious.

"In a way, yes—"

"Actually no, Posy, you aren't like the rest of us." Lucas laughed sharply. She gasped and looked at his face. Now there was the expression she recognised from their school days: a pained envy that was clearly spiking to his core. "*You'll* never be on your own when it comes to money."

Posy jutted her chin. "That's a little unfair," she said. "Do you know how tough it is to have your own father tell you he doesn't believe in your dreams?"

Lucas snorted. "Tough? I don't think you know what tough is."

"Hey!" Posy spluttered, rising to her feet. "I'm not going to apologise for my father's wealth! It's not my fault—"

"I swear to God," Lucas said slowly, his teeth gritted, "I cannot spend another minute here and listen to this."

"Listen!" Posy yanked off Lucas's jacket and shoved it into his chest. "I know how lucky I am. You think I don't? But I've had my father's legacy hanging over my head my entire life. You try living up to that. And don't even get me started on my preternaturally talented siblings."

"Forgive me if I don't weep for you," Lucas said with an eyeroll and he downed the rest of his whisky. "I can't be sad for someone who has squandered a lifetime of immense privilege and then blames it on daddy issues."

"That's not what I'm doing." Posy was outraged. "At least I'm not some rigid arse with a massive chip on my shoulder. You think I've wasted my privilege? I'm here tonight to try and make the best of it."

Lucas froze as he was putting on his blazer – only for a second but Posy didn't miss it. But he didn't elaborate.

"Well." He did up the buttons on his jacket. "Best of luck with that. Somehow, I don't think you'll need it." And with that he stalked off, his powerful form soon melding with the encroaching darkness until she could no longer see him.

Posy dropped back down to the bench alone, bringing the roil of emotions within her to some kind of calm. How was it possible Lucas O'Rourke *still* had a massive stick up his arse when it came to her? Posy knew how lucky she was to have had the upbringing she had, but it wasn't as if Lucas had been raised in a cave, was it? As she jiggled her leg in irritation, something flicked against her foot. Glancing down, she saw the edge of one of his cards sticking out from under her shoe. Mud had stuck it to the sole. She lifted it out with her fingertips. The card was stiff yet almost cashmere soft to the touch. Where it wasn't crusted with mud, that was.

"Huh. It really is premium stock." Just then her phone buzzed from the depths of her bag and, dropping the card in, she reached for the phone, her lips curving when she saw who it was.

"Hey babe." Henry's voice was husky and deep, sending a shiver down her spine that had nothing to do with the temperature. "How's the party?"

"Lame. Your offer still on?" she asked.

"You bet," he replied throatily, and anticipation made her heart trip.

"See you soon." Posy hung up with a satisfied smile. Screw Arundel, and screw Lucas O'Rourke. She didn't need to be told how to live her life. Posy Edwins would be just fine.

## Chapter Six

M onday morning gifted Lucas with a serious funk that even a punishing dawn session in the gym couldn't vanquish. As he rifled through his bedroom drawer for the perfect tie, he couldn't help ruing that he'd had not a single bite from that evening at Arundel and the subsequent spat with Posy had done nothing to amend the feeling of failure. The universe had gifted him the chance to speak to her alone, but she'd started whining about her bad luck and he'd not been able to stand it. How could someone be so oblivious? The whole train journey back to London, he'd kept trying to work out how he would inform Fred of his failure to get any business leads but each time his mind slipped back to Posy blithely whinging about her mega-rich father's failure to fund her whimsy. How could someone be so oblivious? What must it be like to charge through life without any thought or strategy, to do whatever you fancied because you knew Daddy would foot the bill?

After a quick shower, he was just slipping into his suit

when the phone rang; one glance told him it was Jackie, their PA. It wasn't even 7am yet and she was on the blower? Couldn't be a good sign. Steeling himself, he answered.

"Lucas?" Jackie was sobbing.

"What's wrong?" he answered.

"It's Fred. He… he…" Her words dissolved into snot and sobs. Lucas felt something tilt inside him. Staring out of his bedroom window across the rooftops of East London, he had a harrowing sense that there was about to be some very unwelcome change in his life. He swallowed, steeling himself.

"Jac, what happened?"

"He's in A&E at St Thomas'," she gulped. "I'm here… I'm waiting for Suzi but I'm all alone and I don't know what to do."

"I'm on my way now." Lucas hung up and swiftly ordered an Uber, knowing that the hospital was a short twenty-minute cab journey from his flat but easily double that on public transport.

Soon, he was at the impressive and enormous institution that was St Thomas' Hospital, a sprawling mass of buildings situated right by the Thames. He charged into the Emergency Department and found Jackie huddled on one of the seats in the waiting area, which appeared mercifully quiet at that time of the morning. As soon as she clocked Lucas, her eyes screwed up tight and fresh tears slid down her cheeks.

"Jac, what happened?" Lucas enfolded his assistant in a supportive hug and she collapsed against him, her shoulders trembling.

"I got in about six to set up for the day," Jackie sobbed into Lucas's chest. "Because of Dorfman coming in at eight.

And Fred was on the floor in his office – his lips were purple! Paramedics think it was a heart attack."

"Oh no," Lucas groaned, clinging to her tighter. Fred frequently liked to arrive super early; for him to be in the office around six to prepare for an 8am meeting was very typical. He remembered the tablet he'd seen Fred take in the kitchen the other day. Was that connected? It occurred to Lucas that Fred may have been secretly battling something for some time now and Lucas being the oblivious idiot he was hadn't noticed! He cursed himself for the neglect. He could have forced Fred to take a holiday, review his medical care, anything that could have avoided this living nightmare. He closed his eyes against the glare of the overhead lights, shut out the constant slap of feet on the tiled floor and let Jackie shudder out her anguish.

"Excuse me?"

Lucas opened his eyes. A petite, red-haired doctor in scrubs had arrived, her tired face arranged in a polite smile. She said, "Are you the family of Mr Fred Jones?"

"We're his colleagues and friends. His wife isn't here yet." Jackie lifted her phone. "She has to get in from West London and there's the kids to sort. She might be a while yet."

"I can only speak to next of kin, I'm afraid," the doctor said, chewing her lip. Her name badge read Dr Kim Lee.

"I'm his best friend *and* business partner." Lucas hated how clinical and exclusionary 'next of kin' sounded. Fred was a brother in all but blood, not that it would matter to Dr Lee. "Please, can you tell me anything?"

"Your friend is stable," Dr Lee replied. "That much I can say. And we will be admitting him to Cardiology. May I get his wife's details so I can call her with all the information?" She handed a notepad over to Jackie, who began scribbling down the details.

"Cardiology?" Lucas breathed. "You should know there's family history there. His dad was about Fred's age when he died from a heart attack. At least, I think that's what it was."

"That's useful," Dr Lee allowed Lucas a grim nod of thanks. "Look, if his wife gives permission, I don't see why we can't let you say hello to him, if he's up for that. I'll be right back." After another kindly smile she headed to the nurses' station, her rubber shoes squeaking on the lino floor.

"Coffee?" Jackie said hoarsely, thumbing down the corridor. "Saw a Costa down there."

"I can get you one," Lucas said, jamming his hand into his pocket for his wallet. "What would you like?"

"Oh, let me go," Jackie said. "I want to stretch my legs." She accepted the tenner Lucas proffered with an assurance she'd treat herself to whatever she liked.

As she trudged off, Lucas slumped back in his seat. It was all too much. A world without Fred wasn't one Lucas wanted to envisage. And Suzi! Fred had met her at university and had never looked at another woman since. Lucas couldn't imagine how frantic she must be.

Moments later, the doctor came back, saying she'd spoken to Suzi and they could pop in to see Fred but only one visitor at a time was permitted. He dropped Jackie a text to let her know where he'd gone and followed Dr Lee onto the ward.

"Oh, mate." Lucas's legs buckled at the sight of Fred, wan against the hospital regulation bedding. He had a nasal cannula fastened to his face, a drip in one arm, and a host of wires connecting him to a rather terrifying-looking monitor with all manner of lights and beeps.

"Hi," Fred rasped.

"I haven't got long," Lucas told him, taking a seat at Fred's side. "What happened?"

"My heart pulled a dick move and I passed out," Fred rasped.

"Or what we in the medical profession call arrhythmia," Dr Lee corrected, glancing at his monitor.

"Yes, mein Herr," Fred wheezed.

"Two minutes." The doctor pointed at Lucas and slipped out through the privacy curtain.

"Shit." Lucas took a deep breath. "Can they treat this thing?" Silently he vowed to research the condition and all associated illnesses as soon as he got home. There was no way he could live with himself if he didn't examine all the possibilities for Fred's wellbeing. And there had to be steps they could take at Align: in-office therapies, relaxing candles, heart-healthy snacks on hand. The cost didn't matter. Anything to keep his friend in one piece.

"Yeah," Fred said. "It's common. But getting back to full health might take time and... oh boy."

"What?" Lucas half rose, ready to buzz for help but then he saw Fred wave his hand.

"Chill." Fred coughed. "I can already see your mind going at a mile a minute. It's going to mean I need to take a step back from everything for a little while."

"Right. Of course. Whatever you need." Lucas was certain Align could cope without Fred there for a few weeks.

"It's just... they think part of the problem came from

stress," Fred said. "And I know when Suzi gets here, she's gonna stick the boot in about me working too hard."

"We'll manage, mate," Lucas assured him with a fervour he didn't feel. "You take some time. I can handle everything." He fought the urge to chew his thumbnail as he mentally reviewed each critical business decision he'd made of late. Was this his fault? He didn't want to think about a world where he wasn't working side by side with his best friend.

"Oi." Fred poked him with all the strength of a tired kitten. "This shit is mainly genetic. Don't start blaming yourself."

"I'm not," Lucas lied and forced a laugh. "Just thinking about what I can do to help."

"What would really help me is hearing how you got on at that school reunion." Fred's eyes glimmered with hope and Lucas's heart sank.

"Oh." Lucas managed a stiff nod. No point in worrying the man. Best that he believe the business was in safe hands for now. "Early days but should have some good news in the next week or so."

"That's fantastic," Fred gushed, a slow smile spreading his features. "And, whilst you're here, you should know I had a call from Lim Management last night."

"Lim?" Lucas's mind boggled. Lim was an Asian outfit – globally successful, with various offshoots of investment funds and wealth management.

"Yeah, you know I used to work with Evie Wong? She's one of their top M&A officers. She called me."

"What did she want?" There were few things a company like Lim could be after, in Lucas's opinion, but a buyout was the likely goal.

"Not sure," Fred admitted. "Seemed merely exploratory but—"

"Hey!" Dr Lee had yanked back the curtain and was eyeballing her patient with amused sternness. "What did I say about relaxing?"

"Okay, I think time's up," Lucas said. "Suzi's on her way here anyway."

"We're moving you to Cardiology," the doctor said firmly. "I'll make sure your wife finds you there."

After Lucas instructed a still shaken Jackie to take the day off, he headed into the office, booting up his computer with a whirling mind. After calling Dorfman to apologise for the last-minute cancellation, he spent some time splitting up Fred's responsibilities between himself and his team. Then he took a moment to breathe. Ticking off this necessary task should have given him comfort, but the gnawing in his stomach didn't let up. He'd nearly lost his dearest friend and now Lucas had to keep their struggling company afloat whilst he recovered, without anyone to turn to. Although keeping stress from Fred was important, Lucas knew he couldn't hide any problems from him for too long. He'd wise up to it sooner rather than later and who knew what effect that would have on Fred's wellbeing? God, if only Lucas been able to drum up some business from the reunion! But not only had he failed to spark any interest, he'd managed to upset the daughter of the key target Fred had begged him to win! Lucas straightened his notebook and brushed a loose bit of thread off his desk. He checked the angle of his desk and the recline of his chair. Still optimum. He opened up several programmes on his computer and swallowed his vitamin cocktail, mind racing all the while. As his email application opened up he saw a note from Steven Lazslo at

Maine Jewels pop in, high-priority. A nauseating wave engulfed him as he saw the ebullient jeweller had peppered the email subject line with a number of emojis and not happy ones at that.

"Oh, Fred." With a groan, Lucas dropped his head to the desk.

## Chapter Seven

Posy stretched her body along the bed in languorous pleasure at the sight of Henry padding back into his bedroom with two mugs of aromatic coffee. He looked so delicious at this time of morning – his dirty blond hair rumpled fetchingly, chiselled torso just visible through his unzipped sweater and matching sweatpants. His pink lips curved into a lascivious smile as he passed a mug over to her.

"Oh, lovely." Posy pulled herself to a sitting position, leaning against the silken headboard and took the drink.

"Fresh from the press," Henry purred, brushing her cheek with a gentle kiss. Posy grinned, inhaling the coffee he'd imported from overseas at great expense. Crashing at his after the reunion had been a total balm, soothing her jangled nerves from the party. There hadn't been much talking; Henry had been mentally taxed from whatever he'd been up to whilst away and Posy had only been interested in banging the stress away. And the latter activity was something Henry was exceptional at. So exceptional, in fact, that she'd spent the entirety of Sunday in his bed and Monday morning had snuck up on them almost unexpectedly.

"Thanks darling," she said, licking her lips in appreciation. "You always know exactly what I need."

"I thought you'd need the energy after yesterday." Henry raised his neat eyebrows suggestively. Posy could only agree. She really had needed a distraction from the fact that she had quite spectacularly failed the task her father had set her. And now, as Henry nuzzled her neck, she had trouble remembering what that had even been.

"Well, you know, your flat is just a short hop from Arundel," she said casually. "Convenience, and all that."

"Is that all it is?" He smirked. "More like you missed me whilst I was away." He paused his devouring of her neck to gulp coffee.

"If you say so." Posy smiled indulgently. Yes, Henry was the whole package – in every way – and the trouble was he knew it. But so long as he continued to deliver the fun, Posy was prepared to overlook the self-satisfied comments.

"So, how was it, seeing the old gang again?" he asked, settling back onto the bed next to her.

"It was an experience," Posy replied carefully. "You know the saying 'peaked at school'? Definitely applies to like, ninety per cent of my year." She was still reeling from how alien it had felt to be with Dee and Honor again. As teens they'd shared everything – secrets and emotions and trials and victories. When Posy had lost her virginity to Archie Tremayne-Webb, Dee had been the first person she'd told after Tara. And Honor had practically lived in the Edwins's summerhouse for a month after an epic falling out with her parents over an illegal tattoo. But yesterday, they'd been so apart from her that it had been impossible to imagine those days. And then there was Lucas, who'd arguably had a rough time of it at Arundel yet had seemingly emerged as the most together alumnus of them all.

"Yikes," Henry said. "That must have been quite the situation."

"It really was." Posy nestled against his solid bicep, drinking in the scent of coffee and detergent from his Under Armour hoodie. "Henners, do you think I'm…?" As she mulled over the accusations Lucas had thrown at her, her eyes stung. "Never mind."

"No, go on." He nudged her.

She lifted her head and looked at his chiselled features. "Do you think I have daddy issues?"

"What?" Henry frowned.

"Well… an old schoolfriend of mine said I've been, like, wasting my life. And that instead of taking responsibility for that I'm just blaming my dad." She bit her lip, almost afraid to meet her boyfriend's eye.

"That friend sounds like a dick," Henry snorted. "Was it Tara? I know she hates me."

"No, not Tara," Posy snapped. "And she's definitely not a dick, thank you very much." Although, now Henry mentioned it, Tara generally didn't speak of Henry all that much, which was odd considering that Posy and Tara discussed everything. "Tara doesn't hate you. What makes you think that?"

"Just her general tone and demeanour." Henry shrugged. "That night in Leeds she barely looked at me."

"She's kind of reserved," Posy said. "Besides, she didn't even go to Arundel so she wasn't at the reunion. Anyway, can we get back to this—"

81

"I try my best to get on with people, you know?" Henry pouted. "And don't I treat you well?"

"Of course you do!" Posy stroked his shoulder. "But I—"

"I'd hate for any of your friends to think so little of me," he went on, his lips curving even further south.

Posy sighed. As much as she wanted his opinion on her argument on Lucas, Henry was clearly troubled by the thought of just one friend not liking him. He wanted to get on well with the people who mattered to his girlfriend, she thought with a rush of affection. "I'll talk to Tara," she said, pushing the Lucas matter to one side. "But I think you're being paranoid."

"You're the best." He leaned over and kissed her, briefly sending all thoughts of Lucas O'Rourke out of Posy's mind. As they pulled apart, he gazed deep into her eyes. "Beautiful, darling Posy," he said. "I am the luckiest guy in the world."

Posy preened in the glow of his admiration. "Well, if you have some time this morning, let me show you just how lucky you are…" Hungrily, she reached for him.

Henry's eyes flicked to the clock by his bed and he jolted back. "Oh Jesus, is that the time?"

Posy glanced back to the clock. It was just 8am. A dull foreboding ached through her. "What's wrong?"

"Crumbs, I have to shoot off back to Norfolk," Henry replied glumly. "I'm flying to Belgium tomorrow night so I said I'd spend some time with Mother first."

"You're going back already?" Posy tried to hide her disappointment. He'd been gone for well over a week and they'd had just two precious nights together. Was that all she was getting this month?

"Work is insane!" Henry drawled regretfully. "I'm so sorry. But it's just until Thursday."

Posy forced herself to smile. How could she understand the pressures of being a jet-set broker for the rich and powerful? "I get it." Then she had an idea. "Belgium, huh? Want any company?" She was so desperate to put off facing her father that she'd contemplate meeting her boyfriend's parents for the first time.

A look of horror flitted across Henry's face. "What?"

"Your country pile sounds amazing," Posy continued with an insouciant shrug. "And I can always take in a bit of sightseeing around Brussels whilst you're working?"

"Oh, darling, we've been over this." Henry settled on the bed next to her and cupped her cheek. "Mummy and Daddy are so old and, well, they don't adjust to surprises or new people very well. Do you mind if we don't do this right now? Maybe in a few weeks when Mummy's new medication finally kicks in?"

"Oh, for God's sake Henry, I was kidding." Posy flapped a dismissive hand, trying not to let her hurt show. She wasn't in any rush to meet his parents per se, but the fact Henry actively didn't want her to come to Norfolk was unflattering to say the least.

"It's just, we're still rather new as a couple," Henry babbled. "I don't want anything to ruin this. We're good taking our time, aren't we?"

"Seriously darling, it's fine." Posy gulped her coffee despondently. A showdown with her pops it was then. "When do you need to set off?"

Henry winced. "Well, once we've finished these, I'm afraid."

"Oh." She had been hoping to squeeze a few more

hours out of him. But, she told herself, that was the hallmark of their relationship, right? Two independent individuals making no demands on each other and fitting their time together in when it suited.

"I know, I'm sorry." Henry flicked his hair out of his eyes. "But Mother does insist that I visit before I travel abroad. She frets – you know how old dears are. She'd worry herself sick if I didn't pop in."

"It's fine," Posy said. "You can just call me when you get to Belgium."

"I'll try," he said. "But I have to go straight from the airport to the boardroom and Wouter is meeting me at the airport so it might be late evening before I get the chance." He shrugged. "In fact, I probably can't talk until late most nights. The meetings I have lined up… argh!" He pushed his forehead against hers. "But I'll be thinking about you non-stop, as always."

"That's sweet," Posy said, bestowing his pillowed lips with a kiss. "When are you back?"

"Well, the meetings finish Thursday, as I said, but I may need to swing through Luxembourg for a day or two after that," Henry replied. "I'll let you know." He edged off the bed and started going through his drawers, pulling out freshly scented T-shirts and socks.

"No problem," she said eventually. "I'll probably be pretty busy anyway, figuring out how to get to Hawaii."

"By plane, I'd have thought!" Henry guffawed, but then seeing Posy's expression, his laughter stopped abruptly. "I mean, what's happening in Hawaii?"

"I mentioned the International Photography Achievement Festival, right?" Posy said, almost slopping coffee down herself. She could have sworn she'd mentioned it recently and more than once. "Remember? It's this really cool, really well-respected photography festival that's held in a different country every year," she said. "This year, Hawaii. And the festival director reached out to me on Insta and asked me to participate! They want me to show my work, sit on some panels and be an overall ambassador. Isn't that amazing?"

"That's stupendous!" Henry cheered, laying his clothes neatly into his LV case. "So when do you go?"

"That's the thing." Posy flushed. "Pops won't give me the money for the ticket. It'll be high season and flights are so expensive nowadays that just to fly economy for the week it would be around two grand at *least*, and that's flying at really shitty times. The festival will provide accommodation, but I'd obviously need some spends. Trouble is, I don't have it."

"Well, surely your allowance could cover that?" Henry said. "What do you think of this tie?" He held up a piece of cream Hermes silk.

"Draining against your complexion," Posy advised. "Anyway, the invite came so late I'd already spent my allowance, plus I got those new lenses that cost an absolute bomb. Normally if I need extra money I only have to ask – so I did and very nicely, by the way – but Pops said no. He doesn't believe this festival could be my big career break and he's kind of cutting me off. Thinks I need to learn about jobs and money management and blah blah blah." She curled her lip. "What does he know anyway?"

"Use savings then," Henry said, holding up some brogues to the light and checking for marks.

"I don't have any. I never thought I would need them." Posy wanted to sink through the bed and into a black hole as Henry's jaw dropped. She knew as a grown woman it was somewhat scandalous to not have any savings. But as the daughter of an incredibly wealthy man she'd never seen the point of trying.

Henry placed the leather shoes into a dust-bag and sighed. "Sorry my darling, I'm just a little flummoxed by the daughter of Jesper Edwins not having a penny to her name."

Posy's cheeks turned scarlet. "Forward planning hasn't always been my thing," she said. "I think that's kind of Pops's point."

Henry brushed her cheek with a gentle hand. "You know, I find it's better to beg forgiveness rather than ask permission." He smiled wickedly. "So why not use your credit card and explain later? When the bill comes in for the tickets, you'll have thought of a way to pay for them."

"I really shouldn't," Posy said miserably. "Pops was pretty adamant about not using his money." But then she wondered. Could she? By the time her pops noticed, she may well already be in Hawaii, proving to everyone what she was made of, and he couldn't be mad at her. But as a solution it was so underhand. As Posy watched Henry fold more shirts, his Rolex caught the light and an idea popped into her head. "Or…" She lay across the bed, drawing a hand down her hips. "Perhaps you'd consider loaning me the money?"

"What?" he spluttered, dropping the clothes to the floor.

Posy paused. She hadn't expected such a reaction. Henry thought nothing of spending wads of cash on extravagant dates; plane tickets were surely a minor expense to someone like him.

"Look," she said quickly, "I know we've only been seeing each other a few months and me asking for this much money is a big deal, but you know I'm good for it. I'll wangle it out of Pops eventually, I'm sure." Henry still seemed utterly taken aback so Posy reached for her phone. "Check out my Insta. All these people looking to buy this picture and this one and this one... After the festival I'll have such a name that I could command hundreds for a print!" She scrolled through her timeline of images for him, trying not to freak out at the unmoving expression on Henry's face as he examined them. "I reckon you add up all these sales, I'd have enough to pay you back in no time. Whack on some more sales from the festival, why, I'd even have enough to pay you interest. What do you think?" Henry was still rigid, so Posy leaned forward, her fingers hovering at the drawstring of his trousers. "I'd be extremely grateful?"

"Wait a minute, Posy." Henry grabbed her hand. "I— Well, that is to say..." His lips narrowed and Posy felt a flutter of uncertainty. This hesitation was most unlike him. Finally, Henry sighed. "Darling, I'm just not that liquid at the moment. Business hasn't been booming recently."

"But you bought those Prada shoes for me last month," she blurted in confusion. "And dinner at Les Trois Garçons that time?" Henry flashed her a wounded look and she raised her hands in apology. "I'm sorry, I shouldn't police how you spend, I just didn't realise you were going through a tough patch." She kicked herself. What kind of girlfriend was she that she couldn't notice such things?

"Don't mention it," Henry said. "But this is why my trip is so important. Could really right the ship, as it were." He leaned in for a sweet kiss, then pulled back to study her face. "Your photos are lovely," he added. "You know I think that. I just can't invest in anything right now. God. I'm so sorry."

Posy masked her disappointment by hugging him tightly. His heart pounded strongly against her forehead and a deep sigh racked his body. She bit her lip. It really wasn't fair to put this on him. "Don't worry," she said, wrapping her arms round his muscular back. "Just thought I'd ask. And I'm sorry, again."

"Any other time Posy, I'd help, I really would." Henry dropped a kiss on the top of her head. "It's not the best time for me right now. Gosh, I wish I could help."

"Seriously," Posy said, her voice muffled by his jumper. "It'll be fine."

"So, why not try the Amex and book online?" Henry said with a reassuring squeeze. "Go on, use my laptop. Remember? Forgiveness, not permission."

---

A little later, Posy quietly shut the front door to her home and tiptoed to the stairs. She still wore her Halston dress from the reunion and despite throwing on one of Henry's old Hugo Boss shirts over the top, it was clear she'd done a walk of shame. The soft voices of her father's favourite radio show meandered out from the kitchen and she breathed a sigh of relief; the odds of making it upstairs unscathed were good.

Or so she thought. Just as Posy made it halfway up the stairs, a door slammed open and Jesper's voice ricocheted up the hallway.

"Posy? Is that you?"

Holding her breath, Posy carried on ascending, hoping he wouldn't come out to investigate, but seconds later there he was, owlish eyes furious behind his wire-rimmed glasses.

"Oh, hi Pops!" she said breezily.

"Don't you dare 'Hi Pops' me," he snapped, his voice breaking. "How could you?"

"What do you mean?" Posy slowly walked down towards him, her insides plummeting. She was pretty sure she knew though.

"I didn't want to believe…" Jesper went on, his face blanching. "Ines told me I was being overly reactive, but I needed to be sure."

"Pops—"

"Did you use the Amex to book a flight to Hawaii this morning?" Jesper demanded. "On beachflights.com?"

"Pops, I can explain," Posy began, panic running through her veins. She had to make him understand otherwise he would cancel the flights and she couldn't allow that to happen.

"What, you didn't think I'd put an alert on your cards?" he said, folding his arms. "You thought you could just do whatever you wanted despite my wishes?"

"I thought if you could only see what I'm capable of you'd understand," Posy said, rushing to his side. Jesper stepped back from her, his eyes reddened. It hit her then that her father wasn't simply angry, he was hurt. Betrayed. Posy swallowed hard. The odds of talking her way out of this seemed small. "Please Pops, I just wanted to—"

"It's always about what you want, isn't it Posy?" Jesper quavered. "What Posy wants, Posy gets. Who cares what anyone else wants or thinks? You doing this just shows me you aren't serious about this festival. It's just another bloody yoga retreat, isn't it? You can't be bothered to put the hard graft in."

"That's not true!" Now it was Posy's turn to snap. "Have you not seen my photos? I have almost twenty thousand followers on Insta now. After a stint at this festival I can double that easily. I can start selling the pictures, get some marketing going… That's a business!"

"Your photos? You mean, the ones taken with the camera *I* bought you," Jesper said. "Edited and manipulated on the laptop *I* got you. The phone you're constantly glued to? Paid for by *me*. What's next, Posy? Want me to start a fashion label for you? Buy you a house to start your property empire?"

"That's not what this is," Posy cried. "But why are you putting your foot down now? You've always helped me!"

"Is it help?" Jesper said. "Is it really helping you just giving you whatever you want all the time?"

"This is Ines, isn't it?" Posy's stepmother was the only person Jesper listened to apart from Sebastien.

"Ines has nothing to do with this," Jesper snapped. "*I'm* taking responsibility for you. Finally."

Posy stopped, her throat dry. "Responsibility?" she repeated. "What, like I'm some mistake to be corrected?"

"Don't be so dramatic," Jesper said. "But I have to accept the role I've played in your life so far. I look at your siblings and the paths they are on… and then I look at you. You're a woman now, Posy, not a child. Things have to change, and it starts now. I mean it. Time to get serious about something, anything."

"There's nothing I can say, is there?" she croaked. "To convince you how much I want this."

"Not this time," Jesper said. "I can't keep throwing money your way in the hope you'll knuckle down. And as for spending *my* money when I specifically forbade it? I'm disgusted."

"Pops… Dad. Please. I'm sorry, really I am." Posy

grabbed at his arm but he jerked away. That stung. She shrank back, dreading what was coming next.

"You may be sorry but I'm cancelling both your credit cards and getting a refund from beachflights.com for that ticket," Jesper said with a sniff. "Your debit card is active for emergencies but I will be examining every purchase on it and if I see one item that doesn't look absolutely essential, so help me I'll take that off you and you'll get cash in hand at the start of every day until you have a job or some meaningful endeavour. God, I'd even be happy if you decided to marry that fellow of yours instead of merely partying with him until the small hours. When I'm satisfied that you're not wasting this life you've been blessed with we can talk about money, but for now, the Bank of Dad is closed."

Posy's eyes filled with hot tears. She'd never seen her dad so dejected. "Pops, please. Can't we talk about this?"

"Your mother only wanted you to live a fulfilled life, Posy," Jesper said bitterly. "Every time I look at you, I wonder what she would think of the choices you've made. I hope she wouldn't be disappointed."

Posy reeled, grabbing the bannister for support. Her father rarely spoke about Celia and when he did, it was only in the loosest, glowing terms. "Take that back." Sobs racked her voice. Her mother would understand, Posy knew. Celia would have understood that Posy needed time and support as she worked out her path in life. Support that Jesper was more than able to provide, only he'd now decided he didn't want to do so.

But Jesper had spoken and the effort had clearly hurt him. With shoulders slumped, he backed away down the hallway and closed the kitchen door with a silent thud. Posy could only watch him walk away, tears coursing down her face. How could this be? How was it her life was reduced to living off pennies?

The front door rattled behind her and from the silhouette in the frosted glass she could see it was Florence. With a groan, Posy flung herself upstairs. She had absolutely no desire to see her smugly engaged big sister and, more to the point, Posy had yet to feed back on the bridesmaid dresses anyway.

Posy slammed her bedroom door shut and dropped onto her bed, her mind racing. With another sob, she reached to her bedside table and found the framed picture that had pride of place – one of the few that existed of her and her mother together. Celia cradled a baby Posy in a yellowing shawl that had been worn by several generations of Edwins.

"Oh Mum," Posy sighed. "Would you really be ashamed of me?" Of course, her mother didn't answer, her sweet smile frozen in time. Celia had been a traveller, a rider of horses and climber of mountains. She'd laughed and cooked and sung – always constantly singing. Surely a soul as expressive as that would have understood that each of her children was unique and needed space to grow into the adult they would become? How could her pops think otherwise? What would it take to make him proud of her?

Posy lifted her chin; she just had to show her father that she could be worthy of his approval. If he wouldn't help get her to Hawaii, she would have to find her own way there. As her fingers brushed her expensive clutch bag, inspiration struck. Surely, amongst all her designer clothing and accessories, she had some items that she could part with? Energised, she hurried to her wardrobe and flung it open, cheered as ever by the sight of the rainbow of fabrics. There had to be some clothes she didn't wear anymore that could fetch plenty of money on eBay or perhaps one of those specialist designer sites?

After a solid half an hour, Posy had a couple of Rixo dresses, a Chloe sweater and an ancient McQueen skirt that she felt able to part with. It had occurred to her as she looked that despite the immense pleasure she took from beautiful clothes, the bulk of her allowance went on travel and photography, meaning there wasn't an excess of clothing to sell. It surprised even Posy. Frowning at a loose hem on the skirt, she then went to her jewellery box, bracing herself for the sight of her mother's ring nestled pride of place in the middle of it. Posy allowed her fingers to brush the Cartier-branded box. It was by far and away the most valuable piece she owned, and by no means was it up for sale. Brushing aside the memories of her mother, Posy found a simple gold chain an ex-boyfriend had once gifted her and some gaudy Chanel earrings that had seemed like a really good idea that time she and Honor had partied hard in Monaco one summer, just before Honor got married.

Dumping her haul on the bed, Posy felt somewhat deflated. She might be able to scrape together a few hundred for this lot; the clothes were well worn, the jewellery nothing special. No way would this get her the fast cash she needed. Ironically, the only things worth enough to pay for a plane ticket and expenses were the very things she needed for Hawaii: her laptop and camera. Posy stared disconsolately at the rumpled clothing. She had so little that was tangible to show for the money she'd been given over the years. With a huff, she dropped to the bed and closed her eyes. What on earth was she to do?

Just then, her phone chirruped. Hoping it was Henry with something to cheer her up, Posy upended her clutch bag to find it, but in her prone position the contents of her bag went everywhere, some landing on her face. Growling, Posy shoved everything back in her bag, but the last item caught her eye and made her pause: Lucas O'Rourke's business card.

"Great," she muttered.

It was an unwelcome reminder of the harsh words they'd exchanged that night. But then another thought popped into her mind, a memory that was soon followed by a plan so outrageous she almost dismissed it outright.

But not quite.

## Chapter Eight

The City of London was as busy as ever. Lucas hustled out of Liverpool Street station, cursing the train with the faulty doors that had made the entire service grind to a halt and as a result, caused him to be woefully rushed to get ready for a 9.30am conference call. So far this week had been manic, dealing with the fallout of Fred's absence.

He strode down Commercial Street, thanking his lucky stars that Align's offices were a short walk from the station. Dodging slow-moving tourists, he nipped down Charlotte Alley, a narrow little street that surely once upon a time housed all manner of nefarious deeds but now played host to several fledgling companies looking to make their mark on the financial centre of London, including Align. Lucas loved the sudden hush that the tall buildings afforded, the history wrought in the faded bricks and uneven pavements.

He stopped in his tracks, for there was something he hadn't expected, not at all: Posy Edwins, curled up on the small flight of stone steps that led to Align's front door. She was busy fiddling with what appeared to be a state-of-the-art

SLR, a thermos at her elbow. Her thick, honeyed hair was piled on top of her head in a style that he knew had taken probably seconds yet still managed to look chic and considered, showing off her graceful neck and high cheekbones. She was dressed warmly for the spring morning in a thick olive cardigan that slipped off freckled shoulders to show a bright jungle-print vest-top and distressed jeans with studded boots.

"Posy?" he said. "What are you…? How long…? Are you waiting for *me*?"

Posy's head jolted up in surprise. She looked tired, but there was excitement in her eyes. "Hello there! Why yes, yes I am here for you. Do you have a moment?"

Lucas knew the gentlemanly thing would be to invite her in but after their encounter by the lake mere days ago, there was no one he wanted to see less. "Not really," he said, honestly. "I have a call soon that I really need to prepare for."

"Please." Posy's hazel eyes widened. "I know we parted on bad terms at the reunion, but I have a proposition that I think could be of interest to you." She cleared her throat. "Like, financially and stuff."

"What?" Lucas tried to hide his scepticism. Unless Jesper Edwins was currently hiding in that tote bag she was hauling, it was doubtful Posy had anything to offer that Lucas could want.

"Please hear me out." She lifted placatory hands. "I only need five minutes."

"It must be serious if you've trekked all the way down to London," Lucas said. "Daddy's helicopter provide a nice ride, did it?"

Posy's face hardened. "Are you interested in my proposal or not?"

Lucas stared at her determined expression. If enduring five minutes with Posy Edwins could garner a lead to save Align, then Lucas owed Fred that sacrifice. "Fine," he sighed. "I can give you a little time."

He flashed his swipe card on the security lock and ushered her in through the lobby. Within moments they were in his office and Posy was face-up to the window, admiring the same view Lucas did every day. Feeling like the situation was increasingly surreal, he hung up his jacket and switched on his computer.

"Don't suppose you have any coffee?" Posy asked, swinging her thermos at him. "I've been up since two and I'm gasping."

"2am?" Now Lucas was intrigued. "Fine," he said with a shrug that he hoped masked his curiosity. He pushed the intercom on his phone. "Jac, can you bring a pot of coffee in please? Two cups. And is the VC link up for the nine-thirty?"

"Coffee is no problem," Jackie said. "But the Moskowitz Brothers cancelled."

"Fuck." Lucas palmed his face. "That's so last minute. Did they say why?"

"Swear jar!" Jackie barked and Posy stared at the phone in surprise.

"Fine, fine." Lucas dug around in his pocket for his wallet and dropped a pound onto the table. "There. So, tell me, why?"

"No, their assistant didn't say why," Jackie went on. "She said she'd call back with new time suggestions later."

"Double fuck." Lucas made a fist. "Yes, sorry Jac, another quid coming your way. Just the coffee then, cheers." He hung up and rubbed his face again. From what he knew of the Moskowitzes, if they were cancelling the call with no rush to rearrange, it meant they had no need of Align's services anymore, he could feel it. If Fred were here, he would merely lift the phone to woo them back with his magical charm. That morning however, Lucas felt about as un-magical as it was possible to feel. Lucas pointed at his visitors' chair. "Let's get this over with."

"Charming. But yes. Let's." Posy curled up on the stiff leather chair opposite him. The effect was somewhat disarming: Posy with all her bohemian chic, looking totally out of place in an environment created to serve people of her wealth and background. Ironic really, Lucas thought to himself as Jackie bustled in with a cafetière and two cups.

"Here you go," Jackie said as she popped the tray down. "I'll have those pounds for the share jar please."

Lucas handed the money over. "I'm going to be bankrupt at this rate," he said and then winced. His joke wasn't too far off reality. With a satisfied smile, Jackie took the coins and hurried out, not without a curious glance at his guest, who was going straight for the coffee. "Right," he said to Posy, as she got busy plunging the cafetière. "What's all this about?"

"It's a little mad," she said, "so please bear with me." She poured out the coffee into both cups and handed Lucas one. "I think we can help each other."

"You're going to have to explain," Lucas muttered. "And quickly." He took a deep mouthful of coffee, wincing as the roof of his mouth complained at the heat.

"Right," she said. "Remember at the reunion *before* I put my giant foot in my mouth, I told you about my dad sort of cutting me off? He's now gone a step further and pretty much frozen *all* my cards. Not even an overdraft. Nightmare."

"Hang on." Lucas held up a hand in disbelief and Posy sighed loudly. "You're telling me, as a woman nearing her thirties, educated at one of the best private schools in England, that your father still gives you an allowance?"

"Yes, like everyone else we went to school with, Lucas." Posy's cheeks pinked, throwing her freckles into stark relief. "The point is, I have a major opportunity coming up that could well be my break for an actual career. A step towards being a proper photographer. But I need a plane ticket. One that my father won't pay for."

"Right." Lucas put his coffee down. After the experience with Fred, Lucas had little patience to indulgence her. "I really don't see how—"

"Just let me finish," Posy begged. "I can't get a loan, because my credit rating isn't great. It's awful, actually."

"Christ, how?" Lucas had spent his whole adult life conscious of his credit score. Nowadays it was actually considered trendy to flaunt your thriftiness but when he'd been a student, such behaviour hadn't been at all sexy. Not even a little bit. Only Sally had appreciated Lucas's expert wielding of a household budget spreadsheet, but that was mainly due to her data-driven job as a corporate lawyer. And that was over now. So how could Posy, born into more money than most people would see in a lifetime, end up with a poor rating? It beggared belief.

Posy yawned and picked at a nail. "There was this time when I opened a new card and then someone pinched it from my yurt in Bali and went on a massive spree across the world." Posy waved a hand dismissively. "And a dispute with the Maserati garage which actually was not my fault. All sorted now but there's apparently still, like, red marks against my name or something? Believe me, I've checked and without a regular source of income or Pops being a guarantor, I can borrow the grand total of zero pounds. Not only that, it turns out I have bugger all of value worth selling apart from my camera."

"Sorry I asked," Lucas said wearily.

"Anyway," she went on, "this photography event, the one that will massively boost my career, it takes place in Hawaii."

"Glamorous," Lucas remarked, still curious as to why he needed to know all this.

"I know, right? It's the most exciting thing to ever happen to me and you're talking to someone who once got a personal invitation onto Leo DiCaprio's yacht."

"So how can I help?" Lucas said, irritation pricking at his tone. "I'm not lending you any money – certainly not based on the pitch of the past few minutes." He didn't add that he needed every penny at that moment. "Now, if that's all…?" He flicked on his computer and began to enter his password.

"I don't need your money," Posy said, a hesitant smile stretching across her features. "I just need your hand in marriage."

Lucas blinked. Had he heard her correctly? "Excuse me?"

"Hear me out," she went on calmly. "You need clients. Now more than ever now those Moskoshits have—"

"Moskowitzes," Lucas croaked. His eyes locked, panicked, upon hers.

"Whatever," Posy said. "You need business." When Lucas opened his mouth to deny it she wrinkled her nose.

"Don't lie, it's obvious. You were clearly trying to recruit clients at the reunion." Lucas had no idea Posy could be so perceptive. She grinned infuriatingly, clearly smug she'd nailed the truth. "Now it just so happens my brother is looking for a new wealth manager to manage my father's funds."

Lucas's curiosity edged its way past the shock. "*Really*?"

"Yes. Sebastien is utterly clueless on things like this. He would jump for joy if I plonked a keen, experienced, trustworthy wealth manager in his lap." Posy leaned back in her seat, one perfect eyebrow arched. Lucas seethed. She knew she had him.

"You'd connect me with your brother?" Lucas could only dream of getting such a meeting through his own efforts. "But there's no guarantee he'd offer me his business."

"Trust me when I say he's panicking and doesn't trust any of the usual candidates. He wants someone new but reliable and experienced. I can talk you up," Posy said. "You give me some success stories I can brag about... and trust me, I can sell you."

"Right." Trust Posy Edwins? Lucas thought. How could he?

"And if that's not good enough, I'm willing to offer up my entire social circle for you to mine," Posy went on. "Like, my ex. He's the owner of Shulware – have you heard of it?"

"I'm still stuck on— Hang on, you did say Shulware?" Lucas repeated hoarsely. "The software giant?"

"Yup." Posy nodded. "Fenny and I are on excellent terms. He'd take a meeting with you if I told him to."

"You refer to Fenton Shulman – the sixteenth richest person in the world – as Fenny?" Lucas felt as though his head might explode.

"Yes." Posy rolled her eyes. "He isn't royalty or anything. His idea of a wild night was completing the *Times* crossword in under an hour. Total dork." She took a sip of coffee and dabbed her lip. "You'd really get along."

Lucas was curious enough to let that dig slide. "So, what, you'd simply call him up?"

"Yes." Posy flicked her hair. "We talk loads. There's him, there's the Farrellys, the Withenshawes, there's, oh, a ton of the art collector gang from my uni days. They're all just as bad with money as I am. You'd clean up, I'm sure of it." She paused, a hopeful smile creasing her face. "And I'd give you the intro of your dreams to all of them."

"I see." Lucas sagged back in his chair, his mind reeling. "But why do I have to *marry* you to get all this?"

"The Prefect Marriage Rule. Remember?" Posy said jubilantly. "We marry, and the school has to pay for the wedding *and* the honeymoon."

Lucas finally understood. "You're suggesting the honeymoon would be Hawaii."

"Exactly." She nodded.

Lucas lifted a hand. "You do realise how crazy this sounds? Abuse the institution of marriage just to secure some flights you should be able to afford anyway? Plus, what happens if we want to marry someone else?" Marrying Posy Edwins was a farcical enough idea, but the inevitable divorce was just plain nightmarish.

"I hear you, but my thinking is we don't need to marry for real." Posy's face contorted. "As if. We'd just, like, fake it somehow."

Lucas wasn't sure whether to laugh at the unsurprisingly slipshod nature of her plan. "How much have you looked into this?" Posy looked at him blankly, so he tried again.

"Did you speak to, I don't know, a lawyer? Did you even dig out the contract your father signed upon confirming your attendance at Arundel? Read the bylaws?"

"There's an actual contract?" Posy gaped and Lucas had to resist the urge to smash his head into his desk, the earlier excitement over the clients fading into frustration.

"Think about it," Lucas said, not bothering to disguise the scorn he felt. "You suggest faking it? How exactly would that go? We merely tell them we're getting married and they just hand over wads of cash based on our word?" When Posy didn't answer immediately, he snorted. "I am not interested. This is crazy." How deluded could one person be?

"Believe me, I have no desire to be your wife for real," Posy replied. "I'm suggesting there might be a way to fake it. If Arundel imposes too many restrictions or we don't feel we can get away with it, we can bail. But think of what we could both gain if we went ahead with it. It could be so simple."

"There's nothing simple about getting married," Lucas said ruefully. It wasn't lost on him that Posy was sitting in the exact spot Sally had been in when she'd finally dumped him.

"Wait, what?" Posy's eyes darted to his ring finger. "What are you saying? This won't work if you're married already."

"No, I'm not married." Lucas wished he hadn't said anything. "I *was* engaged. For a while. It's over now."

"Oh." Posy appeared largely unconcerned by this revelation. "What did you do?"

"It just went—" He stopped and frowned. "Hang on, who said I did anything wrong?" When Posy merely responded with an eyebrow raise, he dismissed her with a wave, unwilling to let Posy in on the very recent pain of it all. "I may not have made it down the aisle, but I do know weddings can be a lot of work."

"Doesn't have to be." Posy leaned forward. "Listen, if Arundel approves, maybe we can knock up something that just looks like a wedding and take some photos to show as proof afterwards. I'll wear a nice dress, carry a bunch of flowers—"

"Christ." Lucas steepled his fingers and pushed them to his lips, taking deep breaths. "This is possibly the maddest idea I've ever heard."

"Why are you so negative all the time?" Posy threw her hands up in the air. "Is it really that mad? We can send them the photos of a fake ceremony, and we can at least try and look happy." When Lucas didn't immediately respond she went on. "Happiness is an emotion that people with blood flowing through their veins and not data—"

"You really don't see why?" Lucas interrupted. "You seriously expect Arundel to hand over free money based on us promising to send a few photos of a staged ceremony? That's even if this stupid marriage rule still exists. You haven't thought this through at all." He tapped at his computer in a show of indignation. "Perhaps you should leave. I have a business to run."

But Posy didn't go.

"No, *you* haven't thought this through. Come on, consider it. So what if they did want to see a proper wedding?" she demanded. "If we can fake photos, why not the real thing?"

"You mean arrange an actual wedding of sorts that Arundel staff could attend?"

"Yeah."

"Where do I even begin to describe the lunacy?" Lucas

gripped the arms of chair. "What if Arundel requests a real marriage certificate? Banns? You know, legal documentation that we're married?" When Posy remained silent, he snorted derisively. "See?"

"Okay, maybe I should have dug out the contract," she admitted. "And there may well be some complications. We might have to think on our feet and go with the flow, but I think this could actually work!"

Lucas couldn't believe she was describing a fake wedding, an act of fraud, as something they could just fumble their way through. A real one took months of planning and that was when genuine emotion was involved. "Maybe, maybe," he tutted. "Great plan Posy, glad to see you're still capable of putting in the hard graft."

"Hey!" Posy lifted her chin. "There's no need to be such a dick about it. You know, technically, you can do whatever you like and call it a wedding. My friend Yaz got married in the middle of a Wyoming meadow on the solstice, officiated by a peyote dealer in full biker gear. It was awesome, and ten years later, all people can talk about is that wedding. Was it legal? Nope. Was it *real*? For Yaz and Hugo, yes. Arundel can't force us to have a legal ceremony if our beliefs demand we do it in a non-legal way."

"I take your point on circumventing the issue of the legality of it all," Lucas said impatiently. "But what of our reputations? I don't want people thinking I'm married when I'm not!" He shuddered at the thought of his clients finding out about such a scheme. It could ruin him.

"Who has to find out apart from Arundel?" Posy demanded.

"You're Posy Edwins," Lucas tutted. "Everyone will find out about your wedding in seconds. And what would I tell my parents?" His parents had been so upset over the breakup with Sally. The idea that Lucas was embarking on a fake marriage for professional gain would no doubt devastate them.

"We'll find a way around that," Posy breezed. "Look, I need an answer on this. I have to confirm my flights to the festival ASAP. It's in July and we're already getting to the end of May."

"I'm a serious businessman," he said darkly. "I can't be getting my business from... from prostituting myself like this."

"Hey, whoa!" Posy flapped her hands. "I only want to marry you! I have no interest in getting into your pants."

"Believe me, I was not offering," Lucas growled.

Posy arched a perfect eyebrow. "You're totally safe from my attentions, I assure you. Strictly business is this. I have a boyfriend."

"Ah yes, Mr Foremost Insurance Broker," Lucas said. "Why can't *he* fund this dream holiday of yours?"

"It's not a holiday. And I already asked. He can't," Posy said with a huff. "He's going through a lean phase at the moment and really, one shouldn't involve money in matters of love."

"Oh, but involving marriage in the matters of money, sure, he's fine with that," Lucas snarked. He knew if it were *his* girlfriend embarking on a scheme such as this, he'd have a real problem with it. But then Henry probably operated at a similar level as Posy did, coming from the same world as she.

"All marriages are just transactions anyway," Posy said with a casual shrug.

"Before we embark on complicated social theory," Lucas

said, "let's look at the fact that this represents a real risk with no guarantee of reward." Fred's face danced across his mind's eye. If only he were fit and well. Fred would make light work of Posy's contacts in minutes, but these deals would have to be closed by Lucas alone and that was not his strength. If he got it wrong, he could really damage Align's reputation. But if he succeeded? Align could thrive as a real force to be reckoned with in the financial services industry. They wouldn't need to consider selling it off.

Posy leaned forward again, her freckled face animated. "Lucas. This festival is coming up fast. I can't get a loan, and there's not enough time to sell my prints to raise the money I need for my flights. But there *is* enough time to knock up a fake wedding!" She knitted her hands together in hope. "A few weeks of your life, a wedding that isn't real, and then you will be meeting some of the most influential people in the world. After that, you and I can go our separate ways forever. What do you say?"

## Chapter Nine

"Well, this is nice," Tara said, pointedly looking at the empty seat at their table.

"I'm sure he'll be here any minute," Posy said, checking her phone for the millionth time. Still nothing from Henry. "It was his idea for us to brunch together." Well, it was somewhat Henry's idea. He'd suggested a boozy lunch date with Posy, and she'd convinced him that Tara simply had to come along. Well, how else were her two favourites ever going to get along unless Posy forced the matter? Alfie's was the best brunch venue in Coaldale, if not the county, and the fact Posy had managed to score a table on a Saturday morning was nothing short of miraculous – a clear sign that this was a brilliant idea of hers. Yet Henry was over twenty minutes late with no word. She sighed. Alfie's was as bustling as ever – tables exquisitely decorated with fine crystal and fresh flowers, the air rich with the scent of expensive perfume and fine cooking.

"You said he was returning from Belgium last night – perhaps his flight was delayed?" Tara said.

"Maybe, but he should have told me," Posy sighed. She didn't miss the barely concealed eyeroll her response elicited. "What?"

"Nothing," Tara replied quickly.

Posy remembered the morning after their big weekend. Tara had been just as evasive then and this time she couldn't blame it on a hangover. "Spit it out."

Tara puffed out her cheeks. "I just... I have a feeling about Henry, is all."

"A feeling?" Posy glared at Tara. "Like a bad one? You barely know him!"

"No, I know, and that's why I'm here." Tara toyed with her water glass. "There's no denying how hot he is but every time I talk to him, I feel like I'm getting a show. You know? Like, is he being straight with me?"

Posy took a breath. "I think he just wants to impress you." Henry was a charmer for sure, but as an insurance broker he was always selling and pitching. "It's just part of his character. He's so much fun. We laugh, like, all the time."

Tara threw up her hands. "I know, I know. I'm sorry. Just doing my job as the best friend." But still, she glanced at her watch and twisted her lips.

Posy decided to bat the issue aside. Tara had gone through a toxic divorce; it had to have skewed her judgement of men, particularly eloquent and affluent men, no doubt. Posy couldn't blame her for that. But Henry was very late, and they only had the table for two hours. "Why don't we just order?" she said. "Henry will soon catch up."

"Right," Tara said brightly. "Eggs Benedict it is."

"Some things never change," Posy giggled.

"It's their best dish!" Tara shot back in mock outrage. "What are you having?"

"It'll have to be the soup," Posy said miserably. It was the cheapest thing on the menu. Posy suspected her father wouldn't view a brunch with friends as an essential purchase.

"What?" Tara looked at her sharply. "When you could have pea pancakes and creme fraiche?"

"Oh Tar." Posy found herself spilling the truth about her father's decision, withholding only the solution she'd proposed to Lucas. As close as they were, Posy wasn't sure she'd understand.

"Wow." Tara shook her head. "I did think you were moaning about him more than usual. I suppose our bender the other week was the last straw?"

"Kind of," Posy answered. "But don't blame yourself."

Just then the waiter appeared and Tara promptly ordered, demanding that Posy have the pancakes. "If Henry doesn't show, it's on me," she said. "To say sorry for playing a part in your disagreement with Jesper."

"You're too kind, Tar," Posy said.

"Not at all!" Tara said, then, once the waiter had left them alone; "I'm just so sorry about the other day. We did kind of go a little potty, didn't we?"

"Don't apologise," Posy said. "I wanted to show you a good time."

"And you did, as always, but your dad was so upset with you after." Tara's dark eyes turned sorrowful. "I feel terrible."

"Oh, I think his outburst was a long time coming." Posy forced the lump in her throat back down. How long had her pops been observing her with such disappointment in his heart? "You know the expectations he has."

"Don't I just." Tara shuddered. She was an alumnus of the Swiss boarding-school variety so knew very well the sort of world the Edwins moved in. Her divorce had not gone down well amongst the sophisticated Sastri family and Tara was currently managing the crushing weight of her parents' dismay. "Speaking of expectations, what's the latest on Florence's wedding?"

"Ugh." Posy took a gulp of water. "You'd think she was having it featured in *Tatler* the way she's carrying on. Poor Inigo is such a dear. I don't know how he puts up with it."

"That's society weddings for you," Tara said. "I swear, if I ever walk down the aisle again… well, there's not going to be an aisle. I'll bloody well elope. Too much stress."

"You know Pops even said if I get married that would be enough for him," Posy said.

Tara's jaw slackened. "Hang on, he's forcing you to work or get married? What the fuck?"

"He says he just wants me to have a purpose." Posy picked up a napkin and threaded it through her fingers. Her mind flitted to Lucas; she'd never met anyone with more vision or drive. But the effort of that must be exhausting. The idea of every second of your life being planned out… Posy couldn't imagine living her life that way. How could her father want that existence for her?

"So what, your dad thinks simply getting married is purpose?" Tara went on. "Trust me, if he wants you to be happy and live with purpose, forcing you to rush into marriage is not the answer. Take it from me."

"The thing is I *do* have direction. Yes, I party hard, but my photography is everything to me. He's barely paid any attention to it. He just assumes I'm messing about." Posy took a deep breath. "Do you think Mum would be disappointed in me, Tar?" The napkin was now mangled in her lap.

Tara gasped in horror, dragging her chair over to Posy's side. "Oh, hell no!" She gripped Posy's face in her hands. "Don't ever say that! You are warm and funny and kind and... okay, I'm never going to take financial advice from you or, honestly, be a passenger in any car you're driving"— she paused as they dissolved into teary giggles—"but you're fab just as you are."

"It's just that Pops said... Pops said..." Posy took a juddering breath. "He said in not so many words that she would be disappointed in me. In my choices."

Tara's lips flattened into a bloodless line and she took a moment to compose the emotions Posy could see roiling in her eyes. "Then that's really shitty of him," she said. "I know he's probably only worried about you, but still. Do you want me to speak to him?"

Posy grabbed her friend's hands, genuine alarm coursing through her. "No, please don't!"

"Because I can, if you need me to." Tara lifted her chin defiantly.

"No, really, but thank you." Gratitude flushed through Posy's heart. "You're the best. I don't think Pops would appreciate me talking about this with anyone, even you."

"I'm glad you said that because honestly Jesper terrifies me." Tara gulped theatrically. "So what are you going to do about the money for this trip to Hawaii?" she continued. "Because if I had it, you know I'd give it to you but since the divorce I have to be—"

"Hey, whoa, no!" Posy flapped her hands in horror. "So sweet of you to offer but no. I have to work this out myself. And—"

"Morning ladies." A voice broke their conversation and

the friends swivelled to see Dee standing there, gripping her crocodile-skin purse under her arm like a lance.

"Dee!" Posy flushed. She'd been meaning to touch base with her old friend "What a nice surprise!"

"Isn't it?" Dee's grin was fixed. "Just grabbing an early lunch with the mother-in-law." She indicated across the room to where a wisp of a woman was buckling under the weight of a bottle of champagne. "Lionel would be with us, but his practice is OVERRUN. Poor darling. But you should see his monthly billings!" Dee's mother-in-law cast her eyes over to them with an expression that could sour vinegar.

"I'm sure," Tara murmured with a smile. "Does your mother-in-law need help pouring her drink?"

"She's fine." Dee didn't even look. "Tara, isn't it? I was so sorry to hear about your divorce from Ben. He's just joined our members' club. Terrific fellow."

Tara pasted on a smile that showed considerably more teeth than normal. "Thanks."

"Dee, we really should let you get back to Lionel's mother." Posy recognised the murderous glint in Tara's eye. "Our food will be here soon anyway."

"Now, you seem to be missing a member of your party." Dee nodded at Henry's empty chair. "Who are you expecting?"

"My boyfriend," Posy replied.

"Do I know him?" Dee quickly asked.

Posy sighed. The problem with the circles she moved in was that everyone knew everyone else and as a result immediately had opinions on any relationships that occurred. It was beyond claustrophobic. That's what made Henry so refreshing, as he wasn't technically part of said circle. "I doubt it," she said. "Henry Allardyce? He's not local, just stays up here for work. Spends a lot of time in Norfolk with his elderly parents. He's in insurance."

Dee tapped her chin. "Allardyce. Hmm. No, not ringing a bell. I say, he didn't board at Charterhouse, did he?"

"Well, you can ask him yourself," Posy said with relief, realising she actually wasn't sure herself. "As he's here now!"

Henry barrelled across the restaurant, his suit a little rumpled, his skin pale. "Posy, sweetheart!" He swept past Dee and dragged Posy into a tight hug. "Forgive me, the M1 was impossible."

"Don't mention it." Posy's words were muffled by his silk scarf. Henry smelled a little unwashed but he was warm and solid, his hug much needed after all the unpleasantness with her father.

"I thought you had a place in Leeds?" Tara said, clearly baffled.

"I do but I had to drive here straight from the airport." Henry's deep voice resonated through every inch of Posy's body.

"He's been abroad on business," Posy reminded Tara.

Henry bristled at Tara. "My mother will be worried sick I haven't called her since I landed but I was so desperate to get to Posy I drove straight here. And hello to you too."

"Sorry." Tara flushed. "Posy was worried, that's all."

Dee watched the exchange with a tilted head and when Henry finally untangled himself from his embrace with Posy, she proffered her hand.

"Desdemona Carrington-Goodman," she said. "But you can call me Dee."

Henry shook her hand. "Henry Allardyce. A pleasure. Wait, Dee?" He beamed. "You're an Arundel alum. Posy was telling me all about the friends she'd reconnected with at the reunion." And he winked down at Posy, who stifled a grin. Yes, she had been telling him about her friends but not all of it had been complimentary.

"Indeed." Dee patted her stiffly sprayed hair. "Posy and I have been pals for simply years." She side-eyed Posy with an impressed smile. "My word Posy, where have you been hiding this one? You said nothing of Henry at the reunion!"

"Ah, I guess I didn't get a chance." Posy's phone flashed with a text from Lucas – probably some yawn-fest about the statistical probability of her plan failing or some other buzzkill. She discreetly flipped it over. "We've not been dating that long; we met in Leeds. You know the new cock-tail lounge?"

"Yes, this one just walked into that place and stole my heart," Henry added, dramatically grabbing Posy's hand and placing it on his chest. "And now here I am dining with her and her best pal."

"Lovely." Dee's smile iced over somewhat. "Posy owes me a lunch too but has yet to give me a call."

Posy's cheeks grew hot. Yes, she'd promised a catch-up with her old friend but whenever she'd picked up the phone to call Dee, words had failed her. Dee had a life full of responsibility and obligations, a life far removed from anything Posy had experienced. But as she looked at Dee's ill-concealed indignation, she wondered if that was truly her reason for not calling.

"Lunch, hey?" Henry said with a chuckle. "She'd have to run that expense by her father!" His face dropped when he realised no one was laughing with him.

"Oh?" Dee leaned closer, indignation giving way to intrigue. "Do tell."

"It's nothing," Posy said.

"Now I wouldn't say that," Henry went on kindly. "It's kind of a big deal. He won't pay for anything; he won't even pay for Hawaii and that's a huge opportunity for you, darling."

"Jesper has cut you off?" Dee's eyes bulged and Posy wanted to scream with the humiliation of it. It was one thing Tara and Henry knowing what her father had done but quite another for Dee to know. Soon enough everyone she knew – and plenty she didn't – would hear about it.

"No, not really." Posy tried to laugh it off. "Honestly it's not worth mentioning."

"And Hawaii? What's happening there?" Dee tapped Henry's arm playfully. "Oh, you aren't going to make an honest woman of her, are you? Kona Beach is the most wonderful location. I could put you in touch wi—"

"Oh no," Henry was quick to refute. "It's just a fabulous professional opportunity for Posy that her father won't pay for."

"Yes, it is," Posy jumped in before Henry could babble any more. "But I'll tell you at our lunch, right Dee?"

"But I'm here now…" Dee said, sounding almost desperate but, luckily for Posy, just then Dee's name was called from across the room. Dee's mother-in-law was waving an almost empty flute in the air. "Great," Dee muttered. "She's already quaffed all that champers." She turned back to the group with a forced smile. "Delightful to see you all. I'd best get back to Meredith. Posy, Tara." She laid her hand on Henry's arm and fluttered her eyelashes. "Hope to encounter you again, Henry."

"Have a wonderful day," he responded politely, and with that, Dee strutted back to her impatient and increasingly tipsy mother-in-law. Once she was out of earshot, Henry pulled a comical face at Posy and Tara. "Yikes." He nudged Posy. "Seems like you owe her a lunch."

"I know, I know." Posy was keen to change the subject. Fortuitously, she spied the waiter coming over, bearing their food. "Come on, let's sit down. Henry, you should order."

As Henry perused the menu and queried the waiter about the origins of their free-range beef, Posy quietly turned her phone back over. As expected, there were several texts from Lucas, all starting with questions that made her head spin. What was wrong with him? Why couldn't he see the simple brilliance of her plan for what it was and just go with it? Why did he have to complicate it with this boring nonsense? As soon as Tara excused herself for the bathroom, Henry lunged to kiss Posy's cheek.

"What was that for?" She squealed in mock outrage.

"I just hate to see you frown." He nuzzled her neck. "Fuck, you smell amazing. Shall we ditch this crowd and head back to mine?"

"This crowd is *Tara*." Posy was disappointed.

"Yes, and she doesn't like me," Henry murmured. "The look she gave me when I walked in!"

"She's just protective," Posy said. "I want you to get to know each other. She'll soon thaw out, you'll see."

"No wonder her husband left her." Henry's mouth grazed her earlobe and Posy had to push aside the resulting wave of lust in order to stick up for Tara.

"Hey." She placed a palm against Henry's chest. "Ben is a grade-A shit. A cheating, lying scumbag who thinks his money places him above decent behaviour. Any woman would be traumatised after being with someone like that."

Henry blinked and leaned back. "Oh."

"Yes, oh." Posy fixed him with a stern gaze. "Tara's too

good for him. So she's a little sensitive – can you blame her?"

Henry swiped a menu and cast his eyes down it. "Guess not."

Posy tilted a finger under his chin to make him look at her. "So will you make an effort with her?"

Henry pursed his lips then grinned. "Only if you wear that black thing in bed tonight."

"Fine." Posy rolled her eyes indulgently. If that was what it took to get Henry to push through the awkwardness with Tara, she'd gladly do it. But when Tara returned to her seat and a frosty atmosphere descended once more, Posy began to regret her brunch scheme. Were two of the most important people in her life ever going to see eye to eye?

## Chapter Ten

Fred eyed the proffered hamper with suspicion. "What the hell is that?"

Lucas tutted. "Don't be obtuse, mate. It's not your eyes you need to worry about." He pointed. "Selection of freeze-dried herbs and spices, plus the best green tea that Whole Foods had to offer. You need to avoid salt as well as up your vitamin K intake."

Fred held up a white packet with terror in his eyes. "I cannot believe you brought tofu into my house."

Lucas snatched it from him. "Lean, plant-based protein," he said, lobbing it back into the hamper. "It'll help." Ever since Fred had become ill, Lucas had spent time researching arrythmia and how to manage it. Virtually all the websites and medical journals he consulted had told him much of it was genetic, but that recovery was given greater odds with the right diet. So he'd created a custom hamper full of the best ingredients plus the new *Heart Healthy Eats* recipe book by Doctor Lakshmi Burke.

"Thank you, Lucas." Suzi leaned in and removed the hamper, grimacing under its weight. "We appreciate the effort you've made." Her expressive eyes widened at Fred. "Don't we?"

"We do," Fred intoned dutifully. "But you needn't worry. Sooz is taking good care of me."

"No, I know," Lucas said. "I just wanted to help and…" Emotion closed his throat, so he offered a helpless shrug, afraid that if he spoke further he'd cry.

"You were doing a Lucas," Fred said affectionately. "Over thinking, over worrying, over planning. It's what you do when you really care." His voice became gruff and he patted Lucas's shoulder. "Thank you."

"Just want you to be okay," Lucas warbled. It was still so alien. His best mate was curled up childlike on his sofa under a blanket, his face drawn. Not the guy Lucas was used to. Fred was the person you noticed first at a party, the one who made everything fun and easy, the one who could instantly convince you he'd do anything for you if asked. It wasn't right that someone like him, with the most love to give, had a heart that might not be up to the task.

"And I will be." Fred gestured around him. They were in the living room of his Victorian terrace in North London, which had been decorated mainly by Suzi who favoured a clean, almost Scandinavian aesthetic. Their eldest two were twins named Esme and Pippa, who were lolling on the grey wool rug, lost in their Nintendo devices, whilst the force of nature that was Rudy lurked somewhere on the upper floor. Lucas's back twinged in anticipation just thinking about the lad, despite the extremely comfortable sofa he was sitting on next to Fred. Nestled into Lucas's side was Gene, two years old and adorably fast asleep. Fred smiled and went on. "Got everything that's important right here with me."

The smile transformed Fred's face and it gave Lucas hope. "What have the doctors said?"

"They're saying lots of things," Fred replied with a tut.

"*Fred.*" Suzi had returned from offloading the hamper to the kitchen with a tray of hot drinks and biscuits. She fixed her husband with a stern eye as she lowered the tray to the coffee table. "What they are saying is that he needs to keep his blood pressure steady and have lots of rest. Perhaps lose a little weight."

"Says the woman bringing in sugar-laden morsels of death." Fred gestured at the plate of biscuits.

"These are Weight Watchers, actually." Suzi handed over a small, chocolate-coloured square. "One is fine, especially when washed down with green tea."

Lucas accepted his own diet biscuit and green tea with a smile, relieved that Suzi was already in control of Fred's recovery. He'd suspected that it would be as such. Suzi was a university lecturer, specialising in economics. She could plan like no one else and was the perfect foil to Fred's lad-about-town persona.

"You on Warfarin?" Lucas thought back to his research,

"He is. It's really taking a toll," Suzi added, flicking back her coppery ringlets. "But clots are a serious threat with his condition."

"Necessary evil," Fred chimed in.

As Lucas murmured his understanding, he became aware of a silent communication between the two people sitting either side of him. Suzi's eyes were intent upon her husband, lips fixed in the rictus of a polite smile.

Lucas set his mug down on the bleached-pine coffee

table. "What's up, guys?" Suzi arched her eyebrows meaningfully at Fred and with a wary sigh, Lucas swivelled to face him. "Come on," he said. Trepidation coursed through him. How could there be more bad news?

"It's about Align." Fred cleared his throat. "Specifically, my role at Align."

Lucas frowned. "Yes, you need to take a step back. We agreed. I can run things until you return."

"That's just it." Fred had difficulty meeting Lucas's eye. "I don't think I can. Come back, that is."

"What?" Lucas's reply sounded very far away, as if someone else were saying it. Align had been their baby, his and Fred's. It worked because the two of them worked and without Fred, there was no way Lucas could save it from the current trajectory.

"At least, not in my current… form," Fred added quickly. "I can't keep it up. The hours, the late-night calls, the travel."

"It's the stress," Suzi said. "He makes it look so easy, but the workload does a real number on him."

"But… but…" Lucas was stumped. He'd done so much research for this visit, purely to show Fred how he was going to facilitate his rehab. Sure, he'd expected a lengthy recovery period, but this? "It sounds like you're giving up," he said.

"No." Fred shook his head. "Not at all. But something has to change. Like, maybe I work as a consultant. Pitch in a few hours a month or something."

Lucas's mind whirled. "Surely that would mean renegotiating the terms of your ownership. Or me buying you out?" Neither of which sounded appealing to Lucas.

"Or Fred sells his share to another buyer?" Suzi suggested hopefully.

"What?" Lucas whirled on her. "Align is mine and Fred's; you know how I feel about selling out."

"We did broach this the other day," Fred said gently. "Remember, Lim Management?"

"But I thought we agreed selling was a last resort?" Lucas had the visceral sense of things moving too fast, that horrid change was coming for him whether he liked it or not. "Why not give it some time, mate?" he said desperately. "See how you feel. You love this job, this company."

"I love my life more," Fred said simply. "And time? I just got a very real reminder of how much time I might have left on this planet. Yeah, Align has been my dream for years, but dreams change. People change."

*I don't*, Lucas thought angrily. He hadn't changed at all! And yet Fred's decision was going to possibly force some very unwelcome changes into his life. But as he looked at his best friend's face, notably thinner than it had been just a couple of weeks before, the indignation faded.

"I hear you," Lucas said eventually. "So, my options are to buy you out, though, as you know, raising any more capital will be tricky because of the current state of business."

"Or, we sell my share to someone else," Fred went on.

"Or sell the entire company," Lucas gulped.

"What sounds best to you, Lucas?" Suzi asked, her voice soothing. "Out of those options, what would work best?"

Lucas pondered for a moment. Beside him, Gene snuffled and buried his nose into Lucas's arm, and his heart squeezed at the sensation. He couldn't blame Fred for wanting to hold on to every second of this. "If I have to choose, I'd own Align outright," he said eventually. "Keep Fred on as a consultant, so you could help me retain our vision." But as he said it, he knew it was far more likely that an outside buyer would be most feasible. Being able to make the company more successful and boosting his own wealth would make it far easier to raise the funds needed to buy Fred out.

"The thing is," Fred said reluctantly. "I'd like to get this resolved as soon as we can. Don't want to rush you, mate, and of course, we'll do whatever we can to make this right for you as well as me, but the sooner I'm free of the responsibility, the better."

Fred spoke kindly, but each word was like a weight on Lucas's shoulders. "I get it," he said quietly. "But getting to a position to buy you out will take time." *Time we don't have,* he thought to himself.

Fred shrugged apologetically, but his face was resolute. Then his eyes twinkled wickedly. "Shame you didn't marry Sally, eh? She's loaded. Could have lent you a few quid."

"Oh don't," Lucas groaned. But Fred's jibe triggered something, a thought of Posy Edwins, cross-legged on his office chair asking for Lucas's hand in marriage. He couldn't hide the snort of laughter that escaped from his mouth.

"What?" Fred asked.

"Oh, nothing." How on earth could he put into words Posy's outrageous plan?

"No, that's a face of *something*," Fred wheedled. "Out with it."

"It's just a mad get-rich-quick scheme a former classmate from Arundel proposed – quite literally – to me the other day," Lucas said with an eyeroll for good measure. "Like, the maddest thing ever."

"Ooh that sounds intriguing." Suzi reached for another biscuit, eyes wide. "Go on."

"No, it's ridiculous!" Lucas protested.

"Seriously, I just got out of hospital because my heart is a flimsy bastard," Fred said, ignoring Suzi's hush noises. "I could really do with some silliness."

"You asked for it." How could Lucas refuse such a plea? "As you know, I was head boy at a very old and elite private school and they have this archaic rule that if the head boy and girl were ever to marry, the school would pay for the wedding and honeymoon."

"What?" Suzi laughed, slopping tea over her jeans. "That's crazy. Who does that?"

"Spoken like a true child of the state education system," Fred said indulgently. "There's a guy I once worked with whose school used to make all the pupils fight over horsehair pancakes at Easter in order to win a day off. A free wedding doesn't sound that mad to me."

"Right," Lucas agreed, wondering what on earth a horsehair pancake would taste like. "Well, if you remember, Fred, the head girl during my time was Posy Edwins…"

"Wait." Fred's eyes bulged. "Are you saying *she* asked you to marry her?"

"Basically, yeah," Lucas said, his face growing hot. "She's been cut off financially by Daddy Dearest but needs to get to Hawaii for a business opportunity ASAP."

Suzi squealed with glee. "So, what, you'd marry her and she'd use the honeymoon funds to get to Hawaii?"

Lucas nodded tightly, aware of how mad it sounded. "And in return, she can practically guarantee me the task of managing her family's wealth as well as access to her little black book of some seriously rich folks." He swallowed. "A life-changing number of clients."

"What?" Fred cried. Beside Lucas, Gene shifted in his

sleep. Fred lowered his voice but his eyes remained bright. "The Edwins fortune? How can she guarantee *that*?"

"She reckons her brother is all at sea with the responsibility and doesn't know where to begin. Posy is sure she can get him to agree to give us a go." With mounting horror, Lucas noticed the set of Fred's expression and recognised that his brain was working away. Could his friend be seriously contemplating this? "It's a joke Fred; she hasn't thought it through. Arundel College isn't run by idiots – they're sure to see right through it."

"But still." Fred waggled his eyebrows. "There are worse ways to make money."

"Not many," Lucas growled.

"Fred!" Suzi chastised. "Don't encourage him, seriously."

"Let's just think for a moment," Fred said. "The Edwins are serious money. Stupidly rich. Here we are, desperate to improve our fortunes and along comes Posy with a potential save." Fred leaned towards Lucas. "What exactly would you have to do?"

"Well, I presume we'd take a meeting with the headteacher, try to convince them we are legit and need the money." Discussing strategy – madcap as it was – had its usual calming effect on Lucas. "Then it depends on what demands they make. Posy thinks she just needs to wear a white dress and send some photos of us looking happy but I don't think it will be that simple."

"What if it is though?" Fred's eyes were darting. "A photo… I mean, where's the harm in that?"

"Wow, she's beautiful!" Suzi suddenly thrust her phone at Lucas and Fred. There was a paparazzi shot of Posy clad in a scrap of grey lace, strutting down the street with a collection of ladies whom the showbiz journalist assured readers were the *Real Housewives of Leeds*.

"Oh, come on!" Fred pointed at the picture. "She's not just minted, she's a stone-cold fox. Why not hang out with her for a few weeks? Who knows, you might have some fun for once."

"Fun?" Lucas said. "We *hated* each other at school. Imagine the exact opposite of me in human form and that is Posy Edwins. *So* not my type. Anyway, she has a boyfriend."

"He can't be a serious boyfriend if he won't help finance this scheme of hers," Fred said with a snort.

"She's one of *them*, Fred," Lucas went on vehemently. "A mickey-taking toff. You don't know what it was like, working alongside her day after day knowing that I could turn water into wine; she still wouldn't give me an ounce of respect."

"Teenage girls," Fred snorted dismissively.

Lucas felt pretty certain Fred wouldn't be so blasé if he actually met Posy. "Whatever. It wouldn't matter if she were single, I am not going there."

"She looks way more fun than Sally," Fred smirked.

Lucas shook his head. "You can't compare them." But Fred was already launching into his ever so predictable critique of Sally.

"Sally wouldn't let you drink on a weeknight," Fred said, lifting his fingers to tick off her attributes. "Sally didn't approve of cinema that wasn't arthouse as everything else was 'brainrot'. Sally also didn't want you to fly to that stag in Budapest because she was worried about your collective carbon footprint being too high that year." He threw up his hand – case closed.

"Yeah well, she didn't *actually* stop me going to said stag in the end," Lucas muttered sheepishly.

"Only because she had that conference in Geneva or somewhere and couldn't stop you." Fred said. "Bit hypocritical if you ask me."

"Sally just has strong morals," Lucas said defensively. It had been something he'd admired but now, post-break-up, hearing Fred list her traits like that was kind of illuminating. Had Sally really made him boring?

"Fine, if you want to call it that." Fred sighed. "Sorry, I didn't mean to bring up painful memories. But what's the harm in speaking to the school? Finding out how far you'd have to take this charade? If it gets too much, back out."

Lucas opened his mouth to protest but then he saw the pain behind Fred's cheeky grin, the laboured way his friend's chest rose and fell. There was no question that Fred needed out of Align and quickly. Even this friendly catch-up was costing him. Waves of guilt crashed over Lucas.

"I guess I could at least find out more," he murmured, and tried not to weep when he saw the relief flood Fred's face.

"That's all I ask," Fred beamed.

---

Sometime later, Lucas was back home, nursing a medicinal beer. Seeing Fred so weak, so quick to pounce on Posy's plan, had been disconcerting. How much longer could the guy hold on to his health with the fate of Align so uncertain? Fred's eagerness at the sound of Posy's plan had also set Lucas thinking. Could they even get away with what Posy was suggesting? Lucas was reasonably sure the contract for Arundel would be in his father's files at home and before he could even countenance going through with this plan, he had to review it.

Lucas went to his desk and pulled out his laptop, then quickly navigated to the Arundel website. As expected, it had an overarching breakdown of certain codes of conduct they expected students to abide by, but it was by no means exhaustive and made no reference to the marriage bylaw. It was possible the bylaws were archived online but that would take some intense digging. It was clear that the most accurate way to check would be to meet with Arundel themselves. Lucas shuddered. How would one even *open* that conversation?

This whole scheme was bonkers, no question about it. And then there was the question of word getting out. What would people think? He would definitely have to explain to his parents that it wasn't a real marriage so they wouldn't get their hopes up. His mother had been particularly crushed when his engagement to Sally had fallen through. Or perhaps he could keep it from them entirely? Then he shook his head again. The news of the Prefect Marriage Rule actually being invoked would be sure to make it into the alumni newsletter and as former employees of the school, his parents read each one avidly, usually over their breakfast. Lucas's heart softened at the image of them hand in hand, sipping tea and reminiscing over their years at Arundel. Would they understand him doing something like this?

Fred's deathly pale face danced across his vision again. There was no doubt Lucas had to do something quick to save Align before they were forced to sell it off. What harm could it do just to explore the possibility by meeting someone from Arundel? After all, if Arundel had changed the bylaws, they could walk away from the meeting consequence-free.

And at least it would be a good excuse to get up north and see his parents for the first time in months.

Lucas sat up. Took a deep breath. Then, before he could talk himself out of it, sent Posy a text consisting of two words:

*I'm in.*

## Chapter Eleven

The Hand and Flower hadn't changed much over the years, Lucas reflected. The cramped Yorkshire boozer had been a surprisingly popular haunt for the pampered student body of Arundel College, mainly due to its histori-cally lax approach to checking ID but also because it was walking distance from the school itself, tucked away in the rugged little village of Much Alderton. The village was a genteel cluster of old mill cottages, battling the often unfor-giving winds coming off the peaks, and The Hand and Flower was a monument to longevity. It was still small and dark, its walls crowded with faded beer adverts, the same sticky red carpet and mismatched stools crowded around a corner bar staffed by Edna and Dave. The couple hadn't changed much during the intervening years: Dave was still a pudgy sphere of a man, his egg-like head free of hair apart from a salty rim of persistent hairs clinging to the base of his scalp; Edna, as ever, perched on her high stool like a gin-soaked vulture, her large nose invariably dipping into a sample of her favourite liquor.

Lucas ordered a pint of bitter and took a seat in the far corner, soon realising that it was the seat he'd liked to occupy on the few occasions he'd visited as a student. It was still the optimum seat though; it allowed a good view of the entrance and was far enough from the toilets that the smell of bleach and drains was just faint enough not be a deterrent.

He realised the churning in his gut was nerves and so he took a fortifying sip of his drink. This was just an exploratory meeting, he told himself. Just to see what was possible. Because there was no way Arundel would agree to this, right? He and Posy could just play the part, ask the question about the money and take it from there. No pressure, he assured himself. But there was pressure of course, pressure in the form of his seriously ill friend and their collapsing business.

The door cranked open, bringing in a whoosh of warm air. It was Posy, unexpectedly bang on time but looking different to how Lucas had expected her. Her honeyed tresses were tamed back into a demure low knot and she was simply clad in wide-leg trousers and a plain ivory blouse. She'd even slicked on a peach lipstick and added rather old-fashioned pearl earrings. The overall effect was oddly familiar, but Lucas couldn't say why.

"Ah good, you're here!" She leaned over the bar, oblivious to Lucas rolling his eyes at her total lack of a greeting. "Dave darling, can I get a lemonade?"

"Bloody 'ell, Posy Edwins, is that you?" The landlord's face broke into a smile Lucas hadn't known was physically possible for the man.

"It's been too long, hasn't it?" She proffered a hand and Dave patted it affectionately.

"I'll bring yer drink over," he said and as she reached

into her purse, he lifted his hands. "Hey, yer money's no good here, after everything you've done for us. What's a lemonade?"

"That's so kind of you!" Posy trilled and positively skipped over to Lucas, flopping dramatically into the seat opposite him with a happy sigh.

"I didn't think Dave had the facial muscles required to smile," Lucas remarked by way of a greeting. "What's your secret?"

"Um, I partied here every weekend for several years," Posy said with a smirk. "Probably spent a fortune. Oh, and that raffle we did for the graduation ball? The money went to the hospice that cared for his sister. She had Down's Syndrome – such a sweetheart."

"Oh." Lucas tightened his grip on his beer. "I didn't know that." Posy had won the coin toss for that particular decision and if Lucas remembered rightly, he'd stormed out after losing best of three. He hadn't understood why supporting the local mayor's election fund hadn't been a worthy cause.

"Yeah. We stayed in touch for a while but she died a few years after we graduated." Posy's lips downturned. "Lovely funeral."

Lucas was taken aback. He had a hard time picturing Posy socialising with anyone not of her social standing, certainly not to the extent of being invited to a family funeral. He'd had no idea about Posy's motivations for her choice of raffle donation; at the time he hadn't considered her option was worth considering. As he watched the portly landlord hurry over a pint of lemonade with slices of lemon, glacé cherries and a cocktail umbrella, he felt a pang of guilt that he hadn't known about the man's sister.

"This place really hasn't changed much, has it?" Posy said as she took a deep gulp of lemonade.

Lucas had to agree with her. It even smelled the same. "Anyway, thanks for meeting early." He rapped the table. "I wanted to go over a few things before we get to Arundel."

"What's to go over? They can't dispute the fact we are former head boy and girl," Posy said, edging lipstick with her little finger. "And the rule is still in effect, right? So, they can't say no. They *have* to give us the money."

"The rule is still in effect, yes," Lucas said. Since their meeting just over a week ago, he had done a lot of research. Lucas had had to do some extensive checking with the local council who had been able to direct him to a sub-directory of the local education authority's website. Astonishingly, a scanned PDF of the original bylaws from over a hundred years ago existed online and Lucas had painstakingly studied it, half hoping that the bylaw might have been struck out. It hadn't. In fact, he'd managed to find a lot of information that led him to believe Posy's mad plan wasn't quite so mad after all. "The language is vague but doesn't specify a church wedding or indeed, place any restrictions upon us at all. Quite remarkable the clause even exists in this state."

Posy blinked, a delighted smile spreading across her face. "So that means they can't force us to get legally married in order to be eligible for the cash?"

"Seems so." Lucas nodded. "Despite that, I reckon Mrs Paddington is going to want to be pretty sure of all the facts before she hands over any cash. And I'd be amazed if some faked photos would help her have that certainty. Now, did you read the *about me* information pack I emailed?" He tried not to panic as Posy yawned. "We need to ensure we know everything there is about each other, just like an actual couple in love would do."

"I glanced at it," Posy said. "An excellent sleeping aid, I must say."

Lucas gritted his teeth. She was insufferable. "Did you read it properly?" It had contained all the key points a future wife should know.

"I'm well rested, aren't I?" Posy said. "Did you get my reply?" She snapped her compact shut.

"You sent me a link to a Wikipedia page."

"Yes, *my* Wikipedia page," she shot back. "It's mostly accurate."

"Why is there even a page dedicated to *you*?" It had made for quick reading: a summary of her education and family, mention of her relationship with Fenton Shulman, and the 'fun fact' that she was rumoured to have once stood in for one half of Daft Punk at a Croatian music festival, but no one knew because of the famous masks.

"Yeah well, you turn up to one of Jonathan Ross's Halloween parties and that'll happen to you," she said with another yawn.

"Right." Lucas once more had to marvel at the insanity of this woman's life. "It was only mildly useful. Did you have any questions about me?"

"I didn't know your family was Irish," she said.

"My surname is O'Rourke," he said, his disbelief tinged with relief she'd clearly read the email. "Also, you did meet my parents when they worked at our school. You heard their accents, right? Kind of hard to miss."

"Oh, yeah." She drew the second word out, an indication of the effort of memory. "Hang on, I do know something. You like managing money."

Lucas resisted the urge to smash his head into the table. "That's my job, not a personality trait."

"Well, forgive me if that's the overwhelming takeaway from our interactions," Posy snorted. "It's reassuring that your love of spreadsheets keeps you company to this day."

"Posy." Lucas levelled his gaze at her. "If you really want me to do this with you, you could start by being less of a colossal prick. Great impression we're going to make strolling into Arundel at this rate."

Posy pursed her lips then nodded grudgingly. "Fair point."

Lucas pushed. "Seriously. And the whole background knowledge thing is key. They aren't going to hand over money to us just like that." He snapped his fingers. "We need to be prepared for every approach. We can't mess it up."

"You think I'm not taking this seriously? Look at me." Posy took a deep pull on her straw. "Do I not look like someone who's ready to be a wife and mother?"

Lucas finally understood what it was about her appearance that had given him pause. "You're an Arundel mum." Her sensible form of chic was what every mother had looked like when attending PTA events. He had to admit it was a nice touch.

"Exactly!" Posy snorted. "You know in my world, if you aren't married and sprogged up by thirty, it's something of a scandal. I thought dressing like this would help convince them that's why we're so desperate to marry quickly."

"Come on," Lucas scoffed. "We're not in the 1950s anymore."

"I know, but that's the way it is." Posy shrugged. "A fulfilling career is the next best thing but really, if you aren't married, you aren't considered a whole person, I sometimes think. So bloody archaic and what's worse my father agrees with it."

"Archaic is the word." Lucas downed the rest of his drink then frowned as his head swam in reaction. His breakfast had been a dry piece of toast as his nerves hadn't let him consume anything else and, in the haste to meet Posy on time, he'd forgotten about lunch.

"Here." Posy pushed her lemonade at him. "I really can't drink this much sugar. Oh!" As Lucas took a sip of the refreshing drink, she reached into her bag again and pulled out a little red box – unmistakably Cartier. "Here's the finishing touch!"

"Wow." Lucas breathed as she opened it to reveal a chunky yellow-gold ring in an Art Deco style, with an enormous emerald at the centre and diamond baguettes spiralling away from it. It seemed to single-handedly light up the entire room. "Is that…?"

"Real? Yes. It was my mother's." Posy lowered her head as she put it on. "Her engagement ring went to my sister, but she left me her favourite cocktail ring."

"Should you be walking around with that?" Lucas took another sip of lemonade to moisten his suddenly dry mouth. "I mean, it must be worth thousands."

"Yes, it's worth a whole heap of change." Posy twiddled with it so the refracted light beams played along her features. "But no one will believe we're engaged if I don't have a proper ring. And girls like me never say yes to anything less than Cartier."

"Right." Lucas nodded. "Sound logic, I guess." He'd bet it cost ten times what he paid for Sally's ring and that had come from a top-rated jeweller in Hatton Garden.

"I thought so," Posy agreed. "You proposed with it after asking my father for permission and he gave it to you."

"Yes," Lucas went on. "We connected at the reunion after years apart and finally confessed our love for each other. So we decided to get married right away."

Their eyes locked. Flecks of gold rimmed her hazel irises. "I realised I couldn't live another day without being yours," Posy said softly.

Lucas swallowed. Goosebumps teased the back of his neck. "Right," he said hoarsely. Posy's voice was so sensual, even a bleary-eyed Edna roused herself to glance their way.

"Nailed it!" Posy honked, and Lucas snapped out of the mini trance her act had put upon him. Taking another gulp of lemonade to allow him to re-calibrate, he told himself what he was feeling was relief; they might just be able to pull this off.

Posy glanced down at her watch, a slim gold piece with the unmistakable red and green of the Gucci brand. She leapt up. "Crumbs! If we start walking now we'll get to Arundel with time to spare. I'm sure Mrs Paddington appreciates punctuality in people about to fleece her for money. We can go over my family because the Wiki for some reason thinks I'm part Russian when actually I'm part Swedish. Let's start with my brother, Seb…"

## Chapter Twelve

Matilda Paddington took a deep, appreciative sniff of her Earl Grey. The delicate aroma and warmth of her ritual pre-lunch tea never failed to rally her spirits after a morning of dealing with parents. During her thirty years as a teacher in the private school system, ten of that as a head-teacher, Matilda had learned that by far the worst thing about private education was the parents. Certainly, their privileged little darlings could be a handful, but the parents were often beyond frightful. It was how she imagined invest-ment bankers had to operate, providing updates to clients on how the money was being spent and the rate of return they could expect to receive. For some, no answer could ever be good enough.

But today's round of calls had been managed and Paddington now had a few minutes until her next appoint-ment. She leaned back in her seat and cradled her tea, taking in the grandeur of her office. Her office was so magnificently leather-bound it positively reeked of prestige. Along one wall, she had mounted all her accreditations and certifications, as well as prized photos of herself with famous former pupils: two actresses, an MP, and a bishop! As she took her first delightful sip of Earl Grey, there was a timid knock at the door and Paddington regretfully lowered her cup.

"Yes?" she called.

The heavy wooden door creaked open and executive assistant Alma Waldron's mousey head of curls poked through.

"Your 12pm is here," Alma said, her Scottish accent a gentle burr.

"Hmm." Paddington glanced down at her black Smythson diary. Sure enough, there was an appointment with Posy Edwins and Lucas O'Rourke, who, according to Mr Day's impeccable records, had been head boy and girl over ten years ago. They hadn't specified what they wanted to discuss, but due to their former standing at the school, she had felt duty-bound to see them. "Sure. Fetch Viv, would you?"

"Absolutely, I'll get her first." Alma nodded obediently and vanished. Minutes later Vivienne Hardstark bounded in, bringing with her the smell of fresh air and mown grass.

"Hello." Hardstark settled herself in one of Paddington's guest chairs. "I was just checking in with the head gardener. He thinks some of the Austin roses on the north lawn have canker." Her chin wobbled with distress. "Big job on our hands with that one. May need to bring in some experts. Anyway, what can I do for you?"

"We have alumni coming in for a visit," Paddington said. "Our former head boy and girl from 2008."

"That would be Posy and… Lucas," Hardstark said, her

smile turning triumphant as Matilda nodded in confirmation.

"I thought that as you were teaching here back then you should join us, seeing as how you know them." The head-mistress swirled her tea, closing her eyes again to enjoy the scent released into the air.

"Of course," Hardstark agreed, adjusting the front of her tweed jacket. "Prepare to get very uncomfortable."

"Oh?" Paddington arched an eyebrow.

"Well, the pair of them are like chalk and cheese, as they say," Hardstark said. "They never got on during their prefec-ture. Now *her* father is incredibly wealthy – Posy was Little Miss Popularity for her entire time here, but Lucas is quite the opposite. His parents worked at the school for many years and he got in on a scholarship as a result. Bright lad if I remember correctly, but how do I put this? He struggled to fit in socially. A diligent head boy though. Ambitious."

"Curious." Paddington lowered her tea and nibbled her lower lip. "I suppose all we can do is find out what on earth they want." She buzzed her intercom and Alma popped her head back in. "Send them in," Paddington ordered. Her assistant nodded obediently and went to collect the pair.

## Chapter Thirteen

As Posy entered the headmistress's office, she was immediately transported back in time. The dark wood walls still looked the same, and the imposing bookcase that Mr Day had loaded with his fencing trophies also remained, although it seemed Mrs Paddington favoured actual books and weighty tomes. The lady herself rose elegantly from behind the same enormous oak desk, formidably clad in a Chanel skirt suit, the pristine edge of her bob grazing a sharp jaw.

"Welcome," Paddington said, adjusting her Prada spectacles. "Always a pleasure to see former students, a real pleasure." She extended a delicate hand with long plum-coloured nails.

"Good afternoon." Posy modulated her tone to sound as cultured as the woman before her. Paddington smiled in response, but it didn't reach her pale-blue eyes. They stayed narrow and assessing, causing Posy's heart rate to speed up. Surely, Paddington wouldn't have an inkling of what they were about to attempt? "Thank you for making the time."

"Not at all," Paddington said and gestured to the rotund woman to her right. "You remember Ms Hardstark, Deputy Head?"

"Of course." Posy shook the other woman's hand in awe. Hardstark hadn't changed at all. A solid mass of a woman with russet hair blow-dried into stiff curls, Hardstark still had those tiny grey eyes that never seemed to blink behind thick, unflattering glasses. And today, as she'd always done, she wore a tweed skirt suit in drab green. No matter the weather, you could rely on Hardstark to be in a tweed ensemble. "Lovely to see you again."

"Likewise." Hardstark extended her hand for a shake and as Posy took it, she saw thin seams of dark earth beneath the woman's nails.

"And Lucas!" Paddington turned a shark-like smile to him. "How are your parents? Enjoying retirement?"

"Do send them my best," Hardstark added, reaching over to shake his hand.

"They're, um, great, thanks," Lucas stammered. Posy frowned. Was it her imagination or was he sweating? They hadn't even broached the question of marriage yet and he was already losing his cool.

"Anyway," Posy said loudly, to draw the women's gaze to her and not the flailing Lucas. "Thank you for seeing us."

"Please be seated," Paddington said. "I must admit I am somewhat curious."

"Well." Posy lowered herself gracefully into her seat and balanced her bag on her lap, ensuring that the stunning Cartier ring was visible. "It's big news for Arundel." She took a dramatic pause, her heart pounding. Here it was, the moment their audacious plan went into action. Everything rode on this moment. "You see, Lucas and I have recently got engaged." She extended her ring finger to show off the Cartier in what she hoped resembled an excited bride's manner.

"Oh, my word!" Paddington's hand fluttered to her throat, and she smiled politely, if hesitantly. "My warmest congratulations! But, ah, don't take this the wrong way but why are you here?"

"They've read the bylaws," Ms Hardstark declared, folding her arms.

"Bylaws?" Paddington repeated.

"Yes." Hardstark nodded. "There is one in particular that states if ever a head boy and head girl marry, Arundel will pay for the wedding and honeymoon."

"What?" Paddington tittered nervously. "Viv, did you just say *we* have to pay for *their* wedding? How hilarious!"

Hardstark said, "Not that funny. It's genuinely an old school bylaw."

"Is it one we actually have to abide by?" Paddington's mirth faltered and she gripped the edge of her desk. Posy glanced at Lucas, who seemed to be in some kind of wide-eyed trance.

"One moment." Ms. Hardstark hurried over to the bookcase and pulled out a slim leather volume titled *The Arundel Handbook*.

"It is indeed a charming old tradition," Posy said as sweetly as she could. "One that, as proud alumni, we'd love to honour."

"I'm sure that bylaw is purely for ceremonial purposes." Paddington sounded as if her throat was closing. "It must be as ancient as the school. You can't possibly think that we would actually use school funds on a *wedding*." Her eyes widened. "Thrilled as we are that you would think of us at this wonderful time of your lives."

"Here." Ms Hardstark dropped the old book on the desk in front of Paddington, releasing a stale smell of dust. She pointed to a section of the open page. "See?"

Paddington adjusted her glasses and studied the page, then looked up at Hardstark. "And this clause hasn't been revised since this was written?"

"So it would seem," Hardstark said. "As far as I know it's never been invoked. Easily forgotten."

"Right." Paddington took a sip of tea, her forehead creasing in a minute frown. "Posy, Lucas, I just don't see how we can possibly use funds intended for the education of children to finance a wedding—"

"And a honeymoon," Posy said.

Paddington glanced up at Hardstark who nodded confirmation and she bared her teeth in a brief show of frustration. "Oh for—" Paddington cleared her throat. "As I was saying, the school's money is to pay for the services we provide. We would be taking money from *children* to pay for a *wedding* – that with all due respect I am sure the two of you can afford between yourselves – and I don't feel comfortable with that notion." She pushed the leather book towards them as if to say 'case closed' and set her chin.

"The funny thing is, we, ah, can't afford a wedding," Lucas said, his upper lip damp with sweat.

"What?" Paddington's eyes went so narrow they were virtually slits.

"Long story." He tapped his thigh, foot jiggling. "It's ultimately, um, that is to say, well, it's personal."

Posy lifted up her tote to hide her face and glared at Lucas. "Get it together!" she mouthed, fighting a desire to shake him by the shoulders. There was no way they were failing at this because Lucas lost his nerve. Posy could see it was going to be down to her to get this argument won.

Posy lowered her bag and turned back to Paddington. "Listen, you can't refuse us. It's in the rules. We're entitled to that money. Surely we can come to some agreement?"

"I'm sorry," Paddington said with a thin smile. "But I am not paying for a wedding because of some nonsense old bylaw that to be honest needs to be done away with." She glanced up at Ms Hardstark. "Viv, remind me to call our lawyer and the board this afternoon. And now, you two, I think that has to be an end to that. Don't you?"

"Wait, please!" Posy gasped as Paddington rose to her feet to show them out. "We're so very much depending on… I mean, if you don't honour the contract, isn't that, like, breaking the law?"

"In effect." Lucas spoke suddenly and they all whipped their heads to look at him.

"Excuse me, Mr O'Rourke?" Paddington said with a voice of steel.

Lucas lifted his chin, his nerves seemingly calmed. "It's all very well saying you can't honour this tradition because it's taking away resources from current pupils, but the fact remains that this school and you, as its current headteacher, didn't see fit to revise the rules in order to prevent such a thing ever happening, did you?"

"Well, no, but it's so underused, it's obsolete! I never even knew it existed and if I had, I'd have brought it up to the board!" Paddington laughed sharply. "So when all is said and done—"

"When all is said and done, it *is* underused, and perhaps

it *should* be obsolete but under contract law," Lucas said, "you have to honour it."

"I think our lawyer would disagree," Hardstark remarked savagely.

"Not if they're any good they won't." Lucas met the woman's eye fearlessly and Posy couldn't help but be impressed. He was practically a different man now; the sweaty lip was gone, his hands and voice steady. "Arundel is classed as a business, not a charity. You lost that status a few years ago. And so, your business is providing education. You sign a contract with each pupil and the feepayer, do you not?"

"Well, yes," Paddington said. "But in that contract we don't say, 'Oh by the way, if you become head boy and then marry the head girl, we'll pay for it!'" She laughed again. "Come on!"

"No, the contract says that both parties agree to honour the bylaws to the letter as established circa 1873 from now until perpetuity." Lucas nodded at the leather tome on Paddington's desk. "Those bylaws in fact." Lucas pulled out a sheaf of paper from his back pocket. "I double checked my own contract just to be sure. We may not be students here anymore but the promises you made to us in this contract are binding until the day we die."

"But... but..." Paddington's mouth flapped.

"So, by all means, get your lawyers to check this all out and you can try to wriggle out of it"—Lucas adjusted the cuff of his shirt and flashed a stern grimace—"but I'm sure they will echo what I'm telling you. If you don't fund the wedding and honeymoon, you will be in breach of contract and we can sue should we feel aggrieved enough." He looked at Posy, who was having a hard time hiding her astonishment. "And we will be aggrieved, won't we?" He bared his teeth. "*Darling*?"

"Absolutely," Posy squeaked.

Paddington sank back into her seat, her mouth still opening and closing. Hardstark tugged the book off the desk and clasped it close to her chest.

"Obviously Mrs Paddington and I need to consult on this matter." She darted a side-eye at the now speechless headmistress. "Please could you give us a moment?"

Wordlessly, Posy and Lucas scurried out, barely able to meet each other's eyes. They took a seat in the foyer outside, just as they had done all those years ago when they took the fateful step of becoming head boy and head girl. As Posy looked around the hushed lobby, she could hear the faint calls and laughter from the playing field that stretched around the rear of the building they were in. It was probably a PE class she realised, and a wave of nostalgia washed over her. She'd loved hockey and lacrosse. Posy felt a pang for her teenage self, who'd walked these corridors brimming with optimism about her future as the world was spread at her feet. Would she have been so optimistic had she known what the future held, the way her family would view her? Next to her Lucas sat staring at the floor, arms folded. She could tell by the way his lips moved he was reliving every word of his argument. Posy nudged him.

"Do you think we did enough?" she whispered.

Startled, he glanced up. "I think so. They haven't got a leg to stand on," he said. "I bet they're on the phone to their lawyer now and he will tell them to abide by the rules."

"What if they contest it?" Posy hadn't even considered that would be a possibility, but Paddington had been far more resistant than she had imagined.

"The language in our contracts with the school is pretty black and white," Lucas said confidently. "As hard as it was for me to believe, they'd have to find a hell of a reason not to comply and—" he halted as the door opened abruptly.

Hardstark leaned out, her face grave. "Could you please come in?"

Posy leapt up, making sure to take Lucas's hand as they walked the few feet back to Paddington's office. The headmistress was still behind her desk and gave them a reluctant smile as they took the visitor seats once more.

"Now then." Paddington cleared her throat. "We have checked with our lawyer and yes, Mr O'Rourke, you're quite right. To deny your request would be a breach of contract and we have to honour it. However, he pointed out that there are no guidelines with regard to budget and so as such we aren't duty bound to pay for the kind of society wedding Miss Edwins is no doubt expecting."

"Understood," Lucas said.

Posy's heart thudded. She recognised the calculating look in Paddington's eye; if they offered her a tenner she'd scream. "As I told you, Mrs Paddington," Posy said authoritatively, "for the wedding we aren't looking for anything fancy. But when it comes to the honeymoon... well, if you want to fly anywhere nowadays it's hugely expensive and we do have our heart set on—"

"We can offer you three thousand pounds in budget," Paddington went on. "With the assumption that you will subsidise that with your own funds." A faint note of amusement trickled through her voice.

"Three?" Posy laughed, but she felt no humour. That little money wouldn't cover a flight to Hawaii! "That's an insult. We will take ten."

149

"Miss Edwins, are you *actually* negotiating?" Paddington said.

"I don't know, are you *actually* offering to pay for a wedding or trying to take me for a fool?" Posy snapped.

"Five," Paddington snarled.

"Eight."

"Seven and that's my final offer," Paddington said. "One more word and I'll go back down to three."

Posy had to clamp her lips together. Seven grand! Tara's dress alone had cost that when she'd got married! True, this was a fake wedding, but such a measly amount was an insult. That money would easily cover the cost of one ticket to Hawaii but for the sake of appearances they'd probably have to buy two and that would leave little else to cover even the most basic of fake weddings. But at least it was something. It was seven thousand pounds that she'd not had before.

"Ah, thank you," Lucas said, when it became clear Posy was not yet willing to speak.

"But here's the thing," Paddington went on. "We have conditions."

"Tell us," Lucas said authoritatively. "If we comfortable with them then we can accept."

Paddington bristled. "First of all, we want an invite."

"Oh." Posy kept her face neutral. There went the idea of hoping that some photos would suffice. No, this ruse had to go all the way.

"Very well," Lucas agreed, ice running through his words.

"What church are you intending to have it at?" Paddington picked up a pen.

"No church," Lucas replied curtly.

"What?" Paddington exchanged alarmed glances with

Hardstark. "So where…? You understand we need this to be done properly."

"You can call your lawyers again to verify," Lucas said confidently. "But nowhere in the bylaws does it stipulate what kind of wedding we have. We would like a Humanist wedding. No church or registry offices."

"We want it to be sublimely unique," Posy chimed in, stroking Lucas's arm for good measure. "Just about us."

"I…" Paddington looked back at Hardstark, who shrugged helplessly. Posy felt a surge of triumph. Lucas being such a mega-nerd had actually paid off!

"Right." Paddington cleared her throat, clearly irritated. "Anyway. This is an *Arundel* wedding and we have an obligation to our community to inform everyone by newsletter. You understand."

"Of course." Lucas nodded. He turned to Posy. "We expected that, right?"

"Mmm." Posy made a noise through gritted teeth.

"And obviously, we need to know the good name of Arundel isn't being smeared by something, well, inappropriate or debauched," Paddington continued.

"What's that supposed to mean?" Posy found her voice. "Isn't this something of an over-reaction?"

Paddington lifted a finger. "I'm stipulating that Ms Hardstark attends your appointments to, how shall I put it? Ah, yes, *reassure* us that this will be a wedding Arundel can really be proud of. My lawyers tell us we can in no way dictate what kind of wedding you have but I must insist that you are mindful of the school's good name. This could be a nice little bit of PR for us if handled correctly and naturally we would want to use any images or footage in our newsletters or branding. I must warn you that if Ms Hardstark feels at any time you are besmirching Arundel's good name, then under the morality clause that you signed upon confirming your place at Arundel, we have every right to withdraw our investment in you."

"Hang on." Posy reeled back to gaze at Lucas, knowing her horrified expression was a mirror image of his. "I want to make sure I've got this right. You're going to be checking up on us? Coming to every appointment?" She gripped the arms of her chair. Not only were they going to have to go through the rigmarole of organising a fake wedding with a paltry budget, they now had to do it under a microscope? She glanced at Lucas with horror. How on earth were they to spend so much time together without ripping each other's head off and giving the entire ruse away?

"Well, the main ones," Hardstark chimed in. "Dress, venue, and such. I'll be there with the credit card to pay for them too." She chuckled. "But these things take time to organise, don't they? I daresay you'll barely notice me when all's said and done."

"Oh, well, that's just it," Posy said, her voice cracking. "We want to get married very quickly. In a month!"

"What?" Paddington's voice dropped. "A month! Why on earth…?"

"Does it matter?" Posy yelped.

"Well, it's most irregular," Paddington said. "Most society weddings take months of planning!"

"We want lots of babies right away!" Posy shrieked, startling Hardstark so much she sat down with a heavy plop. "I want to have my moment in a white dress before I start popping out all the kids." It seemed as good a reason as any to have a hasty wedding.

"Right," Paddington said eventually and Posy let out a sigh of relief.

"When you know, you know, right?" Lucas quipped weakly. But no one laughed. For a few seconds they sat in silence. Posy's cheeks burned. The very *idea* of procreating with Lucas…

"I can be available over the course of the next month as and when you need then," Ms Hardstark said distantly.

Lucas and Posy exchanged glances. Posy thought back to that day in his office in London, when she'd boasted how easy it would be to fake a wedding. That day and her confidence suddenly seemed very far away.

"This isn't going to be a problem, is it?" Paddington asked coolly. "Because all of this is an absolute condition of us funding your wedding. I don't want to be embarrassed."

"And you're sure we can't just elope?" Posy reckoned it was worth at least having one last stab. "Have a fun little ceremony just the two of us?" As Lucas had warned her, this scheme was rapidly spiralling out of control.

"Oh no." Paddington shook her head. "No. I realise that legally there are only so many impediments I can place upon you – after all, it is your wedding – but elopement won't work for us. We need to be present at the ceremony and if you elope that can't happen, can it?"

"Right." Posy was suddenly very desperate to get out of the stiflingly warm room. It stank of tea and wood polish and the walls were closing in on her. "Well, we'll be in touch." She rose to her feet and hurried to the door.

"We have your contact details," Paddington went on smoothly to Lucas. "So do let us know how you'd like to proceed."

"Lucas!" Posy was desperate to escape, and the man was seemingly rooted into his chair.

"Yep." Lucas jumped up, nodding at the teachers. "Thanks for your time and, er, generosity."

Posy didn't wait to exchange any more niceties. She whirled on her heel and stormed out, but not without glimpsing the imperious smirk that blossomed across Paddington's face. She heard Lucas make some kind of stammering farewell behind her but she was out of the great door and down the stone steps before he caught up with her.

"Hey, slow down!" he called. "Christ, you move fast."

"This is a nightmare!" Posy snapped. "We can't have Hardstark watching us drop most of that budget on tickets to Hawaii! It'll be obvious we're full of shit and they'll pull the plug. And as for attending the wedding themselves? They'll know we're fake the minute you have to kiss the bride and I throw up in my mouth."

"I should have known it would come to this." Lucas rolled his eyes. "We don't just have to fake a ceremony; we have to fake an entire relationship! We have to convince them that we're so in love that we don't care what size wedding we get, only that we're married so we can run off and make lots of babies in the romantic setting of Hawaii."

"That's quite the fairy tale," Posy snarled. Making babies with Lucas O'Rourke? Hah! If her teenage self could see how far she'd fallen… It didn't matter that Lucas had clearly undergone something of a glow-up since leaving school, the challenge of displaying any emotion beyond irritation in his presence felt monumental. How on earth would they pull this off?

Lucas grimaced. "Tell me about it. But we have to try.

We're in it now." He dipped his head to catch Posy's eye. "Right?"

"Yes, yes," she grumped. "Ugh! I thought they'd just hand us the money and ask to see some snapshots for the newsletter. I didn't think they'd be this involved."

'Well, they are," Lucas said. "So we need to put on the show of our lives. Can you handle that?"

# Chapter Fourteen

Back at Arundel, Paddington turned narrow eyes towards Viv Hardstark, who was ruminating in the chair recently vacated by Posy.

"What do you make of that then?" she asked her deputy.

"Miss Edwins did not seem happy about our involvement now, did she?" Hardstark wagged her finger. "And I'm not sure I believe the babies explanation either. I mean... no matter how in love you are or how desperate you are to get married, you take more than a month! Especially someone of her standing. I can't imagine Jesper Edwins wanting his daughter marrying in such a manner."

"I doubt she's ever even attended a wedding that cost less than twenty grand, let alone one that costs seven," Paddington said. "No wonder she sounded surprised!"

"Her brother's wedding was in *Hello!*" Hardstark said. "He married a Rothschild and they must have spent at least a hundred grand on the whole affair."

"I get the feeling we're missing something here." Paddington tapped her chin. "Is Jesper Edwins suddenly broke?" When Hardstark shook her head in the negative, Paddington threw her hands up. "So why would they go to all this bother for a few measly grand? Has she been disowned by her family?"

"I doubt it," Hardstark replied. "That sort of scandal would be all over the grapevine and I haven't heard so much as a whisper on that front."

"Well, what on earth is going on then?" Paddington said.

"Perhaps they really are in love and for whatever reason want to involve the school?" Hardstark suggested. "This is, after all, where they met."

"Don't be ridiculous!" Paddington rolled her eyes. "No, I have an instinct here. Something isn't right." She pointed at her deputy, who straightened her back in response. "You have to watch them like a hawk. You see anything that makes you doubt the sincerity of their union, let me know immediately. Got it?"

## Chapter Fifteen

A couple of days after the Arundel meeting, Lucas was sighing with delight over the breakfast his mother had served. Annie O'Rourke never failed to deliver when it came to mealtimes and today was no exception. Juicy links of sausage and runny poached eggs were on the menu today, served with homemade English muffins and a pot of tea.

"Not that I'm not thrilled to have you here, son," Annie was saying as she loaded up his and his father's plates. "You don't visit enough, to my mind. But it's all a little mysterious you spending so much time with that Posy Edwins. You and she weren't exactly best friends from what I recall."

"Just catching up, Ma," Lucas said, mentally calculating the length of the run he'd have to do that evening to make up for the extravagant breakfast.

"Posy Edwins?" Brian's eyebrow twitched. "Her dad has that big house over on Clifton Mews, doesn't he?"

"And she's still as beautiful as ever," Annie added.

Lucas shovelled a forkful of sausage in his mouth and

shrugged. He knew he had to let his parents in on the scheme with Posy at some point so there were no horrid shocks, but honestly, he wasn't sure how to handle it. His parents were still devoted to Arundel even in their retirement and there was a chance they'd see this marriage as pure exploitation of the school. They could even stop the thing from going ahead and Lucas knew if that happened, there was no way he'd get his hands on the business Posy was offering. But looking into his mother's curious eyes, he lost the bottle. Perhaps when a date was set, he could tell her then.

"Posy is helping me develop my business network," he said. It was somewhat true after all. "She's very well connected, not just through her family but socially too."

"Oh." Annie didn't seem convinced. "I don't remember her being particularly business-minded as a child. In fact, I have a vivid memory of her breaking into the kitchen to steal biscuits for some party or other."

"Sounds like her," Lucas conceded. He broke open an egg to reveal a golden-orange yolk that flowed gently onto his muffin. He hummed in ecstasy. "Ma, these eggs are perfect."

"I should hope so." Annie watched her son fondly as he demolished his meal. "I can't imagine you eat like this too often. Too many protein shakes, I bet." From behind the kitchen door came a cacophony of demented yapping and Annie rolled her eyes. "Pablo! Minty! You'll get yours later. If these two leave you any, that is."

Lucas exchanged amused glances with his dad. Generally, sausages and lavishly buttered muffins were not part of his usual diet. But when your mum had been a head chef at a prestigious school for decades, you made exceptions for her cooking. Unfortunately for the two family dogs, that'd mean less scraps for the duration of his stay.

"So how long are you with us?" Brian asked, yolk dribbling down his chin.

"Probably a week or so," Lucas said. "Maybe more."

Brian's face brightened. "That's great news. But what about Align?"

"All in hand." His team was more than capable of keeping things going in the office. Besides, he wanted to give Fred a bumper crop of good news to aid his recovery. "I can work from home well enough. I may need to pop to London on the train once or twice, but that's no bother." He glanced at his watch and his insides leapt. He was already late for his first wedding appointment – a venue that Posy had said would be just the ticket. "Well, look at the time." He swallowed the last chunk of sausage and stood up. "Thanks for breakfast, Ma. See you both later." And, leaving his mother to dab at Brian's eggy face with a tea-towel with loving irritation, Lucas made his exit.

---

"What *is* that smell?" Posy complained for approximately the fourteenth time in five minutes. Ever since he'd picked her up outside her yoga class, she'd been moaning the entire drive.

"As I said, probably from the dogs!" Lucas glowered. He'd been delighted when his dad had offered him the loan of his old car whilst Lucas was visiting. The drive up from London was always a bore, and he could get hours of work done on the train. But the ancient Nissan needed a tune-up and a deep-clean valet. The off-beige seat fabric had trapped all manner of odours over the years, not least the pungent stink of wet dog. With a sigh, he thought of his top-of-the-range BMW currently languishing in his garage awaiting his return. As they pulled up to a junction, he looked over at her. "Which way now?"

"Turn right here," she said with a small smile.

"Tell me, what is this place we're viewing?" Lucas drove as he was told.

"Oh, just a little pile I thought might make for a lovely venue," she said casually.

Lucas frowned. "A little pile?" he repeated. He knew what a 'pile' meant to privileged folk like Posy. "What the hell does that mean?"

"Hey, you asked me to find local venues that could host a wedding cheaply, and I had an idea!" She splayed her hands proudly. "Oh, keep left here."

"When you say cheap, I did mean like, a couple hundred quid, yeah?" Lucas fought to keep his voice calm. "Remember the budget spreadsheet? The line item for venues was—"

"Do stop talking like a walking calculator!" Posy snapped. "Spreadsheets my eye! I'm telling you, Sumpter Hall will do us a favourable rate—"

Lucas almost slammed his foot on the brakes. "You've got to be kidding me!" Sumpter Hall was a local stately home, frequently used for period dramas and more than one episode of *Antiques Roadshow*. It was quite simply the pride of West Yorkshire and Lucas would be amazed if they'd even let them set foot on the grounds for the size of the budget they had. "You told me you could arrange a fake wedding with ease," he eked out the words through gritted teeth. "So I did you a budget that would cover the basics, leaving enough for flights to Hawaii." Because Hardstark was closely monitoring, they would have to buy two tickets and not one, so they had even less wiggle room when it came to paying for the ceremony, which had to look as convincing as possible. Thankfully, his Excel skills had come to the rescue. He didn't mention he'd used the template from the aborted wedding plans he'd made with Sally.

"You did do a budget," Posy said mutinously.

"So then why…?"

"Because Sumpter is lovely!" Posy cried. "This may be a fake wedding, Lucas, but it's *my* fake wedding and I'll be damned if I have to fake marry in… in… a public toilet or wherever it is *you* want to do it!"

"For fuck's sake," Lucas groaned. "You know perfectly well I don't want to marry in a public toilet. Don't be facetious." Posy remained ominously silent. Lucas tutted. "Facetious means treating serious—"

"Very funny," Posy barked. "I went to the same school as you; I know exactly what it means."

"I put enough in for a cheap venue hire." He fought to keep his tone level. "An hour or two in a village hall perhaps. A room above a pub. That's all we need."

"A room above a—" Posy reared back against the car door as if to get distance from the very idea of it. "Why don't I just wear my dressing gown on the big day instead of a dress? Use a bunch of weeds as a bouquet? I'd fit right in, wouldn't I?"

"You know that's not what I'm saying," Lucas muttered.

"I bet we won't even be allowed in Sumpter anyway, pulling up in this heap of a car," Posy grumbled, cranking the window even lower. Lucas could see her point. She was out of place in the dingy little car; all that piled up hair was brushing against the roof, gaining more and more in static charge.

"I know you're not used to worrying about money," he went on, slowing down to allow a trundling pheasant time to get out of harm's way. The bird ambled to the crumbling stone wall and pecked at its base, blissfully unaware of its proximity to certain death. "But you have to face facts. We cannot afford Sumpter Hall." He stopped at a junction, fingers tapping the wheel. "Call and cancel. There's no point to this."

"Can't." Posy shrugged sheepishly. "Ms Hardstark is coming too. Might it not seem a little suspicious?"

"Oh for fu—" Lucas clamped his lips shut before the curses could start flowing. "You're right. We can't risk that."

"Look, Sebastien got married here a few years ago," Posy went on, evidently gleeful to get her own way. "We spent an absolute fortune. I bet they'll do us a favour."

"A favour?" Lucas said. "For somewhere like Sumpter Hall we'll need more than a favour. We need a bloody miracle. Maybe you could sell a kidney to pay for it. Although I doubt we'd get much for your champagne-riddled organs."

"I'm a whisky girl," she growled. "And you'd get a fortune for lungs like mine; my yoga teacher says I have astonishing breath capacity."

Lucas almost choked on his laughter. "Astonishing is right," he spluttered once he calmed down. Jesus, rich people.

"Anyway, let's be a bit more positive." Posy's cheeks pinked. "Surely it won't cost that much just to use a room for, like, an hour?"

Lucas shot her a side glance, incredulous that someone who hailed from such wealth could be so out of touch with how much things cost. "Still way out of our league. Is Hardstark meeting us there or do we need to pick her up?"

"She'll meet us there." Posy harrumphed. "Maybe we'll lose her in the maize maze."

"Not if she dies from laughter at our even trying this," Lucas muttered.

Minutes later they pulled up at Sumpter Hall. It was as grand as Lucas remembered from his younger days – a dignified mansion in the Gothic style, its stark magnificence only compounded by the acres of green lawn and exquisite rose gardens surrounding it. A long stable block to the far side of the driveway was draped in the most luscious wisteria and fat bees buzzed lazily around the vibrant flowers as if they had all the time in the world. It was, he reflected grimly, the sort of place Sally would have chosen as their wedding venue, had she stuck around long enough to see things through. As the battered old Nissan puttered down the great, lemon-coloured drive, Lucas stole another glance at Posy. She was looking up at the beautiful old building with awe softening her face and excitement curving her lips. Lucas felt nothing but encroaching gloom; how could she think this would be a viable option for them?

Lucas pulled into a parking space and no sooner were they out of the car than Ms Hardstark was upon them. Dressed in an ankle-length wool skirt and clumpy hiking boots, she looked as though she was ready to tackle a mountain race rather than view one of Yorkshire's most treasured institutions.

"Morning!" Hardstark boomed right into Lucas's ear.

"Morning." Lucas winced.

"Hello, Ms Hardstark," Posy said, trying not to giggle.

"Lovely day for a hike, isn't it?" She received a glare in response.

"Who's our appointment with?" Lucas asked Posy, tugging at his ear with a pained expression.

"Miles Purslow," Posy answered. "His office must be that way." She pointed at a neat English Heritage branded sign directing them down a narrow path to the manager's office. With a noise akin to a horse's whinny, Hardstark led the way. Lucas dawdled down the path, taking a moment to drink in the delicate scent of the flowers lining the path. It was truly a stunning place.

The path led them round the back of the imposing building to a small courtyard sheltered from the tourist tracks, with high hedges blocking views of the gardens. A door with chipped white paint was ahead of them, a laminated sign saying 'Office' tacked to the side of it. Hardstark, with all the delicacy of a sergeant major, stomped up and banged a fist against the door.

The man who answered the knock was slight but tall, with intelligent grey eyes. He regarded Ms Hardstark with a curious wonder.

"Ah, hello?" he said.

"Mr Purslow?" Posy waved. "I'm Posy. We spoke yesterday?"

"Oh yes!" The man nodded genially, a warm smile revealing endearing dimples in his cheeks. "Do come in. And call me Miles, please." Miles's office was small and overstuffed with furniture. A small desk housed a laptop and desk phone, as well as a large blotter and several curious plastic toys. "Love a fiendishly hard brain teaser," Miles explained, tossing a small Rubik's Cube in the air and catching it deftly. He directed the trio to a large velvet couch scattered with embroidered cushions and then moved to a battered sideboard where a small tea station had been established. "Drink?" he asked. "No coffee today, but tea I can manage."

Lucas, who was wedged against the rigid arm of the couch and Hardstark's unyielding form, shook his head frantically. Best to get this over and done with.

"A tea would be delightful," Hardstark said and Lucas wheezed with despair.

"Splendid." Miles flicked the kettle on, then rooted around in the sideboard's cupboard, withdrawing a pack of Hobnobs with relish. "Can I tempt anyone?" Posy and Lucas both declined in unison, but Hardstark took two biscuits with a coquettish nod. "Now." Miles settled himself once all the pleasantry was out of the way. "How can I help?"

"They're looking for a wedding venue," Hardstark interjected, swirling her tea daintily. "But only have a small budget as donated by my employer, who I am here representing. Arundel College."

"Arundel?" Miles's neat eyebrows leapt. "I say."

"If I may," Posy said, shifting to find a more comfortable spot. "You may remember my family, the Edwins? We've hosted a number of events at this venue. I have such a place in my heart for Sumpter Hall, so many happy memories."

"Right." Miles scratched his head through his thatch of grey hair. "I take it there is to be a spot of negotiation?"

"As I said," Posy went on blithely. "I *love* this place. My brother Sebastien got married here… gosh, some time ago now. My family did spend a great deal on the day, as I said."

"Sebastien Edwins?" Miles nodded in recognition. "Yes,

I remember. His best man was the one who got spectacularly drunk, right?" His amiable expression darkened somewhat.

"Patrick, yes," she giggled. "I seem to remember he bought at least two bottles of top-shelf whisky for our guests."

"Yes, and promptly passed out in the Latimer Garden causing untold damage to our prize roses," Miles said, primly folding his hands in his lap. Hardstark gasped audibly, her teacup clattering back in its saucer.

"Oh." Posy seemed to fold in on herself with embarrassment. Lucas dropped his head into his hands. Posy offered Miles a meek smile. "Sorry. Didn't know that."

"Please, don't worry." Miles's sombre expression melted. "It was a long time ago and it's not the worst thing to happen at a wedding here. The roses survived with a little nurture."

"And some quality mulch, I imagine!" Hardstark piped up with a girlish titter.

"I see we have an expert in the room." Miles nodded approvingly. "I worked very closely with the head gardener on the issue. Roses are a particular passion of mine. I'm somewhat of a fanatic, in fact."

"The soil recipe is so important," Hardstark sympathised. "It's been a tough year for Austins. You should see the troubles we're having at Arundel with this year's blooms."

Posy leaned behind Hardstark's back and caught Lucas's eye. *Soil recipe?* she mouthed with derision.

"Anyway," Lucas barked, desperate to get off the couch so he could breathe, "very glad the roses are okay. But back to the wedding?"

"Right." Miles seemed deflated at the change of subject

167

and tore his attention away from Hardstark. "I will say though that we can't really offer much of a discount, even for special friends of Sumpter," Miles went on. He stood up abruptly. "But let's take a walk. Come with me." Two long strides took him out of the office and Hardstark was up with a bound to follow him. Posy and Lucas extricated themselves from the low couch with some difficulty, but before they could leave the office, Lucas snagged Posy's arm.

"How did you not know that guy trashed this place at the wedding?" Lucas asked, incredulity stretching his eyes wide.

"Oh my God, it was like five years ago," Posy whispered. "Can you remember stuff that happened five years ago?"

Lucas stared at her incredulously. "Yes. Many things. Easily."

"Oh whatever," Posy said. "Is there a spreadsheet for that?"

"I don't think you even know what a spreadsheet is," Lucas said with despair.

Posy brightened. "What I do remember is the chocolate cheesecake they served for dessert. My word, you should have tasted it. I'd marry *Hardstark* for another slice of that bad boy."

Lucas tutted. "God, if you want cheesecake so bad, we can pick one up at Iceland for our wedding. They do two for a fiver."

"Eww," Posy shuddered. "The signature dessert for my wedding will not be freezer food."

"Signature?!" Lucas spluttered. "Did you even look at the budget?"

Posy slumped dramatically against the doorframe as if

she were about to pass out. "I swear, you should marry Excel instead of me."

"It's the most efficient way of drawing up a budget," Lucas hissed at her. "It's what people do when they plan a wedding!"

"And what do you know about weddings?" Posy asked irritably, shrugging off his arm as they followed Miles and Hardstark.

"I know enough," Lucas said. He thought of Sally, of the tears she'd shed that day. He walked ahead of Posy, suddenly unable to look at her. Did Posy even know what it felt like to let someone down so badly, the way he'd done with Sally? Would she even care? But then hurried footsteps tapped behind him and she was back by his side.

"Sorry. I forgot you'd been engaged before," she said softly.

"Clearly," Lucas snapped.

Posy's annoyance obviously overrode her sympathy. "Seems to me she had a lucky escape."

"Don't tempt me with the idea of *escape*," he said, clenching his jaw. "Now, pipe down and hold my fucking hand."

And so, hand in hand, they caught up with Miles and Hardstark, who were enthusiastically discussing the merits of different compost brands with regards to rose growing with an uncharacteristic amount of laughter from the normally dour teacher. As Lucas and Posy did their best to mimic the air of a loving couple, Miles led them down a path of neatly swept flags and pointed towards the manicured lawns that rolled down to a river sparkling in the distance. There were so many delightfully old trees – splendiferous willows, gnarled oaks and elegant beeches, their majesty a perfect foil to the exacting boxed hedges and artfully placed statues in varying states of crumbling ruin. Even at the mid-morning hour, numerous tourists and groups meandered around the many pathways, children darting and playing as their parents appreciated the scenery around them.

"Look up there." Miles indicated a copse of ancient and massive oaks. "See the treehouses?" Posy gasped in delight as she saw state-of-the-art wooden huts built in and amongst the weighty branches, with walkways between each tree. "If you're feeling nimble, those make very scenic spots for photos and in fact, you can even get married in one of our state-of-the-art treehouses. They're fully licensed for ceremonies, although you can't get much of a crowd up there."

Eyes wide, Posy turned to Lucas. "Now that sounds awesome. We could—" She stopped as she clocked his grimace. "What now?"

Lucas was well aware of Hardstark watching them. "Heights, darling. Heights," he said through a rigid smile.

Posy pulled a face and Lucas crossed his fingers, hoping she could rectify her error, but Hardstark swooped.

"You weren't aware that your fiancé has a phobia of heights?" Hardstark commented, a cocky smile blossoming. "How odd."

Lucas, out of Hardstark's view, mouthed furiously at Posy. "Fix this!"

Posy shrugged an insouciant shoulder. "Oh, no I do know that actually, I just forgot that it was all heights, you know and not just buildings, ladders, mountains."

"You thought that going up a tall tree didn't count as a height?" Hardstark said slowly.

"Um. Yeah."

"I give up," Lucas whispered, so only Posy could hear.

"Onward!" Miles interjected politely, leading them a little further along the path. "Here we are. This is the Great Hall where we hold most of our ceremonies." He gestured at a large wooden door set into the back of the building where they had arrived. He opened the door with a flourish. "We're currently setting up for a wedding tomorrow, so you can get an idea of what we do here. Come on in."

Lucas gasped. Now he could see why Posy had wanted to take such a punt; the place was glorious. The hall was a wide, high-ceilinged room with exposed beams and brick-work. Ten rows of antique chairs were arranged to face a matching table, behind which two larger, throne-like chairs were placed. Golden candelabra had been placed strategically about the place, their thick pillar candles artfully drip-ping wax. Staff were arranging flowers on the backs of each chair whilst two burly men unrolled a long white carpet down the floor of immaculate grey stone to form the aisle.

"This is quite a simple set up," Miles went on, waving at the activity. "But we can do all sorts. Light shows, live music… whatever you want."

Lucas glanced over at Posy; her face was soft with imagi-nation. "Lovely," he said automatically.

"It really is," Posy breathed. "We could have fabric draped over that far wall to create a really sensual atmosphere." She then whirled to look at the altar. "I'd have a ton of fresh flowers here; get rid of those fairy lights, get some festoons up there." She clapped her hands like an excited child.

"All possible," Miles said. "After the ceremony you'd have pictures outside or elsewhere, even in the main house should you so wish. Then back in here for the wedding breakfast, with banqueting to your specifications." Posy smiled broadly and Lucas had to take a deep breath. Why was she being so positive about this when she knew how little money they had? He had to stop her and now.

"How much does all that cost then?" Lucas said bluntly and Posy looked at him with wounded eyes. He clenched his jaw. Let her bleat all she wanted; this was the biggest waste of time and exactly what he'd feared when agreeing to this plan.

"Well, we have various packages," Miles was replying. "And I have brochures back in the office which detail them all. But for, say, fifty guests, ceremony and reception, you're in the realm of about fifteen thousand pounds dry hire. We have in-house catering you can use if you wish and that starts at eighty pounds per head for the breakfast."

Posy looked as if all the breath had been sucked out of her body and Lucas almost wanted to shake her. "Well, that's that then," he said. "Come on. *Darling*."

Posy stood obstinately, fists clenched. "Are you telling me there's no wiggle room there?" She wheedled. "Say... just the ceremony for half an hour on a Monday afternoon or something? We could bung you a few hundred for that?"

Miles rewarded her with a strange look. "I appreciate you may be on a tight budget, but we are a premium venue," he replied, aggrieved. "Weddings booked here provide revenue to help restore and maintain this historic building and if we book a ceremony then that whole day is yours, regardless of the length of the event. We can't drop the price by that much."

Posy huffed, her shoulders drooping. "But my family have spent so much in the past – doesn't that count for anything?"

"We have truly valued your family's custom." Miles

lowered his head in a polite nod. "But I can't give you anything for a bung of a few hundred." He shot an exasperatedly kind glance at Lucas, who smiled indulgently back. There was no way he was fighting Posy's corner on this. "Even if it would clearly be a cultured event of good taste." Miles beamed at Hardstark who merely sniffed.

"So what do we do now?" Posy muttered to Lucas. Hardstark saw her dejection and pounced.

"It doesn't matter where you marry does it, as you're so in love?" she said viciously. "You told me that you don't need anything ostentatious."

"Yes." Posy bared her teeth. "I did say that."

"All right then," the older woman said, holding out her phone. "Then why not look at this delightful registry office in the council building? It needs a lick of paint but surely it'd do?" As Posy mournfully took in the brightly lit, wide-angle lens photos that did nothing to disguise the bleakness of that particular registry office, Ms Hardstark's victorious grin became practically wolfish. "Or better yet," she went on, "why not postpone, take some time? Save up your own damn money."

Posy's face turned puce, and Lucas stepped in hurriedly.

"You're right, Ms Hardstark, we really don't need much," he said. "This place is great, Miles, but we have a minimal budget. We're looking to get married in four weeks' time, too."

"We're SO in love you see." Posy grabbed Lucas's arm so hard he yelped, wrapping it around her waist.

"Er, quite." Miles looked totally bemused. "Well, even if you did have the money, we have no availability that soon anyway."

"Okay, so." Lucas squeezed Posy to him and she gazed

up at him, her sweet vanilla perfume filling his nose. "You hear that, darling? We really cannot get married here."

Miles raised a finger. "I may have a solution."

Posy lurched out of Lucas's grasp. "You do? We can have it here then?"

"Well, not as it stands." Miles said. "Not unless you have a suitable budget and can wait until the summer after next." Before Posy could protest, he lifted a hand. "However, I do know of another place that would suit your... er... situation," he went on. "It's obviously nowhere near the scale of Sumpter but I'm sure it will be available at short notice and ripe for someone with this young lady's imagination." He reached into his linen jacket and pulled out a clip of business cards, rifling through until he found one, offering it to Lucas. "Here, why not give my friend a call?"

## Chapter Sixteen

"Okay, turn right down here." Posy squinted at the directions she'd hastily penned on the palm of her hand. Lucas obliged and as the car turned down the meandering Yorkshire lanes, Posy caught a glimpse of Hardstark following their car in her little Boxster. Watching the woman fold herself into it had been almost as intriguing as predicting what kind of venue Miles had set them up with. Lucas had called the proprietor then and there, setting up a viewing straight away. The lady at the end of the phone had been so excited to get his call she'd almost burst into tears. And so, the directions had led them to Lower Thicket, a village roughly ten miles from Arundel College, tucked deep into the hills of the Peak District.

"I don't think I even knew this place existed!" Lucas remarked as they passed a rather shabby and rusted 'Welcome to Lower Thicket' sign, or rather, a sign that had clearly once had such a greeting. Most of the lettering was so faded it appeared to read 'Wel Thick' which caused Posy no end of giggles.

"I don't know this place at all," she said once her mirth had subsided. "But I mean… wow, it's so picturesque."

"It's tiny." Lucas slowed down to 20mph as per the road sign, which allowed them to get a better look at the village. The houses seemed to be mostly small, low-roofed cottages with neat little gardens. The verges brimmed with tall grasses and verdant wildflowers that swayed gently in the summer breeze. They passed a homely church attached to a quaint little school and there, tucked off the road onto a tidy green was their destination: Lower Thicket Town Hall.

Lucas turned the car into a patch of tarmac optimistically signposted as the car park and turned off the engine. As the engine cooled, Posy stared at her potential wedding venue in disbelief. The building before her was one step away from a Portakabin, a one-storey building with rough white cladding and net-curtain rimmed windows with frames badly requiring repair. A small set of stone steps – all of them cracked and worn – led up to a door that perhaps had once been red but was now a murky shade of salmon-pink. The portico above it sagged and was laced with thick spiderwebs.

"No." Posy folded her arms. "Nope, nope, nope. I know this is a fake wedding but this is… this is just sad, Lucas."

"We haven't seen inside yet," Lucas said. His tone was defensive, but Posy could detect a faint note of despair. "And you're right. This is a fake wedding, yeah? It doesn't matter what this place looks like, so long as it'll host a sham wedding for peanuts. I'm sure it'll be fine."

Posy turned on him. "Do you even have eyes Lucas?" she cried. "It's a dump! I was willing to endure a cheap wedding for the sake of my career, but this is too far. It's testing my limits of acting."

"Yes, but if we spend all our money on a flash venue we can't afford plane tickets. You *do* understand that, don't you?" From somewhere behind them came the roar of Hardstark's car pulling into the car park. Lucas sighed. "Look, if we don't get out there and put on a show Hardstark is almost certainly going to know something is up. And if she does, no Hawaii. Is that what you want?"

Posy pondered her options. How on earth would she make this festival happen otherwise? "All right, all right. God, I forgot how persistent you can be. And by persistent, I mean the most annoying human on the planet." Posy took a deep breath and looked him firmly in the eye. "Let's do this."

As they climbed out of the car, the door to the building opened. A petite lady trundled down the steps, pulling a moth-eaten cardigan of indiscriminate brown around her wiry frame.

"Hello!" She waved frantically as if she were lost at sea and hailing help. Interestingly, despite the vigour of her movement, her solid wedge of greying hair didn't move; it stayed still like snap-on Lego hair. "Lucas O'Rourke?"

"Yes!" He walked towards the woman with hand outstretched. "You must be Mrs Jones?"

"Patricia, please," she said. "Oh, no handshake dear – I don't do touching. Germs, you know."

"Right." Lucas withdrew his hand and rocked on his heels.

"And this must be your lucky fiancée!" Patricia cooed, offering a wave to Hardstark, who had advanced ahead of Posy. "My, you certainly eat your greens, don't you?"

"I beg your pardon?" Hardstark trumpeted as Posy unsuccessfully attempted to hold back a snort of laughter.

"It's me actually. I'm Posy." She stepped out from behind Hardstark and offered a little wave.

"Ah, of course, of course." Patricia's eyes lit up at the sight of Posy. "Now *you* are a picture! Oh!" She clapped her hands together. "A very handsome couple indeed. Now, come on in. I don't have long, I'm afraid; the bridge club will be along shortly to set up."

Posy and Lucas followed Patricia into the building. The hallway was compact, with a bristled grey carpet worn thin in places from the tread of many visitors. A lightbulb in an off-white lampshade highlighted the walls where cork notice-boards advertised various services and events in the local area. To the left was a closed door marked 'Office' and directly ahead double doors led to an open space, from where Patricia and Hardstark's voices echoed.

"Eww." Posy pulled a face at more dust-coated cobwebs in the corner of the hallway.

"Do come on." Lucas led the way and Posy trailed behind, gathering her blazer around her. As they entered the main hall, Posy could sense Lucas brightening at what they saw but she couldn't match his reaction. True, the inside of the hall was surprisingly light and neat, especially when compared to the scruffy exterior. The walls were a basic off-white, the floor scuffed wood rendered dark by years and years of poorly applied varnish. At one end, garish orange plastic chairs were stacked and braced against the wall and to the right of the entrance was a long serving-hatch upon which was an ancient tea-urn surrounded by concerning scorch marks. The one saving grace was the long wall being taken up mostly by floor-to-ceiling windows that looked across the green to the bucolic old church at the other side. It filled the room with a gentle, golden light that was admittedly rather pleasant. But Posy couldn't help remembering the glory of Sumpter Hall and compared to that, this place was severely lacking.

Lucas ambled over. "Buck up, dear," he murmured and Posy lifted her chin mutinously.

"What do you think?" Patricia asked, gesturing around the room with obvious pride.

"You really want to know?" Posy squeaked, arms folded. From behind Patricia, Hardstark grinned.

"As I understand it, this place is available in four weeks," Hardstark said. "And if you really want to get married as soon as possible, why not book this place? One might think you aren't serious."

"We are," Lucas said hurriedly. "Posy? *Darling*."

"Yes." Posy knew she had no choice. She gave Patricia a saccharine smile. "Super serious."

"It's a blank canvas just as Miles told us," Lucas said with a nod and he looked at Patricia. "What's the damage?"

"Well, for a full afternoon, that is to say, noon till five, we could do it for three hundred," Patricia answered, fishing into her shapeless cardigan's pocket for a notepad. "For four hundred, you'd get use of all the chairs and tables, myself and my daughter to help set up, serve any food and drink for two hours, as well as our clean-up services at the end. We'd also need a security deposit of one hundred, which we would repay once the event is over presuming there's no damage."

Lucas shoved his hands in his pockets and Posy could tell by the furrowing of his brow that he was mentally consulting his beloved budget spreadsheet. "We can manage that," he said eventually. "And when is the next available date?"

"We do actually have a Saturday available at the end of

next month," Patricia continued with a warm smile. "June 30th. It was supposed to be the Wingers' fortieth wedding anniversary party but ever since Goldie took up with the salsa instructor... well..." Patricia flapped a hand. "It all goes on around here," she remarked. Posy very much doubted anything of merit went on around here, but she saw Lucas's logic.

"Let's do it." Posy knew she was being a child about a wedding that actually meant nothing at the end of the day and that every moment she kicked up a fuss she ran the risk of Hardstark rumbling the game. The problem was she'd underestimated how much working to such a tight budget was going to restrict her natural flair and tastes. It may have been a fake wedding, but it was still *Posy Edwins's* fake wedding. She closed her eyes and imagined Hawaii, and the boost her career would get. That was all that mattered.

"Are you sure?" Hardstark said in obvious disbelief.

Posy opened her eyes and met the older woman's gaze. "Oh, I'm sure."

"Very well," Hardstark said with a huff. "Patricia, allow me to get the financial details from you as I'll be coordinating the payment side of things."

"Oh." Patricia blinked at her and then looked back at Posy and Lucas. "I'm a little confused. Miles wasn't clear. You're from the school but, are you mother of the... bride?" She squeaked the last word with some trepidation.

"I'll explain in your office," Hardstark said with a leaden expression. "Lead the way."

As soon as they were out of room, Lucas rounded on Posy with wide eyes. "Can you keep it together?"

"I'm trying," she said. "But come on, this place is a dump."

"Obviously it's not as fancy as the previous venue," he admitted. "Thing is, we don't need it to be, remember? I didn't step away from my business and temporarily move in with my parents only to have the whole thing blown by a temper tantrum."

Posy gave him her best scornful look. "Is that what you think? That I'd ruin my chances by throwing a tantrum?"

"Well, what do you call this?" He gestured at her.

"Fine, okay fine." Posy dismissed him with a shake of her head and wandered over to the window. It really was a pretty view and beyond the church there was a delightful-looking pub that gleamed in the light of the sun. She took out her phone to take a snapshot, only to see an email pop up on the screen. The Arundel newsletter had come in and even though she usually ignored them, this one she opened. "Lucas?" she croaked.

"What now?" he grunted.

"Our wedding made the newsletter!" She began to read the text as Lucas hurried to her side, his nose already in his phone.

Time to buy a hat! In a first for Arundel College, we are delighted to announce the marriage of former head boy, Lucas O'Rourke, and head girl, Posy Edwins. This wonderful pair served in their prefect roles for academic year 2008-2009 and recently decided to tie the knot, setting the date for this summer. Arundel are proud to part-sponsor the nuptials as per a soon-to-be-defunct ancient clause in our school bylaws. Lucas currently works for a start-up wealth management operation and Posy takes pictures for social media. Please, join us in offering our heartiest congratulations to the happy couple!

Posy exploded.

"That's fucking savage! *Takes pictures for social media?*" Posy wanted to scream. "Why don't they simply call me a jobless waste of space and be done with it?"

"*Works for a start-up?*" Lucas quoted with a frown. "That makes me sound like a graduate, for crying out loud!"

"The shade of it!" Posy could see full well what Arundel was doing. This was a petty retaliation for what she and Lucas had managed to do.

"Posy, I think you're missing the issue here," Lucas gripped her shoulders. "The word is out. Everyone we went to school with will soon know. Our *parents* will know."

"My dad hasn't read the newsletter in, like, a gazillion years! And I bet none of our friends do." Posy hoped she sounded more confident than she felt.

"Good for you, because my parents read it religiously," Lucas said.

"Jesus, why?"

"Because Arundel actually means something to them." Lucas took his hands off her shoulders and stepped away. "They care about that place, even in retirement." He looked back at her and guilt twisted his face. "I don't think they'll take kindly to learning about it like this. They were so disappointed when Sally left me; this'll just be the icing on the cake."

Posy looked at Lucas. The newsletter's arrival had knocked the vim out of him and it was strange to see. Posy felt an additional frisson of guilt at the notion that his parents would be upset by what she and Lucas were doing; that wasn't fair.

"Go," she said. "Talk to them. I'll finish up here and get Hardstark to drop me at home."

"Are you sure?" he said. "I thought we would research officiants this afternoon?"

"I can do that," Posy said.

Lucas fixed her with a stern glare. "Remember to—"

"Check the budget, yeah, yeah." She made a shoo-ing motion. "Make sure your parents are all right. I'll firm things up here."

"Okay then." He smiled gratefully and lifted his eyes to hers. "Thanks."

"No worries," she said. "I know a little something about disappointing one's parents."

Lucas frowned at her, then softened. "Yeah, well, let's prove them wrong, shall we?"

## Chapter Seventeen

The house was quiet when Lucas arrived home, but the kitchen was warm with the scent of cinnamon buns. He wasn't sure where his parents were but he could see two freshly washed mugs by the sink so guessed they might have popped out for a post-lunch walk. He exhaled in relief; perhaps they hadn't seen the email yet. He hurried up to his room intent on catching up on work but half an hour later found himself staring into space with very little actually done. He couldn't concentrate. There had been such a weird moment at the end of their visit to the hall. Posy had been gracious enough to let him duck out and get home, showing something akin to empathy, which he'd never imagined he'd see.

Just then, his laptop began to ping with an incoming video call: it was Fred. Grateful for the excuse to suspend the pretence at work, Lucas answered the call.

"Fred?" His best friend was barely visible in the gloom on the screen; indeed, it seemed as if he was making the call in the dark. "Mate, are you under your duvet or something?"

"Shhh!" Fred hissed. "Suzi will hear!"

"You're supposed to be resting," Lucas chided, failing to control his laughter. "She's going to kill you."

"Ah, what does she know?" Fred said affectionately. "Listen, I don't have long. Did you read through the email from Lim today?"

"They sent another one?" Lucas shook his head and opened up his emails on his phone. "When? They want to meet?"

"So it would seem," Fred answered. "I reckon they'll make an offer."

"Right." Lucas searched for the email. Indeed, there it was – a very complimentary email asking for a conference call about 'an exciting future together.' There was such a smugness about their tone, as if the deal were already done; Lucas's instincts immediately recoiled. But there was no disguising the hope in Fred's eyes. Swallowing, Lucas bit his tongue. "I guess there's no harm in having an exploratory call."

"Great." A relieved smile spread across Fred's face.

"I'll ask Jackie to set it up," Lucas said tightly.

"Spit it out." Fred loomed closer to the screen. It wasn't a flattering angle.

"Spit what out?"

"You're disappointed," Fred said. "I know selling up has never been in your life plan and up until recently it wasn't in mine but here we are. Unless Posy's introduced you to a ton of new clients?"

Lucas sighed. "Not yet, not until the wedding day. The date has been set though. End of June."

"Interesting." Fred waggled his eyebrows. "So how are you getting on with the wife-to-be?"

"Like a dream," Lucas said sarcastically. "I asked her to find a budget venue and she promptly booked a viewing at a stately home." He laughed bitterly. "She has no idea what doing things on the cheap even means. How we're going to get through this without being rumbled, I do not know."

"Ah, rich kids," Fred said with a grin. "Play our cards right and ours could grow up that stupid."

"Funny," Lucas said. "I just can't wait for it all to be over. "

Just then, Fred's screen lightened as the duvet was suddenly ripped off his head and there in the background was Suzi, her expressive eyes rolling as she saw what Fred was doing.

"I leave you alone for ten minutes," she said, deadpan.

"It was just a quick catch-up, my little periwinkle," Fred pleaded. "No work, I promise."

"Then why are you hiding under a duvet?" She failed to hide her grin. "Hi Lucas."

"Hi mate," Lucas greeted her. "You all right? How are the kids?"

"Yeah." She stifled a yawn. "We're all fine. Just worried about this one."

"Tell me about it." Lucas looked at her tired face and felt even more pressure rest upon him. Fred could really do with cashing out and taking it easy – Suzi too by the looks of it. "Listen, I'd best go." Downstairs he heard the front door crash open and Annie roar his name.

"Was that your mum?" Fred asked.

"There's a chance she's found out about the wedding," Lucas replied with a wince.

"Nice knowing you," Fred said, pulling a face.

Lucas ended the call with a promise to speak soon and stood up but his bedroom door was flung open and there was his mother. Her expression brooked no pleasantry.

Lucas gulped. "You read the newsletter."

"I did." Annie entered the room, rubbing her wiry arms as if she were cold. "I had to check my email to see when my Tesco delivery was scheduled for and it popped up. Imagine my surprise to see your name in the email subject. What in blazes is going on? You're engaged?"

"Ma, sit down." Lucas guided her to the edge of his bed, his heart turning over at her resulting scowl. "Let's just—"

"Don't *let's just*." Annie batted his hand away. "You're engaged! And you didn't see fit to tell your parents?"

"Does Pa know?" Lucas asked.

"Not as yet; he's gone fishing. But when he comes back one of us will have to explain." She tugged at her hair. "How on earth will we do that?"

"It's complicated," Lucas said, knowing as he said it how much that would enrage her.

"Are you or are you not marrying Posy Edwins?" Annie snapped.

"In a manner of speaking, yes." Lucas watched with horror as his mum's eyes filled with tears. "Oh Ma, come on, let me explain!"

"What is happening?" Annie sank to rest on his bed. "First Sally leaves you..."

"Yes, she did, but this is—"

"And now you're going to marry someone who, for all intents and purposes, hates you?"

"Ma." Lucas took a deep breath. "I'll tell you everything

but it's all hush-hush, okay? You can't tell any of your old pals from Arundel about this."

"What has gotten into—? You know what?" Annie flapped her hands. "Never mind, just tell me."

"Align is in big trouble," Lucas began. His mother's eyes narrowed and he wanted to hide under the duvet just like Fred had. "I've failed and…" He stopped, his throat closing. How could he explain to his ever so proud mother that the big dream was slipping away from him?

Annie chucked his chin so she could meet his gaze. "Oi. You're no failure. You got a first from LSE. You won the entrepreneur's prize at—"

"Ma. Stop." Lucas couldn't bear to endure a roll call of his accolades. "You don't get it. The company lost some major clients this quarter and we don't have the cashflow to sustain us beyond another six months."

"How has this happened?" Annie said.

"I'm not even sure," Lucas replied. "I did all the calculations, Fred brought in some good clients…" He shrugged. "I clearly did something wrong, didn't I?"

"Not necessarily," Annie said. "Sometimes these things happen in business. You can't get any more capital or borrow?"

"Fred has been trying for a while, but we don't have the assets. We're leveraged to the hilt as is." Lucas allowed the crashing guilt to rack him for a wordless moment. "There's a chance that we could be bought out, but Ma, selling Align has never been the plan. What we need is clients, and lots of them, but Fred's ill so it's on me to bring them in. You know that's not my strength."

"Poor Fred," Annie said with a sympathetic nod. "I hope he's taking care of himself."

"He is, but he has to rest." Lucas gestured at himself. "Now I'm the only one who can pick Align up. Otherwise, we sell."

"But you're always so busy!" Annie gestured at his laptop that even now was pinging with emails. "I thought business was good."

"I am busy," Lucas admitted. "And honestly, being away from London has weirdly allowed me to be really productive, but it's not enough." He met his mother's eye. "We need clients. Big-money clients."

His mother tilted her head. "Big money like... Posy Edwins?"

"In a manner of speaking," Lucas replied, wondering how best to explain their plan. But Annie's face twisted in revulsion.

"Are you saying you're marrying her for her money?" Annie's face creased with revulsion.

Lucas could see the conclusions she'd leapt to and rushed to placate her. "No, it's not like that."

"Ah, Jesus!" Annie said. "When you said you were marrying Posy Edwins, I thought Lord help me, he's depressed or something, a psychotic break perhaps, that's what has caused him to do this. But marrying your childhood nemesis for money? That's way worse!"

"Ma, that's—" Lucas frowned as her words sank in. "Wait, really? Being a kept man would be worse to you than having a mental breakdown?"

"From where I'm standing," Annie snapped. "Lucas, you are to call this off. I mean it!"

"Ma!" Lucas yelled, making her jump.

"Lucas." Annie pressed her lips together. "Do you love the girl or not?"

"Just... listen." Lucas had forgotten how tenacious his Ma could be. "Arundel have an old bylaw dating back from the early years of the school's inception. If ever a head boy and girl marry, at any time of their life post-graduation, Arundel pledges to pay for the whole wedding and honeymoon. It's all in the T&Cs when you sign the contract to attend."

"The Prefect Marriage Rule?" Annie sank back onto the bed with a gasp.

"That's the one." Lucas nodded. "It's never been removed from the bylaws. Now Posy has been cut off from her father's money; she's broke. But she needs to get to Hawaii for a job opportunity – a photography thing."

"And let me guess, the honeymoon will be in Hawaii?" Annie folded her arms and leaned back.

"That's it." Lucas thought he saw a smidge of understanding in his mother's expression so he carried on. "In return, she introduces me to her social circle. *Clients*, Ma. She'll vouch for me, big me up... She knows anyone and everyone. People that can save Align."

"Why didn't she just ask you to pay for her flights?" Annie said. "If her cashflow is that bad?"

Lucas hung his head. "Plane tickets are several grand a pop," he said. "Every spare penny I have is tied up in Align. My savings are keeping the lights on, quite literally." But then it occurred to him Posy hadn't even asked him for the money. She'd gone straight for the madcap scheme, headfirst. "But it's a fair question."

"I don't like this," Annie said sadly.

"I know." Lucas hung his head. "But please remember, it's not a real marriage. Legal or otherwise. It's business, pure and simple. Ma, you have to understand, her idea seemed the quickest and surest way to meet the right sort of clients."

"Oh, I understand that." Annie's eyes went distant as she smoothed an errant strand of his hair back. "Funnily enough, those things don't worry me so much as the other thing."

Lucas frowned. "What thing?"

"I have this awful feeling you're going to get hurt."

"Hurt?" he scoffed. "How? It's a business deal, plain and simple."

"I remember Posy Edwins," Annie said. "She's from a different world to you and me, and she's dragging you into it with this crazy idea. You're too blinded by your ambition to see the danger."

"Danger?" Lucas echoed. "She's not going to kill me, Ma. I won't be jumping out of airplanes or deep-sea diving."

"There's no need to patronise me," Annie said. "I'm telling you I smell trouble."

"Whatever." Lucas had expected condemnation, but the vague warnings exhausted him. "Just, promise me you won't rat us out to Arundel." Annie thinned her lips, fixing him with a glare Lucas was sure he'd be able to picture for the rest of his life. "Ma, please."

"I won't tell on you. But only because your business and Fred's health depend on your plan working." His mother's eyes were hollow, and Lucas felt like the worst person in the world. "Don't ask me to lie for you like this again."

## Chapter Eighteen

It was a grey day, drizzling and cool, when Posy set out on the mission to buy a budget wedding dress. She was tired, mainly thanks to Henry waking her up with a 2am booty call from Belgium. She should be used to the late-night phone sex by now – they were the norm when Henry was away – but Belgium was only an hour ahead of England. Surely he didn't have to call quite so late? But some of her pops's ultra-strong coffee had fortified her and she was looking forward to the morning ahead. She'd briefly considered pulling one of her mother's vintage ballgowns out of their archive instead of forking out for a dress but she and Lucas had agreed that a day of 'saying yes to the dress' might help convince Hardstark of their legitimacy. So Lucas had adapted the spreadsheet to accommodate a little purchase and so here Posy was, ready for the strangest dress shop of her life. In addition to Hardstark tagging along, Posy had roped Tara in for support at the last minute, but as Tara had been in the midst of dropping off her kids with her mother-in-law, there hadn't been time to explain the matter thoroughly.

As she trundled down the main street of Coaldale town centre, she spied Tara waiting outside Symphony of Chiffon, taking what appeared to be a very fraught call.

"No, no Loretta, I don't want Angus to eat any of that," Tara declared into her phone, rolling her eyes at Posy in greeting. "Because he'll throw it all right back up again, you mark my words. Yes... Yes, I know he's asking nicely. He always does." She lowered the phone and mouthed *sorry.* Posy smiled and checked her own phone as Tara berated her former mother-in-law further. She glanced at the revised budget that Lucas had sent, hoping she'd read it wrong the first time but no, she hadn't. A measly hundred quid for a wedding dress. She shuddered. That wouldn't even cover a basic frock from the likes of – ye Gods – Coast! She gazed in the window of the high-end wedding boutique, her heart aching at the sight of Chantilly lace and pristine satin. There wasn't a chance of her tiny budget stretching to a single thing in that shop – even Posy knew that. But, thanks to the power of social media, she may have discovered a work-around to find something special.

"Argh!" Tara finished her call and threw her hands up in the air. "My fucking ex-mother-in-law, I swear to fucking God!"

"What's she done now?" Posy breezily air-kissed her friend.

"Just the usual, trying to feed my lactose-intolerant child ice-cream," Tara said. "Well, I almost hope Angus *does* have a reaction. See how she likes Cherry Madness splattered all over her bloody Le Corbusier." She closed her eyes and let out a long breath. "Anyway. Enough of Loretta. Why am I meeting you outside a bridal shop?" Her eyes widened in trepidation. "Did Henry…?"

"Ah no, I have a confession to make." Posy took a deep breath. "You remember that festival I told you about? The one Pops won't give me airfare for?"

"Yeeees." Tara drew the word out slowly. "I am still unsure what that has to do with—"

"I don't have much time, Tar," Posy interrupted. "I have a plan to get me there which is either totally ingenious or certifiably mad." She quickly rolled out the details, leaving out the disastrous trip to Sumpter Hall.

"Crikey," Tara said, moments later. "How does Henry feel about this?"

Posy bared her teeth in a wordless show of embarrassment. She had hoped Tara would somehow make her feel magically less guilty about how she was handling things with Henry.

"Oh my God." Tara clapped a hand over her mouth. "He doesn't know? Henry doesn't *know*!"

"I'll tell him at some point!" Posy squealed. "It's all happened so fast is all and he's in Belgium, working. He'll be away for days. So it's fine, right?"

"Huh. Right," Tara harrumphed. "Funny how he shoots off overseas when his girl needs funds for a business venture."

"Not like that," Posy said with a squirm. "He's often away for long periods of time; his work is super busy right now." Tara remained unmoved and it bothered Posy. "Seriously. You know what our relationship is like. No pressure, just really, really chill." Posy added a carefree laugh, but it stuck in her throat.

"If you say so," Tara said primly.

"I do." Posy grabbed Tara's hand. "So don't say anything to him please. I'll tell him at some point."

"Your secret is safe with me." Tara squeezed her hand. "So, are you going to tell me why you've dragged me along on this crazy scheme?"

"Well." Posy was relieved to be off the topic of Henry. "To confess... I'm involving you as I need you to help pad the lie to Ms Hardstark."

Tara's eyes bulged. "What? I'm a terrible liar!" she protested. "I'll give the game away!"

"No, you won't." Posy pulled on Tara's hand again. "An excitable girlfriend will really help sell the story. Feel free to bang on about how you've never seen me so happy and that you're totally supportive of this marriage, yeah? Say stuff like, 'Oh, Posy's always wanted babies, so badly' and 'It's the perfect match'. Blah blah blah."

"Sell the story, huh? Is that why you're wearing *that*?" Tara pointed at Posy's outfit. Posy was once more aiming for a 'society woman desperate to get married' image and was wearing an ankle-length skirt reminiscent of a newly engaged Diana Spencer paired with a wholesome pink cashmere sweater. "You look like you've never seen anyone naked, like you don't even look down in the shower. Who are you trying to kid?"

"Oi!" Posy giggled at Tara's mock outrage. "I have to consider every angle. Hardstark is suspicious and Lucas would flog me to pieces if I didn't cover off every eventuality to ensure success."

"Cover off...?" Tara gaped. "You don't talk like that. Are you channelling him right now? Is he actually controlling you, with his hand up your backside?" She made a big show of trying to shove her head up Posy's skirt, calling out; "Lucas, come out, all is forgiven, I know everything!"

"Get out of there, you nutter!" Posy tried to dance out of Tara's reach but her friend just laughed and dove under even more.

"Ahem!" The deep, phlegmy rumble of a throat clearing startled Tara and she jumped, her head unfortunately colliding with Posy's crotch.

"Oof!" Posy crumpled in half, only to see a bulky tweed torso hove into view. "Hi Ms Hardstark," she wheezed. "Lovely morning."

Tara awkwardly edged her way out and offered a hand as if she hadn't just been diving up Posy's skirt. "Hullo. Tara. Best friend. Maid of honour."

Posy whipped her head around to Tara. They hadn't discussed Tara having a role in the wedding but there was no going back now. And it did make things seem more legit. "Er yes, this is my maid of honour! Tara, Ms Hardstark, Ms Hardstark, my dear friend Tara."

Hardstark allowed Tara an icy smile, her gaze drilling right into Tara. "Charmed."

"Did you know Posy wants lots of babies?" Tara squeaked in panic.

Hardstark regarded Tara for a little longer, then her eyes lifted to the frontage of the shop behind them. "This is a little high-end for your budget, wouldn't you say Posy? Didn't we learn *anything* after the Sumpter Hall visit?"

"Yes, actually," Posy told her. "We may be meeting here but we're actually going down there." She pointed down a little alleyway to the left of the boutique. "Rumour has it Symphony of Chiffon gives away damaged frocks to a vintage shop in this alley, so we might snap up a bargain."

"A vintage shop? Here?" Tara pulled a face. "Who told you *that*?"

"Twitter," Posy said. She'd patted herself on the back when she'd sent an enquiring tweet out about bargain wedding dresses and a user named @Yorkshirenana had told her about a 'gem' of a thrift shop on Pipkin Alley. She shoved her phone at Tara. "Look."

"Posy, there's no vintage shop down there," Tara said. "Unless Twitter meant the animal rescue charity shop?"

"Charity shop?" Posy said faintly.

"Yes…" Hardstark drew out the word with evident pleasure. "You know, where people donate their old baby clothes and the like? To raise money for good causes?"

Posy gulped. "I've never been in a charity shop."

"Well, you're in for a treat!" Hardstark gestured down the narrow alley, then, much to Posy's horror, added, "I've picked up a few bargains at this one myself. Lead the way!"

With mounting trepidation, Posy trekked down the narrow alley, wishing the walls would spontaneously collapse in on her and end this living nightmare. The alley opened up into a dingy courtyard, where there was a pet shop, a dry-cleaner's and, as Tara had said, the animal rescue charity shop.

Posy buried her face in Tara's shoulder. "I can't do it." The village hall had been bad enough but this shop was next-level drab. The charity shop had a low window display showcasing what Posy assumed were their most attractive donations. If that was the case, then she could only imagine how bad the bridal offerings were, if indeed there were any.

"Yes, you can." Tara patted her arm. "Think of why you're doing this."

Miserably, Posy lifted her face and took a breath. "Well

yeah, if you're going to make me use logic." Clenching her fists, Posy opened the shop door, a quaint little bell tinkling as she did. Once inside she had to take a moment for her eyes to adjust to the dim light. The floor was crowded with multiple circular rails wedged tight with clothes of all colours. One wall was dedicated to shoes and handbags, lined up proudly on high shelves as if that would hide their pre-loved weariness. The air was musty and too warm, filled with chatter from Goldie FM on the radio at the till. A tired-looking woman pushed a sleeping toddler in a buggy as she mulled over a battered paperback from a rack in the corner.

"I see what happened here." Tara was looking at the tweet Posy had insisted she check. "This tweeter's bio says she's a grandma of six who loves a bargain. This is, like, her natural habitat." She squinted at the screen. "She might be a hoarder, Posy. I'm not even joking."

"It smells in here," Posy whispered. Her remark wasn't quiet enough however, as it caught the attention of the lady working the counter, who rewarded Posy with a stern pout.

"Don't be so negative," Hardstark said. "Look, here's the bridal rail." She pointed at an area to their left.

"Just one rail?" Posy's shoulders slumped as she pictured the enchanting boutique window just a few yards away from the charity shop.

"I mean, it's a whole rail," Hardstark said, as if that was reassuring. She led the way to where a mass of gowns was tightly wedged into a corner space and began to rifle through. Posy was pretty certain she saw a cloud of dust rise up from a particularly poufy number. "Now, these seem promising!" Hardstark crowed. "And the prices even more so! This one is only twenty pounds." She pulled out a 60s-style, white minidress with a high neck and crispy polyester sleeves. A yellowing floral appliqué decorated the hem.

"Looks like a bloody doily," Posy said morosely, wondering when the house that was surely destined to land on Hardstark's head would arrive.

"Oh, come on," Tara huffed. "Let's have a rummage." Elbowing Hardstark out of the way, she dove in. "Now that's not bad." She fingered ivory fabric. "Although it looks like an elephant wore it – it's huge. And— Oh, hang on!" Her face lighting up, she pulled out something grand and frothy. Reacting to Posy's devastated expression, Tara lifted a finger. "Now bear with me on this." She called over to the lady at the till. "Got a changing room?"

Moments later Posy was in a narrow cubicle, a thin curtain the only barrier between her and the rest of the shop. Resignedly, she stepped out of her clothes and pulled on the dress, the stiff material scraping her legs as she pulled it up her body. The sleeves were starched with age, clinging tight to her arms and puffing out at her shoulders. The skirt was seemingly reams and reams of net-like fabric that made her skin itch whenever she brushed against it. Posy regarded herself in the smeared full-length mirror and wanted to weep. She'd seen toilet-roll covers chicer than this.

"You know what, Tar?" she called. "I'll dig something out of my wardrobe. I don't need a new dress. Nothing is worth this."

"Show me," Tara demanded.

So, Posy stepped out onto the shop floor. Hardstark laughed, not even trying to conceal her derision.

Posy flapped her arms. "Tar, come on. I know I have no budget, but I can't stoop to this. It looks like Princess Di's offcuts threw up on me."

"No, *you* come on." Tara wagged a finger. "Open your mind a bit. It's got a lovely scooped back. And that bow on the arse is the most gorgeous chiffon."

"Bow?" Posy angled herself towards the mirror in the changing room and craned her neck. Indeed, Tara was right. The back was almost daringly low cut, with an enormous bow of diaphanous fabric positioned at the base of her spine. "That's not so bad," Posy allowed. "But this massive skirt? The gross sleeves?"

"Get your needle and thread out," Tara suggested.

"I can't sew," Posy said. "Remember? Lottie Moss and I tried to do our own knicker line, but she broke it off when I destroyed her sewing machine."

"Well, isn't Florence a dab hand at this sort of thing?" Tara said.

Posy grunted. Florence actually was a skilled needleworker, as well as a very good baker, dog-groomer, quilt-maker and cross-stitcher. "She's planning her own wedding right now. Guaranteed if I ask her to help me, she'll say no." Plus there was the awkward matter of no one in the Edwins family having any clue what Posy was up to.

"Well, then I could do it," Tara said with a deep breath.

"You?" Posy looked at her friend in surprise. "I know you used to sew but how long has it been?"

"Listen, the daughter of Gaya Sastri was trained to be a perfect wife and mother," Tara said exasperatedly. "I may not have succeeded at marriage but it wasn't because I'm not domesticated. I made all my boys' clothes at one time before I started spending my free time coming up with ways to piss off their dad."

"Oh yeah, I remember now." Posy nodded. "But you think you can handle a wedding dress?"

"I absolutely can."

"I'm not really in a position to say no, am I?" Posy looked down at the outdated monstrosity adorning her body and sighed. "I can't wait to see you work a miracle."

Once Posy had managed to extract herself from the dress, the trio headed to the till, where, much to Hardstark's consternation, there were no Amex card facilities to be had.

"I thought you were a regular here? Surprised you didn't know about this rule." Posy smirked, earning a glare from Hardstark.

The kindly shop assistant offered a sweet smile. "Corporate Amex charges just eat into our profits, I'm afraid."

"I'm not using my personal cards," Hardstark spluttered. "And who carries cash nowadays? Surely in this instance you could make an exception?"

But the shop assistant was un-moving. "Those charges take money away from proceeds that help some very vulnerable animals. Surely you can't condone that?"

Red-faced, Hardstark had to admit she did not condone such corporate greed and also humbly agreed to sign a petition to aid some awareness-raising efforts the shop was engaged in. Grumpily, she hurried out to the High Street to withdraw cash and came back flustered and muttering about withdrawal fees.

Soon enough, the three women tumbled out onto the pavement, the dress unceremoniously stuffed into a carrier bag. Posy sucked in the cool air gratefully. The shop had been so stuffy.

"Any other appointments today?" Hardstark asked, tucking her purse back into her lizard-skin bag.

"That's it," Posy said. "Thanks for the dress, Ms Hardstark."

Hardstark leaned in, her eyes narrow. "You're up to something," she said. "I can smell it."

"The only thing you should be able to smell on me is Dior," Posy sniffed. "And need I remind you that you are contractually obliged to be doing this?"

"You'll slip up," Hardstark said. "And when you do, I'll be there to save Arundel's reputation." She delivered a stern glare to Tara and then marched off down the High Street.

"Yikes." Tara watched the woman leave with trepidation. "You know, I'm not surprised you've ended up the way you have if that's the quality of teachers you had growing up."

"Shut up, Tar," Posy said good-naturedly.

Tara stuck her tongue out, her retort interrupted by the persistent irritation of her phone pinging with multiple texts. They ambled towards the High Street as Tara impatiently rifled through her overflowing handbag, emerging out of the alley to see the street was already busy with the usual parade of well-to-do mums in expensive activewear and harried nannies ferrying their charges to various activities.

"Coffee?" Posy asked.

"I wish, but I'd best get back to the kids." Tara had found her phone and was scrolling her new messages with exasperation. She flashed a texted picture of a stunning black Le Corbusier-style sofa splattered with a violently pink and creamy vomit. "My poor baby."

"Absolutely, you go." As Posy kissed her friend goodbye, she had this powerful sense of the world moving on with purpose around her and it was not a feeling she liked. Unmoored, she reached for her own phone. She'd spoken to Henry in the early hours of the morning, but suddenly needed him for more than dirty talk and whispered fantasies. She needed *him*.

Strangely enough, for someone supposed to be in Belgium, she didn't get an international ring tone. The call rang out. Posy frowned. Odd. Henry usually had his phone glued to his side in case an urgent work issue came up. She hit re-dial and once more, it went unanswered. Just as she was about to hang up, the phone was picked up.

"Hello sexy," Posy cooed. Oddly, she was met with silence. "Henry? Hellooo?"

"Who is this?" The voice was female; cultured yet icy.

"Posy." She pulled her head back to check she had indeed dialled Henry's number. Yes, she had. Which begged the terrible question: "Sorry, who is this?"

"Posy? Your name is *Posy*?" The speaker's voice curdled around her name.

"Yes." A sickness billowed in her gut. "Are you… Henry's mum?" But the lady on the other end of the phone was not a doddery old lady – far from it. Posy braced herself for the response she guessed was coming.

"I'm his wife," was the reply. "Jacinta. The mother of his children. And you are?" The woman spoke with poise but Posy could hear despair seeping through, threatening to crack her composure.

"Wife?" Posy shook her head, even though she'd suspected this the moment she'd heard Jacinta's voice. "His *wife*? Please tell me this is all a joke?" But she knew it wasn't. A wife. Kids. Posy's stomach vaulted.

"Let me guess," Jacinta said, "you're the bit of fluff he keeps up in Leeds. The one he thinks I don't know about. All that bullshit about his work being so demanding when the whole time…" The ice in her tone splintered.

"I didn't know he was married!" Posy insisted, tears springing to her eyes. "Honestly, I never knew! He doesn't even wear a ring."

"I know." From the background of the call, Posy could hear the deep rumble of Henry's voice, the volume growing as he realised who his wife was talking to. "I saw your phone ringing and thought I'd take a message for you," Jacinta yelled at Henry. "P Edwins seemed like it might have been a work call and I didn't want you to miss it but oh no, it's your fucking mistress!" There was an almighty clatter and a thud as Jacinta – presumably, as far as Posy could tell – threw the phone at Henry. "And what kind of a fucking name is POSY?" Jacinta screamed as loud footsteps – hers – receded away and for a moment all Posy could hear was Henry's ragged breathing as he picked up the phone.

"Posy?" he croaked. "What on earth—? Why did you—? We normally speak at night…" His voice trailed off, panicked.

"Are you married?" Posy demanded. "Is it true?"

"I'm sorry," he moaned. "I didn't intend for this to happen. Why did you call at this time?"

"Hang on," Posy said. "You don't get to be the annoyed one here!"

"I had things under control!" Henry snapped. "If you'd just given me time, done things the way I asked…" He sighed heavily. "We could have made this work."

"Made *this* work?" Posy remembered his protestations about his elderly parents. "It's not your parents' house you're staying at, is it? It's your family home. *That's* why you didn't want me to come to Norfolk with you. That's why you never talk to me until late at night. You're waiting"—she thought she might throw up—"you're waiting for your family to go to sleep!"

"I'm sorry," Henry said. "I'll call you later. We can talk about this."

"No," Posy said desperately. "We really can't."

"Posy, please don't do this," Henry begged. "Give me a—"

But Posy didn't hear what he wanted her to give him because she'd hung up. Henry was married. Her sexy, funny, generous boyfriend had a wife and children and Posy had stomped all over that. She stood on the pavement, tears flowing as shoppers streamed around her. She didn't care about the curious looks, the concerned whispers. All Posy knew was that she had destroyed a family.

## Chapter Nineteen

For possibly the hundredth time in recent days, Lucas wondered what on earth was going on with Posy. True, they were standing in a shop far from her natural habitat — a pound-shop — but it was the party decorations section at least. The wide, brightly lit aisle was gaudy with tinsel banners, lurid balloons and a wall of fake flowers in hues not often found in nature. One would have thought the inflatable champagne bottles might have raised a smile at least, but Posy had just stared gloomily through them. After Posy's dispirited reaction to the hall, Lucas saw the wisdom of disguising the tatty walls and neon lighting with some colour of sorts, if only to suggest to Arundel their union was a joyous one at least. But their budget didn't extend to the sort of extravagant displays Posy longed for, hence the pair of them finding themselves in Coaldale's only pound shop.

"We could string up a load of these rainbow balloons over the door," Lucas suggested, after a protracted silence. She didn't reply, her phone chirruping for the fifth time since entering the shop. She silenced it with a huff. Despite the thunderous expression on her face, Lucas tried again.

"So, what do you think?" He held two balloon packets aloft. "Rainbow party selection? Or rose-gold hearts?"

"Whatever." She idly fingered a garish plume of feathers that Lucas hoped was a duster and not a serious décor idea.

"Posy." Lucas slung a couple of packets of heart balloons in his basket. "We're only here because you threw such a tantrum about the state of the hall. I'd happily do the ceremony without contributing to the climate crisis if you'd rather be elsewhere right now."

"Crisis is about the right word." A turquoise feather detached from the thing Posy was fiddling with and she grimaced. "Jesus Christ, an animal was plucked for this. The indignity of it."

Lucas waited for her to elaborate on what was upsetting her, but she remained mute. He tutted. "Fine, don't tell me, but you could be less of a brat. This isn't exactly my ideal day out either."

Her eyes flashed. "I don't want to talk about it."

"Fine." Lucas stuffed a few bunches of fake daisies into his basket and made to stalk away, before stopping. It really wasn't fine. In the few days since their appointment at the Little Thicket Village Hall, he'd been consumed with work, trying to keep his and Fred's remaining clients happy as well as remotely managing his team. Today, he was meant to be carrying out employee performance reviews – which were already overdue – but instead, he was here in this unpleasant shop with an overgrown toddler. His life and his career were in huge upheaval and all Posy could do was sulk. "You know, we don't have to do this."

Posy looked up, dazed. "What?"

"Any of it." Lucas tried to keep his voice level, but it was a feat nigh on impossible in the face of such disinterest. "Look at me, buying plastic tat in an effort to make this ridiculous plan of ours more palatable but you couldn't give a toss, could you?"

Posy wrapped her arms around herself. "That's not fair."

"The least you can do is meet me halfway!" The basket clattered at Lucas's feet. "I'm putting my reputation, my *everything*, on the line and all you can do is mope whilst I try to make a go of this. I've had it!" Posy said nothing, her hazel eyes widening. "So if you want out just say now and put me out of—"

"Henry and I split up," she blurted, eyes filling with tears.

"Oh."

"Yeah."

Sympathy began to temper Lucas's anger. "I'm sorry."

"I'm not." She sniffed then bobbed her head. "Well, I am. He was… he was married." Her voice gave out on the last word.

"Right." Lucas hadn't expected that. "I take it you didn't know?"

Posy turned agonised eyes on him. "Of course not!"

"Okay, okay. Sorry. How did you find out?"

Posy fiddled with a silver and green 'Congratulations' banner. "I decided to spontaneously call him outside of our pre-determined call times. I thought he was in Belgium and I just really missed him. His wife answered."

Lucas grimaced as he picked up his basket. He could only imagine the horror both women had felt at hearing the other's voice. "That must have been really hard."

"Not as hard as finding out he has kids," Posy intoned.

She shoved her hands in the pockets of her decidedly un-Posy-like hoodie and scuffed her feet. "His wife sounded so broken. And *I* did that."

"Wow." Lucas blindly shoved a few more flowers in the basket and together they ambled to the till. "What a shit."

"Yeah." Posy managed a weak laugh. "And I swear, the moment I found out I ditched him."

"I'm sure." Lucas dumped the basket in front of an obviously bored teenager whose yellow shirt clashed rather unflatteringly with his red hair. "Just these please."

"And now he won't stop phoning me." Posy lifted her phone to show Lucas that, indeed, Henry was calling yet again. "I don't know what he wants me to say."

"I'd have thought 'fuck right off' would have sufficed?" Lucas said.

"Bag for 10p?" the shop assistant droned through a golf-ball-sized wad of chewing gum. Lucas nodded.

"I told him where to go," Posy assured Lucas. "Like, I know you think I'm some vapid party girl but I'd never knowingly break up a family."

Lucas stared at her. "I never thought you would."

Posy arched an eyebrow. "Your low opinion of me radiates from you like the sun, you know that?"

"Hey." Lucas winced under her painful glare. "We've never been friends, Posy. And you were a total cow to me at Arundel, but seriously, I've never taken you for a home-wrecker. I don't think that now either." A flicker of guilt registered. "You're not a monster, for God's sake."

The shop assistant lifted a bunch of luminous flowers, not bothering to hide his fascination at their conversation. "Two for one on these?"

"Nah, you're all right." Lucas waved him off and turned back to Posy. "This isn't your fault. You didn't know."

Posy helped scoop their pitiful decorations into the plastic bag. "I know that. Like, intellectually, I know that. But I just keep hearing his wife's voice over and over in my head. Then I go back to feeling like total shit and there's no rationale that can make that go away."

Lucas paid the agog shop assistant the exact change required for their purchase. "It might take some time. My fiancée dumped me just a few weeks ago, so trust me, I know."

Posy bit her lip, the neat incisor stark white against her full mouth. "It's just so much guilt. And I— Oh you have to be kidding!" Henry was calling for the seventh time.

"Give it." Lucas held his hand out. An idea was taking shape – one that might lift Posy out of her funk and alleviate the shame he felt at having added to her pain.

A hint of a smile played across Posy's face. "What are you going to do?"

"I'm your fiancé, aren't I?" Lucas took the phone and hit the green button, clearing his throat and putting the call on loud-speaker. "Who the fuck is this?" he growled in his best hardman imitation. Judging by Posy's resulting stifled giggles his imper-sonation hadn't quite hit the masculine mark he'd intended.

"Henry Allar— Who on earth is this?" Henry sounded exactly as Lucas had imagined: haughty, cultured and extremely entitled.

"Posy's boyfriend, innit." Lucas had become an East-End hardman in the few seconds since he'd picked up the phone.

"That's impossible," Henry sneered. "Posy couldn't

possibly have moved on so quickly. It's not even been a week."

"She's my bird now." Lucas had to look away from Posy who was dissolving with silent laughter against the counter. "And she told me what you done to 'er."

The shop assistant piped up. "Er, there are other customers waiting?"

Lucas glanced back to where a small queue was forming. "Listen 'Arry—"

"Actually, it's Henry," the man snarled. "And I demand to speak to Posy. This isn't finished."

"'Arry, 'Enry, whatever. I suggest you toddle off back to that poor wife o' yours and hope she takes you back." Lucas didn't find it hard to inject menace into his tone as he spoke those words. The man was despicable. "And leave my girl alone. She deserves better."

"Listen, you reprehensible—"

Posy snatched the phone back, her face suddenly resolute. "You heard him, Henry. I never want to hear from you again." And she shut the phone off, to be met with a round of applause from the now five-deep queue snaking through the shop behind them. Posy's reddened eyes widened in delight, and she took a bow.

"Good for you, love!" A little old lady cheered, clutching a novelty teapot that looked like a fat hen. A few other customers cheered along with her.

As they hurried out of the shop, Lucas could barely believe what he'd done. But in that moment, the arrogance of Henry and his oblivious bulldozering of Posy's emotional wellbeing had bothered him greatly. Posy was clearly hurting, drowning in her guilt over being party to breaking up a marriage, but her twat of an ex couldn't care less about her pain.

Posy and Lucas walked down the street in silence. It was just past midday, and the lunchtime crowd was emerging to patronise the many delightful bistros and cafes that Coaldale excelled at. The sun shone down on the cobbled streets and glistening windows of the picturesque market town and Lucas was suddenly infused with a glorious sense of wellbeing. Posy was smiling; he'd done a good thing.

"Thanks for that," she said suddenly. "With Henry, I mean."

"You're welcome," he said. "I hope he leaves you alone now."

"Oh, I have no doubt he won't," Posy replied. "But you gave me a solid laugh. I needed that, thank you."

"I'm glad," he said. They arrived at a bus stop and Posy began to rifle through her pockets.

"I can get the next bus," she said. Then she glared at Lucas. "Don't be so shocked that I deign to use public transport every now and again to save cash."

Lucas raised his hands. "Wasn't going to say anything." Although he vowed to watch her board the bus just so he could say he'd witnessed her do such a previously unthinkable thing.

"If you say so." She fished out a crumpled ticket and sighed despondently at the sight of it. "Oh, the joys of public transport."

"I meant what I said, by the way," Lucas told her. "You do deserve better." When Posy regarded him strangely, he hastened to qualify. "I mean, Henry is obviously an awful person who only cares about himself, least of all you or his wife and kids. You should be with someone who cares and listens." His voice petered out under the intensity of her stare. "Look at it this way, you can focus on Hawaii now. No looking back."

Posy seemed to shake herself and she nodded. "Right. No looking back," she agreed. The bus rumbled towards them, and she stuck her arm out. Lucas chuckled. "What?" She flushed.

"The one and only Posy Edwins hailing a bus," he said. "Now that's something I'd love to read about in the Arundel newsletter."

Rolling her eyes, Posy boarded the bus, pausing in the doorway. "Well, I guess I'll see you soon for the next instalment of the nightmare wedding. The decorations were a really good idea, by the way. Garish, but good."

"Not bad for a scholarship kid, eh?" Lucas said with a dry chuckle. He thought it was quite a funny remark, but she didn't laugh.

Instead, Posy remained in the doorway, much to the annoyance of the bus driver and fixed him with intense eyes. "Lucas. Just so you know, I never disliked you at school because your parents worked there. Plenty did, but not me."

Lucas was taken aback. "Right," he said curiously. Her smile was soft and new. His heart thudded in anticipation.

"My problem with you was that you were a colossally boring pain in the arse."

"Oh," he said. "I see." He wasn't sure what he'd expected her to say, but it wasn't that. He exhaled and looked away. "Thanks for that."

"Look at me Lucas." They locked gazes. "I said *were*. You *were* a colossally boring pain in the arse."

"But not anymore?" He asked.

"Not anymore." Her gentle smile broke so wide and bright it almost hurt to look at it.

"Excuse me, but do you actually intend on traveling with us today, love?" The bus driver bellowed from behind her.

Posy giggled and waved to the man apologetically. "Sorry." She turned back to Lucas. "That's my cue."

"I'll be in touch," Lucas promised.

"Thanks again," she said softly. As the doors hissed shut, Lucas waved, watching the bus disappear down the winding road. He had the vague sense that things had shifted between them. He just didn't know what that meant.

## Chapter Twenty

"**A**re you JOKING?" Tara had never looked so thunderous, standing there with pins in her sleeve and a tape measure looped over her shoulder. Posy and Tara were in Tara's cramped office space in the two-bed flat she'd moved into after her split. Despite it being a lot smaller than her marital home, Posy much preferred it. The house Tara had shared with Ben had been an ode to beige luxury, all rounded edges and muted colour schemes. But Tara's home as a single mother burst with colour, Tara's vibrant personality stamped on every room.

Posy, currently standing in her underwear, felt exposed, like an admonished child under the blaze of Tara's outrage. Telling her about Henry's infidelity had landed exactly the way she'd thought it would. "Nah. Won't leave me alone."

"The audacity." Tara checked Posy's waist measurement again. "Has he even apologised for being a cheating bastard?"

Posy's sadness hollowed out her stomach. "No. Well, I've

only allowed him to say a few words at a time and none of those have been *sorry*."

"His poor wife." Tara wound the tape around Posy's hips.

"I'm so sorry, Tar," Posy blurted. Tara looked at her in surprise. "I promise I didn't know he was married."

"I believe you," Tara said gently. She offered Posy a small smile and carried on with her work. But Posy still felt rotten. Although the cracks in Tara's marriage had been long-forming, Ben's affair with a much younger colleague had still been a nasty shock that had devastated Tara. The very idea Posy could have caused a similar kind of pain to a woman she didn't even know was eating away at her and Posy desperately needed her best friend to understand how terrible that made her feel. Tara made some notes then turned back to Posy. "Has Henry offered any explanation as to why?"

"Just that he saw me that night and couldn't resist. That he had no choice but to be with me." Posy mimicked being sick. "As if flattery would get him out of it."

"Pretty sure there's no clause in the wedding vows that makes allowances for meeting irresistible hotties in bars," Tara snarled.

"And it seems to me that the thing that really bothers Henry is not the fact I caught him in his lie, rather that I walked away from him, you know? Like, his pride is more important than the people he's hurt." Posy watched as Tara ran the tape down her legs.

"Oh, I get that," Tara replied with a bitter laugh. "Ben was so shocked that *I* filed for divorce first and not him. I think he expected me to cling on until the bitter end, until he got the chance to bring the axe down. As if I was going to let him have that ego boost."

"What a prick," Posy said vehemently.

"Which one?" Tara quipped. "Seriously, if Henry were here now, God, I'd give him a piece of my mind. I've half a mind to call him and let rip."

"Oh, Lucas has already done that," Posy said with a chuckle.

"You can get dressed now," Tara said. Then she started. "Wait, *Lucas* spoke to him? As in, the fake fiancé who bores you to tears?"

"Yes." Posy pulled on her jeans. "It was really funny actually. He took my phone and pretended to be my new boyfriend, only, like a real tough guy. Told Henry I deserved better and to leave me alone." Something softened within Posy as she recalled the way Lucas had thrown himself into the ruse, screwing up his face and swaggering like an actual hardman. It had been a true act of kindness on his part.

"Hmm." Tara walked over to the mannequin where Posy's charity shop dress was displayed and began pinning the hem. "Lucas intrigues me more and more."

"Why do you say that?" Posy asked.

"Well, you claim to loathe the man and, believe me, I remember how you used to talk about him when you were head girl," Tara said. "But since this marriage thing, I don't know, you seem to be going a bit easier on him."

"Easier?" Posy fiddled with the buttons on her silk blouse. "I mean, sure he's grown up a bit since school. But he's still an absolute square. So boring his fiancée left him."

"I don't know, pretending to be your new boyfriend to chase off Henry doesn't sound boring to me," Tara remarked. "Seems like Lucas maybe has a fun streak in him that you bring out."

"Lucas? A fun streak?" Posy waved the suggestion off. "As if."

"All I'm saying is, that was a nice thing for Lucas to do." Tara finished pinning the dress and stood up straight. "For someone who's supposed to be your mortal enemy, he showed himself to be a true friend. Is it possible you got him all wrong?"

## Chapter Twenty-One

The roses really were struggling, Ms Hardstark fretted. She was in the top meadow of Arundel College's acreage, the rolling hills of the Peaks surrounding her. A hundred yards away, the Year Ten group were engaged in a lively match of lacrosse, their shrieking voices filling the air and startling a meandering group of starlings that had chosen that moment to drift across the sky. As much as the display of teenage exuberance lifted Ms Hardstark's heart, she was weighed down somewhat by the obvious signs of decay in front of her. Increasingly, the stems were darkening, the normally velvety petals struggling to retain their usual glory. Her mind flashed to that charming gentleman she'd met at Sumpter Hall. He'd know what steps to take here; there was no doubt the fellow was an expert. And, if she wasn't mistaken, he'd welcome another rousing conversation with her about rose maintenance. Indeed, she couldn't deny the thrill she got from the thought of engaging in such repartee again.

As her mind raced with ways she could get back in contact with Miles Purslow, Mrs Paddington appeared at her side.

"Morning," the headmistress greeted her. "Glorious day, isn't it?"

"Truly," Ms Hardstark agreed. It was a quintessentially delightful English spring day.

The headmistress's eyes narrowed. "These roses are a state; you should get the gardeners on this."

Ms Hardstark gritted her teeth. "Believe me, I'm on the case."

"And how are our lovebirds?" Mrs Paddington went on.

Ms Hardstark blinked. For some reason, Miles Purslow's face drifted into her mind again. Then she realised Mrs Paddington was referring to Posy and Lucas and she batted the image of Miles away. "Apparently they have to go back to the venue tomorrow," she said. "The proprietor wants to review decorations or something. I don't even understand the point of it, to be honest. I think that Patricia woman just wants attention."

Mrs Paddington sighed. "I had hoped the newsletter announcement would have stirred up some reaction amongst the Arundel community, that someone might have come forward with… oh, I don't know, some little clue that could tell us what the hell is going on."

"Give it time," Ms Hardstark advised gently. "It's not been long since we had this dropped on us."

"Actually, it's been two weeks," Mrs Paddington barked, tapping her Prada boot against the ground. Ms Hardstark noted with irritation that the motion was disturbing the nearby rose bush, sending delicate petals to the soil. "I don't care how irrelevant tomorrow's appointment may be," Mrs Paddington said. "Watch them like a hawk. I want to hear everything."

## Chapter Twenty-Two

Lucas pulled up to the Little Thicket Village Hall in the stinky Nissan. Nothing much had changed in the week since they'd visited. The village green was as tranquil as ever, a light breeze stirring the venerable willow trees that lined the edge. When Patricia had asked him and Posy to stop by for a quick meeting regarding details for the big day, Lucas had figured it wouldn't hurt to put in a bit of effort to make sure things seemed legit. However, Hardstark had caught wind of the meeting and, naturally, she'd insisted upon attending. If he was honest, Lucas was glad of the distraction. Overnight, Lim Management had made a formal offer to buy up Align Management. The money being offered was substantial and if Lucas wished, he could also take a position as a very well-salaried employee at his pick of any of Lim's international outposts. Singapore was being touted as a regional hub that could really benefit from his expertise. Lucas had to admit it was attractive. Fred was definitely tempted to take the money and run; after all, what was being offered would give him the ability to recuperate with no financial pressure. But at what cost? The loss of their vision, the ability to be their own boss, which had been the dream all along. The team at Lim was gracious enough to recognise the significance of the decision and had given them some time to consider, but not long. In fact, Lucas and Fred needed to submit their final response by the end of June – the day of the wedding. Lucas didn't know which way to turn, but his mother felt very sure he should take the deal. All Lucas knew at this point was that he'd kill for a cold beer and the chance to forget the pressures of life for a few hours. But there was much to be done, so here he was.

As he got out of the car, he immediately recognised Hardstark's Porsche and a shiny cherry-red Mini that had to be Posy's. He wondered if he should run the Lim deal by her, see what she thought about it. He suspected she'd tell him go for it; after all, it involved travel and adventure as well as a great deal of money – things Posy was very familiar with.

With one last admiring glance at the Porsche, he headed into the hall. There in the hallway he saw Hardstark cornered by a talkative Patricia, who was bemoaning a cancellation of some event the day before or something. Hardstark looked at him hopefully, clearly anticipating he would save her from the onslaught of small talk, but Lucas merely gave her a cheerful wave and walked on to find Posy. She was in the hall, standing by the large windows and gazing out to the green. For a moment, he observed her. She was dressed in yet another Arundel-wife-approved ensemble: loose linen trousers and a neat twinset. That golden hair was piled in a chic knot, which expertly highlighted her sharp cheekbones and jaw. He thought back to their encounter at the pound shop and how it had felt to make her laugh in the depths of her sadness. It wasn't the first time since that moment the memory had crossed his mind and he wasn't sure why he kept dwelling on it.

"Hi," he called.

"There you are." Posy smiled.

Lucas walked over. "How are you feeling?"

"Better," she said. "Just the two calls today."

"Glad to see he's showing some restraint." Lucas nodded his head towards the outside. "Saw your car. No bus today?"

"Ha!" Posy shuddered theatrically. "Flo used my car yesterday and kindly topped the tank up. Besides, no buses come out to the arse end of nowhere and let's just say I wanted to make sure I could make a speedy exit if need be."

"But what an arse end." Lucas gestured to the view. "As arses go, it's got some appeal."

"You might say it's growing on me," Posy murmured, and her eyes met his as if challenging him to acknowledge her words.

"Excuse me?" Patricia interrupted them. "Sorry to intrude but I have an appointment in an hour, so I'd like to get started."

"Sorry, of course." Lucas greeted the woman. "Hi, Ms Hardstark."

The teacher merely greeted him with a glare.

If Patricia noticed Hardstark's animosity she didn't show it. "Ms Hardstark here was just telling me about your minimal budget for decorations."

"That's right," Lucas said. "We picked up some budget décor yesterday actually. Are there any restrictions on what we can use?" He hadn't thought to ask, so busy was he revelling in his genius idea of how to decorate the place cheaply.

"Well, we can't have anything nailed to the walls,"

Patricia said. "No Blu Tack or Sellotape. No animals, live or otherwise." Posy and Lucas exchanged a glance. "I must insist on no loud music after 10pm, should you be partying into the night."

Lucas held up a hand, still reeling from the suggestion they'd bring live animals to their wedding. And who knew what the woman meant by *otherwise*? "Please don't worry – we're keeping it simple. We'll have the ceremony, then we thought we'd order pizzas, have some beers and dancing. Make it a party."

"Beers and…" Patricia's eyes flickered. "Pizza?"

"I know it sounds super basic"—Posy was clearly unable to resist poking fun—"but this is Lucas's vision. It's what he wants."

Lucas fixed her with a stare. "That and lots of babies, darling." Then he turned back to Patricia. "And in terms of décor, it'll be just as simple."

"No chair covers?" Patricia said curiously.

"None," Lucas said.

"What about a floor runner for the aisle?"

"Nope."

"Not even… flowers?" Patricia visibly reeled when Lucas replied in the negative.

"What's a wedding without flowers?" Hardstark demanded, and Lucas looked at the woman with surprise.

"I know," Posy agreed, much to Lucas's shock. "My mother loved flowers. Especially roses. You think that Mr Purslow up at Sumpter Hall is potty about roses? Mum would have given him a run for his money. She was obsessed! When I was born, she planted Golden Celebration along the wall of the house."

"Your mother clearly had considerable skill." An uncharacteristically soft smile transformed Hardstark's face. "As well as taste."

"Thanks," Posy said uneasily. Lucas couldn't blame her. Witnessing Hardstark talk with such compassion was unsettling – like watching someone sleeping with their eyes open or a dog walking backwards.

"The Golden Celebration is one of the most fragrant and beautiful roses you'll ever see," Hardstark went on, lacing her fingers across her middle. "But it needs a lot of space to grow and find its strength."

Posy gulped. "My mother didn't mind that," she said in barely a whisper.

"Be that as it may"—Lucas wondered when hell had frozen over to permit Posy and Hardstark to bond over flowers—"we can't fill the hall with roses. We have to keep it simple."

"But you'll at least have music?" Patricia said, looking like she might burst into tears if they didn't.

"Oh yes. I'm building a cracking playlist." Lucas lifted his phone.

Patricia regarded it as if it were a bomb about to go off. "No band?" she asked coolly.

"Nope, just good old Spotify," Lucas said.

"Right." Patricia nodded. "Fine. Okay. Well, you'd best check the sound system then. Come here." She led them over to a corner where there was a rudimentary PA system with a few jacks. After faffing around with the cables, she found one compatible with Lucas's phone and plugged it in. "My daughter's really good with this," she went on. "You can get her to coordinate the songs and press play when you need to. Simple, see?" She tapped at Lucas's phone.

"Good to know," Lucas said just as Bob Dylan's lamentations on the loneliness of being a rolling stone blared out. "We just need to choose the song for Posy to walk down the aisle to and job done."

"Nothing by Dylan, please," Posy said.

"You aren't a fan?" Lucas asked.

"Nah." Posy grabbed the phone to scroll through his music. "I mean, he's okay."

"Bob Dylan is… okay?" Lucas could barely get the words out. "He's the voice—"

"Of a generation, yeah." Posy tutted. "Don't get me started. But, oh—" She tapped at the screen. 'Like a Rolling Stone' ended abruptly and 'Honey' by The Jesus and Mary Chain started. "Now this, *this* is awesome." She handed the phone back then reeled away, hands in the air as she swayed to the music. "How about this for the wedding?"

"A little… inappropriate, isn't it?" Patricia was scandalised.

"It's a classic!" Lucas and Posy chorused back at her, then looked at each other.

"Didn't know you were into alt-rock," Lucas said. For some reason he'd had visions of Posy enjoying trippy dance or pop.

"What, did you think I was about to break out a Britney Spears routine?" She giggled. "Do yourself a favour and get some Smashing Pumpkins or Pixies, then we can talk. But this?" She pointed to the speakers. "Total bop."

Lucas watched Posy dreamily sway about to the kick-snare beat of the classic track. She closed her eyes, the troubles of the idiot ex seemingly far behind her. For a second it was as if all his cares fell away; there was only the music and Posy. Lucas envied her ability to throw herself into the moment, the ability to behave however she wanted as the

227

mood struck. What would Lucas do, should he have such freedom?

"She moves beautifully," Patricia remarked. "Is she a dancer?"

"I don't think so," Lucas said absently, lost in his observation. But then he became aware of a heavy presence at his elbow. It was Hardstark, her face ominous.

"Tell me," she breathed. "How can a man not know his fiancée's music taste? Or, if she's ever been a dancer?"

"Um." Lucas thought quickly. "It's all kind of a whirlwind when you're this in love."

"Is that what you are?" Hardstark immediately asked. "Because I think you're up to something with Arundel's money."

Lucas tried not to let his panic show. "Oh, yes, that massive sum of seven grand, watch how it changes our lives." He affected an unconcerned eyeroll. "Now, if you'll excuse me." He walked over to Posy. "Shall we practise our first dance?" he asked loudly, so that Hardstark could hear. Posy took his hand with more than a little bewilderment.

"What are you doing?" she whispered.

"Dancing with my wife-to-be," he said, very aware that Hardstark was watching their every move. He led her several more feet away then put a hand around her waist, drawing her close. "Ready?" Beyond the open windows, the greenery of Yorkshire's countryside billowed, the sweet scent of mown grass filling the air.

With a swallow, Posy nodded. Cymbals crashed, the Reid brothers' husky voices chorused and Lucas began to move. His steps were tentative at first, the muscle memory rusty to say the least. To the side, to the right then a twirl.

"Since when did you learn to dance like this?" Posy was clearly impressed.

Lucas grimaced. "Sally made me take lessons for our wedding. It was about the only thing we managed to get done before... well, before it ended."

"Sorry," Posy cringed. "Didn't want to stir up old memories."

"It's fine," he said. "If I hadn't taken them, I wouldn't be able to do... *this!*" And without missing a beat, he dipped her into a low lean, and her hair toppled back to brush the floor. "Whoa." Suddenly her face was inches from his, her vanilla perfume filling his head. Uncertain as to what he should do next, the mellow drumbeat of The Jesus and Mary Chain petered out and Chris Isaak's plaintive guitar began.

"This is some dad vibes now," Posy said, seemingly unaffected by their proximity. "Are you sure you made this playlist and not my pops?"

"What? This is a tune! *World was on fire...*" Grateful for her aloofness, Lucas righted her and sang along tunelessly.

"This is going to be a car crash of a first dance." Posy winced. "Thank fuck it's not the first *song*."

"I have the voice of an angel, I'll have you know," Lucas said with a grin. He took her through a few more steps and Posy's natural rhythm seemed to kick in. Their dance became fluid, relaxed. But Lucas couldn't enjoy it. Hardstark's expression of victory hadn't diminished, despite his and Posy's display. "Can't believe we almost gave the game away over music, of all things."

"Oh, we were having a laugh," Posy said. "Don't be too harsh on yourself."

"What if it's the giveaway?" Lucas said. "What if, after

all this planning and pretending, having a laugh is what shows us up? We can't relax; we can't let anything slip whilst she's around." He shot a glower towards Hardstark who was now examining something on her phone.

"Hey." Posy placed a hand over his heart. "Calm down. You could make yourself ill worrying like this."

"Now you sound like my ma when I was at uni," Lucas groaned.

"If you worked yourself up like this at university, I'm surprised you didn't drop from a heart attack before you had a chance to graduate," Posy said.

"Yeah well, one slip-up, one mistake, is all it takes," Lucas said. "You know, Benjamin Franklin said 'By failing to prepare, you are preparing to fail' and…" He trailed off, noting her eyes had gone somewhat glassy. "How much of that did you understand before you stopped listening?"

Posy jolted. "I didn't know it was possible to doze off with boredom whilst dancing."

"Not everything can be non-stop fun," Lucas growled. "Sometimes it's about guaranteeing success."

"I didn't know success *could* be guaranteed," Posy said. "Even when it comes to fake weddings."

"You know what I mean. Safety nets," Lucas said. "Maximising your chances. Leaving nothing to chance so that when it comes to your life choices, the odds are statistically—"

"Statistics?" Posy interrupted with a quirk of her lips. "Stats don't mean anything when it comes to *life*. You know, around ten thousand women die from breast cancer in a year, on average. Five per cent of that figure are younger than forty-four. Those are tiny odds, when you think about it. When my mum found a lump, she and Pops did all the right things, with all the right doctors, and they all told her she'd be fine. She *should* have been fine." Posy's moves stilted. "But she wasn't. She was thirty-nine years old, and she was not fine."

"I'm so sorry," Lucas murmured.

"So, you see," Posy said, her voice airy, "sometimes all the planning and prep in the world can't stop what's going to happen. The worst – and best – things in life can come along when you don't plan for them. You know?" Her tone was light, but her eyes were furious and he could feel her retract within the circle of his arms. It troubled Lucas to see her fold.

"I know." Posy Edwins suddenly made a lot of sense to Lucas.

"Have you quite finished?" Hardstark barked from across the room. "Only, I do have a day job, you know."

Somewhat reluctantly, Lucas stepped back from Posy. "Sorry, yes."

"Now, you're all clear on decorations and music," Patricia checked.

"All sorted," said Lucas. "And don't worry, Ms Hardstark, I was able to stretch to a pack of balloons."

"Be still my heart," Posy muttered.

"Then why am I even here?" Hardstark thundered. "Call me when you actually have a meaningful appointment." And with a grim nod at Patricia, Hardstark marched out.

"A forceful woman, your mother," Patricia murmured.

"She's not— You know what? Never mind." Lucas unplugged his phone and turned to Posy who was tutting at her phone again. A flash of inspiration struck him. "Fancy a drink?" he asked.

Posy lifted her eyes to his and let out a relieved sigh. "God, yes."

"There's a lovely pub on the green," Patricia said. "Can't miss it."

Moments later, Posy and Lucas were ensconced in The Tap on the Green, a homely establishment of old beams, warped floorboards and a roaring fire even in the midst of the delightfully warm day. There were only a few other patrons – mostly of the pensioner demographic. The bar staff seemed barely old enough to drink alcohol legally, let alone serve it, and they welcomed Posy and Lucas with almost total indifference. Without asking, Lucas treated Posy to a double measure of the pub's peatiest malt, which she received with a wry smile.

Nestled in the leather-bound booth that overlooked the green, Posy took a healthy gulp of whisky and then released an exasperated huff. "You ever have, like, multiple experiences in a short space of time that on the face of it are contriving to let you know exactly what an irrelevant piece of shit you are?" she blurted.

Lucas wasn't sure how he kept his face straight at that, but he did. "Try my whole school career," he cracked, but at the sight of her muted expression he decided to limit the sarcasm. "I mean, look, just because your boyfriend turned out to be married doesn't make you a piece of shit." He pondered for a moment. "Shit-adjacent, perhaps."

"Shit-adjacent." Posy swirled the amber liquid in her glass. "I'll take that. So far this month, my father has told me I'm a disappointment, my school reunion was merely a reminder of how little I've achieved and my boyfriend of the past few months obviously agrees because I'm only fit to be his sidepiece."

"Yikes." Lucas exhaled noisily. "I'm not surprised you feel like shit after all that."

"Thanks," Posy said. "Is this meant to be cheering me up?" She downed the rest of her whisky and signalled the nearest bartender. "Two more, please."

"You did forget to mention your upcoming sham marriage to the one person you weren't even friends with at Arundel," Lucas remarked. For one horrible moment he thought Posy was going to cry but then she caught his eye and spluttered into laughter, throwing her head back. The music of it attracted all attention their way and Lucas felt like a specimen under the microscope. The other patrons were probably wondering what on earth Lucas was doing drinking with someone like *her*.

"Your mum probably hates me too," Posy said, unable to control her mirth.

"She does now," Lucas said, without even thinking. Posy's eyes widened in alarm. "She read the newsletter," he added. "She wasn't happy."

"Oh God." Posy lowered her head to the table.

"It's fine." Lucas decided to leave out Annie's less than complimentary remarks about Posy. "She'll keep our secret."

"Great. Now we're having to make your mum lie. Maybe I should just *swim* to Hawaii," Posy said, her voice muffled by the table. "If I make it there, great; if I drown, even better."

"A little dramatic, don't you think?" Lucas quipped.

"Meh." Posy mumbled, lifting her head only when the new whiskies were plonked in front of her.

"But in all seriousness," Lucas said. "Forget Henry. He's clearly an idiot."

"He is."

"Yeah." Lucas picked up his second whisky, his head already swirling from the rapid consumption of his first. "Move on."

"Yeah." Posy swirled her drink, bottom lip jutting. "He was fit though."

"And as for the school reunion, I get it." Lucas charged his glass. "The few people I even managed to engage in conversation soon made a swift exit when they realised I was Helpboy. I bet I could become Prime Minister and I'd still not be worthy of those people."

"You sure it wasn't your riveting chat about spreadsheets that drove them away?" Posy smirked.

"I wasn't the only one hiding down by the lake," Lucas tutted.

"Ha ha. You know what, fuck 'em," Posy said. "Seriously. Fuck people's preconceptions. Here's to not being hurricanes!"

"What?" Lucas thought he'd misheard.

Posy snorted. "My family used to – well they still do – call me Hurricane Posy sometimes. If I make a mistake or have a massive blow-out, they just say, 'Oh look, it's Hurricane, making a mess again.'"

"That's not the worst nickname," Lucas said, deadpan.

"It's hardly flattering though, is it?" Posy fiddled with a lock of tawny hair. "I'm a grown-up. Being compared to a destructive storm is so not what should be happening to me right now."

Lucas swilled liquor in his mouth, enjoying the toffee sensation of it prickling his tongue. "I think I'm learning that worrying about what should be is over-rated," he told her.

"Quite right," Posy said, taking a sip. "God, this is good.

Anyway. I'm sick of talking about my issues. What's new with you?"

"There's a company interested in purchasing Align," Lucas said. "*Very* interested."

"Isn't that good?" Posy said.

Lucas shook his head. "I'm not sure about it. I don't want to be someone's employee. Align is mine. If I sell it, yeah, I'll have no financial worries and yeah, I could have a senior executive role at Lim in one of their international hubs."

"Money *and* travel?" Posy arched an eyebrow. "Not too shabby."

"No." Lucas had to agree. "And Fred, my business partner, could do with the break." The thought of handing over Align, his baby, to strangers made him feel wrong-footed and he wasn't sure how much Posy would understand.

"Sounds like an amazing opportunity," Posy said politely.

"It is." Lucas felt so uncomfortable. He knew very well that he should jump at selling Align; for a start he wouldn't have to go through with this wedding thing. He just knew in his bones that wasn't what he actually wanted. As he frantically searched for a change of topic, he became aware of someone next to him.

"Mr Purslow!" Lucas stood to greet the kindly proprietor of Sumpter Hall.

"Miles, please! I thought it was you!" The gentleman shook Lucas's hand. "I take it Patricia was able to assist you?"

"Yes," Posy replied morosely and took a deep swig of whisky.

"Splendid." If Miles noticed Posy's grumpiness, he didn't show it.

"What brings you here?" Lucas asked.

"Just a little gathering of the local Rose Growers Club." Miles pointed to a little group of men who looked virtually identical to him, huddled in the far corner all clutching pints of bitter. "We meet monthly to discuss all things roses. Sometimes an iris or an orchid gets a special mention, but roses are our passion. A few of those chaps even cater to weddings at Sumpter so we're a real team."

"I'd always imagined my wedding full of roses," Posy said dreamily. "A carpet of them as far as the eye could see. My mother loved them."

"I quite understand. Roses are – to me – the epitome of elegance," Miles said. He craned his neck around the pub. "Your... ah... is Miss Hardstark not with you today?"

"No, thank Christ!" Posy snorted into her glass.

"Ours is not a social relationship," Lucas added. He couldn't fail to be amused by the hope burning in Miles's eyes.

"A pity," Miles said bravely. "Because I'm sure she'd really get a kick out of our growers club."

"No doubt." Lucas was amused by how his concurrence stirred up some excitement in the normally mild-mannered gentleman.

"Might I... do you think I could call her?" Miles asked. "Only, she had some wonderful ideas about propagation that I was really curious to hear more about."

"Propagation." Posy was deadpan. "Is that what they call it?"

Miles's amiable face dimmed with embarrassment and Lucas grimaced at Posy. "I'm sure Ms Hardstark would love to hear from you," he said to Miles. Lucas took out his phone and found Hardstark's number, scrawling it on a cardboard coaster.

Miles accepted it with a reverent smile. "Thank you," he said. "I'll text her right away."

And with a fulsome goodbye, Miles virtually skipped off back to his friends. Lucas sank back into his seat with a chuckle.

"Just call me Cupid." Lucas raised his glass to himself.

"Eww." Posy groaned. "Did you just hook Hardstark *up*? Like, with a date?"

"Don't be miserable," Lucas said. "Old people deserve love too."

"I don't need to think about Hardstark loving anyone," Posy said.

"God." Lucas wished Posy hadn't put those images in his head. "There is not enough whisky in the world to wipe out that mental picture."

"Please tell me your love life is worse than mine," Posy said. "Because that little exchange sent me to the brink of despair."

"You know very well my love life is a farce," Lucas said. "I mean, up until recently I was engaged. For real." Sally's tear-stained face was suddenly very vivid in his memory. He ran a hand over the back of his head. One plus point about being so busy with work and a fake wedding? Less time to ruminate over his ex.

Posy managed a respectful nod. "It's okay, you don't need to tell me what happened."

"It's fine." Lucas waved a hand. "It was all me. Sally was everything a man should want: beautiful, intelligent, success- ful. You know, she was heading up her corporate litigation department before she turned thirty? She ran marathons, skied black-diamond routes and baked to a cordon-bleu level without breaking sweat." His laugh crawled from the wound he'd forgotten existed. "I let all that go."

"You list her qualities like she's a... a competition you lost or something," Posy said, cradling her drink.

Lucas started. "I don't see her that way."

"You know what I mean," Posy said. "Like you said, she was everything you should want. What is it? Ah, yeah, good on paper. Sally was good on paper – am I right?"

"I don't understand." The whisky must have been more effective than he'd expected, as Lucas's brain was already tripping over Posy's words.

"It's the same thing again – the planning and the preparation." Posy slammed her hand down on the table. "You proposed to someone who by all accounts should be what a man of your status should want. But"—Posy leaned over and poked his chest with a finger, the motion surprisingly strong—"you didn't consider who *you* are and that's why the relationship didn't work. Do you even know who you are without a life map or a spreadsheet?"

"You are so down on spreadsheets," Lucas said, his nose in his glass. "I really think you'd benefit from an Excel course. It would change your life."

"I promise you, if ever I'm struggling to fall asleep, I'll take an Excel lesson," Posy said with a tut. "Also, don't ignore the question!"

"I don't even *understand* the question," Lucas said.

"Then we need more whisky." Once more Posy signalled the bartender.

"Another?" Lucas hiccupped. "Are you sure that's sensible?"

"It's good stuff, isn't it?" she said, impishly.

"Yes."

"And you're having fun, with no other plans today?"

"Yes but…" Lucas gestured around them. "Drinking in a pub all afternoon isn't the most constructive use of time."

"You should have stopped after yes," Posy said victoriously. "Sometimes, all you need is *yes*. Listen to your gut and if it says yes, that's correct."

"You think I don't know who I am?" Lucas said defensively. "I've always known. I've built my own business. I've worked hard."

"Okay, then I'll rephrase my point," Posy said. "You don't have *faith* in who you are. That you're good enough without a roadmap. That you can find your way without a plan."

"I—" Lucas wasn't sure if it was the whisky that was stealing his words away or confusion. "I've never looked at it that way."

"I've never met Sally – probably never will," Posy went on, grinning widely as their new drinks were placed on the table. "But is it fair to say she was ready to take that leap into uncharted waters with you, and you weren't?"

"I was ready," he insisted. "I proposed, didn't I?"

"Right." Posy gestured at him. "Because proposing to Sally was good on paper. Intellectually, you knew you should. But your heart obviously wasn't in it, not really."

"I—" Lucas had to admit that Align had become the be-all and end-all, consuming the space Sally should have occupied. "I loved her. I did."

"But?"

The truth was there, staring him in the face. "I didn't

fight for our relationship." Lucas reached for his new drink, taking a grateful sip.

Posy nodded. "Lucas O'Rourke, you may be the most exasperating man I've ever met but what I do know about you is that you fight for what you want. Look at this wedding for goodness' sake! So does the fact you gave up on Sally tell you something?"

Lucas pondered his whisky, examining the lingering guilt that resided within him. "You may have a point."

"He agrees with me! I do have a point!" she cheered, causing more heads to turn. "Instincts can speak volumes but you have to listen to them. Even if it means going against everything you thought you knew."

Lucas took another gulp of whisky, gasping as its sweet heat lit something within. "Another good point."

"And what are you going to do about it?" Posy's cheeks were flushed, her eyes sparkling. Maybe it was Posy's rousing words or the sudden flow of booze, but Lucas was keen to find out where this exhilaration would take him. He leaned forward.

"I'm in your hands," he said.

## Chapter Twenty-Three

"Are you sure we should do this?" Lucas hovered at the front door of the Edwins's home, his eyes wide.

"Don't be weird." Posy grabbed his sleeve and pulled him into the house. It was late evening and they'd spent the entire afternoon in the pub on the green. When the landlady had learned of Posy and Lucas's shared interest in whisky, she'd immediately demanded they do a tasting of the new brands she'd got in. And now the pair of them were quite tipsy, having left their cars in Little Thicket and taxied home. "No one's here anyway."

"I'm in Posy Edwins's house," Lucas babbled, making his way through the hallway and into the kitchen. "Wow, Posy Edwins's kitchen is huge."

"Why are you saying my name like that?" Posy went straight for the fridge, knowing there was at least one bottle of champagne in there left over from Florence's birthday.

"Because I've drunk, like, two pints of whisky," Lucas said, carefully lowering himself onto a kitchen stool.

"Don't exaggerate," Posy said with a hiccup. "It was

barely one. Here, help me open this." She shoved the bottle of Moët under his nose.

Lucas baulked at the sight of it. "Seriously, is your liver made of Teflon?"

"All right, Grandma, I'll serve it with water." Posy left Lucas to wrestle with the bottle whilst she poured out two large glasses of water and fetched the flutes. As she watched him hold the bottle between his strong hands, she wondered for the hundredth time why she'd suggested coming back here. When Lucas had drawn the line at yet another round of whisky, she'd suggested heading back to hers to sober up with pizza and coffee, knowing Jesper and Ines were out for the night. But at some point on the taxi-ride home she'd decided she wasn't quite ready for the irresponsibility to stop. Ever since their trip to the pound shop, Posy had been wondering if she'd got Lucas all wrong. It was as if she were viewing him through a new lens; things were still coming into focus and she wasn't sure what it was she was looking at. What she was certain of, however, was that Lucas wasn't all she'd thought him to be. And she very much wanted to work out exactly what he was.

Lucas grunted. "Having some trouble here," he said.

"I knew those biceps were just for show," Posy smirked and handed him a glass of water. "Drink this. I'll sort the fizz."

Lucas accepted the glass and downed most of it in one gulp. Posy tried to focus all her might on the cork – which was well and truly stuck – instead of admiring the way Lucas's neck corded as he gulped water. She tugged and squeezed on the bottle, but it refused to pop. As she struggled with the cork, Lucas poured himself another glass of water and wandered around the kitchen, taking in the décor with appraising nods. Finally, he stopped by the large archway that led to the hallway and stopped, his jaw loosening. "Oh."

"What?" Posy left the reluctant bottle on the counter and walked over, halting when she saw what had caught his eye. It was a portrait photograph of her mother, taken weeks before her cancer diagnosis. She sat on a traditional Yorkshire dry-stone wall, one denim-clad leg bent. She wore a battered Barbour jacket, her bounteous golden hair bunched up in a sloppy knot. Sunlight kissed high cheekbones, playing across full lips curving with a sensual mischief. Celia Edwins looked off camera and her eyes – the exact same shade and shape as Posy's – were full of love. It was Posy's favourite thing. "Beautiful, wasn't she?" Posy said.

"Yeah." Lucas nodded. "I'm so sorry she's gone."

"Thanks." Posy looked reverently up at her mother. "I don't have many memories of her, but the ones I do"—she gestured at the portrait—"all look like that."

"I can't imagine what it must be like." Lucas sounded almost sober.

"Like a nightmare I wish I could wake up from," Posy said. "I see her in my dreams and she's so real. Then I open my eyes and she's not there. You can imagine how fun that was *not* as a child."

"Your father married again, didn't he?" Lucas asked, gulping back more water.

"Yes. To Ines, when I was about eight."

"Do you guys get along?"

Posy bit her lip. That was the question. "Ines tries," she replied eventually. "I know she wants a closer relationship but…"

"But what?" Lucas looked down at her, his expression soft.

"But Ines is not my mum. She does her best but…" Posy found it hard to meet Lucas's eye so feigned attention on her mother's portrait. "It'd be nice if she fought for me now and again when Pops is on a rampage. I mean, Mum would have been in my corner no matter what."

"Your dad probably thinks he's helping," Lucas said.

"It doesn't feel like that," she said. "It's been really difficult." Even as she said the words she felt like a fraud. She'd had privilege most people could only dream of. Support that could have propelled her anywhere, but she hadn't used it and she could tell from Lucas's face that he was thinking that exact thing.

"Working out a life plan is meant to be hard for most people," he said, his voice turning to steel. "I should know. I had to do it from a young age."

"And don't we all know it," Posy snapped. Her predicament wasn't all her fault, not entirely. And she was quite sick of Lucas's holier-than-thou attitude when it came to the hustle. "But do you know how it feels to have the security you've had your entire life taken from you, purely because the one person who's meant to love you the most is ashamed of you?"

"Your dad said that?" Lucas recoiled.

The sympathy Lucas showed in that instant did nothing to mollify the fire that surged inside Posy.

"Yes, the great Jesper Edwins told his youngest child her own mother would be disappointed in her." As she relived the moment of that bombshell, her father's stern face flickered across her memory, further stoking Posy's fury. "So, forgive me if I'm not in the mood for a lecture from Lucas the Great, okay?"

"Listen," Lucas rounded on her, his eyes flashing, "if I'm great then you'd better believe I worked to be so."

"And, what, I'm some lazy oaf who deserves everything she gets?" Posy snapped, stepping up to him.

"Believe me, I don't think that." Lucas's voice wobbled, rendering his denial empty. Posy nodded to herself. She would always be a disappointment to everyone around her and it was about time she accepted that.

"You've made it pretty clear what you think of me," Posy said. "Perhaps you should leave." And she spun on her heel, hoping he wouldn't see the tears that had suddenly sprung. But Lucas grabbed her arm, stopping her. Posy halted, lowering her gaze to where his fingers gripped her. She was suddenly hit with an undeniable burn of desire at the sight of him touching her. "What are you doing?" Posy barely dared breathe. When she had the nerve to meet his eyes, she saw her yearning matched his.

"I'm not sure." Lucas's gaze dropped to her mouth. "I just… I really don't want you to walk away from me."

The room was totally silent, punctuated only by their heavy breathing. His hand slowly trailed down her arm, his light touch a promise. He stopped when he reached her wrist, his thumb trailing along the back of hers, tracing a path millimetre by millimetre until his fingers were laced through hers.

The moment was broken by a thunderous bang followed by a thud. Posy jolted back to see that the champagne cork had violently burst its way out of the bottle only to slam into the ceiling above. Mounds of white foam frothed over the neck and snaked down, spilling onto the worktop.

Posy stepped towards the mess. "Perhaps I should…" As she moved, Lucas's fingers began to slip from hers and in that instant Posy knew. She whirled around, reaching for him. Lucas's hands tangled in her hair, his fingers warm on her scalp. He tilted her head upwards so he could look into her eyes and brushed his thumb gently over her parted lips.

"Are you sure about this?" Lucas murmured, his nose grazing hers.

"Shut up," Posy gasped. Then she kissed him.

Lucas's kiss was soft, but not for long, the urgency increasing with every second. He moved his hands from her face to her waist, where he wrapped them around her and pulled her tight against him. The fire inside Posy became liquid, spreading through her body, pervading every cell as she pushed herself closer until she was flush against him, yet that still wasn't close enough. She needed skin contact. Her hands moved to his shirt and tugged at the buttons but her fingers were clumsy in their haste.

"Please," she panted against his mouth.

Lucas didn't say a word in response. He lifted her, positioning her legs around his waist until Posy finally could feel the length of him pressed against her. Her head swam at the delicious firmness of him. He pivoted and then she was sitting up on the counter, champagne seeping through her trousers. Lucas's lips moved to her jaw and then her neck as the warmth of his hands worked their way under her top to the curve of her breast.

"Wait," she breathed.

Lucas pulled back, lips swollen, eyes hazy. "What's wrong?"

"I'm sitting on…" She indicated the spilled champagne, the spreading stain on her trousers.

"Oh." His jaw clenched as he reluctantly leaned back. "Sorry, did you want to…?"

She smiled slowly, hopping off the counter. "What I want?" She deftly unbuttoned her cardigan and dropped it to the floor. Lucas's eyes immediately fell to the flimsy lace covering her breasts. Revelling in the craving she saw there, Posy loosened her trousers and allowed them to slip to the ground. She stepped out of them, her feet unsteady but her desire certain. "Follow me upstairs and find out."

## Chapter Twenty-Four

Lucas awoke aware of two things. One, his head hurt beyond belief and two, he wasn't in his bed. The room felt dim and cool, the bedding way softer than he was used to. He was also aware of a third thing. He wasn't alone. And then, suddenly, images from the night before came flooding back. Whisky. A taxi. Overflowing champagne and… He rolled over slowly. Posy slumbered next to him, her face barely visible through the pale-pink bedding cocooned around her.

Lucas let out a long, slow breath. They'd slept together. Then he corrected himself; no, they hadn't *just* slept together. He'd had the most mind-blowing – if a little drunken – sex of his life, with none other than Posy Edwins.

It had to have been the booze, he decided. There was no way she would have entertained doing what they did otherwise, right? And she'd been really into it. Really good at it, too. But this hadn't been part of the plan. They weren't even friends, let alone anything else. They were pretending to be engaged and up until very recently had been in actual relationships with other people! And it had ended rather badly for Posy – how could Lucas be sure she'd really been in the right frame of mind last night? This whole thing was meant to be purely about business and somewhere along the line, they had strayed into pleasure.

And yet… He'd felt something shift in him last night. He couldn't pinpoint when it was that he'd decided he wanted to sleep with Posy or even what it was that had convinced him to make a move the way he did. All he remembered was a thunderbolt certainty that if he didn't kiss her in that moment he would die. Pulling himself up to a seated position and fighting the wave of nausea that followed, he wondered what this meant for their deal. He was *fairly* sure Posy had enjoyed the sex – at least twice, if he was any good at reading body language – but should she feel awkward this morning, there was every chance she might knock their plan on its head.

"I can actually hear you having an internal meltdown over there," Posy grumbled from the depths of her duvet.

"Sorry, I didn't mean to—" Lucas cleared his throat. "I'm not freaking out."

Posy tilted her head, opening one bleary eye. "It's okay if you are."

"I'm fine." He looked about the room. "What's the time?"

"Um." She rolled over, exposing her smooth, freckled back. There was a chrome alarm clock on her crowded bedside table. "9am."

"Jesus." He rubbed a hand across his brow. "How much did we drink last night?"

"Not a—" Posy bolted up. "Fuck."

"What?"

Her face was contorted with panic. "Last night, before we, you know." Her eyes widened and Lucas wasn't sure what that expression meant. "The champagne," she hissed. "My clothes."

"Oh yeah." Lucas vividly recalled the moment Posy had stepped out of her clothes, her lithe body taut and bare.

"*My dad.*" Posy bared her teeth.

"Shit." Lucas saw the reason for her panic. They hadn't bothered to clean up the kitchen. Indeed, they'd only gone to sleep a couple of hours ago and the last thing on their minds had been tidying up the evidence of their deed. As they sat in silenced anguish, Lucas could hear the unmistakable sound of people pottering around downstairs and to his added dismay, a child's voice. "Who's the kid?" he yelped. "I can't do a walk of shame past a child!"

"Oh God no." Posy buried her face in her pillow. "Eamon is here. This is end times." She glanced up at Lucas. "My soon-to-be step-nephew. He's a fucking monster."

"That seems harsh," Lucas said.

"Believe me, it's not," Posy muttered. "You're better off hiding up here until he slithers away."

Lucas wasn't sure if he detected a note of hope in her voice at the prospect of him sticking around. He had to admit there was something appealing about spending extra time in bed with Posy. It was also simultaneously terrifying, and he wasn't sure why. But it didn't matter. He had work to do. "Thanks, but I can't," he said. "I know it's a Saturday, but I have a call at ten-thirty with Align's accountant. I really need to go."

Posy shrugged, her face neutral. "Yeah, good point, I'm

actually frantic today too." She turned to get out of bed then looked back. "Can you, er…"

"Oh, sure, sorry." Lucas averted his eyes until she'd made it into the en suite and shut the door. As soon as he was alone, he grabbed his clothes that he'd managed to help-fully pile on the floor by his side of the bed. Once dressed, he took in Posy's room. It was almost as big as his entire London flat, he realised. Clutter aside, it was a tranquil space, with blush-pink walls, pale wood floors and simple, modern furniture. The wood-framed four-poster bed took up the centre of the room, laden with over-stuffed pillows and silken throws, next to it was a bedside table with yet more photo books, and atop them was the alarm clock and a framed picture of what looked like infant Posy being cradled by her mother. From where Lucas stood, he could see the glass in the picture-frame was well-smudged and it made his heart ache. Soft morning light filtered through a large window with a decorative chaise placed before it, surrounded by numerous stacks of books, seemingly all photography or art based. A selection of photos was spread in a fan shape across the seat and he wandered over to have a look. Most were of stunning vistas; he could see a cascading waterfall, timid deer, and epic sunsets. A tripod and camera were also set up at the window, the lens pointing at the sky outside. Lucas took a seat at the dressing-table and leaned against it, his head full of Posy's vanilla perfume.

"You decent?" Posy called.

"Yup."

Posy emerged from the bathroom in cashmere sweat-pants and a vest top, her hair bunched into a topknot. Her cheeks were scrubbed pink but there was no disguising the shadows under her eyes or the sleepiness in them.

He nodded at the photos displayed across the chaise. "You really are good," he said.

"Excuse me?" Posy's eyes flashed.

"The photos," he said hurriedly. God, how awkward.

"Oh, thanks." Posy smiled. Despite the evidence of a sleepless night, her smile made her more beautiful than he'd ever seen her.

"It would be great to see mo——" He was interrupted by his phone buzzing with a diary reminder. "Shit. I really should go. I have to get my car."

"Okay," she said, stifling a yawn. "If we hurry, I can sneak you out the back."

"Right." Lucas scuffed his feet. That's how it was – he should have known. Perhaps it was the tiredness, but he couldn't help thinking that Henry the dickhead would probably have met all her friends and family, but Lucas, no, Lucas had to be ejected out of the back door.

"Seriously, you don't want to meet my lot," she assured him, as if reading his mind. "It'll just confuse them. They don't know about the wedding and as far as they know I'm still seeing Henry."

"Right, no, I get it," Lucas said, losing the battle against the bitterness that was overtaking him. Best the Edwins family thought Posy was still with Henry rather than Lucas, obviously.

Posy paused at the bedroom door. "You all right?"

"I'm fine," Lucas said tightly. He just wanted to leave and forget whatever it was that churned inside him, the thing that had convinced him to make his move last night. He brushed past her and opened the door, blindly hoping it would be obvious where the back door was.

Lucas emerged onto a wide landing with various doors

leading off it. To the right of him, at either corner, were the newels of a double staircase and the happy noise of family chatter drifted up it. Their innocent cheer only amplified the emotions swirling within him and it seemed mightily unfair.

"Lucas?" Posy barrelled out of her room. He turned, curious. Was she feeling the same as him?

"Yes?" he asked cautiously.

"I thought I might look at flights today online," she said. "See if I can find a deal then send Hardstark the link to book it?"

"Oh." He rocked on his heels. He'd rather hoped Posy would want to talk about last night. But of course, she was so single-minded about Hawaii, of course that would be where her priorities lay. Lucas nodded stiffly. "Sure," he said. Posy was right to be so focused. They both had to keep their eyes on the prize. "See you, then."

Her face softened and she tucked an errant tendril of golden hair behind her ear. "Wait, Lucas, I—"

"Hello?" A male voice hailed them from across the landing. A tall man emerged from what appeared to be a bathroom. He was ruddy and broad-shouldered with rounded spectacles over intelligent eyes and freckled skin. It could only be Jesper Edwins, Lucas realised with a rush of excitement. Jesper approached Posy and Lucas with a curious smile.

"Pops!" Posy's affect instantly changed, her head lowering. "Morning."

"Morning," Jesper sighed, nodding at Lucas. "Is this the mysterious boyfriend then, Posy?"

"Um. Yup." Posy chewed at her lower lip. "He was just about to leave though." She elbowed Lucas towards the stairs. "Bye then."

Jesper gave Posy an odd look and stretched out his hand. "Seems a little rude, Posy. Hi there. Henry, right?"

"No, I'm Lucas." He stepped forward to shake Jesper's hand. "A pleasure."

Jesper frowned at his daughter. "I'm sure I've heard you on the phone to a Henry?"

"Um," Posy swallowed nervously. "Things have, ah, changed."

"I see." Jesper gripped Lucas's hand and gave it an eye-wateringly tight shake. "Nice to meet you."

"And you." Lucas tried not to wring his hand when Jesper finally released it. He couldn't believe it. Jesper was the client of his dreams, and this was how they were meeting, post a one-night stand with the man's youngest daughter.

"How did you two meet?" Jesper asked.

"We were prefects at Arundel," Posy replied, visibly wilting under the interrogation. "And we caught up at the reunion."

"Hmm." Jesper tilted his head, clearly rifling through long-past memories. "Hang on, there was a boy with that name. Wasn't he the kid who you— Oh!" He masked his astonishment with a polite smile and Lucas matched it. It was no surprise teenage Posy would have complained about him to her family. He could only imagine the picture she'd painted in doing so. "Well, this is quite the turn-up. Lucas, won't you join the family downstairs? Have a coffee with us?"

"Oh, Pops, he's really busy," Posy blurted just as Lucas said, "I'd be delighted." He could always be a little late for the accountant meeting. After all, what could be more important than making a good impression on the man who would hopefully be his brand new client?

Trying not to be put off by Posy's warning glower, Lucas followed Jesper downstairs, pretending he wasn't blown away by the beauty of the man's home in the light of sober day. The dual staircase curved round and met in a large atrium of dove-grey walls and bleached-wood floors. Above them, a coloured glass dome welcomed the morning light.

"Everyone, we have a guest!" Jesper announced, ushering Lucas ahead of him. To Lucas's amazement, the breakfast counter that he'd amorously lifted Posy onto the night before was crowded with people. He noticed the champagne had been cleaned up, as had Posy's discarded clothing. Lucas felt his cheeks grow hot. Surely they would all know exactly what had taken place.

"Morning." Lucas waved sheepishly, waiting for a disparaging comment or a cheeky remark. But none came. "I'm Lucas. Hi."

"Hi there." A younger version of Jesper stepped forward, tall and athletic like Posy but with almost white-blond hair worn in loose waves to his chin. "I'm Seb, Posy's big brother. My wife Angharad." He pointed at a heavily pregnant woman with a chic pixie cut and ears heavy with jewelled studs. "That's my son Max." A chubby toddler with golden skin and dimples was trying to force his head up Angharad's flowing maternity dress. "You're dating Hurricane? Good luck with that!" He attempted to ruffle Posy's hair, but she ducked out of his reach with a snarl.

"Ah, Seb, yeah, you were head boy at Arundel too, right?" Lucas shook the man's hand.

"Yes, were you—? Oh!" Seb's eyes widened incredulously, and he glanced at a sullen Posy, who had slouched her way over to the kettle. "*You're* the chap who Posy was head prefect with, right? Yikes." His eyebrows jumped comically. "She did *not* like you back in the day, as I recall. Things really have changed then. Didn't you have a nickname? I seem to remember it was hilarious. Oh, what was it now?"

"Yes. There was a nickname all right." Lucas spoke through gritted teeth as Seb bobbed his head, clearly anticipating that Lucas would share it. There was no way he would, however. "It's a long story," he said instead.

"Nicknames are such bullshit," Posy mumbled as she faffed about with coffee mugs.

"Too right. Who cares about nicknames?" A lady in her fifties appeared at Seb's elbow. Her smile was warm and maternal, her voice betraying the faintest hint of a Spanish accent. "Lucas is a perfectly lovely name. I'm Ines, Jesper's wife." Ines had faded pink stripes in her chestnut hair that clashed with the thick purple lipstick coating her plump lips. Lucas liked her immediately. "We've just finished breakfast, but would you like a coffee, Lucas? I could pop some toast in for you too if you'd like."

"A coffee would be great, thank you," Lucas said. "But please don't worry about feeding me. I have to head off shortly." As Ines joined Posy by the kettle, Lucas noticed the woman offering Posy a gentle smile, which Posy barely reciprocated. Posy merely pushed a cafetière towards her stepmother.

"Come on Pose, won't you introduce me?" At the far end of the counter sat a dark-haired version of Posy, flanked by a ruddy-cheeked man with adoring eyes and a child dressed, rather improbably, in a three-piece suit.

"Yes," Posy said glumly. "Lucas, my sister Florence, Florence this is Lucas."

"A pleasure." Florence cast calculating eyes up and down Lucas. Despite her strong resemblance to Posy, now that Lucas was facing her, the differences were apparent by the second. True, she was beautiful like her sister, but where Posy's looks were effortless, Florence's beauty was considered. Refined. "This is Inigo, my fiancé." She gestured at the older gentleman who affably got up to shake Lucas's hand.

"What a treat," Inigo said. "I've never met one of Posy's beaus before." Out of the corner of his eye Lucas saw Posy scowl. His esteem, which had already taken a beating that morning, sunk even lower.

"Oh Inigo," Florence said indulgently. "They're never here long enough."

Lucas anticipated Posy would pounce on Florence's slight, but Posy merely yawned extra wide to show all her teeth.

"Nice to meet you Inigo," he said.

"And this is my son, Eamon," Inigo said with obvious pride, pointing at the child who was doodling away in an exercise book. "Come on Eamon, say hello."

Eamon bestowed a disdainful look upon Lucas. "I'm in the middle of my homework, Father," he said.

"It's a Saturday!" Posy scoffed.

"Oh, he's working on some stuff for his maths tutor later today," Florence said airily. "He's in the top tier at school you know."

"*Stuff?*" Eamon repeated. "Are you really referring to the Collatz conjecture as stuff?" He turned to Inigo. "Father, I thought your girlfriend went to Cambridge?"

"Florence is my wife-to-be, Eamon – we've talked about this." Inigo's smile stretched his hammy cheeks taut.

"I *did* go to Cambridge." Florence huffily lifted her coffee cup to her lips.

"Oh, that's right, you got a degree in Jane Austen," Eamon said.

"Classical literature of the 1800s, actually," Florence replied.

"So, reading then." Eamon was unimpressed.

Posy let out a loud guffaw that startled everyone and she caught Lucas's eye. "I told you to go out the back," she said.

As Florence gaped at her soon-to-be stepson with agonised impotence, Inigo patted Lucas ineffectually on the back.

"Still, welcome," Inigo said.

"Now then, Lucas, how long have you two been seeing each other?" Jesper asked, forcing Lucas to look away from the fascinating soap opera that was Florence and Inigo.

"Not long," Lucas said, accepting a brightly coloured and rather misshapen mug from Ines.

"And you're already staying the night," Ines said gleefully.

"I wouldn't set much store by that," Florence remarked.

Eamon looked up from his workbook. "Florence says we should put a revolving door on Posy's bedroom." Inigo set his head in his hands.

"That's the sort of thing she *would* say," Posy said. Her face was calm, but Lucas could see the irritation brewing beneath the surface of her skin.

Apparently Jesper could see it too, so he desperately tried again with Lucas. "And what do you do, Lucas?"

"I work in finance," Lucas replied, trying to keep his tone neutral. "Wealth management, to be precise. You know, I read your article just last week about how British business could better handle relationships with EU-based financiers."

"You did?" Jesper's craggy face warmed into a genuine smile. "Thank you. Anyone who cracks *The Economist* once in a while is certainly welcome here. What did you think?"

"Fantastic. Insightful," Lucas nodded, automatically switching into finance mode. It relaxed him instantly. "A little naïve regarding the checks that would—" He paused, clocking that Jesper had stilled, hands on hips. Lucas gulped. "Of course," he babbled, "the notion of setting up a third party to govern sustainability was really well thought out." He was almost panting by the time he finished talking and he searched the older man's face for any sense of reception. Lucas could almost feel beads of sweat pop along his brow. "I'd love to chat more about it sometime," he finished weakly and Jesper laughed loudly, showing slightly crooked teeth. Lucas cursed himself for not simply congratulating the man on a job well done. Flattery always worked with prospective in-laws, even Sally's who had been rather on the severe side. Why did he have to show off?

Jesper clapped a weighty hand on Lucas's shoulder and despite being a couple of inches shorter than Lucas, he had some oomph. "Great stuff!" he said. "Finally, someone who actually read the whole thing and has a cohesive viewpoint."

"Cheers," Lucas said, internally high fiving himself.

"Jesper, I read your article," Ines piped up, her face contorted in an approximation of wounded pride.

"You did," Jesper conceded with an affectionate wink. "Slagged off my use of adjectives but that's what I get for falling in love with a former language teacher."

"Now an artist." Ines pointed at the mug Lucas held. "I made these mugs."

ELIZABETH DRUMMOND

"They're… they're charming," Lucas replied, for want of anything else.

"You can be honest." Seb lifted his own unusual mug with a wink at Ines. "They look like something my son made at school."

"I have a thriving Etsy store, I'll have you know," Ines shot back. She gave Lucas a proud smile. "I also run these amazing classes in self-worth and intimacy," she went on. "If you're ever in the mood for—"

Posy groaned. "Ines, if you mention jade eggs in the next sentence, I swear I'll vom."

Ines laughed. "I wasn't going to." She arched an eyebrow at Lucas. "But if you sign up to my email newsletter you can read all about them."

Posy let out an agonised moan and buried her head in her hands. Lucas had no idea what to say to the older lady about jade eggs but he had a strong desire not to encourage the conversation. Fortunately, he was saved by Posy's brother.

"Come on Posy, give Ines a break," Seb urged. "Anything that keeps her off the pottery wheel has to be a good thing."

"Well, that's the last time I make you a teapot for Christmas!" Ines said with a relieved smile.

Stepmother and stepson exchanged a few more friendly jibes until Eamon's loud whines about not being able to concentrate on his work interrupted them. While a harassed Inigo tried to shush him, Florence moaned to Angharad about not being able to source the same incense holders that Kate Middleton used at her wedding to Prince William. As the family joshed back and forth, Lucas couldn't help noticing that Posy remained on the fringes, watching her family with a faint smile but not joining in.

"Gosh, is that the time?" Posy feigned shock as she glanced at her watch. "Lucas, darling, you have that thing."

"Thing?" He frowned. "I've barely drunk my coffee." It smelled amazing too.

"Yes." Posy flattened her lips. "The thing with your accountant. Here, I'll order a taxi to take you back to your car." Lucas flushed as he remembered the reason why he'd left his car back at the village hall and, judging by the heat rising in Posy's cheeks, she was thinking about it too. She reached for a cordless phone on the wall and dialled.

Lucas sighed, getting the hint. "Fine," he said. "You're right." Posy merely turned her back as she spoke to the taxi operator. Lucas looked at Jesper regretfully. "I have a thing. I should go."

"I'd like to say looking forward to seeing you again," Florence smirked, "but knowing Posy's track record?" She shrugged. "Best of luck."

"Um… thanks." Lucas felt like his cheeks were on fire. He put his coffee on the counter, regretfully barely touched. "Bye everyone."

"Lucas, it was a pleasure." Jesper shook his hand again. "Do come back soon and Flo, don't be mean to your sister."

"She makes it so easy though." Florence pouted.

"Behave." Jesper pointed at Florence. Then he grinned at Lucas. "Maybe next time I'll get you to have a look at the next article I'm writing. *Telegraph*, this time."

Lucas could barely contain his glee. "Absolutely."

"Your car will be here in a couple of minutes. I'll see you out," Posy said to Lucas. Then she glanced at Florence. "I'll leave my sister here with the demonic toddler."

"I'm ten, you imbecile!" Eamon yelled as Posy dragged Lucas out of the kitchen to the front door. Inigo looked like he could have happily accepted being struck dead by lightning after his son's insult.

"Your family are nice," Lucas said as they paused at the door. Florence had come across kind of chilly, but Ines and Jesper were nothing but delightful. "Eamon is… well, he's a character."

"That's one word." Posy's long fingers curled around the door handle, but she didn't open it.

"You seemed kind of distant in there," he said. "Everything okay?"

"Distance is sometimes the best way to handle that lot," she said. "In case you hadn't noticed, everything I do is a joke to them."

"It seemed pretty harmless to me." Lucas hadn't liked the teasing about promiscuity, but he got the sense that ribbing each other was how this family showed love.

"I think you're blinded by the perfection of Jesper Edwins and his eldest two children," Posy said. "Makes it hard to laugh along sometimes."

Lucas looked down at her pale face, his thoughts a jumble. Last night had been incredible and then this morning, to actually meet Jesper himself… it had been a lot to process. He wished he knew what Posy made of it all.

"Posy, I—" Lucas's phone rang. Cursing the intrusion, he checked it. "Oh, it's Fred."

"Your business partner?"

"Yeah." They hadn't spoken much since Lim's offer as Fred had needed to attend multiple hospital appointments. Plus, Lucas had wanted time to digest it, to see how the sale sat with him. He declined the call and sent Fred a quick text to say he'd call him later.

"So, do you think you'll sell the company?"

Lucas looked at Posy sharply. She clearly remembered the conversation in the pub well enough. "It's a generous offer," he said carefully. "The chance to work somewhere like Singapore or New York? That could be amazing. And Fred really needs the funds so he can focus on his health."

Posy nodded curtly. "You should seriously consider it. Getting paid to work abroad? So cool."

"Very cool." Even as Lucas agreed, he felt a disquieting tug at his conscience, but then he heard his taxi pulling into the drive with a crunch of gravel. "I'm considering it." He pushed aside the uneasiness. "But don't worry, I'll keep to our agreement."

"If you're sure?" Posy said. "I'd appreciate that. The festival will be such a break for me." She met his eye, then looked away again.

Lucas hesitated. Was she expecting a hug or kiss good-bye? Lucas had done things to her last night he'd never done with anybody but now he was stressing over a hug. Something about her body language told him it was safer to keep his hands off, so he stepped back. "I'm going to go," he said. "I'll call you?"

"Sure." Posy was already retreating into the house.

"Yeah." Lucas hurried to the cab, sliding into the back. As the driver set off, he sank back into his seat, his knackered mind a whirl. If Posy didn't care what he did, if Fred needed him to sell, what was stopping Lucas from cashing his chips and starting a new life somewhere exciting far away?

## Chapter Twenty-Five

**P**osy leaned her throbbing head against the cool wood of the door. From behind her, the kitchen was full of chatter. Her nephew, Max, chuckled throatily, his cuteness hailed with a chorus of 'aww' from his adoring family. Posy sighed. She was equally desperate for coffee and to avoid the prying natures of everyone in the house. What had she done? A few days separated from Henry and she was already hopping into bed with Lucas of all people?

"Posy?" Ines appeared from the kitchen, a soft smile on her face. "Everything all right?"

"Yep." Posy turned. After the morning she'd had so far, she was in no mood to handle the attentions of her stepmother.

"You look a little pale," Ines said. "Crazy night?" There was a knowing sparkle in her eyes.

"Why do you say that?" Posy asked.

"No judgement, but I did pick up your clothes off the floor when we got in last night." Ines grinned. "Looked like they'd come off in a hurry."

"Fuck!" Posy buried her head in her hands, her cheeks flaming. "I'm so sorry." The thought of Ines and possibly her pops seeing her discarded clothes and spilled champagne was almost too much to bear.

"Don't worry." Ines placed her hand on Posy's arm. "Your father didn't see anything; he was locking up the garage."

Posy exhaled in relief. "That's something."

Ines chuckled. "You're completely forgiven. At your age I'd have no doubt done the same."

"Ines!" Posy gaped at her stepmother. "Don't let Pops hear you talking like that."

"Lucas seems sweet," Ines said. "How long has he been on the scene?"

Posy hesitated. How to answer that question? "It's complicated," she said eventually, and she saw the optimism fade from Ines's eyes. Her stepmother retreated from the burgeoning camaraderie she'd valiantly attempted yet again.

"I see," Ines said. "Well, if you ever want to talk about it, I'm here." She smiled. "I'm always here."

"I know." All of a sudden, Posy didn't mind Ines's over-bearing need to be close. But she didn't feel like she had words for what was going on inside her right now. The sex with Lucas had been like nothing else she'd ever experienced. But it hadn't just been the sex that had blown Posy's mind. There had been a confident looseness to Lucas last night that she couldn't attribute entirely to the booze. Watching him laugh and chat about whisky with the pub staff had been something of a revelation. He'd been the complete antithesis of the Lucas she'd known so far. She honestly felt like it was a side of him she wanted to see more of. But when Lucas had seen Jesper, it was like a force had overcome him, one that excluded her entirely. And it was in that moment Posy had known Lucas was all about the business. Especially with this potential investor or whatever it was circulating Align. Why would he bother with Posy when he had all that going on? No, they had to be strictly business when it came to their wedding.

"Come on," Ines said kindly. "I'll cook you an omelette."

Posy allowed herself to be led into the kitchen, where her family still huddled around the breakfast counter. Max had managed to get hold of Eamon's pencil case and was merrily chucking the contents across the room, much to the older child's annoyance. Angharad was blissfully explaining the merits of her aromatherapy business to a yawning Inigo, cradling her swollen belly in satisfaction.

As Ines busied herself by the Aga, Florence ambled over to Posy. Without even looking at her sister's face, Posy knew she was angling for a gossip.

"So…" Florence leaned against the worktop. "Helpboy, huh?"

"Yup." Posy reached for a mug and the cafetière, which was mercifully still half-full. Naturally, the socially fluent Florence Edwins would have known exactly who Lucas was. "And don't call him that."

"Sorry." Florence lifted her hands in mock regret. "You're right. If he's to be part of the family then I'd better keep my trap shut."

"Who says he will be?" Posy eyed her sharply. Had Florence read the newsletter? Did she know?

"Then again, weren't you with someone called Henry not so long ago?" Florence tapped her chin. "Yes, I suppose I'm being over-optimistic assuming Lucas might finally be the one to get you to settle down."

Posy sighed with relief. She should have guessed that Florence hadn't read the alumni email. Right now, if news wasn't related to her own wedding Florence couldn't even process it. "Ha, that would be quite something," she replied mildly. "Anyway, how *is* all your wedding planning?" Posy didn't really care but continuing to discuss Lucas felt like picking at a scab.

"We're getting there," Florence said brightly. "Still so much to do and only six months to go." She gripped Posy's arm in sudden alarm. "I say, Lucas won't be expecting to come to the wedding, will he?"

"He'll probably be in Singapore by then," Posy replied absently and the realisation that Lucas would soon depart from her life, possibly to another country entirely, made her catch her breath. Their relationship had changed lightning-quick since embarking on this scheme and Posy hadn't taken a moment to fully appreciate how she would feel when the plan was complete. The idea had been to go their separate ways when the whole thing was done but could they truly do that so cleanly now? Last night had definitely changed the boundaries of their relationship but Posy was lost as to what that meant.

"What?" Florence raised an eyebrow.

"Oh, nothing." Posy flapped a hand, unable to articulate the thoughts churning within. "I mean, his work is so busy. I wouldn't worry about it."

"Phew." Florence pretended to wipe her brow. "Because Inigo and I have had so many arguments over the guest list, I refuse to re-do it." She met Posy's eye. "Even for someone as hot as Help— I mean, *Lucas*." And she smirked.

"Yeah, yeah, I get it." Posy took a sip of coffee. Florence's curiosity was palpable, a force demanding recognition, but Posy didn't even know where to start. Fortunately, Florence did.

"Anyway, what's Lucas got going on in Singapore?" her sister asked.

"He might be selling his business and relocating," Posy replied. "He isn't sure yet, but the prospect is keeping him busy. Might not even be Singapore that he ends up in – it was just one option."

"Singapore is, like, so five years ago," Florence said with a grimace. She raised her eyebrows. "Oh my God, would you go with him?"

"He hasn't asked." Posy busied herself reaching for the milk jug, wondering exactly what Lucas would do. If he sold up right now, he wouldn't need to continue with the wedding ruse to keep himself afloat. But if he *didn't* sell, he would certainly need her contacts more than ever. It didn't matter what Posy wanted; Lucas had to do what was right for him and from what she'd learned about Lucas, he always would. He stayed the course.

"I bet he'll ask you," Florence prattled on. "Do you want him to?"

Posy stopped. What *did* she want from Lucas?

The sound of the doorbell ringing stopped Posy from having to address that thought. "I'll get it!" She scurried to the door and yanked it open.

"Posy?"

Posy's heart sank. "Oh, hi Dee."

Her old friend was ensconced in skin-tight leggings and a fuzzy leopard-print sweater, fat pearls at her ears and throat. "So you *are* alive!" Dee trilled.

"What?" Posy was too hungover to comprehend.

"I've been trying to reach you all morning," Dee said,

bundling her way past Posy into the house. "The boys have Mandarin lessons down the road and it occurred to me I'd be in the neighbourhood so I thought I'd check in with you."

"You've been trying to reach me?"

"Your phone keeps going to voicemail." Dee's eyes darted all around the house. "Wow, this place has changed. Is that a Starck?" She pointed at the chandelier overhead.

"My phone must be dead." In Posy's haste to bed Lucas last night, she'd not plugged her phone in to charge. "And... Mandarin?"

"Yes. Competition to get into Arundel is even more intense than it was in our day, if you can believe it," Dee said with a wry chuckle. "Obviously they get priority due to my legacy but there's still no guarantee. And if they are to be doctors then—"

"Aw, they want to be doctors? That's sweet." Posy smiled.

"Well, they haven't said as much, but they will be. Most of Li's family are doctors, you see," Dee explained. "Lionel himself, as you know, runs a medical research facility – private, naturally – and so it's just expected."

"I see." Posy knew she shouldn't react to what Dee was saying, but she was tender this morning, her nerves exposed.

Dee tilted her head. "What do you mean, *I see*?"

"Nothing, it's just..." Posy set her chin. "I mean, aren't they a little young to have their futures dictated to them? I know I would have hated that."

"Well perhaps if you had—" Dee stopped herself then forced a polite smile.

"Perhaps if I had *what*?" A cold dread ticked through Posy's body.

Dee's face turned stony. "Do you know how frustrating it was to be your friend at school?"

Posy's neck ached from the sudden U-turn. "Excuse me?"

"At Arundel. You had it all." Dee gestured at her. "Looks, money, family name."

Posy was confused. Dee's father was Benedict Carrington, and his family could trace their lineage back for generations. Dee's great-great grandfather had set up a world-renowned import-export business worth millions of pounds. The family were Yorkshire legends. Dee had just as much status as Posy could ever claim to have, if not more. "Could say the same for you!"

"Not like Posy Edwins though," Dee said with a grimace. "EVERY boy fancied you, every girl wanted to BE you, and maybe you weren't top of the class, but you're certainly not stupid. Put it this way, Posy, *you* never experienced the indignation of getting picked last for the sports teams."

"Neither did you," Posy said. "You won cross-country three years in a row!"

"What I mean is, you had it ALL!" Dee cried. "All the ingredients. All the potential. I used to wish that some of your glitter would rub off on me because I knew what I would do with it."

"What?" As Posy looked at Dee, memories rolled through her mind like a vicious carousel. The parties, the sleepovers, the secrets. It had meant something to Posy, then. "We were friends. We cared about each other." She didn't even realise she'd used the past tense until the words left her mouth.

Dee bestowed Posy with a pitying smirk. "We were friends because, even as a kid, it made sense for me to hook my wagon to yours, so to speak," she said. "You get that, don't you? We had all the potential to emerge as a force to be reckoned with, but you never seemed to deliver on that promise." She sniffed. "And here you are."

"Here I am." Posy looked down at her sweatpants, feeling inescapably grimy standing next to Dee.

"Unmarried," Dee listed. "Childless. Jobless. And if the rumours are true, your father has cut up all your credit cards. So… you're broke as well."

Posy ran out of politeness. "Did you come here just to talk shit to me, or did you have something else in mind?" Had Dee been this cynical when they were young? She'd been snotty enough at the reunion, but here she was being downright mean.

"Actually, I was hoping for a friendly catch-up, but *clearly* I was aiming too high. You have no business telling me how to raise my children," Dee went on. "Because even if my boys have only a fraction of your potential, I'm going to maximise the hell out of it in a way you never managed for yourself."

Posy was taken aback. Wasn't that the same as what her pops was always saying? "Listen, I might not have married Mr Eligible right out of university but I'm not a complete waste of space. For example, I'm going to be the guest of honour at a major photography festival. In Hawaii no less. Free accommodation too. It could really give my career a boost."

"And here I thought you just 'took photos for social media' now," Dee said.

Posy froze. It was now very clear why Dee had stopped by out of the blue. Trying to remain calm, Posy walked further into the house, hoping to lead Dee away from the kitchen where her family were. "You've read the alumni newsletter then?"

"Yup." Dee smarmed as she followed Posy into the snug. "I know barely anyone reads it nowadays, but my mother certainly does. And she called me, asking 'didn't I associate with Posy Edwins, once upon a time?' So, I looked at it and imagine my surprise." She squealed. "Arundel's golden girl is marrying Hel— I mean, Lucas."

"Uh-huh." Posy perched on a sofa arm, affecting nonchalance. What was Dee going to do with this information?

"That's quite the turn-up for the books," Dee said. "I mean, I saw you just a couple of weeks ago and you were with that dish, Henry."

"Well, you know, this has all happened so fast," Posy said quickly. "You know me. Crazy, Hurricane Posy." When Dee didn't respond, Posy faked a laugh. "A whirlwind romance."

"Clearly." Dee cleared her throat. "So, when is the wedding? Do you have a theme?" Dee let out an appreciative gasp. "I have my eye on an exquisite Marni frock that would be just perfect."

"Who says you're invited?" The words spilled out before Posy even knew she'd spoken, and she was rewarded with an outraged intake of breath from Dee.

"What on earth—?"

Posy opened her mouth, intending to double down on the pre-prepared excuses: it was small, family-only, they were in a hurry. But then Posy realised that if this indeed had been a real wedding, Dee still wouldn't have been a consideration for the guest list. And, in fact, the wedding may be a sham, but Posy wanted it done right. She owed Lucas that much for joining her on this wild ride. "I wouldn't have you there for all the money in the world," she said sweetly. "Not after the way you've just spoken to me."

"What? You came to MINE!" Dee cried, her pearl earrings bobbing with indignation. "It will be expected that I attend yours."

"By whom? *Who* will expect it?" Posy laughed.

"People, of course." Dee gabbled. "I was your *best* friend at Arundel. What will people say if I—?"

Posy stood up. "The way you've just spoken about me it's clear we weren't friends, not truly," she said. "And as for people expecting you to be there, well, this isn't about *you*. It's a wedding. It's about two people and no one else." Her voice cracked on the last word. Posy's heart ached. Who was she to talk on this matter, when she was participating in a sham wedding after breaking up an actual marriage? "What happened to you, Dee?" she asked. "When did you become like this? We were so close."

"I could ask you the same question." For a moment, Dee's eyes watered. "Whilst you were looking the other way, I grew up. We all did. And when I saw you with that catch in Alfie's, I thought you had too."

"That catch?" Posy didn't hide her bitterness at the idea of Henry being described as a catch. "That catch was an arsehole." As Posy spoke she could still hear the splintering of Jacinta's voice the moment she realised her world was crashing down.

Dee smirked. "I don't see how *Helpboy* is any kind of improvement."

"Get out." Posy clenched her fists.

"What?" Dee's chin quivered.

"Lucas O'Rourke is worth a million Henrys." Posy grabbed Dee's arm, propelling her towards the front of the house. "You say you've grown up?" They reached the front door and Posy yanked it open. "If being a snobbish hag is growing up then I'd like to avoid that."

"How dare—" The last words of Dee's outrage were not to be heard, silenced by the slamming of the heavy front door. Posy rested a trembling hand against the wood, adrenaline making her heart pound. There was every chance she'd live to regret kicking Dee out in such a manner, but there had been something so satisfying about finally, literally, closing the door on their relationship.

"Good. I always hated her." Florence's voice cut through the air.

"You did?" Posy looked at her sister in surprise.

"Yeah." Florence ambled over to Posy. "She's not good people. Lucas is."

"Thanks." Posy could only agree whole-heartedly.

"Now come and look at hairstyles with me," Florence ordered, looping her arm through Posy's. "If I have to spend one more second listening to Eamon pontificating about mathematics I am quite literally going to scream."

## Chapter Twenty-Six

Hardstark tapped on Mrs Paddington's door, her mind whirling. What on earth was she going to say to her boss? The events at the village hall had had her convinced at one point that Lucas and Posy were fakers but, frustratingly, she couldn't be sure. As she waited to be allowed in, she checked her phone. Another text from Miles Purslow, confirming the time to come and inspect the canker-prone roses of Arundel later that day. She smiled. He was a kind man.

"Enter!" Paddington's crisp voice intoned. Hardstark did so, shoving her phone back in her pocket. Paddington was at her desk, sipping tea and studying something on her computer. "Morning," she said. "Thanks for popping in on the weekend. The PTA meeting agenda is driving me crackers."

"No problem. I told the gardeners I'd pop by to check on the roses." Hardstark arranged herself in one of the seats facing Paddington. "I presume you want an update on Lucas and Posy?" she said.

"Indeed." Paddington folded her hands on the desk. "How is it going? Any sense they're feeding us a pack of lies?"

"I honestly couldn't call it," Hardstark admitted, chewing the inside of her cheek.

Paddington's right eye ticked. "I see."

"Let me explain," Hardstark rushed. "At the venue, Lucas had no idea about Posy's taste in music or that she liked to dance. Which is odd, isn't it? I mean, you know what your loved ones like, don't you?"

"Yes, I'd say so," Paddington agreed. "Very suspicious."

"Yes," Hardstark harrumphed. She didn't like being taken for a fool any more than the next person, but this situation was so murky she couldn't find a way through. "But then they danced. As in, a slow dance. And the way they held each other, the look in their eyes... I could believe they were in love."

"Well, *I* don't believe it," Paddington snarled. "Everything I've learned about the pair of them sets my teeth on edge. They don't fit." She pointed at her computer screen. "I've gone through Mr Day's logs from their time at Arundel and it seems like they fought on every issue. See here?" She tapped the screen. "October 23rd, 2008. At a meeting to discuss the careers fair, Ms Edwins suggested bringing in a cocktail-making station with DJs to give the event a – and I quote – cosmopolitan air, whereupon Mr O'Rourke called the suggestion a vacuous waste of time and space and said Posy should skip back to the handbag shop from whence she had come. Also a direct quote." Paddington turned her cold eyes back onto Hardstark. "That's one of the milder exchanges. They *hated* each other. And what, they connect at a party as adults and suddenly days later they need to marry? There was never even a whiff of affection from what Mr Day observed!"

"You're right, it's strange," Hardstark said with a sigh. "I don't know what they'd get from such a scheme. But without hard proof, we can't go back on the deal."

"I know that!" Paddington snapped. "And if I were convinced that they were the real thing I wouldn't be so perturbed, but I'm sure there's some kind of scam here. I simply can't ascertain what it is." She leaned back in her chair. "What's their next appointment?"

"Posy wants to book the honeymoon flights," Hardstark said, consulting her emails. "She'll send a link—"

"Insist upon doing it with a travel agent," Paddington ordered. "So you can observe again. If they do it online it's a missed opportunity."

"Good idea." Hardstark shot off a quick email to Posy asking her to proceed in this manner.

"I find it strange that they want to blow precious pennies on a honeymoon abroad," Paddington mused. "If I were them, I'd want to keep everything for the big day."

"They want lots of babies," Hardstark said. "Apparently. One would assume on the honeymoon they'd start—"

"Yes, yes, I appreciate that," Paddington snapped, raising a hand. "Trouble is, I don't buy it. We need to work out what the hell these two are playing at, and soon. I will not have them making a mockery of this school. Understood?"

Hardstark swallowed, her hands clammy in her lap. "Understood," she rasped.

## Chapter Twenty-Seven

Lucas took an energising breath. And another. A few days had passed since his and Posy's night together and now they were about to book the tickets for Hawaii at an actual travel agent's. Lucas couldn't remember the last time he'd set foot in a bricks-and-mortar travel agent's. But Hardstark had insisted upon this as opposed to making bookings online. So, yet again, he had to put on the performance of a lifetime. He had to be a man in love, his only motivation a dedication to the woman he was about to marry, but now it wasn't disdain for Posy he had to mask. What he felt when it came to Posy was something very different and complex, something he couldn't pin down nor examine too closely.

Lucas turned the corner and halted. There she was, outside the travel agent's a hundred yards away. Lucas took a moment, his breath skipping at the sight. Her willowy frame was clad in a pastel-pink shirtdress that fell to mid-shin and she'd twinned it with battered Converse high-tops – not quite a successful portrayal of a society bridezilla then. She was craning her neck up and down the street to see him and he waited until she was turning his way before he stopped staring and headed towards her, eyes on the pavement. His feet moved quickly, as if only responding to the part of him that longed to be in her presence again.

"Morning," he said when he arrived at her side.

"Hi." Her hands tightened around the strap of the distressed handbag she clutched to herself. "You okay?"

"Yeah." Lucas scratched the back of his neck then inspected his shoes. "Work's crazy at the moment. Still not decided what to do." The words rushed out as if desperate to share airspace with her.

"I bet." Her lips quirked. "How's Fred?"

He liked that she asked about Fred. "Getting there, thanks. He's on some new medication but he's not out of the woods."

"A lot of pressure to make the right decision then," Posy remarked gently.

"Yup." Lucas finally dared meet her eyes properly, hoping she'd see the cry for help there. How he wished she would just tell him what she thought about his options. He appreciated that she was being supportive, but did she have any feeling about him leaving the country and starting a new life abroad? But Posy didn't venture any further opinion, she merely shifted from foot to foot and allowed him a small smile that made Lucas dare to think they might find a way to address That Night. Just as he opened his mouth to attempt that discussion, from somewhere behind Posy Hardstark coughed wetly.

"Good morning," Hardstark said.

Posy stalled, her eyes locked on Lucas as if there was more to say. Then she sagged. "Morning Ms Hardstark."

"We should crack on," Lucas said awkwardly.

"Right." Posy abruptly turned on her heel and hurled herself through the peeling, clattering door of the travel agent's. With a greeting to Hardstark, Lucas followed Posy.

Super Travel! was rather drab and quiet for a business that had an exclamation mark in its name. The team operated out of a low-ceilinged office cluttered with dark furniture and a garish carpet stuck in the 80s. Yellowing travel posters adorned the walls and stepping inside was akin to being dropped into a box intent on crushing the life out of you. A member of staff sitting behind a flimsy-looking desk waved them over.

"Welcome to Super Travel!" His thin-lipped smile didn't quite reach sleepy, pale-lashed eyes. "I'm Simon. How can I help you today?"

"Hi Simon." Posy threw herself into one of the chairs. "We're here to book flights for our honeymoon." Simon glanced uncertainly at Hardstark. "Um, Lucas?" Posy dragged Lucas forward from where he'd been concealed by Hardstark. "Meet Simon."

"Right, I see." Simon indicated for them to sit down. After a prolonged and obnoxious glare from Hardstark, he fetched a third chair for her.

"So, where are we traveling to?" Simon asked once everyone was settled.

"Hawaii!" Posy could clearly only just contain her glee.

"Hawaii?" Hardstark's head almost swivelled 360 degrees. "You're planning on Hawaii with this budget?"

"Yeah." Posy fixed Hardstark with a 'well, duh' expression. "My friend invited us over, so we decided to take advantage of her kindness and call the visit our honeymoon."

"Now isn't that delightful." Simon tapped at his computer. "Dates?"

"July 10th, returning five days later," Posy replied. "And the cheapest you can manage, please."

"Okay, let's see what we can do." Simon tapped away some more.

"Simon." Hardstark leaned forward. "I was under the impression flights had become very expensive of late."

"Oh, they are," Simon said with an authoritative nod. "I mean, you wouldn't believe the green taxes a lot of airlines are applying now, but rest assured, I can get you folks a deal."

"Be that as it may," Hardstark said. "Posy and Lucas, why don't you consider a different destination?" She scanned the garish posters Blu-Tacked to the wall. "Belgrade perhaps? Gdansk? Moldova? My, those prices are a steal!"

"It has to be Hawaii." Posy's smile was brittle and Lucas could only back it up with a tight nod. Hardstark huffed and eased back in her chair with a tut.

"Right, here we go." Simon nodded at his screen. "Your best bet is Virgin Atlantic for… £1800 each. Your departure time isn't too bad, but you do arrive late evening in Honolulu. Come back a week later, early morning flight."

Posy looked to the ceiling and Lucas knew she was mentally calculating the festival schedule. Finally, she nodded. "That could work," she said, relief flooding her face. "And that fits our budget, doesn't it?" she asked Lucas.

"It does," he said.

"Great," Simon replied. "And, because we are the best in the biz, this deal I've found you is cancellable up until five days before departure with just a small cost of a hundred pounds per person. I think you'll agree that's pretty good?"

"Absolutely," Posy said. She reached across and patted Lucas's knee. "But there is nothing on earth that could make us want to cancel."

Lucas had to turn his head away. The act Posy was putting on was top class. The expression on her face when she'd touched his leg had been nothing short of euphoric. But it was all fake, wasn't it? In that instant, Lucas couldn't match Posy's look of devotion; he could barely manage a smile. How could she act this way when things were such a mess?

"Will you be needing accommodation?" Simon asked, not taking his eyes from his work.

Posy licked her lips. "We'll be staying at my friend's villa," she said.

"Lovely! Must be nice to have friends in Hawaii." A wistful smile tugged at Simon's features

"What's this friend's name then?" Hardstark demanded.

"Um." Posy blinked. "Irma Copley." Lucas knew that was the name of the festival director, but what he didn't know was why Hardstark was making a note of it. He skidded his chair back, standing.

"Posy? Can we talk outside?" Lucas nodded to the shop exit.

"I'll just need a credit card number…?" Simon said, suddenly alarmed that his customers were leaving.

"She can take care of that." Posy pointed at Hardstark. "Come on." She hooked her hand through Lucas's arm and let him lead her out of the shop, much to Hardstark's apparent irritation; no doubt she was annoyed she wouldn't be able to eavesdrop on whatever conversation was about to commence.

Once outside, they stood on the pavement in awkward

silence as shoppers milled around them. Posy looked at Lucas and he looked at her.

"You all right?" she said.

"Hardstark's not buying this," he replied. "I'm worried."

"We just need to push through," Posy said defiantly. "She needs hard proof to stop the wedding and she doesn't have any. She can be suspicious all she likes, but it won't change a jot."

Lucas palmed his face. "This is harder than I thought it'd be," he said softly.

Posy gulped. "I know," she said. "I never thought it'd be this much *work*..."

"No, no," Lucas shook his head, "not that. The *lying*, Posy. I'm struggling with the lies we're telling."

Posy's cheeks heated, like a scolded child. "You knew what you were signing up for. It's not like I'm enjoying this, is it?"

Lucas rocked back on his heels. There it was. How she really felt. He nodded regretfully. "I thought I knew," he said. "But then, if I can't build my business the honourable way, maybe I shouldn't have it."

"Honourable?" Posy screwed her nose. "We're merely exploiting a loophole; what we're doing isn't *technically* wrong."

"Isn't it?" Lucas retorted. "Because it's making me feel like dirt. I've even asked my own mother to lie. My dad too."

"How is your dad dealing with it?" Posy asked.

"Surprisingly fine," Lucas said. "He says he trusts me to do the right thing. Which is ironic."

"How do you mean?"

Lucas sighed. "I'm lying to all these people in an effort to save my business and even after all this subterfuge I may

283

have to sell it to some big cheese who will probably dismantle the very thing I've dreamed of my entire life to make yet even more money."

Posy folded her arms. "Listen. I do understand if you don't want to keep going with this," she said, her voice small. "I'll find another way to get to Hawaii."

"That's not what I'm saying." Why didn't Posy understand this was tearing him in a million different directions?

"I understand if you want to give up on this," she said, edging closer to him.

"But I don't want to," Lucas said. His lungs swelled. The air was warm. They were inches apart. The fire had gone from their argument but the atmosphere between them was no less charged.

"You don't?" she said.

"No." Lucas had the curious sensation of things falling into place; of a puzzle taking shape, the pleasing tumble of a turning lock. But he had no idea what that meant. Only that he liked it. But he couldn't read Posy's expression. Had he scared her off by even thinking that he might stay put? "I mean, I just want what's best for my company, for my future."

"Right," Posy nodded. "Align."

The shop door clattered open. Startled, Lucas and Posy sprang apart as Hardstark left the shop and approached cautiously, her eyes darting between them.

"I've given him the payment details," she said. "You need to go in and give some personal information so he can confirm the booking and issue tickets."

"Oh, right." Posy scurried into the shop, her gaze on the ground.

Lucas took a moment to watch her go. "What am I going to do?"

Hardstark looked at him strangely. "What?"

Lucas jolted. He hadn't realised he'd spoken out loud. "Nothing." But as he darted after Posy, the question resolutely ricocheted around his head. What *was* he going to do?

## Chapter Twenty-Eight

Posy sifted through her presentation. With what little money she'd had left in her account, she'd managed to blow up some of her best shots and mount them onto large pieces of card. It would mean paying for an extra baggage item at the airport but as she looked at the images of the sunny meadows near her home, she had to admit it was totally worth the effort. They were warm and scenic but also stunningly editorial. As she arranged them in what she hoped would be the most pleasing configuration, she felt her mind drift back to that night with Lucas. She couldn't stop replaying the image of his body in the moonlight shining through her window; firm and lean, muscles in all the right places. But what really struck her, beyond his physical perfection, was his grace. His tenderness coupled with an insatiable wildness that had at times taken her breath away. She'd felt completely at ease with him. Perhaps it was because she knew it could only be a one-time thing, that he was going to head off into his high-powered executive life the moment he could. Perhaps that notion of the temporary had given both of them permission to behave with complete abandon. Forget it and move on, she told herself, because Lucas sure would if his remarks outside the travel agent's were anything to go by.

Her father popped his head through her bedroom door.

"Hi Pops, what's up?"

"Tara is here to see you," her pops said curiously. "Something about a dress?" He pushed her door open further to reveal Tara waiting, a dress-bag over her shoulder.

"Oh!" Posy slapped her forehead. She'd forgotten that she and Tara had made plans to finalise the wedding dress today. And here Tara was, parading said dress under the eye of her unknowing father. "Come in, Tar!" She ushered her friend in, avoiding the inquisitive stare from Jesper. Tara scuttled in, face aflame.

"Oh my God!" Tara hissed once the door was shut. "He doesn't know, does he?"

"Of course not!" Posy said. "Do you think this wedding would be going ahead if he did?"

"Right." Tara thinned her lips. "Anyway, I made some tweaks." She took a deep breath and unzipped the bag. "Here we go." She dragged out the dress, hanging it on the back of the bedroom door. She straightened it out, flared the skirt and then turned to look at Posy. "What do you think?"

Posy couldn't speak. Her mind was too busy trying to reconcile the masterpiece before her with the frothy pile of fabric they'd bought in the charity shop. The poufy skirt had been pared back to fall in a flowing A-line shape. The bodice was simple – sleeveless and high-necked, with no gaudy beading or fripperies. As Posy watched, Tara lifted the dress off the door and turned it around. There was the daring backless feature, with the now pristine white chiffon bow trailing down the back.

"You're a genius is what I think!" Posy clapped her hands. "How on earth did you manage this?"

"As I thought, there was a work of art under all that material." Tara beamed with pride. "I simply removed the sleeves and the overskirts, took out that godawful boning and the chiffon bow really perked up after I starched it." She knitted her fingers together. "So, you're happy?"

"It's truly incredible," Posy answered sincerely. "Can't wait to see what it looks like on."

"Get into it and I'll see where it needs adjusting," Tara said.

Posy snatched the gown off the door and hurried into her bathroom, feeling strangely excited. She didn't think she could be more thrilled than if this were her actual wedding dress. Pulling off her clothes, she slid into it, relishing the soft swish of the material against her legs. Then, she turned to look in the full-length mirror that hung on the door and gasped at what she saw.

"What's up? Do you hate it?" Tara called through the door, her voice tinged with mild panic.

Nothing could be further from the truth, Posy thought as she stared at her reflection. The dress was a little loose around the shoulders but overall, it fit like a dream. Quirky, but elegant, it showed off her long limbs to perfection without being too exposed. "I've never seen anything like it," she blurted, twisting this way and that.

"Is that a good thing?" Tara cried.

In reply, Posy flung open the bathroom door and swept back into the bedroom. "What do you think?" Upon seeing her friend, Tara's face brightened, and she jumped up and down, clapping her hands.

"Oh yay! I wasn't sure the hem would sit right but it seems I needn't have worried!" She walked around Posy, tugging the material here and there. "Looks like I just need to tighten here…" She popped a pin in by Posy's arm. "And here…" She narrowed her eyes, presumably doing some calculations. "But that'll take me all of a few minutes. I can do it now."

"You totally undersold your skills," Posy said admiringly. "Why aren't you doing this professionally?"

Tara's face went blank. "I-I don't know if I've ever considered seamstress work a suitable career," she said. "You know what my family's like. I qualified as a lawyer and when I decided to quit the practice for the kids, well, you'd have thought I'd murdered my grandmother the way they all reacted."

"Ignore them," Posy told her firmly. "Because this is amazing."

"Noted." Tara's eyes were scanning the hem of the skirt. "What shoes will you be wearing?"

"Hang on." Posy dived for her cupboard and fished out the Blahniks she'd earmarked as wedding shoes. The soles were a little battered from a mad weekend of clubbing in Berlin last year but they matched the dress perfectly.

Tara nodded with approval. "Yassss!"

Posy laughed. "You're about a decade too old to say that, you know."

"I blame my kids," Tara said, slumping onto Posy's bed. "Ben's latest girlfriend has got them saying it."

"Wait, latest?" Posy stopped fussing with her shoes and studied her friend. She saw the bags under Tara's eyes, the frizz of her hair. "Is he not with Izzy anymore?" Tara's marriage had ended officially just six months ago, but the rot had set in long before.

"No, it's Allegra now," Tara muttered. "She's a fashion merchandising student."

"A student?" Posy was appalled. "Almost a child then!"

"Barely out of her teens," Tara confirmed, kneading her hands. When she lifted her head, Posy was horrified to see her friend's eyes were brimming with tears. "What am I doing with my life?"

"Oh darling." Posy curled up next to Tara and pulled her in. "Come on."

"I'm a single mum," Tara sniffed. "I gave up my career to be the perfect housewife and I failed there. All my friends – apart from you – have moved on or away. Meanwhile, Ben is off with some... some *foetus* having the time of his life!"

"Men and marriage are not the be-all and end-all." Posy tilted Tara's face to meet her gaze. "You're just grieving the end of your relationship, that's all."

"Says the woman who's marrying a perfect stranger," Tara said with a snotty giggle.

"Ha!" Posy jumped up, the pretence of fetching a tissue a convenient reason to avoid digging into the Lucas issue. "For one thing, he isn't a total stranger." She offered the tissue to Tara, but Tara didn't take it, just stared at Posy. "What?" Posy said. But Tara merely rose to her feet, a strange expression taking over her face. "*What?*"

"You slept with Lucas?" Tara yelped.

Posy dropped the tissue in shock. How did Tara know? "Huh?"

"You did, you slept with Lucas!" Tara pointed an

accusatory finger at her, glee vanquishing her earlier melancholy.

Posy gaped. Myriad excuses fluttered through her mind, but this was Tara here. And Tara was no fool. Posy threw her hands up in the air sheepishly and Tara roared with laughter.

"Oh my God!" Tara cried, clapping her hands. "This is brilliant."

"Look, we don't need to talk about this. We were talking about you." Posy desperately wanted to change the subject. "Tell me about this Allegra, who, by the way, yes, you don't have to ask, I do pledge to hate for eternity."

"No, no!" Tara wagged her finger. "I would rather not talk about my horrendous ex-husband; I want to hear about you *finally* bedding Mr Spreadsheet."

"I—" Tara's expression hardened. "Fine," Posy said. "We were drunk. And it just happened."

"*And?*"

"And nothing," Posy said. "I'm a big girl. Big girls sometimes sleep with big boys." She blushed. "I don't mean… look, you know what I mean."

"We'll get into the *big* comment later," Tara said sternly. "But after what you went through with Henry, I'm surprised you were even ready to look at another guy."

With a sudden and inconvenient clarity, Posy relived the feel of Lucas's fingers trailing down her clavicle, and her breast. The power of his hunger. She swallowed, fiddling with her alarm clock. "Yeah, well. These things happen, don't they?"

"Posy." Tara's voice was stern.

"What?"

"*Posy.*"

Posy met Tara's eye. "Jesus, what?"

Tara's jaw sagged. "You like him."

"No." Although Posy knew her conviction was lacking. "We're friends at best."

"*Friends?*" Tara mimicked her. "Posy, I have met your male friends; I've seen the way you talk about them. This?" She gestured wildly at Posy. "Is different."

"I'm not sure that it is," Posy said. "I mean, it can't be. He has a business that he might very well sell off so he can go and work halfway around the world! I don't fit into those plans."

"You could if you wanted to," Tara pointed out. "Did you ask?"

"God, you sound just like Florence," Posy groaned. "Even if I wanted him to stay, it's not up to me. It must be all up to him. Besides, I have Hawaii and my career." She punctuated the last three words with claps as if to fortify her intent and make it real. "Nothing is getting in the way of that."

"Okay, okay." Tara admitted defeat with a chuckle. "I admire your stance."

"He's a nice guy." Posy's voice was small. "I don't want anyone to get hurt is all."

"No one has to," Tara assured her.

Posy nodded, smoothing down the front of her beautiful dress. The plan had been so simple. And now she'd potentially ruined it. Conscious of Tara's concerned stare, Posy forced a laugh. "Ugh!" She threw her head back comedically. "When did sex get so tricky?"

"It'll be a lot simpler when you marry him," Tara quipped, but her jokey demeanour was instantly replaced by frozen horror as she took in the sight of something behind Posy.

"What are you—?" Posy gulped, turning to face what she knew Tara had seen.

"You're getting married?" Jesper said. He and Ines stood in the doorway, wearing identical expressions of dismay.

"I can explain."

Jesper let out a bark of sarcastic laughter. "Unless you have a fancy-dress party coming up, I think we can assume the explanation is you're getting married without telling anyone!" He turned his ire towards Tara. "Well, anyone apart from Tara."

Tara blanched, but moved closer to Posy, chin high. "She's my best friend, Mr Edwins."

"Leave Tar out of it!" Posy linked arms with Tara, drawing strength from her solid warmth, and the smell of her sandalwood perfume. "She's done nothing wrong."

"Apart from helping you keep this secret from your family," Jesper snapped.

"Why don't we all settle down?" Ines placed a hand upon her husband's arm. "Let's hear Posy out. Calmly."

"How can I be calm?" Jesper cried. But Ines tightened her grip on his arm and Jesper took another deep breath. "Fine, fine, I can be calm." His gaze skewered Posy. "Am I to understand that it's Lucas that you're marrying?"

Posy nodded.

"What?" Jesper's zen didn't last long. "He didn't ask me for your hand!" He gestured at Posy's left hand. "I see no ring. And who's paying for this? His family?" His cheeks turned ruddy. "The bride's father *always* pays for the wedding, and I won't have anyone thinking Jesper Edwins welches on tradition."

"Jesus Christ, Pops!" Posy said. "Never mind about the man I'm marrying, who he is or how he makes me feel." It didn't surprise her that her father's focus immediately strayed to the practical as opposed to the emotional. What surprised her was how much it hurt. "Isn't this what you wanted from me? Making decisions, settling down?"

"I only wanted you to think seriously about your future. I didn't mean that you should run off and find the first man who would have you!" Jesper barked. "If you're that desperate for money, you should have said."

*I did say*, Posy thought but gritted her teeth instead. "It's not like that."

"But what will people think?" Jesper declared. "When they see my daughter marrying in such a manner? Posy, I wanted you to be independent, not, not…"

"Not what, Pops?" Posy's dress swished as she faced off against him. "Not a joke? Not the oddball you had no idea what to do with when her mother died?" Beside her, Tara audibly gasped.

Jesper paled and Ines inserted herself between them. "Let's just take a moment," she demanded. "This isn't helpful."

"I'll tell you what isn't helpful," Jesper snapped. "My daughter constantly proving how right I was to cut her off. Look at how reckless she's being!"

"She's an adult!" Ines planted her feet firmly on the ground. "Jesper, if Posy wants to marry that lovely boy, we should let her."

"*Let* me?" Posy rounded on her stepmother. "You of all people are in no position to tell me wh—"

"Oh, grow up Posy and stop treating Ines like dirt," Jesper interrupted with a growl. "She loves you like a mother, and you talk down to her as if she's no more than an irritation. It was understandable when you were a teenager but as Ines says, you're an adult. Act like it. Take a leaf from your sister's book."

Posy felt like the air had been sucked from her lungs. It was like being a child all over again. Powerless. Reliant on her father for everything and now she couldn't even speak. It didn't occur to her that she might not have to but then Tara stepped forward.

"Mr Edwins," Tara said. "I think you need to give Posy a break."

"Tar." Posy tried to pull her friend back. "Don't bother."

Tara looked back at her. "I can't keep quiet a second longer," she said. She turned back to Jesper. "Yes, what Posy and Lucas are doing is unconventional. And I know that honouring convention is important to you."

Jesper lifted a hand. "With all due respect Tara—"

"I hadn't finished." Tara drew up her shoulders. "Florence and Seb have been good little soldiers, haven't they? I mean, Florence's wedding is set to be the biggest event of the year. A lot to be proud of. Arundel, Cambridge. Blue-blooded fiancé, nice cushy marketing job, which we all know she'll drop the minute Inigo gets her pregnant."

"And what's so wrong with that?" Jesper cried. "That's a nice life!"

"You're right, it is," Tara said. "I mean, I should know. I *had* that life, Mr Edwins." She stretched her arms out, inviting a closer look. "I had the best of everything, you know that. I found the parent-approved husband. I, too, was a good little soldier. But look where it's left me." Tara's voice broke and Posy wrapped her arms around her friend's shoulders.

"Tara, you know we feel so sorry about what happened with you and Ben." Jesper spoke slowly, as if Tara were hard of hearing.

"That's not the point," Tara sighed. "My point is, I did everything right. I was obedient. And my life is a mess right now." She pointed at Posy, her finger shaking. "Granted, she doesn't exactly follow the roadmap that you or… anyone, actually, lays out for her. But she does things her own way. You have every right not to pay for it, but you should respect it. Because God knows, if my family and my husband had respected me, perhaps I'd be in a better place instead of navigating Tinder as a divorced mother of three whilst my ex flaunts his latest bit of fluff in front of everyone." When Tara finished talking, she reeled against Posy, her chest heaving.

"Oh, Tar." Posy squeezed her trembling friend close.

Jesper didn't speak. He pivoted then trudged to the window where Posy's camera was. The line of his shoulders was less certain, his head lowered.

"Nothing about this wedding is traditional," Posy said, relieved that at least this was the truth. "And Tara's right. I don't want any of your money for it." She met her father's troubled eyes. "But your blessing would be nice."

Her father wheeled around and caught Ines's eye. His wife gave him a stern look in response.

Jesper's sigh was laboured. "You have it." He followed up with a tentative smile. "*If* you let me host the pre-wedding dinner."

"No." Posy shook her head. "Pops, this has to be a small affair. In case you hadn't realised, this is low budget and low fuss. I don't want you spending any money." Besides, Lucas would freak.

"Finger sandwiches and one or two bottles of champagne," Jesper insisted. He ambled over and reached for her hand. "Low-key, I promise. We'll only invite family and Lucas. His parents too, of course."

Even though she knew her father's ego was bound up in this offer, Posy recognised an olive branch when she saw one. "You mean it?"

"I do," Jesper said. "You're right. Tara too." Tara acknowledged this with a wide-eyed nod. "Just because you don't do things the same way as your siblings doesn't make you lesser." He clutched her hand to his chest. "You are definitely not lesser, my darling. I only give you a hard time because I love you and worry about you. But it seems I need to listen more. So if marrying Lucas is what you want, then by all means, proceed."

"You... approve?" Posy tightened her fingers in Jesper's warm grasp, his skin rough against hers.

Jesper tilted his head. "I hope to arrive at approval soon. Right now, I'm taking a moment in acceptance."

"How about giving her back those credit cards then?" Tara's laugh died prematurely as Jesper shot her a glare.

"No, that lesson still stands," he said quickly. He dropped Posy's hand and pulled her in for a gentle hug, angling himself so as not to crush the dress. "Posy has to learn how to finance her life responsibly."

"Yes Pops, I get it." Posy wished yet again that he would reinstate her allowance. Because then she could dispense with this whole scheme and distance herself from the insanity of it.

"Well, now it seems we have a party to plan!" Ines clapped her hands joyfully. "Posy, darling, you must let me help in any way I can."

Posy disengaged herself from her father's grasp. "It's mostly done," she said.

Ines tapped her chin. "Cake?"

"We're not having one."

"Bouquet?"

"Um, not bothering."

Ines gulped. "Music?"

"Oh yes!" Posy nodded. "We have a sick playlist on Lucas's phone."

"Right." Ines's smile became fixed. "Are you at least having guests?"

"Oh." Posy realised this hadn't been properly discussed. "We haven't actually discussed the guest list."

"Well then!" Ines was clearly relieved to have found a task she could master. "I insist you send me a list of people and allow me to print up the invites in my studio. I'll send them out for you too." Before Posy could protest, Ines lifted her hand. "I insist! I have a fabulous silk screen set-up that could make something elegant and simple. Free of charge, naturally."

"Are you sure?" Posy had an inescapable sense of things whirling beyond her control. The lie was out there now, amongst those she loved, and threatening to spread.

"Absolutely!" Ines tentatively reached for Posy's arm. "Don't worry. What could possibly go wrong?"

## Chapter Twenty-Nine

Lucas leaned against the side of his parents' house, breathing hard. He'd done a punishing but incredible run through the rolling countryside that surrounded the village and the combination of physical exertion with stunning views had been a balm for his jangled mind. As his lungs took in the fresh air of the Peaks, he'd wondered why he didn't spend more time here. The lush vistas and wide-open sky left him relaxed and motivated like nothing else.

His phone buzzed in his pocket, interrupting the *Business Focus* podcast he was listening to. Lucas concentrated on stretching out his hamstring, resolutely ignoring the call. He knew it would be Fred, pushing for an answer on the Lim Management offer. Despite the work Lucas had put in, despite the research he'd done and despite the overwhelming truth that life would be a lot easier if he just sold up, his gut told him to press pause. Lucas told himself it was purely the fact he was unhappy about giving up Align, but he couldn't deny that Posy was also part of the holdback. He couldn't shake the feeling that there *was* something more there. If he left the country, he might never have the chance to see what it might be. But then, Posy and her mindset was so hard to fathom, Lucas had to wonder if he was being a total idiot for even considering such a thing.

Gasping for a drink, he headed inside. The house was redolent with the smell of sage, warm butter and roasting meat. His stomach growled. But first, hydration. He filled a pint glass with water and downed it, gazing out over the garden through the kitchen window. His mother's vegetable patch was overflowing with leafy greenery; the low green bushes were laden with bean pods and strawberry canes boasting swollen red fruit. His mouth watered.

The back door opened and his mother entered, heaving a truckle loaded with earthy potatoes and numerous sprigs of herb cuttings. Lucas hurried to take her burden, offering a kiss on the cheek in return.

"Thanks love." Annie wrung her hands in relief. "Getting heavy, that old thing."

"No bother." Lucas rested the truckle on the table. "Need help sorting these?"

"And have you sweating all over my veg?" Annie swatted at him. "Get away with yourself and have a shower. I'll do it whilst I wait for the oven timer."

"Fair enough." He sniffed the air appreciatively. "Lunch smells grand." As he headed out of the kitchen, his phone rang again and with a huff of irritation, he answered it. "Fred, mate," he said. "You've got to give me time with this."

The voice that answered was not Fred. "What?"

"Posy." Lucas screeched to a halt in the middle of the living room. "Sorry, I didn't mean you, obviously. You can call whenever…" He was babbling. Lucas took a breath. "What's up?"

"Guest list," she said softly.

"What do you mean?" Lucas was baffled. They'd agreed to have Tara as a de facto maid of honour and Lucas's parents to keep the circle small. Of course, they had to have Hardstark and Paddington. Now Posy wanted more guests? As in… plural?

"Pops found out," she said.

"You told him?" Lucas couldn't believe it. Jesper had the clout to stop this whole scheme after all.

"He walked in on me trying on the wedding dress." Posy's voice hardened.

"Couldn't you have made something up?"

"Well, they also walked in on me whilst Tar was teasing me about marrying you," she said firmly. "Hard to cover that up with anything other than the truth." Before Lucas could start losing his mind, she cleared her throat. "Well, the version of the truth that we told Arundel, anyway."

"They think it's real." Lucas hung his head. "I'm sorry." At least his parents weren't having their hopes raised with the thought of an actual daughter-in-law or grandchildren.

"It's okay," Posy said, a steely thread running through her voice. "The actual truth would be… yeeuch. This is for the best. I've disappointed my father enough."

"Right." A lump formed in Lucas's chest. Of course, marrying someone like Lucas probably wasn't in Jesper Edwins's plans for his daughter. He thudded down on the arm of the sofa. "Fair enough."

If Posy registered the way Lucas's offence clipped his words, then she didn't mention it.

"Ines is knocking up some invites – her suggestion – and I couldn't really say no."

"And you need a guest list from me," Lucas said.

"Yes."

"Annie and Brian O'Rourke."

"Just your parents?" Posy sounded surprised.

"Yes, I've managed to keep a lid on this," he said. *Unlike you*, was his unspoken addition but judging by the audible exhale from Posy's end, she'd heard it.

"Actually, from my side, only Tara knows it's a fake wedding," she said. "Given your parents *and* business partner know, I'd say I'm actually winning in the secrecy department."

"I guess a small crowd would make it seem more legit," Lucas allowed. "So, what, just Tara and your parents?"

"And my siblings. And their kids. And Inigo, Angharad."

Lucas sighed. "That's not witnesses, Posy. That's a crowd."

"I know, I know."

"If something goes wrong…" Lucas could barely contain his dread. Paddington and Hardstark could make things very uncomfortable if they cottoned on. And if Jesper witnessed that, it wouldn't help.

"It won't."

The line fell quiet. But he could hear her there, breathing. "All right, I'm sorry," he said. "It's happened and we can't change it. What can we do?" The line remained silent and yet full, as if his yearning confusion was travelling down the airwaves to Posy. And as the hush continued, his question rang across it, changing meaning with every second. As it burgeoned, Lucas wished Posy would answer what he really wanted to know.

"Everything's going to be fine." She spoke with quiet confidence and Lucas wished he shared it.

"It is?"

"It is." Lucas could practically see Posy's trademark optimism bursting through her words. She went on, "Soon enough this will be over and done with and we'll have everything we want."

*Will we?* Lucas wanted to ask. He nodded, even though he knew she couldn't see it. He didn't know if he wanted to hear what Posy thought.

"Is there any news on Align?" Posy went on.

"Not yet." Lucas could afford to be honest. "Lim are pushing for an answer. So is Fred. I feel I'm just stuck in the middle."

"I'm sure there's a compromise to be reached," Posy said. "I often think the key to resolving stress is keeping things simple. Do what feels best for you."

If Lucas had heard Posy pontificating in such a way a few weeks ago, he'd have laughed out loud. What did she know about keeping things simple, or businesslike? But now her words had weight. "Perhaps you're right," he said. "Maybe there is another way to look at things."

"I usually find there is." She cleared her throat. "You can always talk to me if, you know, you think I can help. I hope you know that."

"Thanks." Silence stretched yet again. But it was comfortable. "Anyway," Lucas said. "I just got back from a run so I'd best shower."

"Right," Posy said. "I'll let you go. We still on for the celebrant on Monday?"

"Yep." Posy had managed to find a humanist celebrant who was available for the ceremony. His emails had been a little odd, so Lucas was a little trepidatious about meeting the guy. "If he turns out to be a serial killer, it's all on you."

After saying goodbye, Lucas hung up and stared at his phone for a full minute. There had been points in that call where it had felt like the pair of them were speaking in code. He wished he'd had the balls to just ask her what she thought he should do. As he turned to head to the shower, he was surprised to see Annie standing there. "You all right, Ma?"

"You're selling Align?" was her acid response. She'd been there for quite some time then.

"We've had an offer," Lucas said.

Annie nodded. She headed over to the mantelpiece over-hanging the ancient log burner that heated the house in winter. As she feigned inspecting the china shepherdesses crowding the shelf, she threw a question over her shoulder, "So what's holding you back?"

"Who says anything is?"

"Is it a fair offer?" Annie narrowed her eyes at a hairline crack at the base of a particularly busty version of Bo Peep.

"More than," Lucas said. "With the option to head up their offices in any financial centre in the world. The buyer is keen on sending me to Singapore or Tokyo."

Annie replaced the china figurine. "Wow."

"Yeah. The money and resulting salary would be more than generous," Lucas went on. "Fred could convalesce, and I could do anything I wanted."

"Except…?" Annie turned to face him.

"Except own the company I built from scratch."

"Which is struggling."

"Yes."

Annie nodded, as if he'd privately confirmed something

for her. "Well, I'm relieved."

Lucas studied her face in confusion. "What do you mean?"

"It's a solution, isn't it?" She walked over to him and cupped his cheek. "You don't have to participate in this ridiculous scheme with Posy Edwins. You can sell your company and achieve great things with the money – hasn't that always been your dream?"

"My dream was to build something," he corrected her gently. "Not hand my business over to the first corporate giant with a chequebook whilst it's still in its infancy."

"You could start a new company, a better one." Annie pressed. "Make new contacts. See the world."

Lucas stepped back from his mother. "You really don't want me to do this wedding thing with Posy, do you?"

"Of course not!" Annie declared. "But I understand why you agreed to it. You didn't have much choice. But now? Now, you have other options."

"It's not a straightforward choice, Ma," Lucas said. "I lose just as much as I gain."

Annie's lips thinned. "It's her, isn't it?"

"What's her?"

"Posy. She's stopping you from agreeing to the sale."

"Ma." Lucas could see his mother was getting agitated. He reached for her shoulders. "She's not stopping me from doing anything."

"Not in so many words. That was her on the phone, wasn't it?" Lucas nodded and she broke out of his grasp. "I knew it. That dopey smile of yours. You used to have the same one when you talked about Sally."

Lucas was surprised not to feel the usual spike of regret at the mention of his ex. "Sally and I—"

"I know, I know. You were too immersed in the business for her." Annie flapped impatiently. "What I mean is, despite all your chat about this wedding being business, I don't believe that anymore." She pointed at him. "Posy Edwins is clouding your judgement. I know that because the old Lucas would have seen this sale as a credible solution."

"No, he wouldn't!" Lucas snapped. "Selling was never in the plan; I'm not sure it's right for me."

"What and marrying your arch-nemesis is?"

"Yeah well, plans change!" Lucas said. "People change!"

"People like her don't!" Annie exploded. "Don't you get it? I worked in that school for most of my career. You think I don't know what she's like? What they're all like?"

"Ma…" He wanted to placate her, but the woman radiated fury.

"No, you listen. People like her chew people like us up and spit us out. They belittle, they demean…" Her eyes watered. "I saw what you went through at that school, the way those kids treated you. I thought I could handle you being amongst them again, I thought you would emerge unscathed, on top. But now?" She splayed her hands. "Now you're considering jeopardising your business because Posy Edwins is batting her lashes at you."

"Ma, you're acting like I'm some hormonal, naive teenager," Lucas said. "I'm capable of making rational business decisions even if someone is batting their lashes – and I'm not saying Posy is." Lucas didn't even know what Posy was doing. He didn't know what she wanted or what she didn't want and it maddened him beyond belief. "I promise you I will do what's right for me, okay? Do you trust me?"

Annie lifted tearful eyes to his. "I used to," she said. "But now I don't even recognise you."

## Chapter Thirty

"**D**amnit," Posy hissed. From her prone position in the back garden, she reached for the water mister, spraying the luscious rose in front of her one more time. Little droplets beaded on the velvety folds and with a grimace of determination, Posy raised the camera again. The warm summer sun beat down on the back of her neck, the smell of baked earth all around her, but Posy was lost in her art, mastering a heretofore unknown style of photography.

"That's a big lens!" Ines declared from behind her, causing Posy to slip and knock her elbow against the hardened ground.

"Yeah." Posy gave up. The moment was gone; the water droplets were vanishing too quickly in the heat for her to capture them. "It's a macro lens."

"Is that the one Jesper bought you last Christmas?"

"What do you want, Ines?" Posy stood and cricked her neck.

"I just wanted to let you know I emailed out the invites,"

307

Ines said. Her voice was as amiable as ever, but a wounding flashed in her eyes.

"Oh. Thanks." Posy smiled. Ines's invites had been simple yet elegant, black calligraphy against a white background with a floral illustration Ines had created herself. "Sorry you didn't get to use your special printing thing. I just thought emails would get out quicker. After all, we're less than two weeks away now."

"No, I understand." Ines was gracious. "I needed to brush up on my computer skills." She cast her eye across the sun-drenched garden to where Florence was sunbathing. "Your sister was very helpful."

"Florence?" Posy pulled a face. Florence famously liked to help herself and no one else.

"Yes. I had trouble exporting my files and she does it all the time at work," Ines went on. "I'd thank her too, if I were you."

"Fine," Posy grumbled. "But only because you asked." Under Ines's watchful gaze, Posy stomped across the lawn, her nose filling with the perfume from the many rose bushes that adorned the garden. When Celia died, the house as well as the funeral had been overloaded by roses. Their smell was as beautiful as it was heartbreaking.

Florence had commandeered one of the sun-loungers on the eastern side of the garden, sprawled across it in her vintage swimsuit, face shaded by a floppy hat and cat-eye sunglasses. On the patio table lay her wedding bible, multiple coloured Post-its flapping in the gentle breeze.

"Ines told me to thank you," Posy said.

Florence jolted awake with a snort. "What?"

Posy waited as her sister inelegantly scooted to an

upright position. "Ines said you helped her with the invites, so thank you for that."

"Well, when she told me you only wanted to invite people by email I felt I had to do something." Florence shuddered. "Honestly, Posy, it's like a car crash. I simply can't look away."

"Hey!" Although Florence was somewhat right. This wedding was careening down a path of its own and Posy was very unsure of where the brakes were. "It's all part of my grand life plan – you'll see."

"A *grand life plan*, is it?" Florence smirked. "Steady on with the romance there, I might swoon."

"That's rich," Posy said. "Considering how much you're making Pops pay for a joint of ham."

"*Iberico*," Florence corrected. "It's the meat of the moment."

"Meat of the…? You mean there's fashionable meat?" Posy had sudden visions of beef and venison joints waddling down catwalks surrounded by ravenous brides.

"Ahem." Florence lowered her glasses, narrowed eyes burning into Posy's. "If you ever managed to be serious about something, you'd know the importance of marrying properly. With integrity."

"Sorry, I didn't realise cured meats were the bedrock of a happy marriage," Posy wheezed. "Please, tell me more, oh wise wedding guru."

"Oh, for God's sake. I'll remember this when you and Lucas thrash out your divorce whilst Inigo and I remain blissfully happy." Florence replaced her glasses and eased back into her lounger.

"We won't be getting divorced, don't worry about that." That much was definitely true. Posy thought of Henry, wondering if he and Jacinta were still together. How his children were. Her mirth soon subsided and, astonishingly, Florence noticed.

"What's wrong?"

"Nothing," Posy replied quickly. But Florence stiffened at the wobble in Posy's voice.

"I was joking, you know." Her sister sat up straight. "And although I think you're crazy for marrying so quickly, I can see the appeal."

"Even though he's the help's kid?" Posy couldn't help but ask.

Florence removed her sunglasses, thoughtfully playing with the arms. "I feel bad I called him that," she said. "It's just… I remember when I was at school with you. He was called that even then and we all found it hilarious. But now? Inigo keeps ribbing me for being a snob and you know what? He's right."

"I didn't know Inigo had the balls to step up to you." Posy had newfound respect for her future brother-in-law.

"Occasionally I do permit him to have possession of them." Florence smirked.

"Ah, he's one of the good ones," Posy said. The sisters shared a look and Posy felt a warmth spread through her.

Posy heard her name being called from the house and saw Ines stick her head out of the French windows.

"Posy, Annie O'Rourke is here!" Ines yelled.

Florence and Posy exchanged another look, although this time it was of confusion. "Okay. Guess I'd better go and see what the mother-in-law wants."

Florence focused on something behind Posy. "Something not good by the looks of it."

Posy turned around to see Annie striding determinedly

across the lawn, eyebrows drawn, lips thin. Posy made her way towards the older woman.

"Hi, Mrs O'Rourke," Posy attempted a breezy greeting, but it was croaky. "How are you?"

"Do you have a minute?" Annie got straight to business.

"Absolutely." After offering her a drink, which Annie refused, Posy led her away from the house and a curious Florence to a more secluded patch of garden where the lavender was in fragrant bloom alongside the rosebushes. Birds sang joyfully, but their mood didn't spread to Posy. "We won't be overheard here. What can I do for you?"

"You can call this wedding off," Annie said brusquely.

Posy couldn't say she was surprised. "I see."

"I don't think you do," Annie replied.

"Of course I do," Posy said. "What mum wants their son to undergo a fake wedding?"

"Listen, the two of you lying to Arundel doesn't bother me as much as I initially thought it would," Annie said, much to Posy's surprise. "I understood the mutual benefit and if it's not a legal wedding then there's nothing stopping you both from moving on once the deal is done."

"So what's the issue?" Posy was rewarded with a look of disgust. Was it because Annie didn't like her? Didn't think Posy was good enough for her precious son? "Lucas knows what he's doing – he's fine."

Annie narrowed her eyes. "Let me tell you something about my boy. Lucas has always worked so hard. It's been that way since he was a child. If he failed at something, he took it badly. He's never been one to take risks." Annie lifted her chin. "But you have been the biggest risk of his life."

Posy suddenly felt small under the gaze of the older

woman. "I don't know what you mean." Although a voice inside her said otherwise.

"You've heard about this potential deal?" Annie said. "To sell his company."

"Yes," Posy said.

"Now, I know it might not have been in his original plan," Annie said. "But it's the most amazing opportunity for him. And it'd stop him going bankrupt!"

"I know that," Posy said, confused. "But he doesn't want to lose his company. He wants to be his own boss. There's a lot more he wants to do with Align."

"He's a bright lad – he could start again," Annie said. "With solid capital behind him from the sale."

"It's a hard decision for him." Posy didn't see the benefit of arguing the toss with Lucas's mother. It was his decision and his alone, after all. "But it's his to make."

"A decision made harder by you." Annie folded her arms, planting sensibly clad feet into the ground.

"I'm not doing *anything*!" Posy couldn't contain her disbelief. "Lucas has his priorities in order, I'm sure of that."

"Does he?" Annie's words reeked of acid. "I suspect that if you weren't on the scene, he'd make the tough but practical choice; he'd sell up and work abroad. Can you imagine a man of his talent in Singapore or New York? But he doesn't want to leave here."

"You think?" A kernel of quiet hope lodged within Posy.

"I do think. I think he's tempted to stay put and slog it out in the hope that you'll be on the scene."

"Again"—Posy tried not to examine the surge of joy Annie's suspicions raised—"the decision to sell is all on Lucas, not me."

"I'm his mother," Annie asserted. "And I know what's right. I'm telling you, clinging on to Align is detrimental. If you care even the tiniest amount about him, you'll let him sell up and achieve his dreams. Please, cancel this wedding for his sake. Stop thinking of only yourself, if that's even possible."

"If Lucas's dreams change, that's up to him." Posy felt her cheeks burn. It wasn't the first time she'd been accused of being selfish but the fact that it was Lucas's mum levelling the charge at her stung beyond words. "I can't force him to do anything, just as he can't force me to give up my photography career."

"Ah yes." Annie's smile was cold. "How could I not mention your soaring ambition? Flying to Hawaii to take your rightful place amongst the world's top photographers, am I right?"

Posy suddenly felt very foolish. "That's not how I'd——"

"Couldn't go and get a job like everyone else, could you?" Annie said. "An internship, a Saturday job? No, you have to go in at the top, don't you? Because why should you work your way up? Why should you wait?"

"That's not fair," Posy said. "I'm talented. I have every right to be there."

"I'm not questioning your talent," Annie barked. "I'm questioning why my brilliant son has to go to university and accrue debt, why he had to work his way up from the bottom and sacrifice his free time with loved ones in order to achieve his goals yet all *you* need to do is fly to Hawaii and be showered with praise. And the funny thing is, you can't even pay for *that* yourself, can you? No, someone else has to pay for it." Her face grew dark, lines of worry knitting tightly around her eyes. "So that's just dandy, isn't it? What concern is Lucas's reputation to you? His goals? So long as Posy Edwins gets what she wants."

"That's not…" Posy wanted to hide from Annie's accusatory glare. It held up the most painful mirror to her choices. Jesper had accused her of not working for what she wanted in life and Posy had believed her wedding plan was a way of proving him wrong. But Annie, with all her maternal defences, had ripped that notion away. "I didn't think I had a choice," she whispered.

"Well, you do," Annie snarled. Then, as if seeing Posy's distress, she cooled. "Anyway, I've said my piece. Do as you please. Those of us that care about Lucas will be here to pick up the pieces."

"If Lucas wants to stop this wedding, he can," Posy said, her voice trembling as she tried to claw back some high ground. "He's under no illusions about me. In fact, I know full well Align is his priority."

"I see it differently." Annie softened. "I know my boy. I see the hesitation when it comes to you. All I'm saying is, if you care at all for him, make it easy for him. Let him go." Her lip wobbled, but Annie reined in the emotion and lifted her head. "I'll see myself out." And with that, Lucas's mother strode off across the garden, head held fearlessly high.

## Chapter Thirty-One

"Is this the right place?" Lucas glanced at Posy, who in turn checked her phone.

"Yes," she replied. "10 Loughton Road."

They peered up at the neat end-terrace house located on a quiet street in Milton Ash, a scenic village not far from Little Thicket. The front garden was a small emerald square, smooth pebbles precisely lining a narrow tarmac path to a glistening white front door.

"This does not look like the home of Edgar Truthteller, humanist celebrant," Lucas remarked.

"Well, what were you expecting in the Leeds suburbs?" Posy rolled her eyes as she unbuckled her seatbelt. "A yurt? An ashram perhaps. You never know, he might have a nudist temple in his back garden."

"Yeah, all right." He should have known better than to expect a straight answer. Posy had been off with him the entire drive, which was frustrating. He really wanted to talk about the sale of Align with someone who wasn't Fred and he'd be lying if he wasn't dying to know what Posy made of it all. Lim had interpreted Lucas's reticence to respond as hardball tactics and had upped their offer, guaranteeing Lucas a role managing in their Singapore outfit with a considerable six-figure salary. Fred could get a similar deal too, if his health could stand it. Trouble was, the deadline still fell on Lucas and Posy's wedding day so time was running out. But judging by Posy's acerbic manner, he wouldn't get much sense from her.

"No really." She slammed the car door. "If Edgar doesn't answer the door in flowing robes, then there's something wrong with him."

"Humanism is a philosophy not a cult," Lucas said. "It's about prioritising concern for the wellbeing of your fellow man, looking to science and not a supernatural source."

"Did you get that from a spreadsheet?" Posy asked.

"No, a book," he shot back as they walked down Edgar's path. "You know, a text-based source of information? If you're not familiar with them—"

"Then it's because I'm never in a library? Never worked a day in my life?" Posy bashed her fist against the glass pane of the door.

Lucas was bewildered. He'd levelled much worse banter at her before and she'd batted it away without a blink. "It was a joke."

"Not a funny one," she said.

"What's with you today?" he asked. "You barely talk to me and when you do, you're all… spiky." A sudden thought gripped him. "Have you changed your mind?"

"Me?" Posy turned to look at him properly, eyes wide with disbelief. "Nothing's changed for me," she said. "Ha-has it changed for you?"

Lucas stared back at her. Everything had changed. How could she not feel that? "I—"

The door cranked open. The man standing there was short and almost entirely spherical with a frosting of strawberry-blond hair atop a rosy-cheeked face. He was dressed in a particularly un-flowing ensemble of khaki trousers and a sensible cashmere sweater. Neatly manicured fingers were unencumbered of jewellery. Lucas lifted his eyebrows at Posy as if to say 'see?' but she was already shaking the man's hand.

"Edgar?" she said.

"That's me," Edgar declared. "And you must be my twelve o'clock."

"I'm Posy and this is Lucas." Posy thumbed over her shoulder.

"Aren't we expecting a Ms Hardstark as well?" Edgar asked.

"Ah, yes," Lucas remembered. "She's running a little late." In reality, they had told Hardstark a time fifteen minutes later than booked. Lucas had had a feeling the conversation with the celebrant might get a little awkward.

"Come in, come in." Edgar beckoned them into a dimly lit hallway of olive walls and dingy carpet, redolent of vinegar and something else, something more cloying and sharper.

Lucas felt his throat tickle. "Do you have cats?"

"Yes," Edgar said. "Fourteen."

Lucas sneezed. Why on earth would someone want fourteen cats?

"They just bring so much elegance to the world, don't you think?" Edgar preened just as a particularly fluffy

317

Persian slunk its way around his ankles. "Anyway, follow me!"

"Abort, abort," Lucas wheezed to Posy as Edgar turned on his heel.

"Oh, definitely nothing cultish about this," Posy muttered. "Edgar and his army of cats, gathering forces to enslave the world."

"What was that, dear?" Edgar blinked up at her, pausing outside a heavily lacquered door.

"Your cats must be your whole world!" Posy improvised.

"Indeed." Edgar beamed and pushed open the door. His office was pristine, airy and bright. A large wooden table served as his command centre with a gleaming Mac computer and, mercifully for Lucas, the air was free of the scent of cats. Edgar showed Lucas and Posy to a break-out area consisting of two plump sofas and a coffee table laden with various candles and crystals. It was now Posy's turn to bestow Lucas with a triumphant expression of 'see?' but he ignored her and took a seat on one of the sofas.

"Anyway, thank you for stopping by," Edgar said after fussing with a jug of water and glasses. "So important to meet my couples before I do a ceremony." He plopped onto the opposite sofa with a fat notebook and pen. "Tell me everything about yourselves and your love."

"Our… love?" Posy looked as if she might choke.

"Yes." Edgar's flinty eyes sparkled kindly. "A humanist ceremony is very much built around the individuals and the promise they are making to each other. I guarantee, it will be the most enriching and moving experience. So"—the pen hovered expectantly—"tell me your story."

"Where do we even begin?" Posy threw a glance.

"The beginning is always best," Edgar said. "The more

detail the better. *Drench* me in your journey." And he gave a delighted little shudder.

Posy made a noise somewhere between a laugh and a gasp of fear and leaned in close to Lucas's ear. "I guess we know why he's available last minute." Her lip brushed his ear lobe. A spike of desire made its way through Lucas's body; his eyes widened and his breath quickened.

None of this was missed by Edgar and he leaned forward, pen waving like a wand. "You are a fine-looking couple," he said. "Tell me, how did you meet?"

"School," Lucas said as calmly as he could. "We were head boy and head girl."

"Oh." Edgar clasped hands to his chest, blue ink smearing across the beige cashmere. "I can see it now." He flapped a hand. "Go on."

"We didn't always see eye to eye." Lucas was unable to take his eyes off the trail of ink now lacing across the man's cheek. "In fact, we were not friends. Total opposites, to tell you the truth, and always butting heads. We had, shall we say, differing approaches to academia."

"What changed?" Edgar asked.

"There was a school reunion," Posy said.

"Hold on!" Edgar wrote slowly, the tip of his tongue protruding between moistened lips. After what seemed like an interminable amount of time, he nodded for her to proceed.

"And we just, I don't know, connected," Posy said. Swallowing visibly, she threaded her fingers through Lucas's, sitting up higher as if on display. "I saw him and it was like... It was like standing in the centre of a hurricane. All around me was the chaos of my life – my lack of a job, lack of, well, anything really. And then, all of a sudden, there he was." Her hazel eyes met Lucas's. "Solid, as if he'd been there all along."

For Lucas, it was as if he was back in that hurricane again, Posy in her pink dress emerging out of the dark. Lucas didn't dare take a breath. He feared if he did, Posy would snap out of whatever this state was, that she'd close the door to wherever these words were coming from.

Edgar, however, had no such reticence. "That's absolute gold!" He began scribbling madly.

Posy side-eyed Edgar and the moment was lost. "Glad you think so," she said. "And then it all went pretty quickly from there. We couldn't spend another day apart."

"Ah ha, ah ha." Edgar chewed on the pen and Lucas watched in horrified fascination as more ink dotted across his lips. "And Lucas, how did it feel to fall in love with Posy?"

"I think hurricane is an apt metaphor," Lucas replied wryly.

"Because it was fast and dramatic?" Edgar said. "Life-altering?"

*Destructive and all-consuming*, was Lucas's first thought. But he smiled. "Exactly that."

Edgar made more notes, pausing only to rub his eye. Blue ink smeared around his eye like a bruise. "Lovely, lovely, I—" The sound of three very precise, loud knocks echoed through the house. Edgar brightened. "That must be the elusive Ms Hardstark," he said, standing up and scurrying out of the room.

"Seriously, what's wrong?" Lucas asked the moment they were alone.

"Nothing's wrong." But Posy withdrew her hand from his, her eyes dull. "I'm just aware that the big day is getting closer and when it's all over, we have to move on with our lives. I'll have to concentrate on getting my career off the ground and you?" She gestured at him. "You'll be in Singapore or New York or... wherever."

"Posy, nothing is decided." Was this why Posy was being off with him? She thought Lucas would just sleep with her and head off into his new life without looking back? She had to have learned by now that he had some integrity. "We both know what's at stake." Lucas reached for her hand again, but to his chagrin, she scooted away.

"I do know," she said softly. "And I want you to be happy with whatever you choose."

"You do?" Lucas was confused.

"Yes." She gestured vaguely. "I don't want to stand in the way of your decision." She fixed him with a determined smile. "Friends make sure friends live their best life, so you make sure you do just that."

"Got it." It was clear where Posy stood on the whole matter of Lucas. He adjusted his sleeves and lifted his chin. "We're nearly at the end of this. Right?"

Posy's lips thinned. "Right."

With a thud of finality, the office door swung open and there was Hardstark, resplendent in her usual tweed armour. However, this time, perhaps in a nod to the occasion, a single pink rosebud was pinned to the lapel of her jacket.

"Hello," Hardstark said coolly.

"Now that your, er, associate, is finally here, we can focus on the structure of the ceremony," Edgar said, escorting Hardstark to a sofa. As she took the seat opposite Posy and Lucas, Edgar pulled over his desk chair. "This wonderful couple were just telling me their love story," he explained to Hardstark. "Truly something."

"That it is," Hardstark growled. "I take it you understand my role in this?"

"Yes, you're from the school they met at, right?" Edgar said.

"That's correct," Hardstark replied. "And as the school is paying for this wedding, everything must pass muster."

"I understand," Edgar said solemnly.

Hardstark pursed her lips. "You have pen all over your face."

Edgar scratched a spot by his cheek and laughed when it came away blue. "It'll be all right on the night. Now, I tend to start the ceremony by describing why we're all gathered in the venue, which is…" He squinted at his notes. "Ah, Little Thicket Village Hall! That's the one by the green, oh, ah." Edgar's face fell as he clearly worked out where they were getting married. "A lovely village," he said diplomatically. "Why did you choose that venue?"

"It was cheap." Lucas was in no mood to lyricise about their choices, even with Hardstark there.

"Right." Edgar frowned minutely, then scribbled a note. "Well, we can make a point about this being all about the love you share. Then I often talk a little about the relationship itself, how it came to be." He grinned at them. "We know all about that, of course. Then we do vows, which you can write yourself or I can supply some boilerplate ones."

"Boilerplates are fine," Lucas said brusquely. He was aware that Posy was staring at him, so he grinned innocently. "Let's keep it simple, hey?"

"My fiancé makes a good point!" Posy's laugh was forced.

"Very well." Edgar scribbled some more. "If you change your mind you can just email me your personal vows. Keep it clean," he tittered. However, his quip was met with three very flat reactions, so he got back to business. "Then you exchange the rings – you *do* have rings?"

"We do," Lucas said. Well, Posy was going to use the Cartier rock and Lucas was using a napkin ring he'd found in his ma's everything drawer. It was too big to stay on his finger but it would do for the ceremony.

"And with those rings we seal the marriage——" Edgar spun in his chair to face Hardstark who had very suddenly and loudly cleared her throat. "Yes, Ms Hardstark?"

"Is there no impediment line?" she asked.

"Impediment?" Lucas repeated.

"Yes." Hardstark shuffled in her seat and clutched her handbag closer. "Should one need to object to the ceremony."

"Ah, I see what you mean." Edgar swivelled in his seat to explain to Lucas and Posy. "It's a line used in religious and civil marriages – that is, legally binding ones – as a line of protection against anything that may invalidate the marriage in addition to the banns. But I don't think we need that here, do we?"

"Nope, so let's not include it," Posy said hurriedly.

"Although, within reason, we can add whatever you want to a ceremony," Edgar said. "So if you both decide to have such a thing, you absolutely can."

"I think you should have it," Hardstark said, causing Edgar to swivel back around.

"We don't need it." Posy bared her teeth.

Edgar turned back to Posy. "Are you sure? It's no trouble to add the line in before we do the ring exchange."

"I think it's very important," Hardstark insisted.

Looking a little green, Edgar rotated back towards her.

"You seem to feel quite strongly about this impediment line. May I ask why?"

"Nothing about this wedding is traditional." Hardstark eyeballed Edgar's ink-smeared face with disdain. "As you may have noticed. I just feel like this would be a nice nod to tradition, so to speak."

"Well?" Edgar refrained from spinning around to look at Posy and Lucas, he merely turned his head.

"If it's important to Arundel, it's important to us," Lucas said with a shrug. "What do we care? Have it in."

"But I can tell you, nothing is stopping this wedding," Posy added defiantly, once more taking Lucas's hand and giving it a gentle squeeze.

"Nothing at all," Lucas agreed, his head full of the scent of vanilla.

## Chapter Thirty-Two

I t was the night before the wedding. Posy perused the photos spread across her desk. She'd rapidly become unhappy with what she had to present at the festival. Images that had once been her pride and joy now seemed flat and joyless. The timid deer she'd snapped creeping around the copse at dawn? Generic. The time-lapse of the stars in Devon? Blah. Nothing was inspiring her anymore. Since the meeting with Edgar, she'd barely eaten, and hardly slept. Although Posy knew she'd done the admirable thing ensuring Lucas made his career decisions for the right reasons, something felt fundamentally unstable.

She was about to shove her phone in her bedside table drawer when she noticed the time: almost six! The pre-wedding dinner was in less than an hour and Posy was still in her sweatpants and no make-up! As she stood and stretched, her phone vibrated and she saw a message from Lucas.

*Good luck tonight. We're almost there!*

Her fingers hovered over the keypad. In terms of time, yes, they had just under twenty-four hours to go. But the 'there' he referred to, the destination? That might just be changing. Trouble was, Posy had no idea what it was changing to. As she dithered over what to say, she had a mental image of Lucas waiting for her response, potentially hinging his future on what she had to say. It wasn't right. With a sigh, she shoved the phone into her bedside drawer.

Once showered, she chose one of her favourite dresses, purchased a couple of years ago from a London boutique but still a classic – midi-length, white, and with a tiny star-pattern print, it had a deep V-neck and balloon sleeves. It was flattering but simple and she always felt aspirational when she wore it. She also thought Lucas would approve; then she mentally kicked herself. That kind of thinking was not helpful! Slipping into soft ballet pumps and leaving her face make-up free, she headed downstairs to see how the decorating was coming along.

Jesper had promised to keep it simple and low-key – family only – but as Posy reached the bottom of the steps, her jaw dropped. Her harried-looking sister was pushing a floral arch into place over the front door, whilst Eamon sullenly arranged gold-confetti-filled balloons along the hallway leading to the dining room. Her heart pounding, Posy followed the decorations to the dining room, where the table groaned with all manner of buffet treats. Although Posy recognised Ines's personal touches amongst the food, it was clear private caterers had been involved. Indeed, three waiters in bowties buzzed around a bar that had been knocked up in the corner of the room where Posy could see champagne and a selection of wines and beers. Sebastien was tacking up a large *Congratulations* banner along one wall, whilst his wife tried to get their son to chew on a cucumber stick and stay out of trouble.

"Ah, you came down early!" Jesper cried as he entered the room, dapper in his favourite suit.

"To see if you needed help getting things together," Posy replied. "Pops… this is too much. I expected a few bottles of wine and some breadsticks!"

"You don't need to worry about helping." Florence stomped past, brushing her hands. "We already did it all."

"Um thanks?" Posy said. "And thanks for coming, I guess."

"Classic Hurricane, isn't it?" Florence snorted. "As if I'd miss it."

"Florence…" Jesper growled.

"Sorry, couldn't resist," Florence sighed.

"Yeah Dad, it's pretty funny when you think about it," Seb called over. "She's essentially marrying the help!"

Posy felt her cheeks flame and she waited for her father to set Seb straight. But he didn't. In fact, he was staring, mortified, at something behind her back.

"Hi everyone." From behind Posy a familiar voice piped up and her heart plummeted. There was Lucas, his parents standing on either side of him. Annie was chic in a pale-blue skirt and blouse, whilst his dad shifted uncomfortably in a suit that was too tight around the shoulders. Annie moved first, her eyes narrowed at Seb.

"What did you just say about my son?" Annie scowled.

"Sorry?" Seb ambled over, stretching out his hand. "I don't think we've met."

"I'm the help's mother," Annie snarled.

Seb stalled, his hand hovering. "Oh, er, that was just a joke. I don't actually think—"

327

"A joke? Is that all people like us are?" Annie interrupted and shot a knowing glance at her son.

Brian reached for his wife's arm, concern radiating from his face. "Steady, love."

"No, I won't be steady," she snarled. "This is exactly what I was afraid of."

Lucas let out a long breath and stared at his feet. Posy wished he would turn back to her, so he would see she did not share the sentiments of the words her brother had thoughtlessly spewed. But Lucas wouldn't meet her eye, his hunched pose reminding Posy so much of the head boy she'd once known.

"Hello, Mrs O' Rourke?" Jesper advanced, his hand outstretched. "I can assure you my son doesn't mean these things. I'm Jesper, Posy's father. It's a pleasure to meet you." He shook Annie and Brian's hands. "I apologise for my son."

"It was just a joke!" Seb said feebly.

"A really bad one," Posy snapped, moving to stand by Lucas, who seemed startled by this. "I expected this shit from Flo, but from you?"

"Thanks!" Florence yelped.

"I didn't mean it," Seb said. "Really." He walked right up to Lucas and extended his hand. "I was being an arse. Genuinely. Can you forgive me?"

"Of course I can." Lucas shook Seb's hand.

"Don't feel like you're obliged to." Posy took Lucas's arm.

Lucas gazed back down at her. "Posy, one thing I've learned recently is that holding onto old beliefs serves no one."

Posy's stomach swooped under the power of his attention. She had never fully appreciated how bewitchingly dark his eyes were, or how long his lashes were. Yet again she was assailed by the memory of Lucas's lips on hers and the ease with which he'd hoisted her up onto the kitchen counter. Aware they were just staring at each other with everyone watching, Posy cleared her throat. "Okay then."

"Anyway." Annie adjusted the front of her blouse primly. "I'm Annie and this is my husband, Brian."

"Wonderful to meet you," Jesper said with obvious relief. "Now, I think we all deserve a drink. Brian, are you a whisky man?"

"I can be tempted," Lucas's father said with a chuckle.

"Allow me," Seb begged, pointing the way to the bar.

As Jesper and Seb led the O'Rourkes to get drinks, Posy turned to Lucas. She found herself throwing her arms around him. He was warm and solid to her touch. "I'm sorry about Seb," she whispered. Lucas seemed a little bewildered by the contact, patting her awkwardly on her back.

"It's okay," he assured her. "I should be used to that sort of thing by now."

Appalled, Posy pulled back. "You should never get used to being treated like that. *Never*."

"Don't worry about it," Lucas said.

The softness in his smile was almost too much to bear. Posy swallowed, reminding herself to keep the conversation on track. "I don't want anything upsetting your mum; she could let the secret out."

"Don't worry about Ma." Lucas's smile faded. "She knows what's at stake. Who else is coming?"

"This is about it," Posy said. "Oh, and Tara, my best

friend." She saw Lucas flinch. "Don't worry, she's nothing like the Arundel lot." She grinned. "Great suit, by the way."

Lucas thanked her awkwardly, clearly pleased by the compliment. It was an easy one to give, Posy thought, as she led him towards the buffet table. His suit was dark green and cut perfectly to fit his lean body. He picked up a plate and she admired the capable strength of his hands against the delicate china. Why, oh why, was she swooning over the man's *hands?*

"This is an amazing spread," Lucas remarked, heaping tiny brioches onto his plate. "You made it sound like Jesper was just going to pour a packet of Doritos into a bowl."

"He assured me it would be low-key," Posy mumbled, nibbling on a cheese muffin and trying not to spray crumbs over his lapels. As a tuxedo-clad waiter offered Lucas a choice of Pol Roger or Bollinger, all she could do was shrug. "This is his version of that."

"You have parsley in your teeth," Lucas said.

"Oh God." Posy was suddenly conscious of the fact she hadn't finished getting ready – her hair was still in a sloppy top-knot and her face bare of make-up. She probably looked as tired as she felt.

"And you have a bit of cheese there, hang on." All of a sudden, Lucas's thumb was grazing the skin beside her mouth. Yet again, Posy flashed back to the night they'd made love, when his hands had done far more wicked things than remove food from her face. She locked eyes with Lucas and her heart began to pound when she saw the exact same dazed lust reflected back at her. What would stop them from sneaking upstairs? There couldn't be any harm in round two… but then Posy became aware that the room had gone quiet, apart from Jesper's booming voice.

"Look at them, so in love they can't even hear my speech!" Jesper declared.

Blinking as if emerging from darkness, Posy turned to see her family and Lucas's parents all staring back at them. "Um, hi."

Ines hurried up, stunning in a cobalt velvet gown. She handed Posy a flute of champagne. "Speech time!"

Aware of Annie's accusing gaze, Posy stepped forward. "Oh, no, really, there's—" But her protests were dismissed. Jesper was centre stage and in his element.

"Welcome everyone!" Jesper called and the room hushed. "I have to say, I always thought I'd be doing the speech at Florence's wedding before Posy's!" From her position in the doorway, Florence muttered inaudibly, causing a reddening Inigo to wrap an affectionate arm around her shoulders. "But Posy has never been one to follow the rules. Or guidelines. She turns up two fingers to most suggestions, if I'm being honest, and whilst charming it can be utterly frustrating. Our little Hurricane."

Posy took a sip of fizz to hide her burning cheeks. Why was her pops making her sound like a naughty child at her own wedding party?

"Listen," Jesper was relishing his moment, "I can't deny I was a little shocked when Posy told me she was getting married. Particularly"—and he bared his teeth—"because Lucas didn't ask for my permission." The assorted guests performed a gasp of outrage and he waved it away. "Just joshing with you. It may be the done thing, but these crazy kids weren't to know."

Lucas slipped his hand into Posy's.

"Now, I know their marriage has been arranged on the quick and cheap, and it isn't what any of us here expected, but I am genuinely proud." Jesper's eyes shone. "Lucas is terrific. Annie, Brian?" He searched out Lucas's parents. "You should be proud too. I am thrilled our families are joining like this. To Posy and Lucas!" He charged his glass and everyone chimed in, raising their glasses high. Everyone that is, apart from Annie, who glowered at Posy across the rim of her still-full flute. Posy shuddered, glad of Lucas's hand which was warm in hers.

"He's quite the orator," Lucas murmured with a quirk of his lips.

"My father is the master of covert shade," Posy said. Lucas's hand tightened in hers.

Jesper was now advancing on them, glass held high. "Lucas," he declared, "the man of the moment. Hope that speech was okay."

Lucas paused. "I think it was more than adequate," he said eventually. Posy hid her smirk in her drink. "And I'm sorry, Jesper," Lucas continued. "I didn't really think asking permission was a thing people did anymore. But I'm pleased you're so… accepting."

"Don't apologise! You're going to learn that when it comes to Posy, you have to make allowances." Jesper swallowed champagne with a hiccup.

"Allowances?" Lucas furrowed his brow. "How so?"

Jesper gestured at Posy. "We used to call her Hur—"

"Hurricane, I know," Lucas said.

"Ah, so you've heard." Jesper laughed. "Simply witness the chaos."

"Hurricanes are forces of nature," Lucas said. "Isn't it best to stand back and let them get on with what they do best?"

Posy glanced sharply at Lucas. What was he doing? No

one questioned Jesper Edwins, least of all about his parenting. Certainly not people hoping to gain his business.

Jesper regarded Lucas curiously. "You make a fine point," he said. "But in an ideal world we'd avoid such destruction, no?"

"I've learned that our world is far from ideal," Lucas replied. "What's that saying? Oh yes, 'when the world zigs, zag.' Seems to me that Posy always zags."

"When the world zigs…" Jesper was impressed. "I've never heard that before! Mind you, from tomorrow, any zagging becomes your problem."

"Is that what I am, Pops?" Posy was sick of being discussed as if she wasn't even there. "Am I a problem?" Her voice cracked. "Your problem?"

"You know I don't think that." Jesper frowned. "All I meant was… it was just a joke!"

"Yeah, I get it, I'm a joke. My photography, my love life." Posy saw Tara entering the room and she thought she might collapse with the relief. "So why don't the two men in my life sort it all out for me whilst I drink with my friend?" And ignoring the pleading expression on Lucas's face, Posy pushed past them and made her way over to Tara, who was dressed in a chic ruby catsuit, a gift bag dangling from her hand.

"Darling!" Tara threw her arms around Posy. "I'm so happy for you—"

"It's okay," Posy mumbled into Tara's capacious bosom. "You don't have to over-egg it. Hardstark isn't here."

"Thank fuck." Tara sighed, sagging into Posy's hug. "Kids have run me ragged all day. I honestly just want a gin and—" Her eyes bugged. "Is that the groom-to-be?" Her eyes drifted up and down Lucas. "You totally undersold him."

"Don't get too enamoured." Posy swiped a bottle of champagne from a passing waiter's tray. "He and Pops are just organising my life, deciding they know everything about me. I need air." She dragged Tara outside to the loungers, where the evening was heavy with the scent of roses. Posy braced herself against her lounger, viciously ripped off the foil and began tackling the cork.

Tara leaned blissfully back on the other lounger. "Oh, before I forget…" She withdrew a large box from the bag in her hands.

Posy paused mid-unscrew. "What's that?"

"Open it," Tara urged.

"You handle this." As Tara got to work on the cork, Posy opened the box. She gasped. Nestled in soft velvet was a gossamer-thin rose-gold chain with luminous pearls threaded through it. It looked like a necklace but with multiple strands. "What is it?"

"It's the head-dress I wanted to wear for my wedding," Tara said, lowering the bottle. "But Loretta didn't want me to. She said it didn't match the style of her son's big day."

"What's wrong with the style?" Posy could barely contain her surprise. "It's so elegant."

"It was my grandmother's." Tara gently lifted it from the box. "She passed away a few weeks before I got married, you remember. She wanted me to wear it, I wanted to wear it, but when it came to the actual wedding, I…" She shrugged and the garden lights glittered off the jewels. "I didn't stand up for myself and so it stayed in the box. I want you to wear it. If you like it, that is."

"Oh Tar. It's simply gorgeous." Posy let the ethereal

piece slide along her skin. "I'm sorry about Loretta; that's frightful of her. But you know what this wedding is, it's a shame to wear something so meaningful to something so, well, not."

"This wedding may be fake but *you* aren't." Tara placed a hand on Posy's knee. "You're going for what you want in a way I never did. That's, like, the realest thing ever. Besides, this can be your something borrowed."

Posy's eyes misted as she laid the headpiece reverently back into the box. "What did I do to deserve a pal like you?"

"Honestly, our mums lived on the same street and ran the PTA together; you didn't have a choice." Tara popped the cork with a cackle. "Let's drink!" She raised the bottle high. "To being real!"

"To being real!" Posy cheered.

"Posy?" Lucas peered through the garden doors. "You here?"

"Hey." Posy accepted the bottle from Tara and took a gulp. "You finished discussing my personality failings with my father?"

"You know that's not what was happening," he said with a soft smile. "Anyway, Ines wants us to come in and take some photos." Faint lines knit in his forehead.

"You okay?" Posy passed the champagne back to Tara and hurried over to Lucas.

"Everything's fine, really." He tucked an errant strand of Posy's hair behind her ear and gave her another smile, but this was strange, wistful. The warmth of his touch made her heart pound.

"Are you sure?"

"They're so happy we're getting married," he said. "And it's all a lie." His eyes blazed with an emotion Posy couldn't identify. Was it hope? Anger? Despair? Lucas rocked on his heels. "Do you think we need to talk?"

"Where would we even begin?" Posy quipped, but she could tell Lucas was serious. Her feelings for him and this entire scheme were one fraught mess as it was, and Annie's scolding had thrown a righteous grenade into the mix. "No, you're right, I think we should—"

Lucas's phone beeped and he pulled it out of his pocket. Checking the screen, his expression morphed from surprise to concern to something utterly unreadable.

"What is it?" Posy caught a glance at who was calling. The screen said *Sally*. "Oh."

Lucas hastily declined the call, shoving his phone back in his pocket. "Timing," he said awkwardly. "I can call her back later."

"Right." Posy withdrew, her mind racing. Was this why Lucas wanted to chat to her? Was Sally back in his life? "I mean, you can speak to her if you want. It might be important."

"It might," he agreed. "But probably a bad idea to talk to another woman at our engagement party."

"Yes, talk about giving the game away!" Posy said with forced cheer. Lucas eyed her strangely, but Posy was in no mood to pick up the strands of conversation from before Sally had called.

"Posy, Lucas!" Florence bellowed from inside the house. "Come on!"

Posy nudged Lucas. "Go on, you head in. I'll be right behind you."

Lucas gave her one last glance and walked back into the house. Posy watched him leave, her insides prickling. What had he wanted to talk about? And why was Sally calling?

Not for the first time, she wondered how her simple plan had become so convoluted in such a short space of time.

"I take it back," Tara intoned from behind Posy.

"What?" Posy couldn't tear her eyes away from the door Lucas had walked through.

"This wedding isn't *that* fake." Tara hiccupped.

"It is!" Posy hurried back to her friend and snatched the champagne.

"You've slept with him," Tara said. "And you look at each other like a pair of lovesick puppies. Are you seriously telling me you aren't interested in him?"

"Even if I were, he's got plans. Plans that don't involve me." Champagne bubbles tickled Posy's tongue. "And what kind of person would I be if I held him back from them?"

"Did you ever think he might *want* to be held back by you?" Tara challenged. "Because the way he looked at you just now, I reckon you'd only have to say the word and he'd be with you."

Posy slumped onto the lounger. "That's just it, in a nutshell. He's worked his whole life, Tar. He's on the cusp of greatness and I won't be the one to take him away from it."

Tara eyeballed her. "You really like him, don't you?"

"What makes you say that?"

"Because the old Posy would have dived straight in, sod the consequences." Tara poked Posy's arm. "But not this time."

"So what if I do like him?" Posy felt so helpless in the face of her feelings. "He has to succeed with his business, and I won't stand in the way. He's gone through so much for it."

Tara shrugged. "I think you should tell him how you feel. At least let him have all the facts."

Posy thought back to the discussion she'd had with Annie, the woman's defiant love for her son and his future. "I don't know, Tar. Maybe he's better off without me in his life."

Tara snorted. "What rot! If you like this guy then by all means, do what you can to help him achieve his dreams. But don't miss out on an opportunity for real happiness."

"Yeah, yeah." Posy was saved by yet another yell from Florence. "Come on, let's get inside." As Tar heaved herself off the lounger, Posy gingerly picked up the hatbox, looking at the headpiece nestled inside. Her heart swelled. It truly was the most beautiful accessory Posy had ever seen. A symbol of self, Tara had proclaimed it, and as Posy gazed upon the heirloom, she knew with sudden clarity that she couldn't wear it as part of a lie, no matter what Tara said.

"Posy?" Tara stood by the French doors. "What are you waiting for?"

Posy looked back at her friend with determination blazing in her heart. "I'm not sure," she said truthfully. "But it's time to make some changes."

# Chapter Thirty-Three

Mrs Paddington leaned back in her chair and massaged her temples. It was Friday night and classes had long since finished, but there was still much work to be done. She glanced down at the behavioural reports waiting on her desk; Paddington liked to be abreast of all the troublemakers at her school and private schools bred troublemakers with great success. Chester Asquith had been caught yet again feeling up his girlfriend in the stationery closet. Alberta Solis had plagiarised her history coursework and the Previn twins had been switching places to mess with their teachers' minds. With a huff, Paddington shoved the paperwork aside. These were run-of-the-mill childish antics – nothing she hadn't encountered before and certainly nothing she would fret about. Still, she added a postscript to the meeting agenda with the Board about ethical methods of marking identical twins in order to tell them apart.

Just then her desk phone rang and with a flash of irritation Paddington snatched up the receiver. "Yes?"

"Oh, you're still at work," a reedy voice gushed. "I wasn't sure you would be."

"Who is this?" It was almost 9pm and Paddington's tolerance for horseplay was at a low.

"Desdemona Carrington-Goodman," came the reply.

Paddington frowned, repeating the name under her breath. "One moment." She tapped at her computer.

"I'm a former student," the woman said indignantly. "My husband and I make regular donations to the alumni fund."

"Desdemona Carrington, you say?"

"Carrington-*Goodman*."

Paddington scoured her database, soon alighting on the student record. "Ah yes, Mrs Carrington-Goodman. You were a student before my time." Interesting, she noted. Desdemona had matriculated the same year as Posy and Lucas.

"Oh, call me Dee."

"Very well." Paddington swallowed. Dee was an awfully twee nickname for a woman with such pedigree. Her grandfather had been a most generous benefactor to Arundel. "I hope the years have treated you with health and prosperity."

"Oh quite," Dee's haughty tone informed her. "I married Lionel Goodman, of Goodness Clinics fame?"

Paddington glanced at her watch. Had the woman called merely to brag of her nuptials? "How wonderful for you."

"Thank you," Dee cooed. "He's very successful, VERY prominent in his field."

"Lovely," Paddington said. "However, I'm not sure I—"

"Listen. I'm calling because I am SO passionate about Arundel. You know it's the only place I would send my darling boys and I simply can't have its good name besmirched."

"Glad to hear you hold us in such regard," Mrs Paddington said, utterly confused. "You believe Arundel is at risk?"

"Why yes," Dee replied. "My dear friend Posy Edwins has had quite a tough time of late. You know she lost her mother young and, well, she never really found her true path. Her poor father had to cut her off financially recently, did you know?"

"Ah." Mrs Paddington had a jolt of clarity. Now the budget wedding made sense. Although she'd never met Jesper Edwins, her respect for him and his stance on parenting spoilt adult children rose considerably.

"And you know she's marrying our former head boy?" Dee's voice was full of thrill. "We had a catch-up recently, what with being bezzies and all. Imagine my shock when she mentioned this last-minute wedding to Lucas O'Rourke, who, as I am sure you are aware, was a scholarship student. They are the unlikeliest of matches. I mean, consider who she *is*."

"I see." Mrs Paddington's lip curled. Dear Lord, some people were terrible snobs.

"So, out of concern, I did a little digging," Dee said. "Posy has been asked to be a guest of honour at some fancy schmancy photography festival somewhere abroad... I forget where... Hang on..." As Dee struggled, something clicked for Paddington.

"Hawaii?" she snarled.

"That's right!" Dee said with a chortle. "And seriously, THRILLED for her so I did some checking on the festival website to research the role she would have. I was curious, you see. But I was quite shocked to learn that she'd have had to pay for her own flight there, even though she's been invited. In return the festival plant, oh I don't know, a dozen trees or something. Then it occurred to me that her father cut all her funds off and if I know Posy, she won't have had a penny saved. So how has she paid for flights to Hawaii? I'm certain she didn't get money from Henry who I am terribly concerned about in all this."

"Henry?" Paddington repeated, befuddled.

"Oh, of course, you won't know him," Dee said. "Just a few weeks ago I was at a brunch spot with Posy – Alfie's? You must go; say my name and you'll get the best table. Anyway, Posy introduced me to her absolute dish of a boyfriend who had driven all the way from the airport just to see her! And this boyfriend obviously wasn't Lucas."

"My goodness," was all a raging Paddington could say.

"And OBVIOUSLY I know all about the Prefect Marriage Rule at Arundel," Dee said. "So it occurred to me that Posy might be exploiting it to get to this festival which, I have to tell you, SICKENS me."

"That's very interesting," Mrs Paddington said. "Because as I am sure you have gathered, the honeymoon that we are paying for is in fact… to Hawaii."

Dee gasped theatrically and Paddington had to force herself to keep her face straight. Like Dee hadn't already worked it out. It honestly made her feel ill, the way Posy's so-called friend was enjoying this moment.

"There you have it," Dee cried, as if swooning. "But then, I wonder. I mean, I don't know what Lucas gets out of this little deal. It seems rather SORDID to me, if you gather my drift." She whimpered, as if fighting back tears. "And

Arundel cannot possibly be party to any such scandal, surely?"

"Of course," said Mrs Paddington. "Thank you for your concern, Mrs Carrington-Goodman."

"Naturally," Dee oozed. "And I DO hope my loyalty to the college will be remembered in a few years' time when it comes to Gabriel and Alec's admissions?"

"I won't forget what you have done," Mrs Paddington answered crisply. After a gushing farewell, Dee hung up.

Paddington replaced the phone in its cradle and sat still for just a moment. She'd known it. She'd bloody well known Lucas and Posy were up to something. Viv Hardstark may have been fooled but Paddington hadn't been. For goodness' sake, as if someone of Posy's status would be happy with a wedding costing less than six figures? That alone should have been enough of a clue that this wedding was not legitimate. Then opting for a humanist ceremony had always bothered her and in the context of what Dee had told her, it made sense that Posy and Lucas didn't want to have a legally binding wedding; the cost and stigma of divorce would be too much all round. It was clear Posy had found a way to get to this festival but what on earth did Lucas get out of it? There was no denying Posy was a great beauty and Paddington shuddered to think what she might have promised Lucas in return for his cooperation. For all her oiliness, Dee had been right; there was no way Arundel could be party to such a scandal.

The wedding was tomorrow. If they were to invoke the morality clause and stop the wedding from going ahead, there was a great deal of work to be done to ensure their bases were covered. Paddington hastily texted her wife to let her know she'd be even later for dinner than planned, then dialled another number.

"Viv?" Paddington greeted her colleague with relish.

"Mrs Paddington?" Hardstark sounded surprised.

"Yes – oh, sorry do you have company?" Paddington heard a male voice in the background.

"Don't worry, I can talk." Hardstark said quickly. "Is everything all right?"

"No," Paddington said ominously. "It most certainly is not."

## Chapter Thirty-Four

Dawn arrived. It was the day of the wedding and Lucas lay in his childhood bed, staring at the ceiling. He hadn't slept a wink for much of the night, wondering what on earth Sally wanted. Several times during the course of the party, he'd reached for his phone to message her, but something had stopped him. He told himself that it would have been improper to talk to Sally, that their first conversation post-break-up should be private. But Lucas knew it was also the guilt. The guilt of the lie he and Posy had perpetuated, blocking him from speaking to the woman whose heart he'd broken not so long ago. How could he hear Sally's voice and not think about the distance he'd put between them in the last starving months of their relationship? Last night's engagement party had been exquisite and Jesper's happiness had been obvious, despite his patronising treatment of Posy. Ines had been so warm and loving towards everyone she met and, after his spectacular boob, Seb had proven to be a charming, funny big brother. Lucas had liked the Edwins family, almost as if he was genuinely marrying into it. Yet he was lying to them all. His and Posy's plan had seemed so simple at its inception. Victimless, really. After all, who cared if an elite school forked out a few grand over a stupid old bylaw that should have been removed years ago? A marriage as a transaction, with no feelings involved and therefore none to be trampled on. But emotions of all kinds had come to the fore. Feelings were about to be hurt and Lucas had to take responsibility for it.

He rolled over and checked the time: 5am. The missed call alerts from Sally stood out on his phone like an angry beacon but she hadn't left a voicemail. Perhaps it wasn't that important. With a groan, Lucas got up and walked to the window, cranking it open. The air that flowed in was already dry and he could tell today would be hot. His whole body ached as he trudged downstairs to the kitchen and flicked on the kettle. The sky through the window was a brilliant glowing pink, the waking sun peeking through the apple blossoms of the trees outside the kitchen window. A perfect day to get married. It was also the day he had to provide his final answer on the sale of his business and Lucas was still very much torn.

The kettle boiled merrily and as Lucas poured himself a strong coffee, his mind drifted back to Sally. Why was she calling? Did she want to take him back? For a moment he allowed himself to imagine the future he'd thought he'd lost, a life in which he was independently wealthy from the sale of Align with a new venture underway. A future in which Sally was his partner, successful just like him, someone he would be proud to have on his arm. It was attractive by anyone's standards, the kind of future you'd be mad to dismiss. Right?

"Thought I heard you." Annie trudged into the kitchen, yawning widely.

"Sorry Ma, didn't mean to wake you."

"You know me, I sleep lighter than air." She took a seat at the table. "Make us a tea, there's a good chap."

Lucas obliged his mother with a tea thicker than tar.

"You all right?" she asked once she'd taken a deep, appreciative gulp.

"Big day." He sank into the chair opposite her, nursing his own drink.

"Isn't it just." Annie cradled her tea and regarded Lucas closely. "Are you sure you want to do this?"

"I'm doing what I need to do." But even as he said the words, Lucas wasn't sure.

Sensing his confusion, his mother leaned over to take his hand. "I only want you to be happy," she said. "If Posy makes you happy then I accept that. If selling Align and moving to another country makes you happy, that's good too. If you don't want to sell Align, that's also grand. I just hate seeing you in limbo when I'm so used to you knowing exactly what you want and staying the course."

"I gave Posy my word I'd see this through," Lucas said, more to himself than to his ma. But then her words sank in. "You think Posy makes me happy?"

"I'm fifty-eight, not blind," Annie cracked. "I was at the party last night. I saw the way you two looked at each other."

"I thought you considered her a bad influence?"

"I'm not saying I've changed my mind on that." Annie took another long sip of tea. "But listening to Jesper talk about Posy as if she were a reckless infant, I realised I've underestimated you too. I have to trust you and your judge-

347

ment. You make good decisions, so if I were you… trust your gut. Listen to it and trust it."

Lucas's heart warmed at his mother's loving words. Then he chuckled.

"What?"

"You sound exactly like Posy," Lucas told her. "She said that I rely too much on spreadsheets and not my gut. That I should trust myself more." He frowned. "At least I think that's what she said. There was whisky involved." A small smile bloomed across Annie's face. "What's that face for?" Lucas tugged her hand.

"Whatever my opinion of Posy Edwins is, it seems she's got the measure of you," his mother replied. "I can't comment on the whisky but she's right about the spreadsheets." Annie glanced at the clock on the wall and winced, patting her hair. "Anyway, what time are you heading to the hall?"

Annie started prattling on about the shoes she was planning to wear to the wedding and whether her ankles could bear the height, but Lucas's mind was soon elsewhere. What did he really want? And how far was he willing to go to get it? A seed of an idea took root in his mind. Lucas drained his coffee and scraped back his chair.

"What's the rush?" Annie demanded as Lucas leapt to his feet.

"What do you think?" Lucas landed a kiss on his mother's head and hurried out of the room. "It's my wedding day!"

By 9am Lucas was at the village hall, his suit hanging up in the gents'. Patricia had opened all the doors and windows, and the sweet smell of the meadows surrounding Lower Thicket permeated the building. As Lucas drank the hot tea she'd kindly prepared in the kitchenette, he explained the last-minute addition to the big day.

Patricia gaped at him over the rim of her mug. "Are you sure we'll have time to sort that?"

Lucas grinned at her, excitement gnawing at his stomach. "I hope so. The guy said he'd have something here soon." He nodded at the decorations he'd brought in the car. "For now, we need to get those set up."

Patricia ambled over to the helium balloons, examining the fake flowers that Posy and Lucas had bought from the pound shop in Coaldale. "Right you are."

Lucas regarded the sad collection of rose-gold balloons, already sagging in the morning's heat and the too-bright plastic flowers that were stiff in the pound-shop carrier bags. The thinking at the time of purchase had been, what could he get for a few quid that could brighten up the village hall. He'd actually patted himself on the back for spending less than £50 on decor. But now, after the fullness of everything he'd experienced, the vigour had gone from his plan. "The balloons can go either side of the window?" he suggested. "They might reflect the sunlight."

"And the flowers?"

Lucas just laughed. "I'll think of something."

"Right you are." Patricia downed the rest of her tea. "The floor still needs a good sweep – fancy lending me a hand?"

"Sure." The next hour or so was taken up by a thorough cleaning, followed by setting up chairs and testing the ancient sound system.

Just as Lucas was considering another fortifying cup of tea, he could hear his phone chirrup. When he saw who was calling, he left the room. "Sally?"

"Is this a bad time?" It was strange to imagine her voice had once been the most familiar thing in the world to him. But now it was odd, jarring to his ears.

"No, I can talk," he said. "How are you?"

"I'm well," she said. "How are things with you?"

Lucas had to hold back a guffaw as he looked up at the village hall with its peeling paint and broken steps. "All things considered, I'm good."

"I'm glad," she said softly. "Look, I'm calling to tell you that I've been appointed by Lim Management to paper their mergers and acquisitions."

Lucas could see where this was going. "Right."

"I thought I should let you know now before… well, just so there aren't any nasty shocks."

"I appreciate it," he said truthfully.

"I thought it would be best," she said. "But can you imagine my surprise when they briefed me about their offer on Align? Something I never thought I'd see."

"Yes, it's quite a turn-up," Lucas admitted.

"The deadline date is today." Disbelief tinged her voice. "And I know there hasn't been any request for an extension."

"Fred has said he will accept my decision as final because he can't work," Lucas said. "It's all down to me and it's not been an easy thing to decide."

"Okay." Sally drew the word out slowly. "So why haven't you asked for an extension if you haven't made your mind up?" When Lucas didn't answer, Sally chuckled. "The Lucas I know always has a plan."

Lucas hesitated. He looked across the green to where the willow tree fronds kissed the pond below them. The Tap on the Green was just beyond, its windows gleaming and welcoming in the sunlight. Swallows flew overhead in the clear azure sky. "I sort of have one," he said.

"Sort of?" Sally repeated with a laugh. "What does that even mean?"

Lucas's eyes followed the lilting movement of the willow tree branches. "Remember the last time I saw you, you begged me to... what was it? Oh yeah, *live*."

"Yes." Sally's voice dropped. "I was pretty harsh."

"You were right though," Lucas said. "I plan everything down to the second. I play it so safe that it's not really living sometimes."

"Lucas, I was hurt, and I lashed out," Sally said. "You're a perfectionist, that's all. And you're only like that because you have such a vision for your future."

"Sally, I am so sorry." Lucas meant every word. "I was so caught up in my career I failed to see what I had, even though it was right in front of me. I never wanted to hurt you, but I did. And you deserve better."

"Thank you for saying that." Sally's breath came out in a shaky stream. "Listen, you should—" She paused, sniffing back tears. "You should know I've started dating someone and, well, it's early days but he's great. I'm having fun."

"I'm pleased for you," Lucas told her. "Seriously."

"Good." Sally let out a nervous giggle. "Whew! I can assure you that any future conversations to do with Align will be far more professional and much less tear-soaked."

"I'm sure they will." Lucas spied a small van trundling its way towards him and his heart lifted. "I have to go, but I promise Lim will get the official response in the next hour. Okay?"

"Okay." Sally's voice was barely a whisper. "Take care, Lucas."

When she hung up, Lucas stared at the phone for a long moment, then shot off a text to Fred, a text that had been sitting in his drafts all morning. He hadn't lied to Sally when he'd said there was a plan of sorts. Although Lucas knew the next steps he was about to take, for once, he had no idea where they would lead. And far from terrifying him, he liked it.

A battered van screeched to a halt, disturbing Lucas from his thoughts, and Miles Purslow's head poked out of the driver's window.

"Morning!" Lucas called.

"Hello there!" Miles said as he parked up and climbed out of the van. "I was most intrigued to get your call at the ungodly hour of 6am."

"Sorry about the early call," Lucas said, "but I wasn't sure who else could help me at the last moment. I can't thank you enough."

Miles beamed. "Don't mention it. Happy to help with something so delightful." He blinked up at the hall. "Hmm. We may have our work cut out for us."

Lucas walked towards him, the summer air fresh. "We might at that," he said. "But if anyone can help me, it's you."

## Chapter Thirty-Five

Posy thought she might be sick all over the back seat of her father's vintage Jaguar. She was finally on her way to the wedding, with Ines beside her chattering incessantly about the beautiful weather. Her pops was chauffeuring, gloved hands on the wheel and a proud smile on his lips. Her father's eyes kept drifting back to her in the rear-view mirror, but Posy didn't dare meet them. She kept her head down, trying to contain the tumult of emotions she felt. There was no anticipation or satisfaction at a plan come to fruition, no victorious sense of gain, just the impending blackness of loss. Even though Posy knew what she was doing was right, it didn't make it any easier.

As they pulled up to Little Thicket Village Hall, Ines gasped audibly. "Is… this… *it*?"

Jesper braked, the motion causing Ines's head to jolt. "This is the place," he confirmed, but he did give the sat-nav a second glance. He turned back to Posy. "You ready?"

"I just need a sec," Posy said, her mouth dry. Her

stomach leapt, as if the car were rolling down a steep hill. But the car wasn't moving anymore.

Ines and Jesper exchanged loaded glances. "I'll give you two some space," Ines whispered. She laced her turquoise manicured fingers through Posy's and Posy met her step-mother's gaze. "Lucas is a very lucky man." Ines's voice was tremulous. "Remember that and you'll be fine."

Posy swallowed. "Thanks," was all she could say in the face of such adoration.

Ines cupped Posy's cheek and brushed it with a kiss then slid out of the car. She paused to steel herself with a deep breath before tottering up the uneven steps of the entrance.

"So." The leather of Jesper's custom bucket seat creaked. "This venue was a choice."

"It's quite lovely inside," Posy said sullenly.

Jesper turned around and leaned through the gap between the front seats, reaching for her hand. "You don't have to do this," he said. "I'd hate to think you were doing this just to impress me or prove a point."

"Believe me, this is not about you." Posy looked up at the grubby little building. In it waited her future, that much she knew. But was that future one she deserved?

"Lucas is a nice lad," Jesper said. "I like him. By all means, marry him one day, but you don't need to rush into it. Take your time, plan things out. Not everything has to be a whirlwind."

Posy laughed bitterly. "Or a hurricane?"

Jesper was quiet for a moment. "You know I mean that affectionately, right?"

Posy frowned. "Yeah, sure."

"Seriously!" Jesper chuckled. "Your mother coined that nickname."

"What?" Posy stared at her father. How had she not known that until now? "Since when? How?"

"The night you were born actually. You know you were born during the biggest storm of the year?"

"Yeah, it was like one of the worst storms to hit Europe, right?"

"Second only to the Burns Storm." Jesper's eyes focused on something beyond Posy. "The ambulance was stuck just a mile down the road. God, I was scared."

"That's when the tree branch smashed the bedroom window, isn't it?" Posy had heard that part of the story before.

"It did," Jesper said. "Bedlam! The drains on our road flooded and Mr Bernstein's boat floated into the Sastris's garden. Total destruction. We could hear the ambulance sirens but you wouldn't wait. You *couldn't* wait. You made your entrance into the world on our bed, screaming your little lungs out. And for one tiny, solitary second, the wind stopped howling. The storm just paused, as if to listen to your arrival. And your mother"—Jesper's voice hitched, his eyes filling with tears—"your mother was out of her mind in pain, but she held you to her breast and said in this funny, delirious voice, '*Watch out for the hurricane*'. Luckily the paramedics arrived then and took care of her and I just held you, with the raging winds destroying the room around us. You were this wild, red-faced elemental thing and I *knew*, the way a father knows, that you'd forge your own path." He rubbed his eyes. "Just like a hurricane."

Her father's words reached down Posy's throat and grasped at her heart, squeezing tight. "How did I not know that?"

"I honestly thought I'd told you." Jesper shrugged. "I

355

suppose once Celia passed, calling you a Hurricane was a way to keep her around, every day. I miss her, even now." He nodded at Posy. "And you look so like her. Especially today."

Posy smoothed down her dress. "You told me she would be disappointed in me. Did you mean that?"

Jesper's face contorted. "No. I didn't mean it like that. I was… God, Posy, no. I was angry, that's all. I spoke out of turn."

"You made me feel so worthless," she croaked. "It's not just the money thing. You talked to me like I was a waste of space."

"I know." Jesper averted his gaze. "I only wanted you to know that you have value beyond money, beyond anything I can give you. I handled it badly. I'm sorry Posy."

Posy shuffled forward in her seat. Close-up, she could see her father's face was heavily lined and it struck her that he wouldn't be around forever. "You did handle it badly, but you were right to cut me off."

Jesper's head jerked up. "What?"

"Don't make me say it again," Posy sighed. "The direction thing. You were spot on. Meeting Lucas has kind of… shone a light on that."

"Well, this is a turn-up for the books." Jesper laughed.

"Don't get used to it." With that, Posy scooted back to open the car door. "Now, I rather need to get in there."

"Whoa!" Jesper jumped out of the car and scurried round to Posy's side. "What kind of bride opens her own car door?" He helped her out and took in the sight of her as she shook out her dress. "You're a vision, my darling." He extended his arm and waited patiently as she fetched her clutch. "Shall we?"

Posy took her father's arm. Her core trembled liked a

taut piano wire, but she forced herself to remain steady as they made their way up the stairs to the hall entrance. Patricia greeted them, curiously dressed in a crumpled linen suit topped with an ostentatious fascinator of peacock feathers and large spirals of electric blue felt.

"You're here!" she squealed. "Wait until you see what he's done with the room! Give me ten seconds to let them know and then you can walk in."

As Patricia hurried off, Jesper looked at Posy. "What's he done with the room?"

"I don't know. We spent the decoration budget at, like, Poundland." Posy couldn't believe Patricia could be so thrilled with what was a few balloons and plastic flowers as wedding décor.

"Here we go then." Jesper tightened his grip. "For what it's worth, I'm proud of you. Taking charge like this… your mother would be proud too."

"Thanks Pops." Posy exhaled shakily, blinking back tears. On wobbly legs, she walked with her father to the doors and pushed them open.

Posy gasped. The first thing that hit her was the scent – the graceful perfume of roses in abundance. The second thing she noticed was that the hall had been transformed. Roses were everywhere she looked, filling every surface. Tables and chairs had been covered with blooms of every shade and the floor was scattered with vibrant red and white petals. A small cluster of chairs faced the floor-to-ceiling windows, with wonderfully neat potted rosebushes lining the aisle leading to the panoramic windows. A large arch coated in pink roses and trailing greenery framed the window, and under this arch stood Lucas.

He turned.

Lucas smiled at Posy and in that instant, Posy could see everything ahead of her with total clarity. She *knew*. Posy understood what her father had meant when he described holding her as a baby and having total certainty as to who she would become. Because Posy had that same feeling when she looked in Lucas's eyes. She experienced the absolute truth of who Lucas was and what he meant to her.

"Ready to get married?" Jesper whispered as the gentle guitar of Smashing Pumpkins's 'Luna' filled the room.

Posy couldn't reply. Their small congregation of her family, Tara and the O'Rourkes might as well have been a million people, such was the intensity of their collective gaze. Under Jesper's gentle urging, her feet began to move, one step, then two. As she made her way down the aisle, Lucas's eyes drank in every inch of her, and with each step she became more and more steady.

When she arrived at Lucas's side, Jesper prised her hand off his arm and brushed the back of it with a gentle kiss. "Congratulations," he murmured to Lucas, placing his daughter's hand in his before taking his seat.

"Hi." Posy could barely get the words out. Lucas looked so damn good in his suit, standing tall and confident with not a trace of concern on his face.

"You look incredible." Lucas handed her a single, perfect rose. "I realised we didn't get you a bouquet."

Posy lifted the bloom to her nose. It smelled divine. "I'm pretty sure there was no line in the budget for flowers," she said. "Where on earth did you get the money for all these roses?"

"Someone did me a deal." Lucas nodded towards the crowd and much to Posy's surprise she saw Miles Purslow.

"Remember his little flower gang from the pub? He helped me call in a few favours."

Posy laughed. A deal? Favours? The hall positively overflowed with fragrance. Everywhere flowers could be displayed, they were displayed. The scratched parquet floor was barely visible under the carpet of petals. "This is beyond stunning. Must have been quite some deal."

"Ah, it was worth it." Lucas's shrug was bashfully proud. "I know this wasn't what we agreed, but a lot has changed for me since we came to our arrangement."

"Me too," Posy said. "In fact—"

"Are we ready?" Edgar's voice cut through the reverie.

"Speaking of changes," Lucas muttered.

Edgar appeared from behind Lucas. The man was dressed in long scarlet robes, his rounded head framed by an extravagant halo of lush peonies that on closer inspection were clearly fake.

"*Robes!*" Posy exclaimed with glee.

The celebrant beamed. "Glad you like them. I believe it is very important to treat every ceremony with the respect it deserves. These robes are made from the finest Egyptian silks, blessed by the grand Yogi Baba Maharishi Sivani." He bowed his head.

Posy could hardly contain her laughter but tried her best as it was apparent Edgar truly believed in what he was saying. "Er, good?"

"Welcome everyone!" Edgar cried, raising his arms high. The room fell silent, apart from poorly concealed titters from Florence's direction. "Be seated— Oh, you are." He reached into the pockets of his capacious robes and pulled out a cloth-bound book. Opening the pages, he withdrew a rather ostentatious bookmark. "We are gathered here today to celebrate the union of Lucas and Posy. The song you heard upon her arrival was chosen by Lucas. You see, Posy loves this band and so Lucas chose a song about taking a chance when it comes to love, the beautiful risk of putting it all out there for the world to see. Something very meaningful for today." Edgar smiled. "My name is Edgar Truthteller"—Florence let rip with another ill-hidden snort of laughter at this—"and I am an accredited humanist celebrant. Lucas and Posy chose a humanist wedding to reflect their inclusive, respectful beliefs. I am delighted to be here and warmed to see so many of you here today."

Posy shot a glance back towards the meagre congregation. Lucas's hand slipped into hers and she looked down at his fingers entwined with hers, savouring the warmth of his skin.

Like it was meant to be, there, next to hers.

"Marriage is a significant occasion," Edgar went on. "An everyday miracle, I like to say. Think of what had to happen for these two souls to come together and take a chance on each other. As head boy and head girl at Arundel College, they didn't get along. But an encounter at a school reunion years later was to lead to this blessed event. Something extraordinary born from the ordinary routine of everyday life." He took a breath. "And now for the vows." He flipped his book around. "Lucas and Posy will use—"

"Actually," Lucas interrupted, causing both Edgar and Posy to look at him with surprise. "I know we said we would use the boilerplate vows but I've written my own. Is that okay?"

"Certainly," Edgar said. He turned to Posy. "So long as you are all right with it?"

Posy wasn't sure what to make of this. What was Lucas up to? All she could do was nod. "Sure."

Lucas produced a sheet of paper from his pocket and began to read from it. His voice was steady, but Posy could see how the paper trembled in his hands. "Posy, if anyone had told me when I was a teenager that I'd be marrying you one day, I'd have laughed in their face. As head girl, you undermined every plan I made; you drove me crazy. We never saw eye to eye on anything. All you wanted to do was party, take photographs and travel. And honestly, you haven't changed. Much." Their guests laughed politely. "The thing is though," Lucas went on, "*I* have. You changed me. I used to spend every day afraid that my plans would fall through, that I'd become my worst nightmare: a failure. I felt the only option was to work night and day to avoid that." He lifted his eyes to hers. "People used to wrongly assume all sorts about me as a kid and I always felt like I had to work twice as hard to overcome their doubts as well as my own. But after everything we've gone through?" He gestured around him with a small laugh. "I feel like I can do anything. That's thanks to you." He swallowed. "You aren't just some chaotic wanderer to be corrected, Posy, you're a force to be reckoned with. And I'm proud to be standing here with you today." As he finished, he let out a relieved breath and nodded at Edgar to confirm his completion.

Edgar regarded Lucas quizzically. "Oh, that's it?" When Lucas nodded again in affirmation Edgar bristled mildly. "Not so much a vow as a statement… but truly beautiful words." He proffered the book with the vows to Posy. "Now, Posy would you like to read—"

Posy lifted a hand. "No, I have something of my own to say." Edgar lowered the book dejectedly. Posy didn't know how to follow Lucas's meaningful words but she knew this was the moment that the truth was needed. She reached for Lucas's hands and lifted them level with her heart. "When we started planning this wedding, everything seemed so simple. We had a plan and all that mattered was completing it. But somewhere along the way, things got… complicated." Here Lucas arched an eyebrow. Posy forged on. "I've never really done complicated. I've always just gone straight for what I wanted without much thought for anyone else." Her mind flashed to Jacinta and Henry. With a grimace she continued. "You've been a real partner through this weird time, the partner I never thought I wanted but the one I truly needed. And all I want is for you to be happy. I hope you remember that."

"Beautiful words," Edgar said. "If a little maudlin," he added under his breath. "And now, if there is no impediment—"

"Wait! Stop!"

All heads turned to the back of the hall to see a victorious-looking Matilda Paddington edging her way out of her seat to stand in the aisle. Hardstark lurked behind her, looking as if she'd much rather be elsewhere.

"Mrs Paddington?" Posy did not like the expression on the woman's face.

"This wedding is not to proceed!" The headmistress brandished a document. "I have here a signed statement from a reliable witness that the bride and groom are marrying purely for financial gain and—"

"Actually." Posy stepped forward, her voice loud. "That's not why this wedding can't go ahead."

Paddington looked like she'd been slapped. "Excuse me?"

362

"Yeah, excuse me?" Lucas grabbed Posy's arm.

"I'm sorry Lucas." Posy hated the sadness filling his eyes. "But I can't marry you."

"Why not?" He moved closer to her and lowered his voice. "I've told you, it doesn't matter what happens with Align. I still want to help you get to—"

"No, I know, and that's very noble of you." Posy couldn't let him finish. Her head swam with the sheer nearness of him and what she was about to say.

"So then why?"

"I can't marry you today because I'm in love with you," Posy said.

A hush fell over the hall. But then chatter. Jesper rose to his feet, red in the face.

"Posy, what on earth?" he demanded, looking around the room in total bewilderment.

Lucas's gaze darted nervously to Paddington and Hardstark. "I second your father's question," he said breathlessly. He leaned closer and lowered his voice. "What are you doing?"

"Like I said." Posy cleared her throat, more nervous than she'd ever been in her life. "I'm in love with you, Lucas."

Lucas pursed his lips, clearly unsure whether Posy was continuing their charade or not. "Isn't that a good thing when it comes to a marriage?"

"Normally." Posy licked her lips. "But you're about to achieve something so important with your career and I refuse to get in your way."

Lucas frowned. "You're not in the way."

"That's not what your mother thinks," Posy whispered. "And she's right." She could sense he was about to erupt at that remark, so she hastened on. "But it's not just the

363

thought that I might influence your decision in any way, this whole thing is just not right. And…" To her horror, tears hijacked her voice, rendering it a croak. "I can't marry you like this when what I feel for you is real."

"Oh." Lucas visibly reeled and Posy's heart sunk even further. Lucas's apparent dismay just showed that Posy was right to distance herself from him, despite her fervent hope he'd want the opposite.

"But I will honour my promise to you." Posy was determined to finish speaking, even if she was reduced to a blubbering mess by the end of it. She fished around in her bag and pulled out a USB. "I stayed up all night and made an Excel sheet of all my contacts. Names, emails, status updates. I've even called and texted a few this morning to make initial introductions. Seb's number is in there too and he's expecting your call." Lucas accepted the flash drive in stunned silence. "I cancelled the Hawaii flights." Posy turned to Paddington. "Your corporate card will get a full refund. And I'll repay all the other costs, so Arundel won't be out of pocket. Might have to be a payment plan but you'll get every penny."

Paddington looked like she might continue to argue, but Hardstark patted her arm and the headmistress merely gave Posy a defeated nod in response.

"I don't understand." Lucas gaped at her.

"Neither do I," Edgar said. "Am I—"

"Please," Posy lifted her hand to silence the celebrant, "let me finish." Sheepishly, Edgar stepped back, clutching his ceremony book like a life ring. "Your mother had a word with me," Posy said. "She taught me that the best things in life are worked for. They're *earned*. If I get myself to Hawaii off the back of this lie, then I haven't earned my place there, not really. Just like I haven't earned the right to be called your wife if we go through with this ceremony." And when Posy finally, fully met Lucas's eyes her tears flowed freely. "I want to deserve the good things in my life, whatever or whoever they may be. You can take these contacts and do something amazing with them. You don't need to be attached to a woman who cheats her way to success. You deserve better than that."

"Posy, I…" Lucas's fingers curled around the USB. "You learned Excel for me?"

Posy laughed through the tears swimming in her eyes. "Like it's difficult?"

He nodded, impressed. "Sounds like you had a busy morning."

"I made some decisions, yes," she said. "And this is final. You can do what you need to for your career without being part of my mad scheme." She raised a shaking hand to caress his cheek. "And thank you."

Lucas looked utterly bewildered. "For what?"

"Showing me a different way." As Lucas stared at her in utter bewilderment, Posy felt the very real need to exit the hall. Turning on her heels, she scurried down the aisle, the guests erupting into confused chatter around her. She could hear Lucas calling her name but there was no way she was stopping to let everyone see her full transition into a snotty, tear-soaked mess. Once out of the hall, Posy ran onto the green, with no clear idea of where she was going, only that she needed to get far away from the scene of her heartbreak. She kicked off her expensive heels, threw the crystal-encrusted bag into the long grass and began to run. Across the expanse of grass, she could see the cosy pub where she and Lucas had spent that one afternoon getting drunk on whisky, and by it the shimmering pond with its graceful willows and serene ducks. Tears blurred her vision, but Posy kept running. It felt good to punish her muscles with exertion, her brain preoccupied with the burning in her lungs.

"Oi!" A powerful hand grabbed Posy's forearm and yanked her back from her headlong sprint.

"Lucas?"

Lucas was breathing hard. Placing his hands on his knees, he took a few deep gulps of air between words. "Did you… mean what… you said… just now?"

Her stomach pitched. "I did."

"Why did you…? Jesus Christ, I thought I was fitter than this." He straightened up and swiped at his damp skin. "Give me a sec."

"Sorry, I suppose running off was a little dramatic," Posy said. "Everyone was looking at me and it was all a bit much."

"Somewhat," he said with a laugh.

"But I did mean what I said," Posy said. "I love you and I don't want you basing any decisions about your career on me."

"Why not?"

"I was scared you liked me," she replied, realising as the words came out that it was probably the dumbest thing she'd ever said. "I worried that you might like me so much you'd make the wrong decision about your career. I suppose I panicked."

"And your solution to this panic was to dump me at the altar?" Lucas thumbed behind him at the hall.

"Hurricane Posy, remember?" She shrugged.

"No, you don't get to write this off as one of your calamities," Lucas said urgently. "Because if you'd just talked to me about it and not my bloody mother, you'd know that—" He grabbed her chin, tilting it so her eyes locked with his. "You'd know that I love you too."

"Oh." Never had a syllable been so ineffectual at conveying total and utter joy. Lucas loved her. He loved *her*.

"Oh?" Lucas's gaze roamed all over her face, knowing and tentative all at once. "Is that all you can say?"

Posy took a deep breath. "How about we get away from that lot and you buy me a whisky?" She pointed to the hall, outside of which their families had gathered to watch from a distance.

Lucas's smile broadened and his fingers moved from her chin to cup her face. For a moment Posy just drank in the sight of him, unable to speak, unable to believe this was happening. Dazed, he nodded imperceptibly, and Posy thought she might explode from the sheer happiness that filled every inch of her body.

"You know what happens when we drink whisky," he said huskily, and desire jolted Posy from her toes up.

"Why do you think I suggested it?" she laughed, feeling like she'd die if she didn't kiss him soon.

Lucas looked over his shoulder at the confused crowd and waved. "The wedding is off!" he yelled.

"But do stay here and enjoy the venue," Posy shouted as Lucas burst into happy laughter. "There's no cake!"

Even at a distance, the confusion of their loved ones was palpable. Jesper was throwing his hands up in the air as a flapping Ines rushed to calm him. Tara high-fived Inigo with such fervour he stumbled.

Lucas turned back to Posy and the jubilation in his face stilled to something more serious. He brushed his hands up her arms and Posy shuddered as his large hands returned to frame her jaw with sensual grace. Posy licked her lips. He really did look good in his suit.

"Are you sure about this?" Lucas said.

"A thousand times yes," Posy said, leaning into his warmth so there could be no doubt.

Lucas inched ever closer. "I'm very happy that you don't want to marry me right now."

"Oh, but you still need to kiss the bride," Posy murmured, her lips brushing his.

"With pleasure," Lucas said.

## Epilogue

### EIGHTEEN MONTHS LATER

The Clary Chapel was every bit a fairy tale, tucked away in the thick snow that had beset the Yorkshire countryside for much of December. A salted path had been cleared to lead around the lake up to the door and the way was festooned with lights strung from tree to tree. The effect was magical.

Inside, despite the heroic effort of several rented heaters, the chapel was as chilly and damp as it ever was, but the guests inside didn't care. The elite of Yorkshire society were transported by the sweet melody from the harpist, the fragrant abundance of the winter rose arrangements and the golden glow of the pillared candles that lent the stern little chapel a homely, welcoming aura.

As the clock struck two, the ancient oak doors groaned open and there was the bride, demure in a simple ivory sheath, a stiff little veil affixed to her head. The groom – dapper in an emerald velvet blazer – went misty-eyed at the sight of his wife-to-be.

"Hardstark looks sensational!" Posy whispered in Lucas's

ear, and he had to admit it was true. Vivienne Hardstark had never been one to entertain fripperies such as satin and lace, but when Miles Purslow had asked for her hand in marriage, everything had changed. To no one's surprise, she used her staff entitlement to wed in Arundel's ancient chapel. As the bride walked down the aisle, one couldn't miss the total joy radiating from every part of her being.

The ceremony was brief and no-nonsense, as one might expect. And once it concluded the crowd stomped their way across the frozen grounds to Arundel's Great Hall where there were drinks, canapés, and music of the highest quality from a string quartet.

Posy accepted a glass of champagne and handed one to Lucas, who had his hand buried in his pocket. "Hey!" she chided. "No phones today, you promised."

"Okay, okay!" He lifted his hands up, phone-free, then winced. "God, I'm still sore from yesterday." Lucas had completed a charity fell run to raise money for Heart Research UK, a cause that had become very dear to him. Although Fred had pulled through his terrifying health scare, the scars of it had stayed with him and all who loved him.

"Well, that will teach you to try and scale a mountain in record time." Posy laughed. "It wasn't a competition!"

"Not a close one," Lucas said with grim satisfaction.

"Show off," she shot back indulgently. "But seriously. Leave the phone alone. Align is in good hands. Hasn't it been since you relocated?" Lucas's decision to work remotely had been an easy one. When Seb Edwins had offered Align the contract to look after the family fortune, it had only solidified the plan Lucas had put into motion. Align wasn't the offices or expensive views of London, Align was its people, all of whom jumped at the chance to manage their own work hours from home offices. Clients loved being visited at their homes or places of business – one didn't need a fancy office to impress them with genius. Thanks to this streamlining and a few more of Posy's contacts agreeing to work with Lucas, Align was healthier and more profitable than ever. More importantly, it was wholly Lucas's business.

"I'm sure that's all fine," Lucas said with a small smile. "I have a good feeling about the future."

"So do I!" Posy agreed. "Right, before I forget, we need to hit up all the engaged ladies at this party."

Lucas frowned. "We do?"

"Yes!" Posy swatted him affectionately. "Tara's still trying to get her wedding dress business off the ground, remember? There must be clients aplenty here."

"Will we ever come to Arundel and not be on the hunt for clients in some shape or other?" Lucas mused.

"Shhh!" Posy giggled, just as the newlyweds arrived to welcome them. "Congratulations Ms Hardstark!" Posy said, raising her glass. "I mean, Mrs Purslow?"

"Oh, I think you mean Mr and Mrs Hardstark," Miles replied with a flourish and he planted a light kiss on his new wife's cheek.

"You took her name? That's so lovely," Posy said, and Lucas watched in astonishment as Hardstark failed to conceal a swoon.

"We wanted to say thank you for coming," Hardstark said with a blush. "You are, after all, the reason we met. Only felt right to invite you, even if you did almost single-handedly destroy the reputation of this college."

"Bit dramatic," Lucas muttered, and Posy elbowed him.

"We put a stop to things though, didn't we?" she

declared. "Cancelled the wedding, refunded pretty much every purchase. No harm done."

"Yes, you just about skirted disaster," Hardstark conceded. "By the way, I saw you've opened your own photography studio in Coaldale now. Congratulations."

"Ah, thank you." Posy tried to shrug the compliment off, but Lucas knew that every time someone mentioned her photography studio and gallery, she got a thrill. She had every right to, in his opinion. Posy had apprenticed with a local photographer in Leeds for the best part of a year, sometimes on the most unglamorous of assignments but she'd prevailed and impressed all she'd worked with. The networking Posy had done, combined with her ever-growing Instagram following, had netted her some third-party investors to aid the set-up of her own studio specialising in bespoke art, perfect for the wealthy residents of the area. Lucas burned with pride at the sight of Posy's glee as she said, "It's a little slow at the moment, but word is getting out."

"I wish you luck," Hardstark said. And with a gentle smile, she moved on to greet other guests.

———

Much later, when the party was over and the Hardstarks had departed for their Provence honeymoon, Lucas and Posy took a few moments to walk the grounds of their alma mater. Bundled up against the cold, they strolled down to the lake to sit on a particular bench. The darkening sky was velvet-blue, dotted with a host of stars. The emerging moon was full and glowing.

"Say what you like about Hardstark, she sure can throw a good party," Posy yawned.

Lucas kissed her head. She still smelled just like vanilla. "Run like a military operation, that wedding," he joked. He delved into his pocket again, earning a tut from Posy.

"Hey, can you stay still? I'm comfy." She let out another yawn. "God, I really ate far too many canapés."

"Sorry, it's these gloves," Lucas groaned. But then he found what he was looking for. His heart thudding, he cleared his throat. "Pose?"

"Yeah?" she replied sleepily.

"Please could you look at me?"

She bolted up, eyeing him strangely. "What?"

Trembling, Lucas held out his hand. A distinctive red velvet box nestled in his palm. "I asked your pops to sneak it out of your room for me. I've had it cleaned and…" With an audible gulp, he opened the box. There was her mother's Cartier ring, bewitching in the moonlight.

"Whoa…" Posy clasped her hands to her mouth, nodding before Lucas could even ask the question he'd wanted to ask for quite some time now.

"Here we go." Lucas eased off the bench and knelt beside her, not even blinking as the cold snow seeped into his trousers. "Posy Edwins, for real this time, will you marry me?"

The smile that spread across Posy's face was the loveliest thing he'd ever seen. She nodded madly and he slid the ring onto her trembling finger. Leaning in for a kiss, Posy spoke the words he'd been longing to hear. "Lucas O'Rourke, for real this time, yes, I will marry you."

# Acknowledgments

Where to begin? Like many authors, being published has been a lifetime dream, held ever since I wrote poor imitations of The Famous Five at the age of 7 and so to be finally writing my acknowledgements for my debut novel feels surreally wonderful.

Firstly, I have to thank my amazing agent, Hannah Schofield at LBA Books, for taking a chance on Posy and Lucas and for seeing the potential in their story. *The Reunion* would not have become the book it is without your support. (How do you feel about them banging? Turns out, pretty great!)

Thanks must also go to the One More Chapter team for giving my story a home, in particular Jennie Rothwell and Charlotte Ledger - whose enthusiasm for *The Reunion* blew me away. The moment I read your pitch will stay with me forever.

I also want to mention Esther Freud and the Faber Academy Writing A Novel class of 2016, in particular Helio Figueiredo, Susan Allott and Jenny Barsby, talented writers themselves who have in one way or the other provided support and friendship over the past few years and not least a safe space to talk about all things writing! The Faber course gave me the tools and the confidence to keep plugging away and the lessons I learned from Esther and my peers have informed my writing ever since. Thanks also to Katie Khan for convincing me to take the Faber course, as well as being a general source of advice, particularly when I was considering signing with Hannah. So glad I sidled up to you at that premiere all those years ago and fangirled over your blog.

I should also thank my family, notably Mum who has bravely read a lot of my writings over the years - volunteered, I hasten to add before anyone thinks I strong-armed her. Couldn't have asked for a better reader as you are never afraid to let me know when something isn't any good. When your response to *The Reunion* was 'I'd forgotten you'd written it' I knew I was on to a winner. Special mention to Grandma Doreen for the subtle pressure over the years, who really just wants to be able to point out my book in Waterstones to her mates. Sorry about the swearing, Grandma. I'll understand if you skip the chapter with the sex.

Last but not least, my husband Neil and my daughters. The kids were actually more of a (delightful) hindrance than any kind of help in getting this book written but given that they will both learn to read in a few short years they should get a mention. Ultimately though, it's fair to say that I absolutely couldn't have achieved this without Neil. The man who takes such good care of me and our beautiful babies and gives me the space to get my writing done. This book was conceived during the horror that was the pandemic in 2020, in those early days when we didn't know what would become of us; our health, our families and our livelihoods. In hindsight, immersing myself in Posy and Lucas's adventures was a coping mechanism and one my husband supported without question. Neil, I love you and to quote Alan Partridge, thanks a lot!